THE MASTER'S TALE

A *Titanic* Ghost Story

Ann Victoria Roberts

The Thorn Press

First published by **The Thorn Press** in 2011

Copyright © Ann Victoria Roberts 2011

The moral right of Ann Victoria Roberts has been asserted.

This book is a work of fiction.
The characters and incidents, though based on historical facts, are largely the product of the author's imagination.
Of course, the story of the *Titanic* is well known, and many of the facts have been used in this book.

ISBN: 978-0-906374-21-4

The Thorn Press Ltd
Lansdowne House
Castle Lane
Southampton SO14 2BU, UK

www.thethornpress.com

To the
volunteer officers and crew
of the British Heritage Steamship

'SHIELDHALL'

Their dedication represents what seafaring is all about.

www.ss-shieldhall.co.uk

Notoriety is a wearisome thing. Our names have been linked together for nigh on a hundred years, always on someone's lips, always with a question attached. I wish they'd let me rest. Those who came with me have long since been released, but I'm still here. As Master, you see, I am responsible. I was in command. The blame will always rest with me.

I failed to grasp it at first, but after a while the message began to make sense.
After a much longer time, I knew who had sent it.

Time & Coincidence
I know the force which draws objects together &
ends with
Destruction
Look back
See how events cluster and collide, drawn in by
the celestial wash of
Time
Leaving nothing but Flotsam bobbing in the
wake...

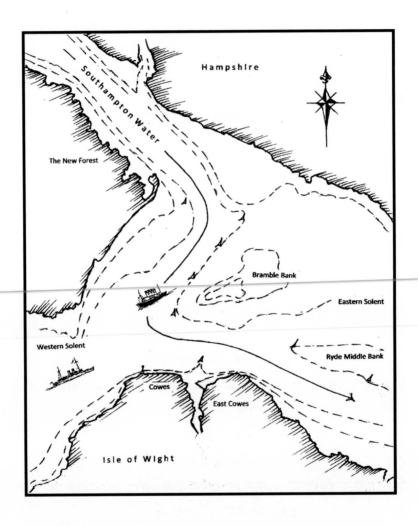

Sketch showing the Deep Water Channel, leading from Southampton, around the Isle of Wight, and towards the open sea. Dotted lines indicate the shallows.

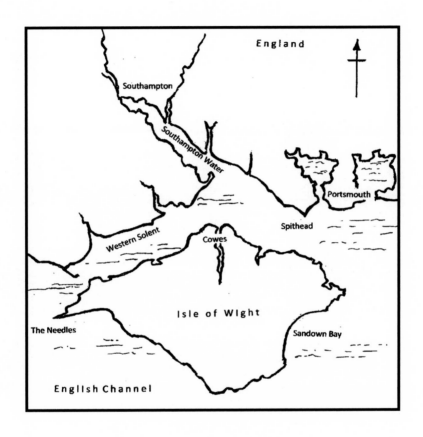

The Solent and
Southampton Water.

1

Memories loom out of the mist like the sails of a schooner off the Grand Banks, skimming past my bridge with a tangible rush and barely a yard to spare. So close I can see the man on watch, and terror in the helmsman's eyes.

A narrow escape: under-breath cursing, heart thundering like the beat of an engine. Each encounter fresh, startling, and then the fading image, slipping away with just a single mast light, until that too is swallowed by the dark.

I looked out on fog. Skeletal trees surrounded the house, lurking like phantoms in the pre-dawn murk. The cab arrived, the usual man stowing my bag while his horse blew patiently between the shafts. As a rule, having said my goodbyes, I didn't look back; but this time, compelled to take one last glance, I rubbed at the glass as though I could clear it with my glove. Turrets and gables became insubstantial as the cab pulled away. Then the cab gathered pace and the house disappeared.

I remember a moment's dismay. Hating mist and fog with the kind of passion most men reserve for long-term enemies, I was tempted to tell the cabbie to stop. But that would have flouted the cardinal rule: once set forth on a voyage, never go back. The house was still there, of course it was; my wife and daughter watching from the turret window. It was simply that mist obscured them from view.

All the way to the docks I was fretting, rubbing my eyes every few

1

minutes, listening to the heavy clip clop of the horse's hooves. Tension rose with every pause, every jingle of the reins, each hacking cough from the cabbie. Would we never get there? Anticipating trouble with the new ship, dreading the slow negotiation into the main channel, my stomach tightened into a knot as I ran through all the likely hazards. Every one made worse by the fog.

At last, red brick and white Portland stone loomed out of the greyness, the South-Western Hotel a familiar landmark heralding my destination. Many of the overnight clientele were similarly bound, about to rise to breakfast and last-minute packing. Perhaps it was my strange mood, but that morning the shrouded line of waiting cabs looked like a funeral procession.

We crossed the junction at Canute Road, turning through the gate by the Harbour Office to enter the realm of ships and the sea. Ahead I saw her, by some alchemy the biggest ship afloat – bigger even than her sister-ship *Olympic* – rising above the sheds, hull black as widow's weeds, funnels veiled by mist and smoke.

Quartermaster Perkis was on the gangway. As I bade him good morning he touched his cap and took my bag, handing it to my steward as he materialised by the main entrance. Paintin followed me along the deck and up the service stairs to the bridge. Beyond the usual greeting, we didn't speak. Paintin knew my moods, understood that with a dozen matters pressing as we prepared to sail at noon, I did not need to know the state of play in the victualling department, nor whether my new uniforms had arrived from the tailor. Most of all I did not want comments on the weather.

My quarters were behind the wheelhouse. Shrugging off my coat, I went through to the bedroom, quickly divesting myself of the civilian clothes I'd worn from home, to don the brass-bound uniform Paintin had laid out for me. As my steward tidied away, I opened the dayroom door and hooked it back, signifying that I was aboard and available to whomsoever should need me.

In my office the paperwork, checked so assiduously in Belfast, was waiting. Certificates of sea-worthiness for the Board of Trade inspector, Customs declarations for every item of cargo; a Southampton crew-list yet to complete; the Articles of Agreement to be prepared for signing by the entire ship's complement.

The new charts had arrived a few days previously. Going through them again I extracted the ones for Southampton Water and the Solent. With the current Tide Tables and Tidal Atlas to hand, I wanted to

2

check the depth of water in the navigable channel. By Calshot Spit especially, where the tide direction and speed could make a huge difference to our approach to the Thorn Channel. Any ship could go aground on that notorious bend around the Bramble Bank, and with something this size it could be disastrous. The pilot would have all the figures to hand, but after that last little difficulty with *HMS Hawke*, I needed to double-check for my own peace of mind.

Halfway through the calculations there came a tap at my dayroom door. I glanced back to see Joseph Bell, the Chief Engineer, standing by with a sheaf of papers in his hand.

'Good morning, Chief – come on through.' I beckoned him in and set my figures aside. 'How are you? Everything going well below?'

'Engine room's just about ready for departure, sir. Bunkers are topped off and signed for. But,' he lowered his voice, 'I'm grieved to say that fire's still smouldering in bunker number 10.'

Fire: the seaman's worst nightmare.

'How serious is it?'

He grimaced, his abundant moustache squirming like a live thing. 'Difficult to say. Like I said yesterday, sir, it's got to be in that Belfast coal at the base, but it's getting to it, that's the trouble. I've had the lads working on it constantly. Could do with another couple of days, to be honest.'

'That's no good.' We were due to sail at noon. I thought for a moment, weighing risk against necessity. 'Is it likely to affect the structure?'

'No,' he said decisively. 'It's against the transverse bulkhead, not the double-bottoms. As soon as we've got it out we'll let Mr Andrews' men have a look.' He drew breath, squared his shoulders and turned for the door. 'Never mind, sir. We'll keep at it.'

'Thanks, Chief. Keep me informed.'

He would, I knew that. A strange breed, engineers, as passionate about their engines as we sailors about our ships. But Joe Bell was sound, he'd been with me before. He knew the situation, knew we couldn't afford *not* to sail on time, and that once under way we had to keep up our speed. We carried 4,500 tons of coal in 20 bunkers, and between them, 90 firemen shovelled around 650 tons a day. They served 29 boilers, providing steam to two giant reciprocating engines and one small turbine driving three propellers. That power was the heart of the ship and Joe Bell knew every single thing that made those engines throb. He knew his men too. If anyone could be guaranteed to solve a problem below decks, Joe Bell was the man.

Even so, it was worrying.

Bunker fires were a common hazard, though no less dangerous for all that. My thoughts turned to my first command, the sweet *Lizzie Fennell*. She'd been lost to fire off Chile in 1881, not long after I moved to White Star. Carrying coal from the Tyne to Valparaiso, she was another victim of spontaneous combustion in the hold. Her Master and crew were rescued, thank God, although it saddened me to think how I'd saved her from foundering with a cargo of cotton, only to have her burn under the man who took over.

In danger of drifting, I dragged my attention back to more immediate problems, countersigned the Chief's paperwork where appropriate, placed my copies with other White Star receipts and returned to my calculations. I was almost done when I became aware of someone moving about in the wheelhouse. Glancing up I saw Henry Wilde's broad back, his thick neck supporting a dark head slightly bowed as he studied something in his hand. The cargo manifest, no doubt, but he was waiting for me to finish what I was doing.

I called him in, thanking him, as soon as we had greeted each other, for agreeing to do this one last trip with me. Less than two weeks since we'd parted when *Olympic* docked, and my Chief Officer was due for the big step up to command. But with all the strikes and so many ships laid up, I felt he'd be better served here in the interim, at least until his future was clear. After taking some leave with his children, he'd joined the ship only the day before, and was still making himself familiar with its layout.

'Shaking down all right?' An oft-repeated question, but it gave an opening for problems or uncertainties to be expressed.

'Yes, sir, I think so. Not exactly like *Olympic*, is she? I thought she would be, but I've managed to lose myself twice so far, just doing the rounds.'

I was having similar problems, despite studying the blueprints and walking the ship. 'You'll manage,' I said with confidence, because I knew he would. Wilde nodded, but I could tell something was bothering him. 'Everything all right at home?'

With the slightest of shrugs and a shake of the head, he managed to indicate that things there were as well as could be expected. Since the loss of his wife and twin babies the year before, his four young children were being cared for by a married sister in Liverpool. Hard for all concerned. My wife Ellie said he needed time at home and I should have let him be until the strike was truly over. But to my mind he was better off here rather than brooding ashore.

'Well,' I said with sympathy, 'I'm sure your sister is doing her best. The children are bound to miss their mother – they'll settle down in time.' He nodded without much conviction. 'It's a disappointment, I know, not getting your command this time. It won't be long though – things will soon return to normal now the pits are starting up again. Meantime, I'm glad to have you here.'

'Yes, sir,' he acknowledged politely, but his eyes were dull.

I had the strangest sense that I should have said something more. Apologised maybe, for cutting short his leave. But this time, faced with a new ship, I had to have my tried and trusted men around me, in positions of experience.

Olympic made good speed across the Atlantic on her maiden voyage, but that was the best part. With regard to service it had been chaotic, everyone strange to the huge new ship, passengers complaining, much time wasted by staff simply trying to find their way about. So for this one trip I'd insisted on having all *Olympic*'s senior officers with me. I told Mr Ismay in plain words, if White Star wanted to make a good impression with this maiden voyage, then everything must work as smoothly as possible. That meant senior officers who knew their way about, and could instruct the juniors accordingly.

Delays over the past few months had given White Star's owners an uncomfortable time. Then there had been the strikes to contend with – the miners had been out since February and had only just agreed to go back to work. For two months the country had been held to ransom as stocks ran down. As Ellie remarked, people at home had been surviving on coal dust and clinkers. Trains were running a limited service at last, but it would be weeks before things returned to normal. As for ships, they were laid up in every port in the land – in Southampton they were two and three deep.

To eliminate further hold-ups, White Star had pulled every string, pushing cargo vessels aside to get to the head of the queue. My previous trip aboard *Olympic*, we'd even carried fuel from America to ensure this maiden voyage got away as advertised.

Despite the tight schedule, *Olympic* had managed to leave on time with her new master – minus a lot of passengers delayed by the strike. With other Atlantic liners also out of service, we had garnered rather more illustrious guests than might have been expected under normal circumstances.

I should have been pleased, but casting my eyes down the Southampton passenger manifest that McElroy brought in, I felt

5

more wearied than inspired. The good, the bad and the downright difficult, all convinced of their own importance, all needing to have it acknowledged on a daily basis. There was one I had never met, but knew by reputation. When I saw his name, Stead, an irrational shudder went through me.

'A Jonah,' I muttered. 'That's all we need.'

'Ah, he'll not bother us,' the Chief Purser grinned. 'We're bigger than that, sir.'

'It's what nonsense he'll put in the other passengers' heads, McElroy – that's what bothers me. You know he's taken up table-rapping and all that claptrap? We don't want any of that on board.'

'Then we'll just have to have a little word, sir, won't we?'

'Be sure you do,' I said firmly.

McElroy would be discreet; jovial but insistent. That was his job and he did it well. Ellie said it was the Irish in him, and maybe she was right. He was a big man in his thirties, his round face and guileless eyes belying the sharp wits behind his smile. But he had charm in abundance, could entertain any company and soothe any fractious situation without raising a hair. Something told me we were going to need his expertise this trip.

As for William T Stead, Esquire, he was no more an esquire than I was, and not renowned for bowing to discretion. Indeed, he had made a profession of shouting his cock-eyed views to the world. I'd read in yesterday's paper that the former editor of the *Pall Mall Gazette* was going to some kind of peace conference in New York – apparently the President himself had invited him to speak. Made me wonder – and I wasn't the only one – just what Taft was thinking.

Almost unconsciously I fingered the medal ribbons on my left breast. Earned during the South African War, transporting troops and evacuating the wounded, I was proud of what my men and I had done in supporting our country. While Mr Stead – and that crony of his, Lloyd George – had clearly been on the side of the Boers. It was just one thing that roused my ire. There were others I'd like to have tackled him with, but my job, apart from seeing us safely from port A to port B, was to play the diplomat. Just occasionally it could be harder work than running the ship.

'Who else have we?' I ran my eye down the Cherbourg list, recognising several of the wealthiest names in America. My eye stopped at Mr and Mrs Morgan. *Not* Mr John Pierpont Morgan – he and Ismay together would have been a strain – but for some reason

JP had already cancelled. I wondered aloud who these other Morgans could be. The Purser winked and quoted a bit of doggerel.

'*Would you like to sin with Elinor Glyn on a tiger skin...?*' At my blank look, McElroy apologised. 'To be honest, sir, it's not the lady author, but the sister, *Lucile*.' Still mystified, I told McElroy to spell it out. '*Lucile*, sir, the famous couturier. Lady Duff-Gordon to you and me, travelling incognito with Sir Cosmo. And a small entourage, of course.' He smiled wickedly. 'Avoiding the newspapermen, I understand.'

'Come to the wrong place, then, hasn't she? She and Mr Stead will be playing cat and mouse all trip.'

'We'll have a word, sir.'

As McElroy left with his passenger lists, I rose from my desk and went outside for a breath of air. The day was brightening. Warmth was beginning to burn off the mist – the bridge was surrounded by drifting, sunlit wraiths. The real world might not have existed, but our funnels, buff and black, were spouting clouds of smoke into a hazy blue sky. Not long now. Making a swift plea to the Almighty, I prayed for the shrouds to lift.

Hearing piping voices and feet on the companionway behind me, I drew breath and found my professional smile. Bruce Ismay's children were having a private tour of the ship before the passengers boarded.

'Feeling nostalgic, EJ?' their father asked as he joined me on the bridge wing. His smoothly polished hair, brows and waxed moustache were perfect but brittle-looking, as though they might chip or break off were he to be so careless as to brush against a doorjamb, say, as the ship rolled. Even his skin was smooth, just a suggestion of a shadow where he'd been shaved that morning. I looked in vain for a nick or scratch that might make him human.

'A little,' I acknowledged, but in truth my feelings were more akin to those of a war-weary general. The past year had been draining and I just wanted this trip to be over. It was not, however, something I would admit to my employer.

'It's not fair,' the boy complained. 'Mama's taking us down to the West Country, but I wanted to come with you, sir. And Papa, of course.'

'Well now, I'm honoured, young man.' This child was fair and round-faced – in looks he reminded me of his grandfather. I ruffled his hair. 'Next time, perhaps.'

'But next time won't be the maiden voyage, will it?'

Bending close to his ear, I said, 'Shall I let you into a little secret?' As he grinned and nodded, I said, 'Maiden voyages are very much overrated.

7

Wait until next trip – I would if I were you.' But he looked at me with disappointment in his eyes, as if to say, *what kind of secret is that?*

In compensation I showed him the telegraphs, the means by which we communicated orders from the bridge to officers in the engine room. I showed him the chart for Southampton Water, and the chronometer from which we took time for our star sights and noon position.

'What's a star sight?'

'One of the mysteries of navigation,' I said. 'We measure the height of the stars above the horizon, and work out where we are from there.'

I was ready for him to ask me how we did that, but after a look that would have withered nettles, he turned his attention to the ship's wheel. He was just a child – not so much like his grandfather, after all. Still, it seemed to me I'd been interested in such things when I was his age, pestering my half-brother Joe to tell me how he found his way by the stars across the oceans of the world.

With a wry smile I turned to greet Mrs Ismay as she came up the steps. Beautiful, rather distant, she had none of Mrs Ismay senior's warmth and charm; *just as Bruce has none of his father's*, I could hear my wife, Ellie, say. We had expressed those reservations many times, but the facts remained the same: this new generation was not the old, and we had little power to influence them.

Noting the time, I left White Star's Chairman to answer his children's questions, and went to attend to more pressing matters. The crew should be signing on. Board of Trade officials would shortly be checking numbers in each department and – with the aid of the ship's doctors – looking for signs of ill-health. First in the crew and then in the emigrant passengers. If they could not pass muster before officials in New York, it was pointless them travelling with us, since we would have to bring them back. Generally without payment. Naturally, the company was not keen on that arrangement.

Food, water and sanitary arrangements suitable for an emigrant ship had been checked and certified earlier. While the crew mustered at their emergency stations for a lifeboat drill, Captain Clarke of the Board of Trade asked to see two of the boats lowered into the water. Fortunately a breeze had sprung up and the fog was rapidly dispersing. The junior officers took eight men each, lowering away with ease before rowing around the grey dock and raising them again with the aid of the steam winch. I'd always thought lifeboats awkward things, but these new Welin Quadrant type, installed for the first time aboard *Olympic*, were a distinct improvement.

With a sharp whistle, the 2nd and 3rd Class Boat Train announced the arrival of several hundred over-excited passengers. Rising noise told me they were pouring off the train and flooding through the Customs shed.

By contrast, the wheelhouse was a sanctuary of calm, woodwork and brassware gleaming, senior officers ready and waiting. I took a sheaf of reports from Mr Wilde. All public areas had been checked; in the cargo holds everything from china to cheese, champagne to sheep skins, was safely stowed. From the victualling department my Chief Steward, Mr Latimer, reported everyone in place and ready to receive the first wave. Our 1st Class guests were due to arrive just half an hour before sailing.

At 11:30 am, above the babble of voices, I heard the whistle of the second train as it approached the crossing on Canute Road. The big green locomotive pulled slowly into the docks and halted with a swish of steam on the far side of the sheds. I felt my stomach tighten in anticipation; but then our pilot, George Bowyer, arrived on the bridge, dispelling anxieties with the warmth of his greeting. George's family had been pilots, he liked to inform me, since Nelson left for Trafalgar, which always prompted a smile. Certainly he'd been piloting our ships since White Star's move to Southampton in 1907, and we knew each other well.

In the chartroom we went through the usual check list, discussing the state of the tide and the offshore breeze; the fact that once we were clear of White Star Dock, there were several ships laid up alongside at Dock Head, reducing the width of the navigable channel. Single moorings were common there but close on the port side were two Atlantic liners, double banked. Neither had been there six days ago, when we came in.

'Could be awkward, getting past,' George said.

I nodded, signifying my awareness of the problem. Out on the bridge the noise was so overwhelming it was difficult to make ourselves heard. A stiffening breeze had cleared the docks of mist and, below us on every deck, people were leaning out and shouting to friends and well-wishers ashore. Every stretch of quay – and indeed, every high point around – seemed to be thronged with waving, laughing people. The windows of the dock offices were alive with flags and handkerchiefs; the Isle of Wight ferry was standing off, its decks crammed with sightseers; there were small boats everywhere.

As the gangway came up, Chief Officer Wilde headed to his station on the fo'c'sle head to supervise tug hawsers and the casting off of mooring ropes, while 1ˢᵗ Officer Murdoch went to the poop on similar duties.

The scent of departure was in the air, firing excitement in the crowd. Steam, smoke, a touch of sulphur adding keenness to blood already roused and impatient for action. As the bridge clock came up to noon I gave orders to sound the steam hooter, three satisfyingly deep-throated roars which brought forth eager grins from all on the bridge and answering calls from vessels around the port. Not so many as last year – not many had steam to blow – but White Star's *Oceanic* was sounding, and even *Majestic*, my favourite command, managed a whoop of farewell from astern.

Laid up ships are a sad sight, and fanciful though it was, their calls sounded to me like cries of appeal as we moved out.

With tugs fore and aft we came off the berth, inching slowly stern first out into the channel where the rivers Test and Itchen meet. With such a massive ship we needed assistance for the turn, but with the manoeuvre complete we were set for Southampton Water, the tugs slacking off. From the bridge wing George gave his advice, 'Slow ahead port and starboard engines, Captain,' and I gave the order to 4ᵗʰ Officer Boxhall operating the telegraphs. It was quite a moment as we felt the response: vibration underfoot as the bronze propellers bit deep and the ship moved forward through the incoming tide.

We were barely under way – in fact we were just abeam of the American Line's *New York*, moored outboard of *Oceanic* at Dock Head – when I heard cracks like gunshots and yells of alarm on every hand. Both ships dipped and rose in the swell, ropes flying everywhere.

God Almighty! 'Full astern both!' I barked.

'Full astern it is, sir!' Boxhall rapped back. With the strident ring of the telegraphs I saw the *New York* had broken free of her moorings and was swinging broadside towards us, sucked in by the wash.

The tug *Vulcan* tried to get a wire aboard to no avail. Slowly – too slowly – we ceased forward movement and began to move back, but the other was still coming on. As George hung over the bridge wing, I took the telegraph, rang down to stop the starboard engine and quickly gave her touch more astern on the port engine to put some water between us. I swear we cleared the *New York's* stern with just a couple of feet to spare. My heart was pounding. George's chest was heaving. The junior, scribbling times and orders for the log book, was the colour of calico. The crowd, like Romans at the arena, elbowed for better views, while we, with grandstand seats, watched tugs struggling to get lines aboard the *New*

York. At last they did, but not before she'd drifted out into the stream, turned in an arc, and ended up in the mouth of the river Itchen.

George could mutter all he liked about idiots who had no idea how to tie up and make a ship safe, but a foot or two closer and the American liner could have finished this maiden voyage before it began. After *Olympic's* run of ill-luck, the consequences of another accident hardly bore thinking about. But even as I clamped imagination shut, anxiety escaped like a swarm of bees. I could hear the buzzing in my ears.

Inevitably, as word rippled through the ship, more and more passengers left the wonder of their cabins to view the wonder of this crisis. Their concern and curiosity touched me on the raw. Squaring my shoulders, I took a deep breath and strode back to the chartroom.

The drama cost us a precious hour, but while George and I occupied ourselves with fresh calculations for the changing state of the tide, Bruce Ismay was pacing the Boat Deck like an expectant father. Not until the *New York* was secured and *Oceanic* tied up like a Christmas parcel, were we able to proceed.

No one mentioned it, but I'm sure Bruce – and my senior officers too – were in mind of the encounter with *HMS Hawke* the previous September. George Bowyer had been pilot that day too.

Suction and the power of the wash. If we'd been in any doubt before, the facts had just been presented in the most heart-stopping way.

George was concentrating on the navigable channel, willing some enthusiastic sailboat owners to sail off elsewhere, and I – yes, I was doing the same. But it was as though only half my mind were engaged. I barely noticed the crowds along the Weston shore, or the staff and patients lined up by the Royal Victoria Hospital. The Hamble on one side and the New Forest on the other might not have existed. It was an April day with the Isle floating ahead of us like a blue-green mirage between sea and sky. Yet all I could see was that September noon, with a cruiser slinking through the haze off Cowes like an old grey cat.

Was it really only half a year ago? It felt like an eternity.

2

We were aboard Olympic then, making the difficult turn by the Bramble when the long narrow lines of a Royal Navy vessel appeared, about three to four miles away, coming up from the Needles. Moving fast, but we were already committed, with Calshot Spit on the starboard quarter and Egypt Point by Cowes dead ahead and looming. That snake-like channel around the Bramble Bank is not a place to hesitate. Not with a fully-laden ship of 45,000 tons.

She was about a point on the port bow when I first saw her. I mentioned it to George, but neither of us anticipated a problem. She was clearly overtaking and bound to keep out of our way. With two short blasts on the hooter, we signalled our intention to turn to port, around the West Bramble Buoy.

'Stop port engine.' As the 4th Officer rang the telegraph, George called 'half astern port engine'; a moment later adding, 'full astern port', to facilitate the manoeuvre. He ordered the quartermaster to put the helm hard over. It was 12:40 pm. With us on the bridge, the 6th Officer was noting times and orders for the deck log. Our starboard engine was still on full speed, but owing to the pull of the turn, we slowed considerably as we came round.

Within three or four minutes we'd steadied on our course, S59°E, to South Ryde. With the port engine once more on full ahead, I looked back to see that our pursuer was a small, twin-funnelled cruiser. Now on the starboard quarter, about half a mile away, she was clearly drawing up fast. No doubt on her way to Portsmouth. I expected she would alter to port and cross astern of us.

I turned forward to check we were running true. But *Olympic* steers well and we were. To starboard, as I turned my head, I could see right down Cowes harbour. Moments later I looked back again. To my astonishment, the cruiser was still with us and catching up, running parallel to our course and turning the foam at a rate of knots. What was she trying to do? Was her commander showing off before my array of passengers, cutting a dash just to prove he could?

He was more than a cable's distance off – maybe 300 yards. Still safe, but with the deep-water channel shelving up ahead as it ran close to shore, I thought he was running a risk. But the cruiser was small, with a much shallower draft – and she came up so quick I thought she was bound to get past. George agreed. Unconcerned, he went to look over the port side.

Suddenly, for no discernible reason, the cruiser dropped back, and, as she lost way, began to turn in. A great wall of spray leapt up along her port side. I shouted to George, 'She's coming to port!' I couldn't believe it: it was utter madness. 'I don't think she'll clear our stern!'

He ordered the helm hard over, but I knew it was too late. The cruiser was coming in at an amazing rate – almost right-angles. I could see her bridge, her starboard guns, her name, *Hawke*, on the quarter, sailors rushing to the side. *She'll never make it*, I thought in that long, long moment of certainty. I caught sight of Murdoch dashing back to the poop. Had she cleared? No. As she struck our starboard quarter I felt the impact like an explosion. For one crazy moment I thought she'd fired on us.

I raced in, pulled the emergency lever to close the watertight doors.

In a cloud of dust and rust, *Hawke* almost turned turtle as she backed off, the rending of steel like the screech of a thousand gulls. But she righted herself, that pugnacious prow of hers a mangled, crumpled mess. I couldn't see the damage to my vessel, but from the look of the cruiser I knew it had to be bad. I could feel it in the dipping of the stern. And she'd knocked us askew. By the time we stopped we were looking at Ryde.

The junior was still scribbling. The time of impact, he told me later, was 12:46.

Shock manifests itself in strange ways. For as long as it took – and

13

it took some considerable time – I was perfectly calm. Spoke to the Chief in the engine room, received assurances that no one below was injured, that the damage below the waterline was confined to two compartments; the pumps were working, and he was trying to assess the damage.

Our passengers appeared to be safe. Other than the spectators on deck, most were busy enjoying lunch, thank God, and wondering why the ship had stopped. With *Hawke*'s prow penetrating just below the Saloon Deck – and cutting through three decks of 2nd and 3rd Class cabins – there might have been some serious injuries. We hailed the cruiser – no injuries there. In the subsequent exchange of messages, I asked Commander Blunt for an explanation. It was a perfectly civil question – it's never a good idea to get into arguments, especially when official enquiries are bound to follow. He replied that I was going too fast, and that his helm had jammed. I sent back that he would be hearing from my owners.

Once I'd spoken to my senior officers and dictated some announcements, I went to find George. He was still out on the bridge, watching the performance going on aboard the cruiser. Dozens of seamen were all over her like ants, trying to secure collision mats to make her seaworthy.

'What the bloody hell was he doing?'

'He said his helm jammed.'

'What? Rubbish!' George followed me into the wheelhouse. 'Lost his nerve, more like! Thought he was running out of sea-room, the silly bugger, and tried to get round our stern.'

'Didn't make a very good job of it, did he?'

'Should have crossed when he had the chance – why didn't he? Bloody amateurs! Put 'em in charge of a bloody gun-boat and they think they know it all! Lunch waiting up in Pompey, I shouldn't wonder!'

George was livid. I was still cold, calculating tasks yet to perform. As my steward came to say he'd made coffee, I offered George some lunch in the Mess and retired to my office to write announcements of our position and inability to proceed. First, a telegraph message to White Star's office in Southampton; one to Trinity House and another to the Board of Trade; also, to the Harbourmaster in Southampton. And a message to the man at Cowes: we would need his assistance in getting my ship to a place of safety – and in getting the passengers off. There was a question of salvage, too. But that could wait: White

Star would probably negotiate terms with the towage company.

With *Hawke* standing by we anchored in Osborne Bay. Then, as she left for Portsmouth – and a sight she was too, like a boxer with a burst nose – we turned and proceeded to the King's Yachts' Moorings at Cowes. Aboard *Olympic*, the pursers and stewards were kept busy, dealing with varying levels of anxiety and disgruntlement. We got our passengers off in the early evening by tender to Cowes, from whence they were conveyed to Southampton. Although I could sympathise, how they were to continue their journeys was not my responsibility. That, fortunately, was White Star's. My concerns were more immediate.

Bob Fleming was Chief Engineer that voyage. With Chief Officer Henry Wilde we went down in a boat to look up at the torn and buckled plates around a hole some 30 feet high. What we saw was a terrible wound. I'd felt the collision, I'd been down the engine room to see the damage; but viewing it from seawards was a far worse shock. Like knowing you've injured yourself, feeling the sting of it, but not actually understanding the pain until you wash away the blood and see flesh gaping to either side.

Our fifth voyage, that's all. Heartbreaking. To my mind, serious repairs always affect a ship – she's never quite the same again. And the wound before us was superficial compared to what was suspected below the waterline.

'It'll be a Belfast job, sir,' Bob Fleming said, outlining his estimation of damage to the starboard propeller and shaft. 'Southampton can't take us – their dry-dock's too small.'

'Expensive,' I commented, 'and time-consuming.'

'They'll have to find us a new prop-shaft, I'm thinking.'

A shaft of late afternoon light cut through the water beside the boat. I looked down, trying to see where *Hawke*'s ram had broken off on penetration and was still embedded in the engine room. Fleming saw it first. As he pointed, I could just make out the device – like some huge, obscene penis wedged in *Olympic*'s most vulnerable parts.

Gazing at it, the Chief muttered with bitter feeling, 'Sorry, sir, but I've got to say it. I feel like I've been well and truly *fucked*.'

His words broke the tension, prompting barks of laughter, however brief. 'Never a truer word, Chief.'

'I hope they strip his bloody rings off!' Wilde had the Commander emasculated, reduced to galley boy and damned to hell besides.

'Oh, they'll have an enquiry,' I prophesied gloomily, 'and probably promote him.' As it transpired, that was precisely what happened. But that was later – much later – at the nadir of my winter, which at that point had yet to begin.

The thought of it – even now – drove the image of that ram right into my vitals.

3

Again, making that snake-like turn by the Bramble – like a great S reversed – we slowed right down. That narrow channel was the very devil with a ship this size. I peered through the binoculars down the western Solent, seeing nothing more than a few yachts coming up from the Needles.

'No grey cats today, Captain,' George murmured with a sly grin as we swept wide past Cowes.

'No, indeed!' But the close shave with the *New York* was still pounding through my veins. 'Nearly caught a whale, though!'

Despite the grim amusement, it struck me that George, like myself, must think of that appalling incident every time he took a ship out towards Spithead. Or did he? Perhaps daily habit had dulled the smarting edge of memory. For me though, it was still fresh. I'd been at sea forty-five years, and rarely put a foot wrong. Appearing before the Admiralty enquiry – having every glance and judgement, every second of those few minutes examined by the Attorney General, three judges, and the newspapers to boot – was like trial by fire. Worse – if worse there could be – I felt I'd blemished my reputation and let the company down.

With the approach of the pilot cutter at the Nab Lightship, I realised this was probably the last time George would see me out. Perhaps he read my thoughts for his handshake was even firmer than usual.

'But I'll see you back in, Captain, never fear.' He turned by the companionway. 'Have a safe voyage!'

Escorted down to E Deck by Mr Boxhall, a moment later George had descended the pilot ladder, was aboard the boat and away. Returning his salute I felt strangely hollow, suspecting that the next three weeks were going to be a series of last things and heartfelt goodbyes.

Even so, having just gone through the hardest winter of my life, I was yearning for peace. Turning my eyes to the curve of Sandown Bay, I longed for a few days with nothing to think about but Ellie and me. For a quiet, old-fashioned retreat where clocks were not in evidence and watches rarely consulted.

Ellie: of course. She would be worried. I glanced at my watch. The early editions of the evening papers would be out in a couple of hours, and if she hadn't heard already about the kerfuffle leaving the dock, she would soon be reading a dramatic version in the local paper. She, like me, would be remembering last September and the *Olympic*. For a moment I wondered whether to send her a message; but then I thought not, it would give the incident more importance than it deserved. No doubt she'd be sensible and telephone the office. They would explain and set her mind at rest.

Normally, once our course was set for Cherbourg I would have quit the bridge, but my attention was caught by a three-masted barque running with the brisk south-westerly. Pitching and rolling she came swiftly towards us, sending great waves of spume across her foredeck. There's somebody who enjoys cracking on, I thought; and my heart lifted in response. For a moment I was a boy again, Cap'n Joe yelling at me to reef that sail and jump to it before the wind tore it to ribbons.

'*Swept along by the breath of God,*' I murmured, quoting my half-brother from all those years ago. To the 2nd Officer I said, 'Give her ten degrees to starboard, Mr Lightoller.'

As he repeated the order for the quartermaster on the wheel, I stood out on the port side to watch the barque come past. She had nice lines and a good set of sails. The men on deck waved to us and I returned their salutes with a grin. Nearby I heard a woman say with a gasp of astonishment, 'Look at that ship – see how it's rolling! But we're not!'

No, indeed. White Star's aims were for smoothness, comfort and luxury: rather different from a sea-passage in the old days. As my eye followed the vessel, already some distance away, I remembered how it felt to be soaking wet for days on end, to feel your arms dislocating as you struggled with canvas in the teeth of a gale. And I knew how it felt

18

to be Master of such a vessel, with your eye constantly raking sea and sky, judging the wind, measuring masts and spars and sail against it.

In good weather there's nothing like the soothing creak of ropes and timbers as a good sea-boat rides the waves, with an occasional flap of canvas to keep the man on the wheel awake. Get it wrong at the height of a storm and the wind could dismast you, never mind rip your canvas to shreds. While idling across a calm ocean with dwindling supplies and a cargo to deliver could turn out worse in the end. As Cap'n Joe never failed to stress, reading the skies and finding the wind was an instinct a good shipmaster worked hard to develop, just as he must read his men and be one with his ship if all are to survive.

Instinctively, I patted the mahogany top of the plated bridge front, just as I used to pat the wooden rail of my first command, the sweet *Lizzie Fennell*. I'd talk to her, urging her along, guiding her through the weather. Ah well, she was gone now. Coal: a great fuel but a dangerous cargo. Too much damp; a sudden shift in weight; a few chips ground to dust, and suddenly there's a smouldering heart you know nothing about. Until it bursts into flame...

With the bunkers in mind my prayer to this new ship was the same as ever: *get us there safely*. It was all I ever asked.

The cliffs of the Cotentin peninsula were looming out of the gathering dusk and I was on the bridge again. With too deep a draft for the fortified harbour at Cherbourg we anchored in the roads, lowering the leeside gangway for our passengers to board from the tenders. Loaded with mail for New York, one of the boats came alongside with representatives of the French press. Eager, like their counterparts in Southampton, to see this brand new liner and garner some suitable quotes. It was necessary publicity, but after the *Hawke* incident, I preferred to steer clear of gentlemen with notebooks and pencils. Fortunately, Bruce Ismay was present to take the brunt of it. No need for me to say a word.

If our noon departure had brought forth a cacophony of noise with whistles blowing and people yelling, Cherbourg after dark was less overwhelming but somehow more strident. Passengers of various nationalities were thrust uneasily together, a long wait ashore adding to nerves already stretched. All intensified after dark by a choppy journey out by tender, and the anxiety of crossing a swelling, watery gap in order to mount the gangway.

A number of our English passengers were leaning over the Boat Deck's rails, watching the new arrivals. A halo of silver hair caught the light; when the man turned I saw his beard was of biblical proportions. Catching my eye, he nodded and came towards me. Normally, I would have bidden him good evening while making it clear I was on duty and not available for small talk, but in this instance there was no such option. I knew who he was before he extended his hand.

'William Stead, Captain. How d'you do?'

His handshake was firm and dry, his glance of the penetrating variety. Interviewed by him, I felt no one would lie, and if so Stead would know it. No wonder he had earned himself a reputation.

'Well,' he began dryly, nodding at the action below, 'I'm glad I boarded in Southampton – although I must say, Captain, I wondered for a while if we would make it as far as the Isle of Wight. The gunshots and all those ropes flying around were most alarming!'

Feeling my hackles rise, I forced my tone to be even. 'Ships not tied up very well, I'm afraid, sir.'

'But no damage done, eh?' He cast his eyes around. 'She's certainly magnificent – and an amazing size. Bigger than *Olympic*, I understand. And just as unsinkable, eh?'

'Yes, indeed.'

His glance took in the bridge and boat deck. Wondering where this conversation was going, I drew breath, ready to make an excuse and depart.

'You know,' he went on pensively, returning that unsettling glance to me, 'I don't like the Atlantic. I've crossed before, several times... but I don't like it. I'd much rather be at home.' He seemed to shake himself, and with wry smile said, 'However, when the President of the United States calls, one cannot refuse...'

Wanting to say I'd read something like that in yesterday's paper, I bit it back. 'Well, Mr Stead, let's hope we can give you a pleasant voyage to New York. And now you really must excuse me. I have duties to attend to.'

'Of course, Captain – don't let me distract you.'

Turning, I caught the 5th and 6th Officers, Messrs Lowe and Moody, indulging in some unseemly whispering and smirking as they looked down on the passengers. Lowe was a Welshman with a pugnacious look, while Moody – a strikingly handsome young man – was from Scarborough. Their names in conjunction had amused me when I signed them on in Belfast, although it was too soon to tell if they were suitably named. So far they'd seemed cheerful enough – decidedly too cheerful at the moment.

Clearing them off with a sharp word, I looked to see what had tickled them. Below, illumined by the gangway lights, an overdressed matron with feathered headgear and fur-collared cape was refusing to cross the gap between ship and tender, despite sturdy sailors on both sides offering support. The tender was in the lee of the ship's side, but inevitably there was some rise and fall, an odd wave splashing between the two vessels, nothing to be alarmed about.

Several other passengers, with varying degrees of impatience, were urging her forward. I thought one woman was about to give her a push; instead, she squeezed past and crossed the gap as though born to it. I was about to send one of the juniors down when I saw Mr Lightoller stepping smartly down the gangway. The 2nd Officer was not a big man but he had authority, and having taken charge he soon had the quivering matron on the right side of the gap. Moments later she was being escorted up the gangway.

For the next half-hour, while stewards were sorting luggage and settling the new arrivals, I was busy in my office trying to dismiss the unease of my meeting with Mr Stead. Since he'd managed to get under my skin with no effort at all, I knew I'd do well to avoid him.

A little later, McElroy chuckled when I asked about the problems boarding. 'I am informed that our lady of the gangway – Mrs Adelaide Burgoyne – is tolerably well, and recovering in her stateroom.' He rolled his eyes. 'Her late husband, I'm given to understand, was head of the Burgoyne distillery.'

I groaned. 'Not *Burgoyne's Bourbon*?'

'Yes, sir.' McElroy gave me one of his old-fashioned looks. 'She insisted on changing her cabin – apparently the one she'd been allocated smells of paint.'

'Hardly surprising. Did Mr Latimer oblige?'

'He did. But then Mrs Burgoyne didn't like the sofa – insisted on having the original one moved to the new cabin...'

There were passengers of that ilk every trip. But with the busy English Channel ahead of us, and St George's Channel beyond that, I put awkward passengers out of my mind and prepared for a watchful, wakeful night. Innumerable small craft going about their lawful business – while carrying less than adequate navigation lights – could make Cherbourg to Queenstown a hazardous passage.

With 1st Officer Murdoch and Henry Wilde sharing the responsibility of the night watch, I managed to rest now and then on the day-bed in my office. Always with one ear cocked and half an eye for the ship. Up with the dawn, and needing a look at that bunker fire, before breakfast I went down in the lifts to E Deck, past the Turkish bath and swimming pool and along to the Chief Engineer's office.

Joe Bell and I donned boiler suits and made our way to the engine room's upper level. Heat like a blast from hell whistled past my ears and sucked my breath away. As the great steel door clanged shut, the air vibrated around us. The Chief led the way down a flight of steel steps, the clang of our boots sharp against the whirring of the fans. Redolent of new paint and hot metal, air was being driven along huge ducts to the six boiler rooms below.

Electric light was feeble here. Below the orlop it seemed feebler still, pinpricks in a glowing, smoky twilight. Silhouettes of men moved back and forth between the rows: trimmers trundling coal in barrows, firemen feeding the huge Scotch boilers, shovels driving, shoulders glistening with sweat. New blazing suns appeared every few seconds, eclipsed again as furnace doors clanged shut.

The heat was fierce. I was sweating as we reached the bottom plates, but Joe Bell was in his own realm and entirely at ease. He indicated two tall bunkers on the starboard side, being emptied as a precaution in case their burning neighbour caused further problems. I saw men standing by with barrows and water buckets while others hauled coals from chutes with rakes and shovels. Smoke was pouring forth. It stank of soot and sulphur. Every now and then a lick of flame sent them reeling back. Like the mythical Wayland's forge, with masked and blackened denizens trundling past with flaring coals. Across the alleyway and into the far boilers; then back to start the raking and loading and burning all over again.

They had been at this since the day before we left Southampton and there was still some way to go. Watching the men – and knowing something of what they endured, for I'd once worked in a forge myself – I felt both humbled and anxious. You can do a lot with a damaged ship, but a serious fire leaves few options.

One man looked up, caught my eye. I nodded. A moment later they were all glancing in my direction. Joe Bell was their boss, a man many of them knew and respected: from these regions the Old Man was a remote figure, seen mostly on inspections and then only fleetingly. Despite my anxiety, I felt an encouraging word was called for. 'Well done there. A brave job. Keep at it.'

Grim though he often seemed, I could see Joe Bell was pleased. We carried on down the alleyway, nodding here and there to the men, stepping through the series of watertight doorways until we came out at last into the well-lit cathedral space of the engine room. There, I allowed myself to cough and blow my nose. My handkerchief was black.

'So how is it?'

The Chief shook his head. 'Well, sir, as you've probably gathered, the whole bunker's afire. We tried pouring water into the hatch up top, but we were getting steam explosions. The only way is to rake it from below.' He sighed wearily. 'What they don't get out will burn. But then there's the clinker to empty – can't leave it in, the bulkhead's too hot. It'll take a while.'

'And it'll need to cool before Tommy Andrews can look at it.' The moment was taut. 'A lot of smoke in there. Are they all right, the men?'

He nodded. 'They'll do. I've got men from each watch on rotation.'

'What about coal stocks? Have we enough to see us through?'

'Well, sir, we loaded plenty…' He pursed his lips, his moustache squirming. 'But the bunker fire's already used more than we planned for…' Finally, he said, 'Yes, there's enough, so long as we don't go daft with it. I mean,' he paused again, 'begging your pardon, sir, but so long as Mr Ismay doesn't want to break any records this trip, we'll be fine.'

'Don't worry about that, Chief.'

If coal was the food, and steam the life-blood, these huge reciprocating engines were the living heart of the ship. Shushing and thudding, the great crankshafts plunged up and down, working propeller shafts, driving us through the water at more than 20 knots. There was surprisingly little noise: it was more a powerful disturbance of air, felt through the ears and nose, the chest and the gut. An awesome power that instilled respect for the men who made those engines work.

Tired after the long night, I was breathless before we were halfway up those interminable steps. Forced to pause, I pretended I was admiring the pristine engine room, but Joe Bell understood. 'A fair climb, sir,' he said gruffly as we continued up to his office.

An hour later we held an emergency drill for the crew – alarm bells, followed by the closing of watertight doors, with the sailors standing by the lifeboats. Mechanically, all went well, although the crew took longer than was desirable to reach their stations. Of course, liners being what they are, most of the victualling department were excused the drill on the grounds of serving passengers. Not ideal.

Afterwards I took coffee with the senior officers in my dayroom. Not simply to discuss the drill. With regard to the fitting-out, everything had been so last-minute, I needed an overall picture of our situation. Usually we were six in all, and the daily meeting was the means by which I kept a check on what was happening aboard; that's when I discovered what had or had not been done to correct faults observed the day before. With a crack Atlantic liner, everything had to be up to the mark all the time.

Usually, coffee was followed at 10:30 by a general inspection of the ship – but, with Cork Harbour and Queenstown on the horizon, the Chief returned to his engine room, while I went through to the bridge to check our course and speed. The Daunt Light Vessel ahead, we slowed to pick up the pilot and, an hour later, anchored in the harbour, the vast rumble of the iron chain like an army of convicts on the march.

As though waiting for that signal, the two paddle-steamers, already loaded with passengers and mails, left Queenstown quay. Carrying journalists too, no doubt, ready to ask the same old questions, this time with an Irish lilt. I spotted Mr Ismay on the Boat Deck and glanced again at the clock. An hour to load, and then the pilot would be back on the bridge to see us out.

Just a handful of First Class guests arrived to be greeted and shown to their staterooms by senior stewards. The majority of the hundred or so who joined us at Queenstown were young Irish emigrants heading for a better life across the water: families with children of varying ages; quite a number of young men travelling in groups, and several young women in their twenties. From past experience I knew there could be trouble, generally fuelled by drink and the licentious behaviour that a sea-voyage seems to release in certain people. As though moral responsibility becomes suspended in the strange gap between one life and another.

Such behaviour was by no means confined to the lower classes, although the young men in steerage were less restrained, more inclined to react with their fists. And young Irishmen, for some reason, appeared to enjoy a good fight more than most. I hoped there might be a priest or two aboard to keep order.

For the benefit of Irish officials we had another lowering of lifeboats and an examination of lifejackets; then, as the final papers were signed, and the tenders left with the mails we'd carried from France and England, a piper began to play.

From aft, the haunting lament drifted over the gathered crowd. More than a few were dabbing their eyes with handkerchiefs they'd brought for waving. Out on the bridge I caught the ripple of sentiment, aware that this was my last trip, and soon I would be saying goodbye to old friends, as well as to a way of life that had sustained me since boyhood.

Whether it was a trick of the light, I don't know, but suddenly I thought I saw Dorothea just a few yards away – slender, dark-haired – amongst a group of ladies on the boat deck. It couldn't be – and yet the profile was hers exactly.

Even as I stood, transfixed, to a screech of gulls some fool of a fireman appeared at the top of the after funnel like a sweep's boy popping out of a chimney. He scared half the company to death. The other half were doubled up with mirth. The ladies, hands to lips, were starting to laugh, but I was not amused. 'Find that man,' I said to Mr Lowe, 'and take his name.'

When I looked again, Dorothea had disappeared.

4

Leaving the huge natural harbour at Queenstown in the early afternoon, we headed into a fresh south-westerly breeze. An hour later we were passing the Old Head of Kinsale – a strange feature on the chart, like a child's drawing of a man, head extended on a matchstick neck. As hills and pastures gave way to the mountains of the west, I checked the course laid down on the new chart, saw that the helm was steady and, handing over the watch to Mr Wilde, left the bridge.

I rang for my steward, ordered some tea to be brought to my office, and reached for the deck log in which orders and conditions pertaining to navigation were recorded. Having entered the relevant details for Queenstown, it was time to write up the additional notes attendant upon our leaving of Southampton.

Pen in hand, I found myself wishing that Joe were still around – the Joe of my youth, full of wisdom and good advice. Once in a while, he would talk about loneliness, the fact that as Master you could have colleagues but never friends. He was right. There was no one else to make decisions; no one to share the responsibility. In command, you are alone.

Since the *Hawke* incident, I'd been acutely aware of it. And yet I was the company's senior master, the one supposed to know it all. I didn't. There were times when I worried that progress was increasing beyond my ability to keep up.

With the brief log entries before me, I began an account of Wednesday's departure from Southampton on a separate sheet of foolscap. Once the incident with the *New York* was written up – and verified by each of my deck officers – it would be attached to the ship's Official Log Book, to be forwarded to the Registrar General of Shipping and used in any subsequent enquiry. By the time it was done my eyes were stinging and I felt like stretching my legs.

The wind howled against the heavy outer door, pushing it shut as I stepped over the threshold. Outside, the familiar rush of cold air buffeting the bridge-front muffled my footsteps. Between the masts, aerials were strung out like laundry lines, whistling and rattling in the wind. Still a rarity, wireless was increasing in coverage and in the last decade Marconi's men had become fixtures on all the Atlantic liners. I had become used to the facility – as I'd also become familiar with the telephone – but whenever I stopped to think of those young lads tapping out their messages across the ether, it seemed extraordinary, miraculous, even. In my young day the only form of communication between one ship and another was by Morse light or semaphore – and then only if you were close enough to be seen. All we could do in fog was ring the ship's bell and pray.

Nowadays though, these boys could send messages over hundreds of miles; thousands at night when the atmospheric conditions were good. The day's financial news, received from Wall Street and the London Stock Exchange, would be printed in tomorrow's *Atlantic Bulletin*. Once upon a time you left port and that was it for news until you got back; now, from this ship, they could make and transmit decisions which kept the wires humming and the financial world turning.

Such refinements kept the businessmen happy. For this maiden voyage we were carrying about half the number of First Class passengers – the bookings were much better for the return leg from New York – but even so we had Benjamin Guggenheim, the iron and steel magnate, and the American railroad kings, Charles Hays and John B Thayer. The bankers George Widener and Washington Dodge were also aboard, as well as the head of Roebling's civil engineering, builders of the Brooklyn Bridge. These were men upon whose empires millions of people depended, and they were all below, dressing for dinner, about to enjoy a relaxed and convivial evening aboard this opulent new liner.

Where else would you find men like these together, in one place and at one time? I glanced at the funnels and thought of the brave souls below, working every hour on that bunker fire. Those up top had no inkling of what it was like, what effort it took to get them safely, time after time, across the Atlantic.

Low down in the west, the dying day was painting spectacular colours across sea and sky. I paused, letting its beauty calm me, cleansing my mind of worry. Suddenly I was caught, almost unbearably, by memories of our old house by the sea, of Eleanor and me walking along the dunes with the dogs, watching the sunset together. How I missed that: how I missed her. It seemed an age since I'd been at home for any length of time.

I closed my eyes for a moment before resuming my walk. Astern of us, Ireland's mountains had become grey, forbidding cliffs, and for some reason they were easier to contemplate.

Earlier, there had been quite a crowd lingering at the taffrail. It would be the last sight of home for many who'd joined at noon. Now there were only two watching the ship's silvery wake and that blue-black silhouette disappearing into night.

In her light-coloured dress the girl looked fragile, wraithlike, as though the wind might sweep her away at any moment. The man, some little distance away, seemed unaware. I studied her, wondering why she seemed so sad, and why so familiar. Was it the girl I'd seen on deck as we were leaving?

Hoping to get a better view, I moved in their direction; but by force of habit, I turned to check the navigation lights were lit. When I looked again, the man was alone, standing motionless as before.

I blinked hard and shook my head, keeping my eyes on the man as I strode aft. Where was the girl? Easy to be mesmerised by the curling of the foam, to be drawn in by the wake. The man would have noticed her, surely? But before I could reach the afterdeck he'd turned, unhurriedly, to go indoors. I couldn't see his face but something about his build and the way he moved made me think he was my half-brother Joe.

I stopped, my head spinning. Leaning heavily against the rail, I could not have said if I was awake or dreaming. Certainly, I was more fatigued than I'd realised.

wraithlike   wraith = an apparition (especially of a living person).

5

If I'd never walked along Liverpool's quays, never caught that wonderful smell of hemp and tar and canvas, I might have spent my life in Hanley. Without Joe – without his salty tales to sharpen my senses – I might not have noticed the pall of ash and smoke hanging over the Five Towns. Or maybe it would just have taken longer to realize that I was not cut out for a potter like my father, nor even a white-collar clerk as my mother would have had me be.

Joe Hancock opened my eyes to what was possible. He was Mother's eldest by her first marriage and already at sea before I was born. I first set foot aboard his ship in Liverpool when I was barely seven years old; by the time he was given his first command I was impatient to follow him. Mother was set against it, as you might imagine. Worrying about her first son away at sea was bad enough: imagining us both wrecked and drowned was not to be borne. As it turned out, Joe survived to become a ship-chandler; but that's by-the-by. Mother was not to know and her plans for me were more prosaic. With my talent for figures, she said, I could have a clean job and a secure future – as though the idea of spending fifty years confined indoors would appeal to a thirteen-year-old boy.

There was little point in argument. I knew what Mother could be like when she had her heart set on something. By unrelenting effort she'd got us out of our two-up, two down terrace house, and persuaded my father, always a stranger to risk, to take on the corner shop at the end of the street. Mind, he kept to his trade well past the day she was making a profit.

Ironically, it was Dad, quiet and undeviating, who made the first chink in Mother's armour. I imagine he was already suffering the lung disease that was to kill him a year or so later – but I, in schoolboy ignorance, presented a long face because what was planned was not what I wanted. There was a strong possibility I might be employed in the offices just down the road, and Mother kept saying what an opportunity, and how fortunate I was. I didn't think so, but dare not complain after all the manipulating she'd done.

Then Joe came home unexpectedly, suntanned as ever, filling the house with his presence. Our sister's children gazed in awe while I begged silently for him to work some magic so I didn't have to labour in the potteries or sit hunched over a desk for the rest of my life.

I remember the sun glaring through a dirty yellow sky, all the doors and windows standing open and Mother sweating over the Sunday roast. Kicking my heels by the kitchen door, I was frustrated because Joe had gone off that morning without me. Usually I knew to keep quiet when Mother was busy, but on this occasion I persisted in complaining that it wasn't fair, Joe had been giving me some lessons in navigation, and I wanted him to look at what I'd done.

Her patience snapped. She waved the basting spoon at me, and I was splashed with hot fat which made me yelp. 'You can forget navigation, my lad, forget ships and the sea, and just put your mind to that job down the road. You've got a good home and a good family – why d'you have to be such an ungrateful creature? Wanting to be somewhere else all the time – what's wrong with here?'

While I struggled to reply, she clicked her tongue and banged the oven door shut. 'I shall be having words with Joe. He's no business filling your head with daft ideas.'

'They're not daft ideas!' I retorted, stung. 'Anyway, why is it always me? You never say he's ungrateful, when he goes off to sea!' At that I had to dodge the back of her hand as I hared down the yard and into the lane.

That afternoon I trudged along by the canal for an hour or more. Pondering miserably on the unfairness of my mother's judgements, it seemed to me that I was always in the wrong, forever punished for my wandering adventures in the local countryside – running off, she called it – while Joe, who'd run off to sea when he wasn't much older than me, was the one she missed, the one she welcomed with open arms.

That day I was planning to do the same: she'd miss me then, I reasoned, and be glad when I came home. If I could be like Joe, with a Master's ticket and the title of Captain – then she'd be proud of me too.

When I dared return my dinner was keeping warm, but for once Mother seemed less cross about that and more concerned with something else. She just sat quiet, elbows on the table, chin resting on clasped hands, looking down at her empty plate, while Dad was holding forth instead. He'd been for his usual Sunday pint and was more talkative than usual. Maybe he'd been looking back while talking to Joe, seeing missed opportunities, adventures he'd foregone in favour of steadiness and security. While I ate my dinner and tried not to be noticed, he was drawing Mother's attention to her elder son, comparing his bright eyes and burly frame to various young men of their acquaintance, all of whom were puny by comparison.

'I don't believe anybody's life is easy,' Dad said, 'but I'd like to think of my own flesh and blood doing well and enjoying life, not labouring in misery at something they hate. If the lad wants to go to sea, well, maybe he should. For all its dangers,' he went on, 'I'd be happier for him doing that than wheezing his life out, here.'

It was a speech I never expected to hear, a speech that fairly bowled me over. It didn't happen at once, of course; mother stuck out and said thirteen was too young by far. So with that promise to spur me on I forgot about running away and made the most of another year at school. I applied myself to Joe's study books at night, and at fourteen, on my father's insistence, went to work at the local forge. Although I was tall for my age, with strong bones, labouring in such an environment was tough, and two years seemed an eternity. The more so since my father's health deteriorated during that time, and our lives, which had seemed dull but secure, changed irrevocably. He died four months before I went to sea.

Mother didn't seem to grieve, she just became silent. My father, upon whom she'd focused all her attention for the best part of a year, was no longer there. The house was quiet as a morgue, only the shop seemed to have any kind of life about it. And that was sluggish, as though our usual customers were afraid to disturb her. Not even my half-sister's children could rouse her, and as for me, well, I didn't know what to say or do. Although I missed my father, I was glad his suffering was over. I tried once or twice to say so, but you'd have

31

thought I'd committed some unpardonable sin. The silence of our evenings became unbearable. When the time came, I was glad to get away.

Dad's advice to build up strength and sinew turned out to be wise. Within days of my first trip to sea I knew he was right to insist on time at the forge. Even so, I often thought that if he had spent a week or so as a young apprentice he might have been less easy about my signing on. Life under sail was hard. And dangerous. *Knowing the ropes?* I'll say. There were well over 200 on a full-rigged ship, and before we left my half-brother made sure I knew the name and function of every single one.

Despite his usual breezy good humour, Cap'n Joe had his serious side. He said you couldn't ignore the Almighty when you were alone on deck, faced with the power of wind and waves, or dazzled by all the stars in the firmament. It was as well, he said, to remember how small and puny a man was, and how terrifying the elements could be.

It was a moment of caution, I felt; perhaps intended to put me off, if put off I was going to be. But words are one thing, reality another. In my ignorance I thought I knew what he meant and couldn't wait to experience it for myself.

Finally I did so, heading off to Liverpool in the early spring of 1867 to be employed by Andrew Gibson & Co, and to join Joe's new command, the *Senator Weber*. Built in Boston, Massachusetts, she was a three-masted, full-rigged sailing ship of well over 1,000 tons, a fine looking vessel with an elegant prow. Spying her from the dockside, my heart leapt with joy. I was suddenly and irrevocably in love.

As my pulse raced and my steps quickened, Joe laid a cautionary hand on my arm. 'Looks are one thing, lad – performance another. And since she's new to the company we'll just have to see how she fares...'

Despite her fifteen years she proved to be a good sea-boat. Fortunate, given that we were bound for Hong Kong with machine parts and materials for the expansion of that distant port: bricks, cast iron window-frames and glass in special boxes. We even carried a master builder and half a dozen bricklayers as passengers.

If they seemed apprehensive at the thought of their first sea-voyage, I'd have done well to feel the same. But with Cap'n Joe by my side I was confident and excited, even though I knew Hong Kong to be a great way off. Not even Joe could say how long we'd take to get there, but he was reckoning the time in months rather than weeks.

The evening before we sailed, just after we'd eaten in a nearby pub, Joe took me into the Sailors' Church at Pier Head. While he knelt to pray for a good voyage and a safe return, my eyes remained open, taking in the great windows, soaring columns and flickering candles. But what impressed itself upon me was the shape of the roof, like the ribs of a great boat upside down, sheltering the folk below. Something in me was stirred. I remembered the story of the storm on the Sea of Galillee, and was suddenly aware that the stones beneath my feet were the last solid ground I would feel for a long time. I wasn't used to praying, but in my unformed way I prayed then for the Lord's protection.

Leaving Liverpool next morning I thought I was the luckiest lad alive. With the waterfront receding as a chuntering little steam tug eased us out of Queen's Dock, I was near bursting with excitement. Towed out into the great River Mersey I thought I'd never seen anything so wonderful as that widening perspective. Joe pointed out various buildings: the public baths by George's Dock – a popular place after a long voyage, he said with a smile – the grand New Customs House and, further along, the Sailor's Church, where we'd been the night before.

'They don't build bigger than that,' he said proudly, tapping the chart and indicating the lantern tower, topped by its spire. 'You know why? It's a navigation mark – on the chart, that is. Been a guide for sailors for hundreds of years.'

Only as we turned into the main channel did I start to feel a little uncertain. The *Senator Weber* had seemed enormous from the quay, but turning under tow she seemed no more than a child's toy being pulled towards the dangers of the estuary and open seas beyond. Feeling the dip and rise of the deck beneath my feet, my stomach churned.

Even as the tug dropped her tow, a score of men who'd seemed unaware, fiddling with ropes or just generally hanging around, were suddenly galvanised by a series of orders from the Mate. Some were up top already, one by one inching out along the yards, releasing lines until the canvas dropped. Others hauled on ropes, turning the sails until they billowed out to catch the breeze.

Joe – Sir, or Captain Hancock, as I learned to address him – seemed to do nothing but stand on the quarterdeck. Only as I watched his sharp eyes following every move from deck to topmast did I realise he was in charge simply by being there. Mr Parsons was doing the Mate's job, getting the ship under way, and the Bo'sun was chivvying the men. I must say they looked a motley bunch. Most in their twenties, I guessed, although Chippy, the carpenter – a man whose skills were invaluable aboard ship – was older than Joe. In his forties, I believe, as was Jim, our cook.

In those first weeks I survived a bad storm across Biscay and a touch of sunstroke off the Canary Isles. Thought the ship was rolling when it was me, staggering down the deck like a drunkard. Cold cloths and Joe's darkened cabin brought me round – and revealed a bond which had probably not been obvious at first. Mind, Jim the cook reckoned he'd known we were brothers all along: we were alike, he said. That seemed odd, given that I was thin as a broom-handle, we had different fathers and our mother was a tiny woman. On the other hand, Joe's blue eyes could be as sharp as Mother's. Maybe it was true of mine, too.

That day of Joe's kindness kept me going through some hard times. He'd explained before we left home that our relationship aboard had to be different, and though I understood that – after all he was the Old Man and I was just the ship's boy – it was something of a shock to find the jolly brother I knew at home so strangely grim and distant at sea. When I saw him prowling the quarterdeck I tried not to mind that we couldn't share a yarn as in the old days.

When the excitement faded I discovered a few realities. If the Master was God, Mr Parsons the Mate was a holy terror, and the Bo'sun his right-hand man. I learned you had to be bright and tough to survive, that it was no good crying for your mother as you clung, dripping wet, to the ratlines – you had to scramble for the yards to miss the next wave. I remember the first time I went up aloft. They said not to look down, but having reached the top platform I saw the ship's deck moving in dizzy sweeps below me, the crested seas surging past, and all at once my head started to spin and my stomach to heave.

A vice-like grip brought me to my senses. It was the Bo'sun. 'Now then, lad – what are you about?'

For a moment I had no idea why I was up aloft, but then I looked around. The sail to my right was furled. I was supposed to edge out along the footrope to release the gaskets – ropes that kept the sail tied to the yard. Stuttering, I said as much.

'Well, then – keep your eyes on what you're doing. Grab that jackstay, twist it round your wrist, edge your way along. Remember – keep one hand for yourself and the other for the job. That way you'll stay alive.'

I thought I would be sick, and only the imagined humiliation of

34

vomiting onto one of my shipmates below made me keep it down. I did the job at snail's pace, but at least I did it. Next time was not so difficult, but there was so much to learn, so much on which your life could depend. Those first weeks were a hard slog of repeated effort. Every muscle screamed in agony, despite the labour I'd done in the forge. But in the forge I was not pulling my weight up vertical masts a dozen times a day, or keeping my balance across a moving, sea-washed deck.

While the brickies hung over the taffrails, vomiting their last meal, or laid in their bunks, groaning like old men, I was finding my sea legs and learning new lessons every day. Not least the practical importance of cleanliness.

'If you get drenched in salt water,' Joe said, 'and you will, at least once a day – the salt will dry on your clothes and skin and cause no end of bother. It's like sandpaper – it rubs and breaks the skin, sets up an infection. I've known men be covered in boils – armpits, waist and groin – agony. Sick as that, you're no good to anybody, least of all the Mate – he'll reckon it's self-inflicted and make your life misery. So keep yourself clean. Use half your water to wash your face and neck and arms – the rest to wash your privates, and then your feet and legs.'

That small allowance was just enough. Clothes were another matter, however: fresh water was too precious to squander on laundry. The first time we had a squall I couldn't believe my eyes. Men dashed out into the rain with soap, stripping off as they went, washing their bodies, rinsing their togs, while those on watch directed rainwater from the sails into the great barrels stationed around the deck. Facing the uncertainty of the Doldrums as we crossed the Equator, with no wind or rain for maybe weeks on end, keeping those barrels topped up was vital.

But sunburn and salt-water sores were bound to happen. With Joe's words in mind, I learned not to mention their unrelieved misery, but paid attention to my ablutions after that and made sure I dozed in the shade. And if I hated the weevils – fresh meat lad! – I was soon tapping my biscuits on the board like any old salt, and waiting for the grubs to drop out.

Often queasy – mostly when swabbing out the passenger cabins – at least I was never seasick. Although in common with most youngsters away from home and family for the first time, I suffered bouts of homesickness for several months. If my mother had often seemed harsh and unbending towards me in the past, it did not take me long to recall her gentler side. And if the house had often felt like a place of restraint, it was the comfort of a cosy nest compared to the close quarters of the fo'c'sle, amongst a score of men who were hardened to the life.

Some were slackers, good at passing work to an innocent, and some were downright brutal, especially when they discovered I was the Old Man's young brother. I was glad to have some muscle on me then, to have developed some strength back in Hanley. Once I'd got the measure of the worst offender – Scouser Rudge, a black-eyed brute of a man – I took the Bo'sun's advice and stood up to him. My left eye took a punch which made the world explode; and my right hand swelled so much after I socked him on the jaw I could barely hold a rope for a week. But at least I had the satisfaction of having knocked one of his rotten teeth out. After that I gained a bit of respect, and mostly the bullying stopped.

Day after day we worked or idled, fought the weather or prayed for wind. Away from England, there were no seasons. Time became meaningless. There was only the rolling sea and the sky. Listening, watching, on that first long voyage it seemed to me that if the breath of God was in the wind, the surging seas held his power. It was transmitted through the ship to all of us aboard. It could thrill, terrify and frustrate in equal measure. I was in awe of how small we were, how much at the mercy of the elements; and yet somehow we achieved our aim. Working like furies, harnessing the winds, with canvas cracking we followed the ocean currents across to Pernambuco, then south to pick up some powerful westerlies. That leg of the voyage was the most exhilarating, skimming across the southern ocean at a rate of knots, racing the seabirds, feeling we were part of the air and the waves, at one with God himself.

I wouldn't have known what day it was, except on Sundays – weather permitting – we gathered on deck for prayers. They were not formal, but followed a similar pattern – prayers for a speedy passage; praise for our survival if the weather had been bad. Joe invariably closed that half hour with a quote from the Psalms:

Thy way is in the sea, O Lord, and thy paths in the great waters: and thy footsteps are not known.

It kept us in mind of our place in the scheme of things.

'Life at sea,' Joe had warned all those months before, 'is composed of both terror and tedium. In just about equal parts, I reckon. With just the odd moment of glory to keep you seeking and sailing on...'

If I was fortunate in having few moments of real terror that first trip, boredom was never a problem. I had too much to learn. Not just practical seamanship, but the finer points of navigation. Under Mr Parson's tuition, I was progressing from the simplicity of plane trigonometry to the complexity of the spherical triangle. Plotting the movements of the stars – learning to recognise and name those lighthouses in the sky – was a challenge that never palled.

As for glory, I found that out on deck at night in the Indian Ocean. The air was warm, every movement like a caress against the skin, the constellations so clear and close you felt you could reach out and pluck them from the sky. I'd never seen a sky like it, never seen such dazzling beauty, nor felt so insignificant and uplifted at the same time.

Once in a long while we caught the smell of land, and next day tropical islands would appear like floating jewels. Every man aboard gazed longingly as we sailed on past, imagining his feet on dry land, the company of beautiful girls, and a banquet of exotic food before him. Such moments – full of promise and frustration – gave rise to desires I'd barely been aware of ashore, although they were no doubt fuelled by the fantasies of others. Men without women, I discovered, are apt to let their imaginations wander.

By the time the extraordinary rocks and islets of the South China Sea appeared, rising like hunched grey monsters out of the deep, we seemed to have been forever at sea. Even so, when we came at last to Hong Kong, it was a surprise to realise that half a year had gone by.

The great crescent of the harbour fairly took my breath away. There were barques and brigantines, Royal Navy warships, Chinese junks and sampans; everywhere I looked there was something different, things I'd never seen before. A feast for the senses, like being let loose in a sweetshop after all those months of open sea. Even as we came in, drawn by a steam tug, we saw Chinese families sailing past, old women cooking with great pans on tiny stoves, little children fishing from boats. At night, with lanterns lit across the harbour, it was like being at the centre of a fairy tale.

But even magic can pall, especially in the humidity of August. We were anchored, awaiting a berth, for more than a week. All quite normal according to Mr Parsons, who'd done this trip before, but it caused problems amongst crew and brickies alike. Hardly surprising, given the length of time they'd been cooped up aboard. Within the confines of the ship the air was heavy with thunder, while from all around us came staccato flashes of Cantonese and a ferocious clacking of what I later discovered to be mah-jong tiles. The locals were addicted to the game and seemed to play – and argue about it – all night.

On heavy air across the bay drifted all the seductive aromas of the east: food, spices, flowers, fish, rotting vegetation. What the men could smell, of course, was freedom, and they wanted ashore. I was keen to get amongst it myself, not least for a change of diet. Hard tack and salt beef stew had long lost their appeal, and the smell of cooking wafting from the sampans had me salivating. Be it cats, rats or birds' nests – whatever the bully boys claimed these folks cooked and ate – I was willing to give it a try.

Joe and I had agreed from the outset that I must carry no tales, nor try to act as go-between in any dispute. Anything of that nature had to be dealt with via the Bo'sun and the Mate. But in this instance desperation made me bold.

'Pardon me, sir,' I said one evening as he clambered back aboard after taking a cooling swim. 'Do you think they'd sell us some of their food, or could we ask them to buy some and cook it for us?' I gestured towards a sampan on our port quarter. 'That old woman over there keeps waving a spoon at me and grinning. I don't know if she's feeling sorry for us or wants me for the pot.'

At that my brother laughed and clapped me on the shoulder. It was the first time I'd seen his good humour in an age and it brought a lump to my throat. When he'd dried himself Joe said he'd certainly think about it, and next morning detailed the Mate to attempt some sort of negotiation. To my delight I was told to clean myself up to go visiting. The jolly boat was lowered, and we rowed across to the sampan. The entire family – at least a dozen people – seemed to be living on this small craft, and they all appeared as we drew alongside. In a mixture of pidgin and sign language we managed to convey what we wanted, and after a little conferring it was smiles and nods all round. Even the baby clapped his hands. As for Grandma, she seemed particularly pleased, grasping my hand and shaking it, even reaching out to touch my face and curly, sun-bleached hair, while her beady black eyes disappeared into a million wrinkles.

Money was the difficulty, of course. We had no real idea how much it would cost to feed so many of us, nor how much we should pay the family for their services. The Mate had a rough idea of what it would cost to eat ashore, so at his suggestion we agreed to work around it. In the end, after a bit of friendly haggling, we paid less and got more for our money. That night a veritable feast was handed across from the sampan, bowls of rice and dish after dish of fish, then some kind of meat and vegetables, rapidly cooked in the big pan and shared out between us. It was the best meal I have ever tasted. So delicious, even those who'd sworn they wouldn't touch a scrap were rapidly tucking in.

The idea of the feast – from Joe's perspective at least – was to end the monotony and break up the frustration, but amongst the malcontents it served only to whet their appetites for feasts of a different nature. They were kept in check for a day or two longer, but once we had our berth and the ship was cleared for entry, several of the crew disappeared. In my youthful innocence I was shocked by such behaviour. Having signed the ship's Articles – a legal document – they were bound to the ship for the duration of the voyage. And liable to arrest if they were found. I felt sorry for Joe – as Captain he was responsible for their welfare as well as their sins and their debts, just as he was liable for everything to do with the ship. Wages, cargo, harbour dues, all had to be accounted for. Including dealings with officials in foreign ports. When men absconded it caused no end of trouble.

With a shrug, the Bo'sun said it happened all the time, but the Mate was furious, chomping on his pipe stem like some angry cannibal. It was my belief the men absconded because of him – he wasn't just hard, he could be vicious, and I think the only reason I got off lightly was because of Joe.

I did wonder why my brother didn't countermand some of Parsons' excesses, but as he explained to me many months later, as Master he had to be seen to uphold the chain of command. He had remonstrated on several occasions – privately – but the men couldn't be allowed to see daylight between the Old Man and the Mate, otherwise the ship would be ungovernable.

'And when I say ungovernable,' my brother emphasised, 'I mean *dangerous*. We need the crew to sail the ship – and they need us to direct it. When the Mate gives an order, it's on my behalf. Therefore it must be obeyed, otherwise discipline's gone. We could run aground, turn turtle, sink. We could all die. It's as plain as that, young man, and don't you ever forget it.'

6

If the heat and humidity of the monsoon region was hard to bear, ahead of us we had the vastness of the Pacific. When I saw the chart, and that huge empty space between the Japanese islands and the western seaboard of America, I swallowed hard.

'It's all right, lad,' Joe said, clamping a heavy hand on my shoulder. 'There are no sea-monsters out there – only big waves and bad weather.' And then he laughed. 'Let's pray the Pacific is well-named!'

Beans and rice formed the bulk of our cargo that voyage, together with crates of luxury goods – Chinese silks and lacquered chests – bound for San Francisco. Since the gold rush of 1849, it was said the town had more millionaires to the mile than almost anywhere else on earth – millionaires who couldn't wait to deck their homes with such expensive finery.

As passengers we were also carrying a large party of Chinese labourers bound for work on the new American railroad. They bunked in the 'tween decks space aft and did their own cooking. Sharing one of the cabins were two English officers, both of whom were returning home due to ill health. The older one was yellow with fever, the younger, a thin, fair-haired man from Cheshire, was suffering from a lung infection. He'd been ill for some time but a sea voyage, with all that salt in the atmosphere, was expected to ease his condition.

'Have these doctors never taken a sea-voyage as a cure?' Joe muttered, grimacing as the chest case coughed with every movement. 'Let's hope we can keep him warm and dry, otherwise he'll be a goner.'

With several hens and a goat penned up on deck, we had eggs and milk to go with the more usual salt fish and cured meats, together with a quantity of dried fruits and Chinese duckling.

The cook was traditionally the doctor aboard – why this should be, I'm not sure, unless it was his involvement with food, and by association, medicines. Perhaps it was simply that he was the most dispensable member of the crew. And I, being the least experienced, was detailed, with Jim, to care for the invalids. As the days passed we could tell the older chap was getting better, but not the other. He had periods of delirium in which he raved about a girl called Dorothea. Some of the stuff he came out with was downright embarrassing. Jim laughed, said he'd like to meet her, but it seemed all wrong to me for a gentleman to talk like that. Anyway, I was still calling him Mr Jones and Lieutenant Jones, trying to get him to eat, until he said one day, 'It's Harry. For God's sake call me Harry.' So after that we were on first name terms.

In his saner moments he talked about his family back home in Cheshire, the fact that his father was a wine and spirit merchant with a business in Liverpool. I talked about my parents and Mother's little shop in Hanley. We both agreed that we'd wanted something different. He'd gone into the army; I'd escaped to sea. Despite the difference in our social stations, for those few weeks we had common ground.

The other chap improved and was soon sitting out on deck, sunning himself. We got poor Harry's fever down, but to my dismay he didn't seem to get better. We did our best with hot poultices and – in desperation – some herbal remedy the Chinese labourers swore by, but his wheezing and choking got worse. If Harry was gaunt when he came aboard, as the days passed he seemed to be drying up like an autumn leaf.

Breathing was such an effort it was hard to watch him. He reminded me of my father in his last days, so I suppose I should have been prepared. But although Jim tried to warn me, when the end came it was horrible. I was nobody's idea of a nurse but I'd tried my best to keep him alive, to cheer him up and ease his suffering. In one sense it was a relief to know it was over, but I felt responsible, felt I'd let him down.

The presence of death aboard the ship was almost palpable. We were all bowed down by it. My father's passing was at the forefront of my mind. At the time, maybe I'd been too scared to believe he was dying. My mother and half-sister did the nursing while I went off to the forge.

When Father died, I took my cue from Mother and did not give way to grief. Instead I tried to shut it out of my mind. Strange to say, out there in the middle of the Pacific I was suddenly inconsolable, weeping like a child for the kind father who'd supported me when I needed it most, the father I had never appreciated until he was gone.

Home seemed an awful long time ago. At my lowest, I wondered if I'd ever see it again.

The carpenter found a length of rusted anchor chain and a few bolts to add weight to the body. Then he took a palm and sailmaker's needle to sew poor Harry into his canvas shroud. In the traditional way, Joe put the final stitch through his nose.

'Just to be sure,' he said grimly. 'They reckon it wakes all but the truly dead.'

The shock of it stopped my grief at once.

We buried the poor fellow at sea. With the ship hove to and rolling gently on the long Pacific swells, we all, including most of our Chinese brethren, stood round the makeshift bier on the foredeck. Knowing so little of the young lieutenant, Joe could hardly deliver a eulogy, but he said a few words about his courage before opening the Prayer Book to the burial service.

Many of crew had been feeling edgy, but through the wind's sighing and the slapping of waves, the old familiar phrases spread their calm and reassurance.

'I am the resurrection and the life, saith the Lord: he that believeth in me, though he were dead, yet shall he live...

'We brought nothing into this world, and it is certain we can carry nothing out...'

Bowed in prayer or respect, several heads nodded at that.

'Man that is born of woman hath but a short time to live,' Joe intoned, *'and is full of misery...'*

More nods, more sighs, but a moment or two later we all took a sudden step forward as the ship lurched on a particularly big swell. My brother's voice took on a note of urgency as he nodded to the carpenter.

'We therefore commit his body to the deep...'

On the next roll the carpenter raised the plank.

'...looking for the resurrection of the body, when the sea shall give up her dead, and the life of the world to come, through our Lord Jesus Christ...'

On a heartfelt *Amen*, the weighted body of Harry Jones was eased over the side. It went with barely a splash.

It was Christmas Eve, too, which made it even more dispiriting. Not that it felt anything like Yuletide at home. The only wrapping up we did was of Harry's uniforms and personal possessions. Joe did a rough sketch of the North Pacific chart, noting the position in Latitude and Longitude, so his family would know exactly where he'd been consigned to the deep.

Jim the cook pulled the necks of some hens which had stopped laying, and since they were too scrawny to roast, made a rich chicken broth for our festive meal. There was a special plum duff for afters, dressed with a piece of red silk ribbon, courtesy of one of our Chinese passengers. We raised a smile and a bit of a cheer for the cook and toasted each other with a drop of rice wine.

My first Christmas at sea – the first of many – and it was nothing like I'd imagined. I went to my bunk that night feeling very sorry for myself. I'm glad to say that no other Christmas ever quite matched it for gloom.

In his delirium, Harry Jones had babbled a lot about the girl who'd jilted him and broken his heart. They say hearts cannot be broken, but she'd broken his hopes and affections, which is much the same. I longed to get hold of that girl and tell her how he'd suffered. After we buried him I took her address from his notebook, thinking I'd write an account of his last days and send it to her. I began, but it was harder than I thought. In the succeeding weeks at least a dozen ruined pages were torn into confetti and thrown over the side.

Seafarers are a superstitious lot, and Harry's unfortunate death aboard the *Senator Weber* was blamed for a host of things from minor accidents to bad weather. The crew began to talk up a storm and none of it was good. Items disappeared and were blamed on poor Harry's ghost. Turned out one of the crew was thieving, but that wasn't proved until we reached California and by then the culprit had disappeared ashore.

After the strangeness of Hong Kong, San Francisco was a heaving, brawling, drunken party of a place, with loose women and gaming tables in every bar. Like all the sin that was ever preached against it was terrifying and tempting all at the same time. I dare say I might have been dragged in head first, but I had a brother as my conscience. Next time round in 'Frisco turned out differently but, as I say, this was my first trip and Joe was determined to keep me on the straight and narrow.

Our thief – one of the Hong Kong replacements – disappeared ashore, along with several others, seduced, as Joe said, by silver-tongued con-men into believing they could make a fortune on the gold-fields. Not just the deck hands, either. Our young 3rd Mate – not much older than me – appeared to have been similarly tempted.

They'll learn, the Mate growled, chomping on his pipe stem, furious at having to whip another crowd of what he called *idle, good-for-nothing lead-swingers,* into some kind of shape. We signed several to replace the absconders but even so we were short of our full complement. And being short-handed meant I was promoted to acting 3rd Mate. Dizzying heights for a first-tripper, but Joe was keen to impress upon me that it was largely because he needed someone he could trust.

'You've done well, lad,' he said that evening before we sailed. 'I'm right pleased with the way you've come on…'

I thought I would never stop grinning. All the way across the Pacific I'd been practising with Joe's sextant, measuring the height of the sun above the horizon, and learning the names of the stars. Running down the coast of South America I would have to learn a whole lot more, but – interrupting my leaping plans, Joe brought me back to earth.

'Hold fast – I don't need another navigator, I just need you to keep a watch. And it won't be easy,' he warned. 'Going from apprentice to 3rd Mate in one trip is a big jump. You'll be on the bridge eight hours a day – 8:00 to 12:00, morning and evening – and you'll be responsible for the safety of the ship. I'll be here, of course – you can call me at any time. In fact,' he added heavily, 'I'd rather you disturbed me for no reason at all, than if you didn't, and a squall turned me out of my bunk…'

He told me a lot more, of course, but that was the essential part – keep watch, and report anything out of the ordinary. For the rest of the time, as ever, I'd be at the Mate's disposal. It sounded fair enough to me. What I didn't bargain for was the hostility from our original crew. Those who'd taken me in, shown me the ropes, accepted me as one of themselves. Suddenly I was raised to the quarterdeck. Become an officer who might in theory order them aloft or even below to the bilges, a man who should have had more experience than they, but who was, in fact, a boy on his first trip.

In reality, it was the Mate did the ordering, and he was usually on deck unless he was sleeping. Even so, the first time I came up against my old adversary, Scouser Rudge, I thought twice about ordering him off his perch. The other men were putting weight on the heavy yards to bring them round, while he was just idling, every so often glancing my way out of the corner of his eye, as if waiting for me to challenge him. Surreptitiously I looked for the Mate but he was nowhere to be seen. But I knew I couldn't let Rudge be – like it or not, he had to be told.

'Lend a hand there,' I called from the quarterdeck, trying to sound forceful.

It was as though I'd not spoken. I called again, louder this time, and at that he did look up. But he didn't rise. Just turned away.

What to do? Shout? Make a fool of myself? No, it was clearly confrontation time. I'd socked him once before: I would have to do it again. Not literally – I was, after all, trying to be a ship's officer. And he was pushing me.

Descending the quarterdeck steps, I was quaking. With no idea what to say, I felt it would have been easier to drag him off his seat and thrust him in the direction of the men working up forward. But I couldn't do that. I clasped my hands behind me, leaning close to Rudge as the ship began to come about. I heard the Mate's voice from somewhere aft, urging the others to look lively. Suddenly I was saved.

'Hear that, Rudge?' My voice was sharp: too close to ignore. He looked up then. I smiled. 'Mr Parsons says to look lively. I should if I were you – otherwise you're liable to find yourself logged.'

With a huff of disgust, the man hauled himself to his feet. I stood back. 'Aye, aye – sir,' he said with all the contempt he could muster.

He ambled off. I regained the quarterdeck, trembling but relieved.

'Next time, kick his arse!' the Mate said in my ear. I jumped and he grinned. 'Well done, lad. You're starting to get the idea.'

In ballast as we left 'Frisco, we were heading south, this time to the Chincha Islands off Peru, for a lucrative cargo of guano.

We could smell the islands at least a couple of days before we saw them, the ammoniac stink growing stronger by the hour. Great cliffs loomed over the horizon, with at least a dozen other iron-hulled ships waiting to load. What we'd come for looked like white powder, but was in fact the mined and crushed deposits of centuries of bird-lime.

Fishy, smelly, sea-bird-droppings. Joe called it the richest fertiliser in the world – almost worth its weight in gold, he said. I wondered why we couldn't have carried the real thing.

'But gold won't increase your crops,' he replied, 'and it's not much use for making gunpowder.' He gave me a sidelong look. 'Refine this stuff, mix it with the right ingredients, and what you get is gunpowder. That's why it's worth a fortune – everybody wants it…' I could see he was already calculating the profits – and his own bonus for bringing it back.

All kinds of steam-driven equipment cut and ground the stuff – while labourers from all points of the compass trundled it from one loading point to another. Receiving our cargo from the cliffs by canvas chutes was simple enough, but the crew – working as trimmers in the holds – could only bear fifteen or twenty minutes at a time below deck, so it was a slow job. For weeks the *Senator* was covered in that stinking, revolting stuff: decks, rigging, cabins, bunks. And for all Jim's obsessive cleaning in the galley, it was even a devilish sort of seasoning on our food.

The stink was even worse ashore, although not as bad as it was in the hold. Supervising the crew, timing their shifts, I had cause to be thankful that our old 3rd Mate had absconded in 'Frisco. Otherwise I'd have been below with the rest.

South of the Equator I learned the path of the southern stars, but as we dropped through the latitudes towards Cape Horn, I dreaded the coming challenge.

The handful of shipmates who'd stood the course from Liverpool were not slow in relating the worst tales they could remember. I knew they were getting back at me for my promotion. Even so, I understood from Mr Parsons that with no land-mass to break the tempests whirling around the globe, the weather in the southern ocean could be appalling. Add to that the terrifying bleakness of Tierra del Fuego, where the wrecks were legendary and great jagged rocks like monstrous teeth lay bared and waiting for the unwary – well, you'll understand how such places strike the fear of God into a man.

Taking the Clipper route, from the Pacific into the Atlantic with the wind at your back, was the easy option; the other way, beating against the wind, ships could be torn apart. Joe said some shipmasters simply gave up after a while, preferring to turn and run before the wind, achieving the Pacific by the longer but less violent passage.

I'm glad to say my first experience was difficult more for a lack of manpower than excess of weather, although battling Cape Horn short-handed in the southern winter felt very much like an initiation into the arcane arts of seamanship. Nevertheless, we did it.

Jim the cook had doused the galley fire beforehand, so we'd been living on cold porridge and bean stew for days, washed down with cold tea. Afterwards, somewhere off the Falkland Islands we had our first hot meal – a sea-pie made of meat and onions and some kind of pepper they grow in Chile. It was so good I can almost taste it now, that and the celebratory mug of hot cocoa made richer with goat's milk and a dash of rum.

The weather was with us after that. We made good speed, arriving in Antwerp at the end of October. Handing over the ship's log, Joe reported the death of Lieutenant Harry Jones to the British Consul.

When we finally reached home, we had been away twenty months. We arrived to an emotional welcome, Mother overjoyed to see her two sons safe and sound. She even hugged me and shed a few tears – couldn't stop exclaiming how well I looked, how much I'd grown and filled out. I was so full at that, I almost shed tears myself; and so eager to relate my adventures I couldn't stop talking, wanting to tell her everything at once.

But I'd barely got started when she dashed off to serve a customer in the shop. When she came back she'd reverted to her usual self. 'Well,' she said, giving me a critical glance, 'you can get that straggly beard shaved off at once. You're not at sea now.' No, indeed. I knew I was home.

Joe had married his Susanna a month or so before we sailed, and on his return found himself the proud father of a bonny one-year-old son. There was much to celebrate with that, and I must say Christmas that year was the best ever, with a fine turkey, and all of us crammed around the table in the back room. By tacit agreement, however, when asked our whereabouts the previous Christmas, Joe and I said mid-Pacific, and skated over the details.

It was so good to be back I thought I'd never want to leave again. But three months in Hanley was too much for me. It was grey even when the sun shone. I missed the open sea and the sky; I'd forgotten how small the house was, and how irksome the demands of the business. Added to which my mother seemed to forget that I'd become a man while I was away, treating me as she'd always done, like a bothersome child who must be set employment to keep him in line.

In Hanley I'd become a stranger almost, and with no regular employment was frequently at a loose end, envied by old pals working in the potteries. In truth, when the time came, I was pleased to be going back to sea. The *Senator Weber* had been laid up in Antwerp for the worst of the winter, having her bottom scraped and treated, her decks re-caulked, and canvas repaired. Joe went aboard a week or so ahead of me and, just after my nineteenth birthday, I re-joined the ship in Cardiff, where she was loading a cargo of pig-iron for the Far East.

I was thrilled to be signed on as 3rd Mate, and a return to Hong Kong seemed fitting, somehow. In the New Year Joe and I had returned Harry Jones's possessions to his parents in Cheshire. The interview was as sad and difficult as I'd imagined, and their distress redoubled my sense of injustice. I made another attempt to write to his girl, but then it occurred to me that by the time she received my ramblings I would probably be in Hong Kong myself. So I waited, and planned to seek her out in person.

Of course, making a vow like that and carrying it through are two completely different things, and what seems reasonable out at sea somehow becomes more complicated when faced with reality ashore.

7

Hong Kong's waterfront at night was just as I remembered it: narrow streets, paper lanterns, strange symbols painted on sign-boards; the clacking of mah-jong tiles and the mouth-watering scents of food drifting across the water. In bars and chop-houses along the Queen's Road I caught half a dozen different tongues and saw as many nationalities passing by. Old Chinamen in caps and high-necked tunics went hobbling along, their white stockings gleaming in the dark.

The colony had grown a little since my first visit two years before, although the settlement was still small. Apart from the garrison and naval base at Victoria, the British residents were mainly merchants and their families. The other Europeans seemed to be a mixed bag of traders and refugees from Macau. There were few women of the professional sort – or so the men complained – since the Chinese mostly kept their wives and daughters locked up. Other than the sampan families, that is, but they lived on the water and seemed a different breed.

On this second visit I noticed more white women about, which struck me as a pleasing novelty. It's surprising just how starved for the sight of a female form a man can be after several months at sea. Finding one specific person, however – even a well-to-do Englishwoman – seemed impossible. I hoped that by day things would be different, that once I got away from the waterfront, the settlement would be easy to reach.

Joe said I was on a fool's errand; nevertheless, he gave permission for a daytime run ashore. Having got Jim the cook to barber me and trim my beard that morning, I sluiced myself down, donned the dark blue cotton suit I'd purchased last time round in Hong Kong, and barely recognised myself in the glass. A little creased perhaps, but with the addition of a straw hat, suddenly the lanky young seaman looked quite the gentleman. I thought so anyway.

Nodding his approval, Jim wished me luck as he straightened my tie. 'But watch yourself,' he said. 'She might not take kindly to being told where she went wrong.'

Grinning, I promised to mind my manners, ignoring whistles from the crew as I crossed the deck.

Apart from the odd pony trap, sedan chairs and litters borne by coolies seemed the chief means of transport, but I ignored them. After being cooped up aboard it was a pleasure just to get off the ship and walk.

The town of Victoria ran along the shoreline in both directions, with a scattering of houses high on the hill. Having roughly established the area of the address I sought, I began working my way upwards from the cheek-by-jowl habitations of the waterside towards the houses of the rich. From below they looked dauntingly grand.

It was hot and the way was steep. I had not gone very far when I began to perceive the folly of my task. Maybe Joe was right. Even if I found my way to this address, there was no guarantee the family would be at home, and even less that I would be allowed to speak to the person concerned. People like that, Joe said, did not generally receive young men without previous introduction, especially those of no account. The most I could expect, he said, was that a note might be accepted.

By the roadside was a small public garden. I took a seat there in the shade, and a moment or two to review things. My plan had been born of some black-and-white notion of justice. Harry Jones had loved this girl but she had rejected him, and he'd died a broken man. At least, that was how I saw it. Therefore, as judge and jury, I had decided she should be told. She deserved to feel guilty.

Those convictions had kept me fired up for several months. But sitting there with the blue hills of China across the bay, I found myself going over Joe's words. What business was it of mine? I was not a relative, so what was I aiming to do? As he'd pointed out, I could be heading for a situation in which I might be made to feel a fool. And at the worst, be thrown out with a flea in my ear. After all, we only had Harry Jones's word to go on. And he was delirious half the time.

But I believed him. I felt she should be told. If I'm honest, my imagination still buzzed with erotic images that had their origins in Harry Jones's delirium. I envisaged some raven-haired siren swathed in Chinese silk, ruby lips promising all the pleasure a man could wish for. In cooler moments I think I understood the image to be, shall we say, *highly coloured*, but even so, I began to question my certainties.

Wrestling with the problem, I reconciled my desire for justice with the heat – and, to be honest, an underlying suspicion that Joe might be right. It was obvious – well, it would have been if only I'd thought of this earlier – that I did not have to present myself in person, I could write something short and to the point and post the letter here. If she wished to discuss the matter further, then she could ask to see me. That would prove whether she cared or not.

With a profound sigh I got to my feet, tapped my straw hat back on my head, and prepared to retrace my steps. Movement caught my eye, and I realised the garden was attached to a building of some kind. It looked more like a hall than a church but there was a cross over the open doorway, and people were moving in and out, carrying cups and plates and glasses. Beneath an awning on the shady side were tables with books and plants and cakes. A signboard announced that it was a bring-and-buy sale in aid of the local mission school.

Well, it was not my usual venue, but I had money in my pocket. Surely they would sell a refreshing drink to a thirsty wayfarer? And maybe, if they were not too expensive, a book to while away the weeks at sea.

I made my way down, returning the greeting of a young man in a dogcollar as I headed for the bookstall. The lady minding it looked me up and down in some surprise before asking if I had any particular interest. When I said ships and the sea, she bent to a box at her feet, saying she was sure she'd seen something along those lines. Huffing a little as she rooted amongst the volumes, she emerged red-faced with *Robinson Crusoe*. Would that do?

I shook my head, imagining the reaction if I took that aboard ship. Somewhat embarrassed, I studied the titles before me and picked out a tattered copy of *Great Expectations*. At just a few pence I could afford that.

'I'll take this,' I said, probably with more emphasis than the sale warranted.

'Are you sure? Oh, well, Mr Dickens is reliable, and always worth a repeat.'

I agreed, not wanting to tell her that I spent so much time studying, my reading matter – and my pocket – rarely stretched to novels.

I was scanning the first few lines when someone at my elbow said, 'May I offer you a cup of tea?'

Surprised, I turned and looked into a pair of dark eyes fringed by the longest, most sweeping lashes I think I have ever seen. That those eyes were set in a pert little face framed by dark curls was something I registered like a physical shock.

'Tea?' she said again, smiling up at me.

It was all I could do to nod and stammer a word of thanks. Heat was rising from my chest, I felt clumsy holding the book, was suddenly all thumbs in my attempt to take a cup and saucer from the tray.

'Oh, how silly of me,' she said at once, 'offering a cup when you have a book in your hand...' She led me to a table. 'Here, do have a seat, then you can enjoy your tea and read in comfort.'

'Thank you.' I got the words straight that time and even managed a smile.

My experience of women at that time was limited. I'd had flirtations at home with local girls, but generally at sea I spoke with men about things pertaining to ships; if we talked about women it was mostly fantasy. Even my brief times ashore had been spent in bars where the girls expected to be paid.

So, finding myself smitten by a beautiful young lady in a white muslin dress, I was at a loss. Pretending to read my book I watched her serving tea, noticed too that the Reverend kept turning his gaze in her direction as she moved amongst the crowd. I wondered if she was his intended, and felt a pang of envy.

After a while I noticed I too was being watched, mostly by older ladies peering critically from under their parasols, and a couple of young girls who kept glancing at me and giggling. There were rather more gentlemen present than might have been expected at home, more the sort who owned ships rather than those who worked them. I began to feel uncomfortable; thought perhaps I should finish my tea and leave.

Just then, a grey-haired man in an immaculate linen suit took a seat close by and engaged me in conversation. His enquiries were carefully phrased but enquiries nonetheless. After a moment I decided a loose kind of honesty could do no harm, and explained that I'd been at sea with someone who knew a local family well, that I had a message for these people, but had lost my way.

'May I know the name? Perhaps I could help?'

'Lang.'

He was clearly surprised. 'But that is my name. I am David Lang.'

It was my turn to flounder. This was not the situation I had envisaged. Gathering my wits I stood to introduce myself, and gave the name of my ship.

He rose at once. 'The *Senator Weber* – yes, I remember. Is your message to do with poor Harry Jones, who passed away last year?'

'You know about that, sir?'

'We had word from his family some time ago. My son was a friend of his. Tragic, quite tragic.'

'I see.' A sudden absence of wind slackened my sails. Had Harry mentioned a male friend by the name of Lang? I could not recall. 'The reason I came – well, it was with news of Harry's death...'

'You were with him?'

'Yes.'

That I had not noticed the girl in white approaching was the measure of my unease. Mr Lang turned and beckoned her closer. 'Dorothea, my dear, come and meet Mr Smith. He hails from the *Senator Weber* – he was with poor Harry last year...'

Dorothea Lang – Harry's intended – the girl of the creamy skin and fathomless dark eyes. Lost for words as my heart leapt and plummeted, I could only bow and mumble some sort of banality about the coincidence.

With an effort I forced myself to concentrate on what was being said. I gathered that Dorothea's brother Nicholas was currently attached to a bank in the City of London, while their father handled the Hong Kong end of things. I had the impression it was some kind of family business, which in itself was daunting. In my private fantasy, I'd had time alone with a faceless young woman, time to spell out Harry's broken dreams, his physical suffering, the number of times he'd called her name. But she was no longer faceless; and in her father's company I could say none of those things.

While people bought plants and books, and cakes were cut up to be served with tea, Dorothea Lang and her father talked to me about Harry Jones, one voice picking up as the other fell away. Dorothea told of his schooldays with her brother Nicholas in England, their firm friendship, and his subsequent posting to Hong Kong... Mr Lang said Harry was delighted to have renewed contact with his old friends, but had been stricken by illness within months, concern mounting as he failed to throw it off. After a lengthy stay in the military hospital, his superiors were forced to arrange his repatriation. Harry had opted for a passage on the *Senator Weber* because it was a Liverpool ship.

'No doubt a sentimental choice,' Mr Lang added, 'his father's business being there.'

They looked to me to carry on the tale. Describing the voyage, the route we'd taken, the sense of helplessness when faced with an endless ocean and imminent death, I felt myself back there again, with a pain in my chest and gravel in my voice.

The sweeping lashes were lowered; tears escaped and Miss Lang covered her face when I spoke of Harry's fortitude. With my eyes on her, I could not believe the things Harry had raved about nor that she would hurt anyone deliberately. And yet even in his saner moments he had spoken of her cruelty, the careless way she'd taken him up and then cast him aside in favour of someone else. I didn't want to believe that.

Instead, I found myself embarrassed by David Lang's thanks for what I'd done for Harry, for coming all this way to let them know what had happened. I caught Dorothea's eye and something passed between us. She knew there was more, and her look begged me to be silent.

'I promised to stay and help here,' she turned to glance at the young Reverend. 'But I would like to talk more about poor Harry. Could you possibly bear to wait for this to be over? Maybe another hour?' She looked appealingly at her father, and then back at me. 'Afterwards, perhaps you could walk me home? We could talk then.'

My heart leapt. This was my opportunity, the moment I'd been planning for months; it might not come again. I saw her father's heavy brows draw together, but before he could protest I said yes, of course I would wait.

Dorothea left us. Aware of tension in her father, that he was viewing me less kindly than before, I felt obliged to mention my working hours, said I was unsure when my next day off would be; or indeed, whether there would be another in Hong Kong. Even now, I added, the Captain was negotiating the next cargo.

Mr Lang smoothed his forehead. I thought he seemed relieved. For some reason he felt it necessary to inform me that there was no Mrs Lang, that his wife had succumbed to the climate and passed away some years before. His sister – the lady on the bookstall – had been like a mother to his children, but life in Hong Kong was not easy. It was not like England.

'You must understand,' he said, 'that in a place like this, where there are so few English ladies, pretty girls are extremely popular. Consequently, in the last year or so – dare I say it? – Dorothea has become a little spoiled. Men of all ages – and ranks,' he added pointedly, 'tend to fall at her feet….'

If his warning found its mark, it could have been because I was already in danger. I told myself I had the ghost of Harry Jones before me, and a mission to accomplish. Despite the heat of embarrassment I tried to look wise.

Deep-set eyes held my gaze for a long moment, as though assessing my reaction. 'Harry Jones was not Dorothea's only admirer. Unfortunately, he thought he should have been. Because he'd known her in England, before she came out to Hong Kong, he thought he had some kind of claim. He hadn't – it was all in his mind.' David Lang paused to examine his fingernails. 'Things became… difficult. And then, when he became ill…'

With a sigh, Mr Lang spread his hands in a gesture that said they had done everything they could, but to no avail. 'So when you talk to my daughter, young man, and she asks you about Harry Jones – do you think you could moderate your reply? She was distressed by his death. I do not want that to happen again.'

Doubt must have shown on my face, because he found it necessary to ask if I understood. As I assured him, David Lang consulted his watch and made his apologies. 'Well now, it's almost four o'clock, and time I returned to my office.'

We both stood. 'I hope I may rely on you?'

'Of course,' I replied earnestly, swayed by the fact that this man of wealth and authority had taken me into his confidence.

I was willing to concede my mistakes until he said firmly, 'Do not stay too long. And once you've had your conversation with Dorothea, let that be it. I want this business to be over. She's been upset enough.' He paused and looked me in the eye. 'It's been interesting talking to you, young man – but I hope you understand me when I say I do not expect to meet you again.'

It was like a slap in the face.

For the next half hour I applied myself to my book, although how much I absorbed of young Pip's encounter with Magwitch, or his later meeting with Estella and Miss Havisham, I do not know. It hardly mattered; I had ample opportunity to digest Mr Dickens' words and wisdom on the long voyage home.

When my own Estella was free, she introduced me to her aunt, Mrs Wilson, and to the Reverend Hawkins, whose mission to bring a Christian education to the orphans of Hong Kong demanded unremitting effort and constant funds. He was an open-faced man with a shock of unruly hair and earnest eyes; full of praise for Dorothea's efforts – and the other ladies, of course – in raising money towards his mission school by the waterfront. In other circumstances I might have taken to him, but his yearning glances towards Dorothea had the opposite effect.

At last, accompanied by Aunt Wilson, we were ready to leave. As we climbed the hill and the way became steeper, she was happy to let us walk on ahead.

'Now,' Dorothea began, 'you must tell me about poor Harry. I felt sure, earlier, that there was more?'

Between my original judgement, her father's insistence that I should spare her, and my present doubts, I was stricken. But she turned to me with such a serious face I knew I had to say something.

'He cared for you,' I began, searching the dusty road for inspiration, 'very deeply. For three weeks you were almost all he talked about.'

'Oh dear,' she moaned, hiding her face beneath her parasol. 'Is that true? What must you think of me?'

'I don't know,' I confessed, trying to see her eyes. 'I don't know what to think. Harry worshipped you. He was convinced there'd been some sort of secret engagement...'

'There was no such thing!' she exclaimed. 'All it was, was – well, we flirted a bit, that's all. It was years ago. I was only fifteen, for heaven's sake, and still at school. He was – what, seventeen, eighteen? He wrote to me, I answered a few of his letters, they were romantic, the sort of thing a girl likes to receive – no more than that. And then I came out here...'

'And later – when he came out...?'

'Yes, Mr Smith, the flirtation resumed. Why wouldn't it? He was my brother's friend. I thought he understood it was just in fun.'

'In fun?' I turned in surprise. 'I don't think Harry saw it like that.'

'I know, I know,' she exclaimed, clearly agitated, her breath coming in short gasps. We reached a level spot and paused where there was a view across the busy harbour. Clouds were gathering and the sea was

56

grey. 'I know how upset he was. It was dreadful, I didn't know what to do. He kept saying I'd promised him all those years ago, and if I didn't set a date to marry him he would kill himself.'

'Kill himself?' I was shocked. 'What did you do?'

'What could I do? I was afraid. He had a gun. I really thought he might do it. I had to tell Daddy – I didn't want to, because I knew he would be cross. Not just with me, but with Harry. And Daddy can be rather alarming when he's cross.'

I could imagine that. 'What did your father do?'

'Spoke to his commanding officer, I believe.' Silence stretched while I waited for her to explain. 'Had poor Harry confined to barracks.'

It took me a moment or two to understand the implications. 'You mean he was under arrest for threatening his own life?' She nodded. 'And that's when he became ill?'

'Yes.' The pain in her eyes found its way to my heart.

There was no chance to say more, even had I been able to find the words. At that moment Aunt Wilson caught up with us, leading me to understand that we were almost at the Lang residence. By the gates she turned to ask, somewhat breathlessly, if I would care for a glass of lemonade before going back. I looked up at the house with its deep eaves and verandas, at the palms and flowering shrubs waving in a health-giving breeze. I imagined large, cool rooms, with servants waiting at table, and was tempted to say yes.

But then I thought of Harry Jones, languishing in the hot, airless barracks below. I couldn't betray him like that. I shook my head. 'Thank you no, Mrs Wilson – I'm expected back at the ship.'

Dorothea glanced up at the sky. 'Are you sure you won't stay for a while? It's quite a walk and bound to rain.' She looked so appealing, a delicate white flower backed by an expanse of greenery, it was hard to believe she'd toyed with Harry deliberately. But I could see why he'd been so besotted.

'I'm used to the elements,' I said boldly, and took my leave. But I had barely reached the town when a sudden rumble of thunder preceded the first huge drops of rain. Drenched within moments, I ran for the shelter of a shop doorway and waited for the downpour to stop. Nothing had gone according to plan, and rubbish tumbling down the gutters looked to me like the remnants of my pride.

8

Through the haze of time and mist, it seemed I'd been dreaming. I came to myself with a sense of confusion. *Pride.* Yes. *Before a fall?* True, I'd fallen all right. Painful memories, jumbled images assailed me. Then I remembered my walk on deck – the stark cliffs of Mizen Head, the curling foam of the wake – and it all slipped into place. With Harry Jones, Joe and Dorothea had even invaded my sleep.

Or was it, I asked as I rose from my bed, that dreams had invaded my waking world?

Shaking off the shadows of the night, I sluiced my face and neck with cold water, donned my uniform and went through to the bridge. It was earlier than usual, just after five, and Henry Wilde was on duty. We exchanged greetings as I surveyed the morning. A gentle swell was running, just enough to give a sense of motion under the feet; the horizon was clear, dawn light streaked like mother-of-pearl over the sea. As beautiful in its way as last night's sunset, but that light cloud cover made the taking of stars a chancy exercise.

'We picked up a couple, sir,' Wilde said in answer to my enquiry. 'Regulus and Arcturus.' As we went back inside he showed me the plotting chart.

'Good altitudes?'

'Yes, good and clear, sir. No sign of a false horizon, so we're reasonably confident."

I nodded, glancing across at the junior officers, busy with pencil and paper. All held Master's Certificates, even down to Moody, who, at 24, had achieved his remarkably young. Our bridge watches were staggered, so that during the hand-over there was always a man alert to the current situation. Between watches, the senior officers, with additional duties to perform, had eight hours away from the bridge, the juniors had only four in which to grab some sleep. Hard, perhaps, but it was all part of the training. I'd done it and so had everyone else.

'How's it looking?' I asked.

Wilde spoke to Mr Lowe and came back to me. 'Good, sir. 21 knots from full away at Queenstown.'

'Excellent.' Mr Ismay would be pleased by that. As the Quartermaster brought me a mug of tea, I took it outside, watching the pearly sky turn pink then gold – then white as the sun showed its fiery rim above the horizon. The promise of a calm day, with barely a flutter across the sea. After a winter in which gales and storms had been the norm, this respite was welcome indeed.

It would have been good to stand and enjoy it, but with a formal ship inspection on the agenda there was no time to linger. Over breakfast in my quarters I checked the Belfast faults' list against Southampton's jobs completed, and made a few notes. Before the usual meeting at 10:00 I wanted an overall picture from Tommy Andrews.

Leaning on his stick as he came in, he looked as though he hadn't slept. For a second I thought we had more problems, but the sleepless night was just Tommy being thorough, checking every single aspect of his latest design.

If sometimes I felt hard pressed, Harland and Wolff's chief naval architect had been working without a break for months. He might have been Lord Pirrie's gifted young nephew, but while the ship lay alongside in Southampton, Tommy Andrews had been labouring like a navvy. No man in the guarantee workforce had put in more hours. Checking everything aboard a ship this size, no wonder he was limping.

Most of the cosmetic details were complete by the time we sailed, but more serious deviations from the original *Olympic* design were still being pored over.

'I'll not be satisfied,' Tommy confided, 'until this ship's done a complete round-trip. I want to see how some of these innovations have worked.'

'Yes, of course, I understand. But you know what bothers me, Tommy? Those windows on the Promenade Deck. They're up forward, right where the weather will hit. What happens if we catch a hurricane off the eastern seaboard? I'm not sure they'll withstand it.'

'Don't worry, sir, the glass is strengthened – I'm assured it will take a hammer blow.'

'What about a wall of water, though?' Having seen what the power of wind and waves could do, I remained to be convinced.

'Well, I agree we won't know for sure until it's tested in real conditions. But believe me, I'm just as concerned about wind turbulence. I need to know how it will affect the structure further aft...'

I shook my head, knowing the idea had been one of Bruce Ismay's last minute changes, inspired, no doubt, by some lady passenger's complaint about wind funnelling down the Promenade Deck. Understandable – the average Atlantic breeze could take your breath away, never mind your hat – but even so, I wished I'd been in Belfast to protest before the job was done.

Having disposed of the technical details, we turned to other matters. When I mentioned our speed from Queenstown, Tommy's tired eyes lit up. 'That's excellent! So, apart from the fire, things are going remarkably well? If the Chief approves we should be able to increase the revs later, bring a couple more boilers on line.'

Since time and weather had been against us in the sea trials off Belfast, Tommy was keen to see what she would do with everything working at full power. I was, too, although – like Joe Bell – first I needed to know that the bunker fire was under control. More importantly, that we had enough coal to fuel a full speed trial before reaching New York. That was a question still to be answered.

As Tommy left, the normal Friday routine took over. My senior officers came in for coffee, we discussed departmental business and prepared for the tour of inspection. I could tell the Chief was less than happy, giving me his report in a leaden tone while chewing on his moustache. The best news he could deliver was that the bunkers either side were now empty. At worst, he said, we could leave the offending one to burn itself out, but there could be a risk of damage to the internal bulkhead.

The engine room was generally last on our morning rounds, with just the Chief and me going below; for once, however, I decided to break with routine and do the inspection in reverse order. 'Finish your coffee, gentlemen – we'll meet you outside the Chief's office in twenty minutes.'

If anything, when we got down there the situation looked worse than the day before. There was far more flame, the heat was overwhelming, the bunker itself appeared to be glowing. The men were bedraggled and dispirited. That worried me as well. Once we'd seen everything and left the area, I suggested they be spelled more often, and ordered up on deck to clear their lungs of smoke.

'It's gone on too long,' I said. 'They look exhausted.'

I was not sure if Joe Bell resented that observation, but the moustache ceased working. 'Right you are, sir,' he said tersely. 'I'll see to it.'

Grimly, we set off back again, up the endless metal steps. In silence we made our way back to the Chief's accommodation. Donning our frock coats, we joined the other senior officers. Time for the morning's rounds, the first proper inspection since leaving Southampton.

It was not entirely satisfactory. We had to retrace our steps two or three times through the lower decks. These were small mistakes, but each wrong turn was disconcerting, reminding me that for all her similarities to *Olympic*, this ship was not quite the same. I made a joke of it, not exactly reassured to hear the others were having similar problems.

'We must study the blueprints, gentlemen! And keep on walking the ship.'

On the plus side, most of the cosmetic work was finished, and the 3rd Class passengers were all comfortably housed in two and four-berth cabins. In the old days, folk travelling steerage were crammed into dormitories with rows of bunks and a communal table. No privacy except in the lavatories. Few bothered to undress or bathe – conditions were worse than in the fo'c'sle of an old sailing ship. In bad weather the stench of vomit was enough to knock a man down.

Here though, everything smelled quite strongly of new paint. And no one was complaining. As Mr Wilde checked fixtures and fittings against a defects list, Chief Steward Latimer and I cast our eyes around the four-berth cabins. Crammed with possessions but clean. Checking for signs of illness, Dr O'Loughlin gave each occupant the benefit of his searching gaze.

'Everything all right?' I asked one passenger after another, mainly mothers of young children, since by mid-morning the men and older offspring were generally out on deck.

Those who understood smiled and nodded, occasionally volunteering a comment. The foreigners tended to be daunted by the array of uniforms, no doubt assuming they'd committed some grave error and were about to be arrested. I often wondered what their circumstances were, what had driven them from their native lands. Some were simply adventurous, others wanted a better life for their children; many were refugees from Eastern Europe. They, poor souls, had suffered from police and military alike, so for these inspections I always put on my best and broadest smile. By the time we reached the last of the cabins I had an aching jaw.

The 3rd Class Promenade was a deck below the 2nd Class Prom, connected by a flight of steps and divided by a gate. Crossing the deck I noticed a young couple standing either side of that waist-high division. He was fair with a short beard; she had soft brown eyes and chestnut hair. Our arrival with keys broke up the close conversation and I apologised for disturbing them.

'Enjoying the voyage?' I asked with a smile.

They both answered shyly; the girl blushed. I imagined they were lovers, the young man unable to afford two Second Class fares.

Having to close the gate between them bothered me. 'It's a damned shame, you know,' I said under my breath as we made our way forward. 'I don't like this segregation business. Never had it in the old days – can't see why we have to have it now.'

'Well now, sir, if you saw how some of the poor devils live ashore,' Billy O'Loughlin ventured, 'tis a wonder they survive at all. I remember now, in Dublin…'

'If it's something serious, like cholera or smallpox,' I protested, turning to emphasise the point, 'how do they think the ship's staff are going to escape? Or the other passengers? Take that couple back there, chatting over the gate. Anyway,' I added, turning to the Chief Steward, 'your people are in and out all the time, Latimer, they could carry any number of diseases. It's pointless – just a nod to quarantine. If you ask me it's quite unnecessary.'

Latimer would never ask; and Billy knew me too well. We'd sailed together for years, ever since he joined me aboard the *Baltic*. Between us we'd seen most of life's dramas and tragedies at sea, from premature births and sudden deaths to a most distressing suicide. Things like that draw you together.

I knew he didn't like Ellis Island any more than I did; it was an unpleasant fact of life to which we simply had to close our eyes. But whenever I was faced with it – when it became personal, as back there – I felt the need to protest. My family hadn't lived in poverty, but my parents hadn't much money either. Had they wanted to emigrate, we'd have been travelling steerage, subject to the same harsh regime.

For the last 20 years, segregation had been required by the American authorities. On docking in New York, 1st and 2nd Class disembarked after a cursory check, while ferries took 3rd Class immigrants across to the island for registration. All right, many of them were tough as old boots, but even folk with young children could be held for hours on those boats, in all weathers, with no protection. And once landed it was often days before they cleared the place. The medical inspections were unpleasant, making our boarding checks seem like a parental once-over. If you had a 1st or 2nd Class ticket though, you were welcomed at once. On the principle that since you clearly had the means to support yourself, you wouldn't be a liability.

I wondered how the young lovers were intending to handle the Ellis Island aspect; how they would manage to meet up again after the separation. 'I think somebody should explain to that young couple back there just what will happen when we dock. They need to be prepared. Mr Latimer – will you see to it?'

'Yes, sir.' I saw him making a note.

'Better do it now, Mr Latimer – in five minutes they'll be gone and you won't know who they are.'

Nameless, seen but once, yet how their earnest faces lingered.

Powdered cheeks, rows of pearls, a bosom plump as a partridge. Her looks spelled wealth not poverty. She looked hard at me, but the lady's face was not familiar. Over lunch in the Saloon with Bruce Ismay, I kept catching a glance from three tables away, a narrow smile and the slightest of nods when I met her gaze. It seemed as though she knew me. Discreetly, I enquired of the steward. Her name was Mrs Burgoyne.

Ah. Our lady of the gangway, as McElroy had dubbed her. The bourbon widow who could not endure the smell of paint. I would have to speak to her at some point, find out when and where we'd met. I glanced here and there, wishing I could see the young lady I'd glimpsed at noon the day before, but the Saloon was busy, ladies and gentlemen coming and going all the time.

Bruce barely turned his immaculately-groomed head. He wasn't interested in passengers – not unless they were multi-millionaires with a stake in White Star. He wanted to know the state of play in the engine room. That was exactly how he put it: *state of play*, as though the fire and the men who battled it were opposing teams in a game of cricket. I would have liked to despatch him below to see the situation for himself, but that would never do. Bruce liked to impress people; he liked to *chat*. Nothing vital or confidential, just odd crumbs of inside information to be lapped up greedily by his cronies and passed on yet again. I felt sure the fire was one thing he wouldn't like to chat about, but there was a danger he might let something slip. So I told him there was no need for anxiety and covered the white lie with something positive.

'We're up to 21 knots now, and Mr Andrews thinks we're ready to bring more of the boilers on line.'

'Really? I must say, that is good news!' Bruce almost smacked his lips over the pudding, and proceeded to wax lyrical about *Olympic*'s record-breaking maiden voyage.

'There is just one thing, sir,' I interjected, lowering my voice. 'About our speed trial. We may have to be careful about fuel stocks.'

He set down his spoon as though nanny had whipped away a special treat. 'Careful?' he demanded. 'Why?'

I raised my brows. 'Well, Mr Ismay, sir, the bunker situation has taken more than we bargained for.'

'Oh. Really?'

For an intelligent man, Bruce could be quite obtuse. 'It would be embarrassing,' I said carefully, 'were we to run short...'

He looked aghast. 'You don't seriously think...'

'No, sir, I do not. Not for one moment. But more speed requires more coal – that's the truth of it. The Chief needs to look at things. Once everything's cooled down, that is.'

'Ah. I see.' Smoothing first his moustache, and then an eyebrow as he considered this, he suddenly said, 'I suppose – I mean, there's *no doubt*, is there, that this situation will be *resolved* by the time we reach New York?' As I hesitated, he added, 'It would be deuced embarrassing to have to call in the fire brigade.'

'It won't come to that,' I replied, more sharply than I intended. Just the thought of it made me sweat.

He looked hard for a moment, then glanced around, catching Mrs Burgoyne's eye as she left with her female companion. Having nodded, he enquired of me who she was. 'Do I know her?'

'She seems to know me, sir.'

Bruce viewed me speculatively, as though I might once have

conducted an illicit liaison with the lady. I gazed back, hoping he could read my thoughts. Evidently, he could. He looked away. 'I'll speak to the Chief,' he said, as though that would solve everything.

We parted by the lifts. I was about to take the stairs to the upper deck when I noticed Mrs Burgoyne close by. With a sense that I should gird myself for this encounter, I bade the ladies good afternoon.

'How are you, Mrs Burgoyne?' I was about to ask where we'd met before, but she didn't give me the chance.

'I thought you were dead,' she said accusingly.

Astounded, I felt my habitual smile slip. I made a show of pulling at my beard. 'No, I think I'm alive...'

'Your name meant nothing to me, sir – Smith being so *common*, you understand. But then I saw you, and recognised you. I have to say, sir, it was a *dreadful* shock.'

'I'm sorry, Mrs Burgoyne, you have me foxed. Clearly you remember me, but...'

'Savannah, Georgia...' She paused, but I was still in the dark. 'You came courting my dear sister – and then disappeared without a word.'

'Savannah?' With surprise, I smiled and said, 'But I haven't been there in thirty years!'

She glared at me, while the companion wilted beside her. 'I guess that's right.'

Thinking longingly of the quiet hour I'd promised myself, I suggested we might sit down and have coffee, rather than discussing old acquaintance by the elevators. To my relief, as soon as we were seated the companion – a sparrow to Mrs Burgoyne's more flamboyant bird of paradise – fluttered away.

'So, Savannah,' I said, waiting for her to fill in the gaps. Savannah to me meant sweltering heat, Colonial houses, vast estates, and *cotton* – bartering with agents, judging the staple, trying to get the best possible quality, watching the stowage as it came aboard. But then she named one of the plantations from which I'd bought when I was Master of the *Lizzie Fennell*, and the circumstances came back to me. Her father had been a big, swaggering man, difficult to deal with. When Mrs Burgoyne named her sister, Marcia, she came to mind at once: Marcia, one of the languid beauties for which the South was famous, and yes – I had been rather keen on her.

As the older woman refreshed my memory – somewhat resentfully, it has to be said – gradually the young Adelaide came to mind, a gawky, wide-eyed girl aged maybe twelve or fourteen, present somewhere in the background when I visited the house. She was hard to recognise in the plump features of the woman before me.

I'd been in my late twenties when Adelaide Burgoyne first knew me, trading from southern ports like Galveston and Savannah. Her father was a bully, used to browbeating his way through negotiations, but I'd refused to be rushed into purchasing my cargo, and, with time on my side, eventually paid a fairer price.

Later, having gained a modicum of respect, I was invited to the estate to see how the crop was harvested and fed through the cotton gin before baling. It was interesting, but then so was his elder daughter Marcia. She knew how to smoulder – and to tease. Alone and frustrated through some warm southern nights, I told myself not to be a fool. If I'd found a liberating sense of acceptance in America, I knew equally well that as a young sea-captain with no assets, my chances with Marcia were virtually nil.

Not until my next visit a few months later, when she began to talk about riverboats, did I realise with a shock how warm things had become. We were by the waterfront, watching cotton bales being loaded onto a barge. The suggestion that I might come ashore, work the boats, was phrased delicately, but I had only to picture her bullying father as my father-in-law to experience a great longing for the open sea.

I felt my memory begin to slide down darker paths, and only as Adelaide Burgoyne enquired, somewhat querulously, about my subsequent disappearance, did I drag myself back to the present.

'You took off that time with never a word – we thought you were dead,' she repeated. 'Poor Marcia was inconsolable for months.'

Even after thirty years, I was sorry to hear that and said so. 'Under the circumstances,' I added gently, 'there was no time for delay – we had to leave at once. But you know, Mrs Burgoyne, I wrote to your father from Liverpool. To advise him the ship and his cargo had arrived safely.' In truth I'd wanted to let Marcia know – through her father – that I was changing my direction.

'Did you?' It was clear she didn't believe me.

'Yes, I did. Since it was largely concerning business matters, perhaps he didn't say?'

'We thought you were lost in that hurricane!' she protested. 'You, the ship, the cargo – lost at sea! He wouldn't have kept that from us!'

Would he not? It was cruel, but perhaps not such a surprise. Looking back, I thought he'd been less keen on the idea of me as a son-in-law than Marcia – and her sister – had imagined. For him, perhaps that hurricane had come at an opportune moment.

Apologising again for having sailed away and left them in the dark, I said, 'You're right in one sense, Mrs Burgoyne. That hurricane nearly finished us. We had quite a job getting home to Liverpool. As it happened, I never went back to Savannah. If I had,' I assured her, 'I would have called on your sister.'

'You'd have been too late,' she snapped. 'Marcia married Beau – the man Father wanted for her all along!' At that she gathered herself together and left me with an untouched cup of coffee.

9

It was the back end of August, hurricane season, a week or so after the conversation about riverboats and pilotage. In Savannah the air had been thick and sticky for days. Folk were watching barometers and battening down in readiness for a bad blow. Every shipmaster in port was trying to get away before the wind hit. No matter how bad the weather, at sea you can ride the storm. Hang around in a confined space and you'll be smashed to smithereens.

We were fortunate in that respect – in fact I was congratulating myself on having most of the cargo aboard, 2,000 bales of cotton stacked in the hold and 'tween deck space, with another 800 to be lashed on deck. If I gave back-word on the deck cargo – always a good move in bad weather – we could be away with the next tide. I sent the 3rd Mate to round up the stragglers ashore, and while the drunks were still reeling to some inner music we were towed out into the river. An hour or so later, having made the open sea, I put her on a north-easterly heading, and with all sail set prepared to put as much sea as possible between me and the land before that weather hit.

I wasn't overly worried. I'd been through some bad blows since my promotion to Master in 1875, and enjoyed the challenge. *I can do this*, was a thought that always got me through, and while I was generally too busy to remember the years of experience, in some quiet backwater of my mind Joe was always there, overseeing every action. I'd expected to do a third trip with him, but with just a few months of sea-time to qualify for my 2nd Mate's exam, he pushed me to sign on for the Atlantic run. Gibson's had no 3rd Mate's job available, so I signed on instead as able seaman aboard the *Amoy*. Those two trips across the North Atlantic, to Norfolk, Virginia, and St John's, Newfoundland, were hard, but I wouldn't have missed them for the world. In those few months I really learned my trade, and could say with the best that I knew how to handle a ship. Not only knew how, but loved the thrill of battling the wind, of finding a way forward when the elements were against us. Better still, cracking on to skim across the waves when everything was in our favour.

At 21 I had my 2nd Mate's ticket, and by 23 my 1st Mate's. By 25, like Joe, I was a qualified Master Mariner, and a year later was given my first command. Sweet *Lizzie Fennell*, a full-rigged ship of just over a thousand tons, built at St John, New Brunswick, with a wooden hull and lines similar to the old *Senator*. She seemed so familiar I loved her from the start, and I swear she responded to that. I soon got to know her little ways and she seemed to know mine; so, with that weather building behind us, I was rightly concerned but not afraid. I knew she'd see us through.

I'd hoped to outrun the weather, but we didn't quite make it. Just two nights later the skies were dense, and with no moon it was as black as pitch on deck. I could feel the seas coming up from starboard in long, oily swells. Hard to see except where they met the ship's quarter in a long, rolling crest of foam. First light was a relief, but the mainmast was describing huge arcs against breaking banks of cumulus, the dark seas presenting bottomless black hollows on every side. For a while the wind remained favourable, but as the sun came up it changed, gusting from every direction; and then I saw the anvil of the storm behind us, growing, flattening, rolling a turbulent shelf of air towards us.

I spoke to the Mate. The men were aloft almost before the orders were given. With part-reefed sails we ran before the tempest, hauling in canvas as we went, great spumes of water leaping over the stern and pouring down the deck. Hard to tell whether we were soaked with spray or hail or driving rain. For a few hours we managed to keep up, always with the fear that if we reefed too much we'd lose control; too little and we'd lose the mast. And meanwhile the wind shrieked through the rigging as though all the devils in hell had turned out to drag us overboard.

The men were working overtime on the bilge pump, but the

cargo was well-battened down, so I had no particular fear for it. It was the ship herself I feared for – and the men, lashed together, struggling with lines and ropes, one after another swept off their feet as poor *Lizzie* was flung about, this way and that. It was like being punched and beaten, hard to breathe, hard to think beyond the need to hold hard and keep your feet. With seas coming green over the starboard quarter, we had two men on the wheel, while Jameson and I were linked to the quarterdeck rail. You expect bad weather in the North Atlantic, but this was more ferocious than anything I'd ever experienced.

While Jameson, drenched, kept his attention forward, I flung stinging water from my eyes and cast my attention aft. The taffrail was away. Alarm shot through me. If the poop should be breached and the rudder damaged, we'd be finished.

There were no clear options. I fretted, knowing I had to depend on the skill of those eastern seaboard shipwrights, but even as I willed my soul into the timbers around me, *Lizzie* climbed a massive wave, teetering on the crest. Black holes appeared on every side, the sea a many-mouthed monster about to swallow us whole. I urged her over the crest with every prayer I could think of. Just as I thought she would do it, a massive sea came up from starboard and shoved us bodily sideways. I yelled at the helmsman, the Mate yelled orders above the screaming of the wind. No use. We were dropping, beam on to those massive waves. Taking them aboard. Going over.

This is it, I thought as my legs went from under me. In the next instant, smacked hard by the sea, everything went black.

When I came to, I was half-strangled and up to my neck in water. I could feel something hard in the middle of my back – that turned out to be the Mate's knees. His hefty fist had hold of my collar, and he was endeavouring to haul me up the deck and out of the water. I grabbed at the quarterdeck rail, using the uprights like a ladder. Incredibly, our *Lizzie* hadn't turned turtle, but was partially submerged and lolling horribly to port.

When I had sense enough to take things in, I saw the masts were at a crazy angle, the lifeboat banging from its lashing amidships, men hanging off ropes like monkeys. Worse, the main hatch-cover was breached – a hasty job sought out by wind and waves – layers of canvas ripping free. As seas crashed over us, I felt the cargo begin to shift. Felt those cotton bales swell and burst their battens. As the ship sank further every man grabbed something better to anchor him. I thought we were done for. Clinging to the quarterdeck rail, I tried and failed to undo the rope around my waist. As though being free to swim could have saved me.

But our *Lizzie* did not go over. She lolled, swamped and helpless, while we poor sailors expected to meet Davy Jones any minute. But we were effectively in the lee of the ship, and, despite the battering, the dreadful exhaustion of our precarious position, by some sweet miracle *Lizzie Fennell* stayed afloat.

The Mate and I were close enough to exchange words. With each switch and shriek of the wind we tried to guess what the hurricane was doing, how long before it might loosen its grasp and let us be.

Gradually the 2nd and 3rd Mates got around the men, establishing that none were lost. All we could do was hang on and pray. Sometime during the night, in the midst of cramp-like agony, we became aware that the noise was less, the devils had stopped shrieking and the rain ceased lashing. I glimpsed the stars for the first time since leaving Savannah, and it came to me that we were being tossed about in the aftermath, that the monstrous thing had curved away, chewed and shaken us like rats but spat us out, indigestible.

We were alive, for which God be praised. Our sweet *Lizzie* hadn't let us down, she'd stayed afloat beyond every expectation. But she was in a bad way. We would have to summon every ounce of energy to get her upright again.

Something Joe never said in so many words – something so basic he probably felt it not worth mentioning – was that a ship can come alive only by virtue of the energy we men invest in her. Unless every man pulls together the ship will founder and fail. And it doesn't matter who we are, whether we hate each other, despise our officers, loathe the work – we must care for our ship. She is our only saviour. Without her, we are all lost.

It was never more evident to me than when we surveyed our position in the morning light. Before the hurricane struck, we'd been in the warm Gulf Stream, approaching Cape Hatteras, some fifty miles or so from the land. When morning came, we could see the black and white lighthouse on the point. It was behind us. Somehow the hurricane had swept us to the north-west, missing the Diamond Shoals – a veritable graveyard for ships – by what can only have been a hair's breadth.

The sea was still hugely disturbed, so we were not yet out of danger.

71

While the 2nd Mate organised teams to man the bilge pump in short spells – it was a brutal job at the best of times, and worse at that angle – Jameson and I worked out how best to catch the prevailing wind and ease us away from the shoals. Just looking at the state of the ship made me sick with apprehension, yet I knew we had to get her right. With the jolly boat gone, all we had was our *Lizzie.* She was our only chance, even though seeing her at this angle it was hard to believe she was still sound. The men were rigid with fear and no wonder, but until we could get her up a bit we wouldn't know the extent of the damage, and we couldn't get her up until we got rid of some water below decks.

With difficulty, the 2nd Mate and I got into the hold. We saw the cotton bales had swollen and sagged to port, increasing the list and holding us down. Pointless hauling them back up again. I figured the bales would gradually drain out into the bilge space – or they would if it wasn't already full of water.

'So,' I gasped to Jameson when he hauled me out, 'we keep pumping bilges, let the bales drain naturally, and she should start coming up. Once we're close to an even keel we can think about repairs and re-stowing the cargo.'

Jameson raised his heavy brows. 'It'll be a hard slog. For the men, I mean.'

'Aye, it will indeed. Spell it out to them – there's no choice. It's that or we slop around here until the food and fresh water run out.'

'We couldn't get back to Wilmington?'

'No. We get straight, survey the damage, then make decisions. Meanwhile, grab the cook and let's see what he can do for us. If they're to work, the men need food…'

We did get straight, we did pull her up, we found the Gulf Stream again and made it back to Liverpool by dint of every man's will and sheer hard labour. It was a slow, sluggish, arduous journey across the Atlantic, despite the current and some good westerlies pushing us along. By the end of those 25 days I felt I'd ground the grit of my determination into the very timbers of the ship. By the time we reached the Mersey I was nauseous with exhaustion, wondering how Joe had managed to be so chipper, coming home from trips like this.

And then came the moment that erased all that. Approaching the Bar Lightship we passed one of the new Atlantic steamers: sleek black hull, white-painted accommodation, four tall masts and a buff and black funnel trailing a long plume of smoke. Her canvas was furled yet *RMS Britannic* was cutting the foam like a tea-clipper. Wallowing in the wake, *Lizzie Fennell* nearly threw me off my feet.

It was like seeing a beautiful woman walk past with a rival. Love, lust and envy, all rolled into one. That ship, that day, spelled the future to me.

A month later I applied to the two most prestigious companies afloat. Cunard had no vacancies but, in the spring of 1880, White Star took me on.

10

'You can smile, Ted,' Joe allowed over a supper of bread and cheese, 'but these infernal steamships are in danger of making us forget our place in the order of things. Praying for good speed and a fair passage keeps a man in touch with the Almighty. A man is never in charge of anything, you know, except by the grace of God.'

I mumbled some sort of acknowledgement as he emphasised the point with his knife. 'This modern preoccupation with clocks and timetables isn't good. You mark my words – get on those steamships, you'll not be the owners' servant, you'll be a slave to time...'

A slave to time... I came to with a shiver, Joe's voice in my ear, startled, disoriented, young again, thinking I knew it all and my brother was getting to be an old fogey...

Aware that I'd drifted into dreams, I roused myself, wondering why my steward hadn't called me. But a glance at the clock said I'd been asleep for barely an hour.

With an effort I got up, went to the bathroom, relieved myself, rinsed hands and face and stared at the reflection in the glass. The weathered old face stared back, white beard, white hair, neater now, with all its youthful curl gone; and a nose that was starting to show signs of good living.

Ellie said I should cut back on the spirits. Not that I drank much at sea – when the weather was bad I needed every wit I could summon. Bending to my shoes, I felt I should really cut back on the meals.

Straightening again, pressing studs into the wing-collar, I fiddled with the bow tie but managed it. Remembering the old days, my struggles to master that one essential item of gentlemen's clothing, I found myself smiling – which brought forth a cheery response from Paintin, my steward, when he came through to assist with waistcoat and mess-jacket.

While he adjusted the epaulettes I stood before the glass wondering where the fit young shipmaster had gone. Time: that word again. A long time since I was surviving on salt beef stew and hard tack, falling into the nearest chop house for a decent meal once we landed ashore. Now it was turtle soup and crown of lamb any day of the week, with some frothy concoction for pudding. Not to mention the best selection in French and English cheeses. I caught Ellie's eye viewing me and sighed, telling her – in my mind, anyway – that it would be easier once I was home for good, once I had her to care for me, to remind me not to have that extra helping or that second nightcap.

In Southampton, when I was showing her the new ship, she'd admired my quarters with its soft carpeting – another of Tommy Andrews' innovations – and said the dayroom with its oak panelling and easy chairs was most attractive, reminding her of my study at home. All it needed, she said, arranging some of my favourite reading matter on the bookshelves, was the scent of cigars to make it mine entirely.

'That won't take long,' I replied with a chuckle, following her through to the bedroom.

'This room looks lonely, though,' she'd commented, giving me one of those quick upward glances that said so much more than words. She meant she was feeling lonely; and guilt swept over me because I'd hardly been at home all winter. I gazed at her portrait by the bed, overwhelmed by love and longing. I needed her so much I ached with it.

Paintin straightened the bedcover and replaced the eiderdown. 'I understand we're in for a calmer voyage, sir?'

'Well, the next day or so, certainly,' I replied, startled out of my reverie. 'Make the most of it while you can.'

The weather reports we had received so far from other ships crossing the Western Ocean were good, extraordinarily so for the time of year. Mad March gales had given way to a period of calm. After a winter spent battling some of the worst storms in living memory, the entire ship's company needed this respite. With a sense that I might just be able to relax a little over the next few days, I went through my office

75

to the bridge and had a word with 2nd Officer Lightoller, told him that if I was needed, I'd be eating in the Saloon.

A few days before, there had been tools and wood shavings wherever we looked, men working, rolls of carpet and furniture stacked up against the walls, the smell of paint overpowering. It was still detectable, but as far as I knew Adelaide Burgoyne had been the only one to insist on being moved to a different cabin. As the Chief Steward frequently claimed, it was like running a grand hotel – in this case, a brand new one offering 24-hour service. But still, after the last few days of strain and anxiety it was good to see things looking as they should. Carpets plush underfoot, woodwork gleaming, glass shining and enough mirrors – as someone said – to rival those at Versailles. Well, that was an exaggeration, but aboard *Olympic*, some thoughtless aristocrat, used to the grand halls of stately homes, had complained that the ceilings were rather low, and wondered why the builders couldn't have made them higher. 'Because it's a ship, sir,' I said briskly, and moved on.

Since this was my first social evening I marked the occasion by taking the grand staircase down to D Deck, running my hands down its gleaming oak balustrade. The great clock on the half landing was impressive with classical figures carved either side in sharp relief. It was grander by far than *Olympic*'s clock – and to my eye the proportions were better. But when Tommy Andrews told me in Belfast what the figures represented – Honour and Glory over Time – I thought it rather ironic. In my experience, Time was king in every case.

Descending to the Reception Room, I slowed my steps to identify familiar faces. I spotted John Jacob Astor's birdlike features – I'd met him before, but not his new young wife. Dr O'Loughlin said she was pregnant, which would set the scandal sheets ablaze again. They'd not long settled down after his divorce. The Astors were in company with Mrs Margaret Brown, her purple satin gown almost as strident as her voice.

Ellie, not usually a snob, said Mrs Brown was a dreadfully common woman whose domineering character had been given untold licence by untold riches. Well, it was close, but still didn't describe her exactly. She was an intelligent woman with more force and energy than a steam train: fuelled, in her case, by a gold mine in Colorado. Get her rolling on the subject of women's rights and I felt she'd quell a riot – or, more likely, start one. That aside, she could be very amusing and I rather liked her. Even so, I was surprised to hear from

McElroy that she was travelling with the Astors – I'd always thought John Jacob rather grand. But perhaps his affair with the 18-year-old Madeleine Force had cost him more dearly than I knew. Maybe he was glad of Margaret Brown's support.

The tall figure of Major Archie Butt stood out. The Presidential aide to Mr Taft was in conversation with his old friend, the artist and writer Frank Millet, another regular with White Star. But suddenly heads were turning as a small man with bushy white hair came into view. As someone moved I saw it was William Stead, smiling at all around him, shaking hands. There was a young woman at his side.

I halted, mid-step. In a lavender gown, her dark hair swept up, she was so like Dorothea Lang. Not an illusion, after all, but flesh and blood. Smiling, her glance moved first to Major Butt, and then to Frank Millet. They were clearly charmed – and why not? Looks like hers have always turned heads.

A little shaken, I made my way down. A steward was passing with a tray of drinks. Champagne. I took a glass, heedless of my usual habits, and drained it almost in one.

What was she doing with Stead? As I wondered, they were joined by Colonel Gracie and James Clinch Smith – both regular patrons – and two ladies in black. The groups melded, stood talking. Dorothea – or so I named her – seemed to know the others, which was puzzling. Stead was English, Gracie from the southern States. I was planning a strategic walk through the crowd when Mrs Burgoyne hove into view, pearls gleaming, feather boa trailing.

She joined them, simpering up to the Colonel as though he were the late Mr Burgoyne's best friend. He may have been, but somehow I doubted it. As I hesitated, a voice beside me said lightly, 'Good evening, sir. Is anything wrong?' And I turned to see Billy O'Loughlin, the one man aboard I could count as a friend.

I hesitated, but something deeply personal prevented me from mentioning Dorothea. 'Not really,' I replied. 'Mrs Burgoyne over there – she collared me at lunchtime. A strange lady. Remembered me from my sailing ship days!'

'Ah, but did you remember her, sir, that's the question?'

I laughed. 'No, Billy, I did not!'

We stood for a few minutes, Bruce Ismay joined us, and together we went through to our respective tables in the Saloon.

The great Jacobean dining room looked magnificent. Jewels shimmered under our bright electric lights, silks and satins rippling and glowing as stewards in white jackets saw guests to their tables. Bruce Ismay and O'Loughlin were shown to theirs, and, accompanied by the senior steward, I walked the length of the room, nodding to familiar faces along the way. Mrs Burgoyne was at the Chief Purser's table, I noticed, as was William Stead. But not my Dorothea. Where was she? I looked around but she was nowhere to be seen.

Again I doubted myself, wondering if I'd imagined her.

Appearing unruffled in company could be difficult sometimes. Even conversation could be a trial. Understanding nothing of a subject – and there were almost as many topics as passengers – the trick was to pay attention and look wise, asking just enough to keep the other person rolling. That first evening in the Saloon, I was fortunate in that my two gentlemen guests, Frank Millet and Archie Butt, were well known to me. The Major had been wintering in Italy after a particularly difficult couple of years in Washington. He'd travelled aboard *Olympic* in January, while Frank Millet had crossed a month later. After their terrible journeys out, the two were keen to offer congratulations – as though I'd arranged it personally – on the present millpond calm.

A New Englander with an impeccable pedigree, Frank Millet was sharp and witty, not known for his tolerance of America's new-made millionaires. Some raised voices drew forth a sardonic comment, not entirely sotto voce. 'Calm weather, Captain,' he said dryly, 'just a pity it couldn't be a *little* more rough this evening…'

I felt myself bridling, until I caught his glance at Bruce Ismay's table, where a vociferous Mrs Brown was making everyone laugh. Bruce, not known for his sense of humour, seemed to be enjoying himself.

Archie Butt frowned. 'Now, Frank…'

I busied myself with the hors d'oeuvres, and turned to the pretty young Countess of Rothes. I asked about her forthcoming journey across Canada to Vancouver, which managed to bring my other guests into the conversation. As they compared cultures and tossed relative values back and forth, I glanced around, noticing fewer tables than usual. The ones set out appeared fully occupied, but still I could not see my lovely Dorothea. . .

An hour later, the meal over, people were beginning to rise. Someone passed close by my table. A swish of blue caught my eye. I glanced up, seeing a profile and the line of a cheek-bone – my heart leapt in recognition. A moment later she'd disappeared amongst a group at the far end of the room.

It cost me something not to follow at once. Hoping to catch sight of her again, I took coffee in the Lounge with the Duchess and her companion. As the ladies retired to the Palm Court to listen to the orchestra, I retired to the Smoke Room. Spying Colonel Gracie alone at one of the other tables, I went to join him. We had been in conversation for a little while when I mentioned Mrs Burgoyne.

The Colonel – a gentleman of the old school – assumed a bland expression. His acquaintance with Mrs Burgoyne was slight, he said, but her connection with his wife's friends, the Enderby sisters, obliged him to offer his protection to all three ladies.

'Quite an entourage,' I remarked lightly.

'An honour, sir, as well as a responsibility, but my old friend Clinch Smith has offered to share it.'

'Did I see you earlier with a younger lady in a blue gown?' I asked. 'I meant to come across and say good evening – felt sure I knew her, but then my attention was distracted, and...'

'Oh, I think you must mean Mrs Carver,' he said, smiling. 'We hadn't met before. I believe her people have some connection with Clinch Smith's.'

'Ah, I see.' So I hadn't imagined her. After a moment's reflection, I said, 'In that case, I must be mistaken.'

Puzzled by the mystery, and no less intrigued by the likeness to Dorothea Lang, I bade the Colonel good night. Before making my way up to the bridge, I went along to the Purser's office and asked to see the First Class Passenger list. *Carver*: yes, there she was. Mrs Lucinda Carver, travelling alone, with an address in New Haven, Connecticut.

If she was a New Englander, I could see no connection with the Langs of Hong Kong. The link with Stead was equally baffling.

It was almost 10:30 pm when I reached the bridge, and 1st Officer Murdoch had taken over the watch. A border Scot from a long line of seafarers, he'd been with me since my time on the *Adriatic*. Could be dour at times, but a good man, dependable. Boxhall and Moody, both East Yorkshiremen, were the juniors. I'd not known them previously, but they came with excellent reports and seemed to have struck up an easy comradeship – no doubt because they shared a similar background.

Murdoch and I went through the usual exchange: weather, sea conditions, course and position. No problems there. I looked at the chart, checked Mr Boxhall's calculations, and went outside.

79

Light cloud had come in after sunset, darkening the horizon and obscuring the stars. There was a slight swell running, with a cool wind behind it. Calm enough though. Looking forward to a good night's sleep I set off on my usual rounds, a habit I'd picked up from Joe when I was first at sea. Sailing ships were smaller, granted, but the principle was the same: see and be seen. Let the crew know you don't leave everything to Mate or the Bo'sun or even the Chief Steward. You use your own eyes and your own instincts to measure the atmosphere aboard.

I paused to look aft, admiring the wake's straight lines of foam curling away as we steamed along, every turn of the screws taking us closer to our destination.

No strange figures tonight, but then I didn't need ghosts to remind me of the past. Not when the image of Dorothea was here in person.

11

Wherever I went ashore, be it St John's or San Francisco, Liverpool or Valparaiso, it seemed Dorothea's face was the one I searched for. In Savannah, too. Looking back, even Marcia bore a passing resemblance: dark hair, dark eyes, a sweet, seductive smile. But none of the ones I briefly courted – even less the ones I bedded – could hold a candle to the original.

Many were the times I picked up my battered copy of *Great Expectations* – the first of a collection of novels – and thought about that afternoon. I did not seriously expect to meet Dorothea again but, having joined White Star to further my career, in the spring of 1882 I was assigned to a ship heading for Hong Kong.

It had been a tough couple of years. With a lot to learn about steamships, I began my time over again as a lowly 4th Officer. The familiar creaks and groans of a wooden ship were exchanged for the heartbeat of reciprocating engines and the hollow ring of an iron hull. For all its residue of sooty grime, its knack of leaving black smears across decks and passengers alike, coal was an expensive commodity. So when the weather was favourable we used sail. But coal gave us steam and, apart from screw propulsion, steam provided power to the steering gear, power to winches to haul up the anchors, lift the sails, wind the ropes. We even had steam-powered derricks to handle our own cargo. The most important factor of all, however: steam drove us through those head-on Atlantic storms.

The engine room was a brutal place, the men who worked there a hard lot. They had to be. It was common for sailors to fall to their deaths from the topgallants, but in feeding the furnaces of steamships men collapsed and died from the heat. And burns – so many burns. You could tell a fireman from a sailor any day of the week – not just from the pallor of his skin, but the scars on his face and arms.

It was an education, working my first steam ship. If I never forgot my first sight of *Britannic* from the wallowing *Lizzie Fennell*, the first time I saw an engine room working at full stretch was another revelation. Everything aft was pounding steel – so close, like the snapping jaws of some mechanical monster – tended by engineers on narrow walkways, adjusting valves, monitoring dials, greasing rods. Hissing bursts of steam escaped as the ship rolled first one way, then another. Adjustments were needed all the time when she started to pitch. Amidships, the big, Scotch boilers – hot, so hot – and forward, the furnaces where men heaved and shovelled in a glowing, ceaseless battle to make more steam.

It made me think a sailor's job was easy. Instilled respect, too. And made me understand what it meant when we up top asked for more speed.

By the time I was promoted to 3rd Officer, I felt I was getting a hold on the job. Even so, in the spring of '82, it was a surprise to be promoted to 2nd Officer and detailed to join *SS Coptic* in Liverpool. Less than a year old, combined sail and steam with some fine passenger accommodation, she was bound for San Francisco and Hong Kong, and expected to remain in the Pacific service for two years.

An exciting prospect. Boosted by the unexpected promotion, I told myself I was keen to see how the island colony had changed. But the thrill of anticipation was more fundamental. Dorothea, rather than Hong Kong, was at the heart of it.

Even by the shortest route, via Cape Horn and Peru, the voyage from Liverpool to San Francisco took three months. Some weeks later, having crossed the Pacific, I saw at once that since my last visit the little colony had expanded in all directions, while the busy harbour was more crowded than ever.

This time there was no hanging around for a berth. As a passenger ship, *Coptic* took on a pilot, steamed boldly past the anchorage and docked on arrival. The central quay was alive with people as we came in, the noonday air buzzing with excited voices. It seemed half Hong Kong's population had turned out to welcome us. After an official reception that evening, the

Captain's plan to throw the ship open to visitors promised to be a success.

The Governor arrived to greet the Captain and senior officers and, with an entourage consisting of Hong Kong's most important officials and their wives, was entertained to a buffet-style supper in the Saloon. Once the speeches were over, our musicians – a string quartet – played some lively airs while the guests enjoyed their coffee. Afterwards the Governor's party was given a tour of the ship.

I was stationed on the bridge. Behind the windows of the chart room, to be precise, with the large-scale chart of Hong Kong open on the table, pretending to be making some corrections with the aid of the latest Admiralty notices. In reality, of course, I was simply waiting for the Old Man to arrive and take over the show.

If I'd spent many idle moments wondering about Dorothea – whether she was still there, married, a mother, even – I have to say the shadow of her father, David Lang, was never far behind. I imagined his position as banker and bullion dealer would warrant an invitation to this little shindy, and with that in mind I'd polished my buttons to a blinding shine. I looked forward to the pleasure of meeting him eye to eye and reminding him who I was. No longer a boy to be dismissed, but a man on his way to the top.

With eyes and ears on the alert, I waited for the tour to reach the wheelhouse, ready to scan the gathered faces as the Old Man began his little speech. I'd often heard him giving passengers a similar lecture, and he was right, a chart was just what it seemed: a map in reverse. Instead of land features it showed the coast and settlements in simple terms, reserving its detail for what lay below the sea, the shallows, the wrecks, the coral reefs and hidden rocks. And most important of all for a ship entering port, the markings of the deep-water channel which allowed safe access to the harbour.

Hearing voices, I stepped back as they entered. I scanned the half dozen male faces behind the Captain: hale, bright-eyed, flushed with whisky and good food, but none was familiar to me. Some were gathered before the windows, peering in as the Old Man indicated the chart and the harbour's unusual features. Above his deeper tones I could hear female voices, but my view of the open bridge was obscured. As the men moved on to the next place of interest, I saw the Chief Officer smiling down at one of the ladies, ushering her along. And then, amidst laughter and the swish of silk skirts, I saw her. Unmistakably Dorothea. No longer a girl but a woman, creamy skin accentuated by dark curls swept up from a slender neck.

Our eyes met. Wide-eyed for a split-second of disbelief, she frowned – no more than a slight drawing together of fine black brows – as though she did not quite believe she knew me. In answer to my ever-broadening smile, there came a tremulous response. My heart pounded. Did she remember me? Had I changed so much? I supposed I had in more than a decade. I saw her glance up at Chief Officer Hines, whose piggy eyes lit on me with astonishment.

She asked a question, he replied, and then she was suddenly beside me, and on a breathless greeting said, 'Mr Smith – it *is* you! But how different you look, how...' She laughed, still not sure, I think, that this man before her was the boy who had dared to bring her to book over her first disastrous love-affair.

With her hand in mine I was beyond words, as dizzy with disbelief as she appeared to be. 'This is too, too extraordinary, Mr Smith. What a strange coincidence that you should be aboard... I never thought...' Again she shook her head, as though civility forbade putting into words what she truly thought, that she never imagined me a man in a well-tailored uniform.

'I must introduce you to my husband, he's...' My heart plummeted as she glanced around, but the husband she sought was not in evidence. 'Ah well, never mind, later will do...' And so we stood and gazed, each, I think, rather liking what we saw. I must have said something during that brief meeting, but my only recollection is of Hines glaring at me over Dorothea's shoulder, indicating that this particular interview had gone on too long.

'We'll meet again, I'm sure. You must come up to the house. That is,' she added, glancing appealingly up at Hines with those melting brown eyes, 'if they allow you some leave while you're here.'

'Oh, I'm sure we can grant him a couple of hours,' Hines replied dryly, giving me a look that said he would find the means to scupper it if he could.

'And you must come too, Mr Hines,' she added with a smile. 'We'll have a little party.' At that she extended her hand for me to bow over, bestowed a heart-stopping smile and was gone.

My limbs went weak. I leaned against the chart table, unable to believe the reality of the last few moments. And then I started to laugh.

Wearing an anxious smile, 3rd Officer Cooper poked his head round the door. 'So what was all that about?'

It was a question that was to be repeated later by others, and to all such enquiries I remained discreet. 'Not sure. My first trip catching up with me, I think.' Of course, they imagined it had been some kind of courtship, a serious flirtation at the very least. How could I explain? And why would they believe that my acquaintance with Dorothea had consisted of just one short afternoon? I could hardly believe it myself.

Each time I pictured her face, a thrill went through me – and that upset my equilibrium even more. She was married, which was no surprise – but if I'd not led the life of a monk in the last few years, as far as I knew adultery had never been one of my sins. That I found myself contemplating it was disturbing.

Dorothea arrived for the open day with a group of lady friends. As navigating officer I was stationed on the bridge, as before. I repeated the Old Man's lecture on charts, we chatted with Cooper – Hines edging his way in before escorting the ladies on the rest of their tour. Later, I learned we'd all been invited to a little soirée at Dorothea's home that evening. There was just one problem: I was Officer of the Watch, so was unable to accept.

Hines could have changed it for me, but, 'Your night off is tomorrow,' he said with a smirk, and that was that. I burned, but refused to beg. A White Star man from his days as an apprentice, the Chief Officer resented the fact that I had previously been a sailing shipmaster and had risen to my present position with apparent ease. Hines the Swine was forever reminding me that steamships were different, and that I could not assume anything, either about the ships or the company. Well aware of that, I found the only reply worth making was to do the job, do it well, and prove him wrong.

Cooper and the 4th Officer expressed sympathy, but there was nothing to be done. Later, a flotilla of chairs borne by coolies carried the lucky few uphill to Dorothea's soirée, while I spent time walking the ship in the moonlight, exchanging an occasional word with the watchmen, and trying to suppress a furious resentment. The younger lads arrived back around midnight, having been to a few bars on the return trip, but there was no sign of the Chief Officer. He'd left with them, they said, but with jealousy burning in my breast I pictured him doubling back and laying siege to the beautiful Dorothea. It was hardly a comfort to hear that her husband had been present – Cooper said he'd left the party before any of them.

From 4:00 in the morning, the next 24 hours were mine in their entirety. I went to bed when I came off duty but barely slept. Being in possession of Dorothea's address, I debated whether to send a note, send flowers, or just turn up. Perhaps, considering her marital status, I should just forget the whole thing. By breakfast time I was morose enough to feel the latter was the only course to take, but then, just as I was about to return to my cabin, a note arrived for me.

'I'm so sorry,' she wrote, *'that you were unable to attend last evening. My friends were looking forward to renewing your acquaintance. Kind Mr Cooper said you had leave from the ship today. I wonder would you like to see something of Hong Kong with Eliza and me? Afterwards we could have lunch here. That is, if you have no firm plans. It would be such a pleasure to talk in more informal surroundings...'*

She went on to name a time when she and her friend would be on the quay, little more than an hour hence, which made me think Cooper had been frank with her about Hines and yesterday's disappointment. Well, I thought happily, it leaves no time to be coy. And with that I showered and changed into fresh whites, presenting myself on the quayside within moments of their arrival. Dorothea was driving a pretty little pony and trap, with just enough room for three.

Formality in such close quarters was impossible. Elation at being ashore for the first time in weeks was heightened almost unbearably by close physical contact with a woman who'd invaded my dreams for years. Aware of Dorothea almost to the point of embarrassment, I gave vent to my high spirits with comments and witticisms as we bowled along the waterfront. Within minutes we were chatting and laughing as though we'd known each other for years.

Dorothea took us along the coast road to a wild but rather sad place, where a tumbling stream ran down to the sea. Here and there, on the slopes of a steep valley, the crumbling remains of grand houses stood like ruined monuments to Hong Kong's early days. Fever, she said bleakly, had killed off most the inhabitants. She indicated the cemetery as we passed, a few tombstones overgrown with creepers and flowering shrubs. It looked as though an age had passed, but I knew it could not have been more than thirty years.

The air of melancholy prompted a recounting of more personal losses: Eliza's husband, a silk merchant, had been killed in China the previous year, while Dorothea's father had died just a year after her marriage. Having expressed my condolences, I said, quite truthfully, 'I'm sorry not to have met him again.'

Perhaps my tone gave something away, for Dorothea gave me a quizzical look. 'Yes,' she replied, 'my father was a remarkable man. He built the business from nothing, you know.' A moment later she said, 'My husband, Curtis, manages things now.' Since her married name was Curtis, I thought it odd she should refer to him by his surname, but she carried on to say that he'd left the party early last evening to board a boat for Canton.

'Why Canton?

'Silver,' she explained. 'We buy silver from China and ship it here – and from here it goes to London.'

It seemed Dorothea's husband spent much of his time there, while her brother Nicholas still handled the London end. Privately, I wondered about the marriage – about her presence here with me, if I'm honest. I could not imagine such freedoms in England. Neither of the ladies mentioned children but, although I was curious, I felt it would have been tactless to ask.

Climbing the valley, admiring the grand views, we took a circuitous route back to Dorothea's home on the Peak. Trees had grown, almost obscuring the entrance, so it took a moment for me to recognise the place. Inside, it was as cool and spacious as I'd once imagined, and heightened awareness made it strange to be in David Lang's old home. Only in a lesser way did I wonder again about this man Curtis. Could I be content to manage my father-in-law's business, and live in his house? I thought not.

A table was set on the veranda overlooking the rear garden, and lunch was served by two male servants. Eliza left us shortly afterwards. It had been a clear morning, but rain was expected and she wanted to be home, she said, before the heavens opened. I felt it was a prompt for me to leave, too, so I rose to my feet, only to be stayed by Dorothea, who claimed lightly that we had never finished the conversation begun all those years before.

The topic I recalled was not one I wished to revive and, in truth, nor did she. She ordered fresh tea and we returned to our seats beneath the deep veranda, content for a while to take in the view of the harbour, with the hills of Kowloon beyond.

Clouds were darkening, reminding me of the day we met. For a little while silence hung between us. Not entirely comfortable, since we were no doubt thinking along similar lines, although from differing points of view. What did we know of each other? Not much, although the background to our acquaintance enabled us to make certain judgements. Already, as a young woman of eighteen or twenty, Dorothea had been the kind of beauty who cuts a swathe through the ranks. Her father had said as much. Back then she'd been unaware of it, possessing an innocence that touched and confused me; perhaps because in those days I was innocent too.

She knew, of course, that I had been attracted to her; just as I'd known, in retrospect, that she had been attracted to me, despite my youth and lack of finesse. That the spark had never been extinguished was clear from our meeting the other day. After a few hours in her company, however, I could see that life had sullied the innocence; there was a brittle edge to her humour, and too often a downward turn to what should have been a pretty smile.

I guessed at an unhappy marriage with too much time in which to brood. I wondered if she saw me as a temporary balm, an adventure to lighten the tedium of her days? Well, that was the way the situation pointed. Whether it was right, what the servants would think, how she would explain it away did not come into it. The air was taut between us, and instinct demanded some kind of resolution.

I turned to look at her, pale against the shadows in her ruffled cotton gown. Rosy lips moved in a slow smile as she extended her hand. I took it, at once aware of the wedding ring. She felt my hesitation and the smile became down-turned as she withdrew her hand – and the ring. Nothing could have made things clearer, but I noticed how easily it slipped off, and wondered if she did that often.

'Please don't ask.'

'A mistake?'

She shook her head, looked vulnerable for a moment, and then as the monsoon rain began to fall, great swathes of it obscuring the harbour, her teasing smile returned. 'Had the weather been more clement,' she said, 'I'd have suggested a tour of the garden. But as it is…'

Servants came to clear away. We rose at once as rain lashed the house, retiring indoors to watch the tempest. I regained her hand, startled by the renewed shock of contact. The morning's suppressed desires leapt afresh between us, her eyes and mouth presenting an invitation I could not refuse. That first light kiss demanded more, but Dorothea drew back, curling her fingers tight between mine, hurrying me along the veranda to the eastern side of the house.

Louvered screens opened into a room she called her boudoir, a place she kept to herself. A desk, an easel, an embroidery frame were things I noticed later; at the time I saw only a day-bed strewn with cushions. She closed the screens, turned, and was in my arms at once. The kiss I'd hungered for filled the void with stars.

I remember the rain drumming on the roof; softness of flesh

beneath the taut material of her gown, small hard nipples beneath my hands, buttons which needed her deft fingers to free. The gown fell in a pool at her feet, leaving just a clinging shift. In the half-light as she unpinned her hair, she looked to me like a creature from some other world, a nymph or naiad come to steal my life, my soul. I gave it willingly, clumsily fumbling with jacket buttons, my skin so hot and damp I needed help to push the heavy linen from my shoulders. She smiled, running her hands over my chest and back, reaching up to pull my head down to hers.

I buried my fingers in her hair and drew her against me. In the moment before we sank onto the bed, she whispered, 'Love me, love me...'

And I did, in every mortal sense of the word. She set fire to my senses in ways that no other woman had ever done. I'd had encounters before – but that's all they were. A meeting, an agreement, the briefest dalliance followed by physical release. Such transactions serviced a need it would be hypocritical to deny. But, for me, that first time with Dorothea might have been the first time ever: like a boy, in my eagerness I even made a fool of myself. We laughed about it afterwards. Then some comment of mine made her ask about my very first experience, and I found myself telling her about San Francisco years ago, about the middle-aged Madam who had decided she wanted to initiate me into the delights of the flesh. Not a happy memory.

Imagining her first time to have been with her husband, naturally I did not ask, but whatever her experience had been in the years since, she was not naïve and did not pretend to innocence. Indeed, my instinct to take control of the proceedings – so sadly cut short – was overturned by her frank but gentle insistence that we do things her way. In the end she taught me not just how to make love, but how to be a lover.

The more we were together, the more I hungered for her. But we were not often together. In port, while we discharged one cargo and loaded another, I had my duties to perform. Mostly, though, I was free after four in the afternoon, and on *Coptic*'s first visit to Hong Kong, Dorothea's husband was away. We found a small hotel on the outskirts of the port, the kind of place where missionaries stayed en route to China. I rather feared running into one of our passengers, but not enough to halt my intent. There Dorothea would come to meet me, her garb as sober as any Nonconformist preacher's wife. Well, as we often joked, we were nonconformists of a kind.

Twelve days, three of which were wasted in the beginning, one at the end. In all we were together seven times. As the days ran out the passion intensified. Our meetings became a bonding of flesh quickened by desire, our partings a tearing that left me aching and bereft.

Leaving her, I was like a man press-ganged into service, as heart-sick as any young husband forced to return to sea and leave his wife behind. But she was not my wife, and the thought of her husband returning from Canton, eager to reclaim his rights, drove me almost mad with jealousy.

For twelve days I'd had little sleep but hardly seemed to need it; on the way to Yokohama, whenever I was not working or eating, I fell into my bunk and slept like a dead man. Even waking, I felt exhausted. Not even Hines's sarcasm could rouse a response. Eventually, he left me alone.

Sailing with the weather rather than against it, we made a much shorter voyage from Yokohama to San Francisco, but never had the Pacific seemed so wide. I did my watches, crossing off the days like a prisoner. We reached 'Frisco by mid-September to say goodbye to one group of passengers and welcome another. According to the Purser, the Americans this time were more of a mixed bag, merchants keen to establish themselves as middlemen, as well as missionaries eager to plough the heathen fields. Both saw China – long forbidden to outsiders – as virgin territory, and the tiny British colony of Hong Kong as the stepping-off point. The bulk, however, were simply keen explorers, planning to head up the Pearl River to Canton just for the pleasure of seeing a strange land for themselves. To my surprise, several of the missionaries and even more of the tourists were sensibly clad women travelling without escorts. I admired their bravery while wondering what the Chinese would make of them.

With every beat of the engines on that return journey, I urged the ship forward. Despite its name the north Pacific was far from peaceful and it took another month to reach Hong Kong. At last, by mid-October, we were back. Knowing nothing of Dorothea since I'd been away, for days I'd been in a fever of anxiety, running through a variety of scenes in which our love-affair had been found out, her husband enraged to the point of violence. What if that were true? Would I be able to see her? And what if she'd simply changed her mind, decided I wasn't worth the risk: what if she wanted to end it?

As before, the quay was thronged with people as we berthed, the air buzzing with anticipation. While sailors made fast the stern ropes,

I scanned the crowd. People were waving and calling. I thought I heard my name. Forced to return to the task in hand, I was already plotting and planning how speedily I could get ashore when suddenly I saw her on the edge of the crowd. She waved and my spirits soared. My answering grin set the seamen laughing.

Changing in my cabin an hour or so later, one of the stewards tapped on the door and handed me a note. It was from Dorothea. *'Meet me tonight if you can – our usual place…'*

And so it began again.

In the beginning she'd begged me not to ask about her husband. But after a tortured absence I had to know where I stood. Our passionate reunion was a balm that lasted no time at all, and later, as we lay together in the closeness of that tiny hotel room, the words, the questions, came tumbling out.

'Is he at home, your husband? Where does he think you are?'

She drew away, studied me in surprise. 'If you mean, is he here, in Hong Kong, then yes, he is.' She paused, held my gaze. 'This evening he could be where he said, at the Hong Kong Club, but he's probably elsewhere, with his mistress.'

'His *mistress?*'

'Yes. She's a Chinese woman, quite well-born, I understand – he met her in Canton, brought her here some years ago.' Sighing, she turned away, reached for her robe. 'Everyone knows. Of course, they pretend not to.'

Absurdly, I was shocked. 'Does he know – that you know?'

She shrugged. 'Probably. We keep up the pretence that I don't. If either of us were to acknowledge it, the house of cards might just fall down.'

Not understanding, I asked what she meant, and she began to explain about the business her father had created. David Lang had come to Hong Kong when the Chinese first granted the British permission to trade from the island. 'He was in Macau,' she went on, 'during the first of the opium wars, working for a silver merchant – that was where he met and married my mother. Mama was Portuguese – her father was a trader. It was quite dangerous then – they were always on the move between here and Macau, having to pack up at a moment's notice, lodging with friends until things calmed down. Or acting host when friends were under threat. Exciting times, I gather,' she added dryly.

'But when all that nonsense about the opium settled down and

Canton became more open, Daddy set up on his own, here in Hong Kong. He'd buy silver from the Chinese and ship the bullion back to London to be sold. The business just kept on growing...'

As she talked, I realised how little I'd known about her. How very few questions I'd asked, how little she had volunteered. I hadn't even known her mother was Portuguese.

'Curtis came to us from Canton not long after you and I first met,' Dorothea went on. 'He became Daddy's right-hand man. Then, as Daddy's health started to break down, he relied on him more and more.'

She bent to turn up the lamp, poured some tonic water into a glass and sipped at it. 'I suppose there was always something between us,' she said slowly, as though speculating on the matter, 'although I never took him seriously because he was so much older...

'But then Daddy spelled it out. The China trade had made him wealthy, but fever and the climate had weakened his heart: he was paying the price, he said, for worldly success. Yes,' she sighed, 'Daddy became surprisingly pious in his latter years. Anyway, he wasn't well, his heart was weak. He said that when he died, he wanted to leave the Hong Kong business in safe hands – for my sake as much as my brother's.'

I understood then what her father's concerns must have been, that when he died the unmarried Dorothea would own half the business and, once married, Dorothea's husband would control it. So she needed a sensible alliance, otherwise all that David Lang had worked for – with the valuable core here, in Hong Kong – would be at risk.

'He was very matter-of-fact,' she went on. 'It was rather frightening. There he was, telling me he was about to die, and in the next breath planning the future as though the business was all that mattered. He was my father and I loved him,' Dorothea declared with a sudden break in her voice. 'He'd always protected me, but suddenly he was talking of death and dying...'

She left my side, paced the room, her shadow moving behind her like a ghost. 'The right man for the business was Curtis. So he was the one to marry.'

I tried to assimilate that and failed. 'But did Curtis want to marry *you*?'

Amused by my thoughtless protest, she laughed; but it had a bitter edge. 'For *that* kind of fortune? My dear, wouldn't you?'

I thought then what an innocent I was, with a mother I'd imagined was ambitious because she wanted her little shop in Hanley, and had manipulated my father into buying it.

I knew nothing.

12

There are no secrets aboard ship, and every time I went ashore there were comments ranging from good-natured ribbing to the frankly envious. Hines, with barbed wit, made it clear he'd have liked to foil my adventures, while the Old Man, handing out an advance of pay, was prompted to deliver a little speech circling around deep waters, weather conditions, and a certain lack of canvas. It was obscure but I got the drift.

Not that it made any difference. Pride made me insist on paying hotel bills, and love made little gifts essential. A length of Chinese silk she admired, a silver vase; a heart-shaped locket for her birthday. My pay barely covered these items, but I refused to worry, just as I ignored the risks I was running. Each return to Hong Kong was a passionate reunion and, if the joy was never as pure as the first time, I considered every moment worth it.

When the ship was in, Dorothea generally gave a small party for the ship's officers and certain local residents with whom they'd become acquainted. She was not the only hostess to do so. Such gestures were seen as a return of hospitality, but in Dorothea's case it was more of a tactic to keep criticism at bay. If Dorothea's husband were likely to be present I would volunteer to stay aboard ship. Whatever the situation between them I had no desire to meet him, nor provide more fuel for gossip.

Evidently, though, he had a desire to meet me. Perhaps the third or fourth time we arrived in Hong Kong, he came, unexpectedly, to one of *Coptic*'s informal receptions. It was a pleasant evening in spring, before the monsoon winds brought summer's heat and crushing humidity. I knew he was about ten years older than his wife, but Dorothea's description was too vague to alert me when he joined the group I was with. The conversation had been about Canton, which I had never visited, but it quickly degenerated into a debate on the opium trade. With ethics versus pragmatism, it was in danger of becoming heated.

'It funds almost everything here,' one man declared. 'Without it, we couldn't live like we do. Ban it, and the whole market collapses.'

'If you'd seen what I've seen,' another said tersely, 'in some of those back rooms off the Queen's Road, you'd know the destruction it wreaks. The families of those people…'

'Oh, you're talking about the addicts…'

'They're all addicts!'

And then the newcomer said lightly, 'But have any of you ever tried it? Smoked occasionally, it's really most relaxing…'

Tension shifted at once. I was aware of it but not sure why. In fact, at that precise moment, I was simply relieved. I'd been at a loss how to divert the discussion, but this stranger had done it for me. I turned in gratitude, just as someone said, 'Oh, it's you, Curtis – might have known you'd have something to say!'

He beamed in response, a clean-shaven, pleasant-faced man with thinning hair and the beginnings of a paunch. Then he turned to me and, on a speculative look, said, 'You must be Mr Smith?'

No choice. I had to shake his outstretched hand. 'I am indeed, sir. How d'you do.'

'I'm just back from Canton,' he said blandly, 'with a party of missionaries glad to be leaving the place. They were talking about the evils of opium, too. I didn't like to tell them the silver in the hold was payment for a cargo from India…'

There was a silence. At a complete loss for words, I glanced over his shoulder, my eyes searching for Dorothea. Someone – the pragmatist – said, 'What did I tell you? This is a man who knows first-hand how the business works…'

Others joined in, and then Dorothea was at her husband's elbow, smiling sweetly, urging him to come and meet the Captain. He bowed to the gathered company, cast an ironic smile in my direction and departed.

I'd been in places that sold opium, had even smoked it once. It did nothing for me, and the after effects were so numbing I had no desire to repeat the experiment. But I'd seen the addicts, hunched in doorways or sprawled, glassy-eyed in some dark alley, and I'd stepped past them, wishing they would find somewhere else to sleep it off. To me opium addicts were in the same bracket as drunken seamen: I felt disgust rather than sympathy, and did not consider that I had anything to do with the state they were in.

With time, of course, one sees the bigger picture. But then, the fact that Dorothea's husband was somehow involved in importing opium to China was less shocking to me than that deliberate introduction.

'He knows,' were almost the first words I said when she and I were alone again.

'Of course he does.'

That afternoon Dorothea had brought a picnic to our assignation on the southern side of the island. She laid out the tartan rug, arranging the plates and a cold collation of chicken and salad leaves as though nothing was wrong.

'What did he say?'

She sat back on her heels, gazing at me as though I were a child needing to have everything explained. 'He just reminded me to be discreet. He said certain little birds were eager to connect the ship to me, and me to you.' She paused, busied herself with the cutlery. 'And yes, he turned up at the reception because he was curious. Wanted to see you for himself.'

Heat flooded my chest and face. I felt like a servant, given the once-over by the master of the house. 'And did I pass the test? Was I considered *good enough* to service the mistress?'

Her eyes flashed as the barb went home. Fingers tightened on the knife in her hand. Slowly, she leaned towards me, the blade pointing at my heart. 'Never,' she hissed, 'speak to me like that again.'

I grabbed her wrist, turned it away until she cried out. 'And don't you ever point a knife at me, madam.'

Tears sprang to her eyes. As she rubbed her wrist I apologised, said she should know not to threaten anyone like that.

She would not say sorry, and we were silent and apart for a while. Eventually, she said, 'It's because it's gone on so long. I gather he's known almost from the first, but expected it to fizzle out.'

'Like the others, you mean?' The words were out before I could stop them: I didn't need the shamefaced nod to confirm it. I was no more a fool than Henry Curtis, and knew there had to have been other men before me. Even so I hated her in that moment. Whatever I'd suspected, I didn't want such confirmation.

It spoiled what should have been a delightful afternoon. There was a half-hearted attempt at reconciliation but I was too sick with jealousy and she, no doubt, too guilt-ridden for it to be successful.

So, having picked at the food and stared at the view, we made our way back in the trap. Somehow, despite its swaying on the uneven road, she managed to keep a distance between us. Bowling along between lush vegetation, dappled sunlight made an ever-changing pattern on clothes and skin. How like Dorothea that was: hard to pin down; never the same for two minutes together. Watching those slender, capable fingers handling the reins, controlling the sturdy little pony, I marvelled at her. She looked almost frail at times, and yet there was a hidden core of strength that allowed her to twist and turn and manoeuvre until she got what she wanted.

I told myself I hated the way she'd snared me so artfully. In truth I despised myself for being such a willing slave.

Like the witch she was, she read my mind. 'Do you hate me?'

'No,' I sighed. 'I hate what I don't know – it torments me. And then you tell me something and I hate it even more.'

A swift glance. 'Have you no past?'

'Only you,' I said softly, knowing it was the truth. I touched the curls at the nape of her neck; her skin was damp and I wanted to taste it. 'I'm a fool, I know.'

She turned soft dark eyes upon me, full of regret. As her hands relaxed, the swaying trap slowed. 'If I were free, it would be different. As it is, I have a past – and responsibilities.' Shortening the reins, urging the pony on again, she said, 'I thought we could have each other – thought we were all that mattered. I imagined...'

'What?'

'Well,' she admitted, 'that the moment would be enough.'

I stared hard at her profile, wondering how she could be so blind. So wilfully blind. Aware of the spectre of Harry Jones, I wanted to say, *you had a past before I knew you – it was your past which brought us together...*

Lacking the courage, I took the opposite tack. 'What of the future? Do you never think about that?'

'Not often,' she said, suddenly brisk. 'In a place like this, anything can happen. Look at my mother, surviving childbirth twice to die of the fever at twenty-five. I've outlived her already. Even had my own brush with death. Who knows how much longer I'll be here? Life's

96

short, my darling – I thought you, above all, would realise that.'

That brash, devil-may-care response typified her. Even so, as the pony's hooves thudded along, I struggled to absorb what she meant. 'A brush with death? When was that?'

Another swift glance, then back at the road. 'Years ago. Didn't I tell you? I was expecting a child – lost it. I was very ill, nearly died. After that...' She shrugged, left the rest unsaid. A bird clattered out of the trees and she clicked her tongue as the pony shied. 'But I thought you knew.'

I shook my head, amazed by her ability to confound me. 'You said you couldn't have children. You didn't say why.'

'Perhaps not.' A brief, enigmatic smile as she negotiated a corner. 'Doesn't do to dwell,' she said.

Feeling inadequate I gave up then, unsure whether the feeling inside was anger or despair.

The future was important to me – or had been, until I met Dorothea. Now the present was paramount. All I wanted was her love, yet with every crossing of the Pacific, the days we had left were falling off the calendar like leaves from a dying tree. I wanted to stop time, hold it back, but there was nothing to grasp.

I learned how short the hours of pleasure could be and, during those endless blue Pacific days, how painful were the days and weeks between. In Dorothea's company I could think of nothing but her; away from her I was consumed by doubt as well as longing. I began to entertain fantasies, to talk about leaving White Star and finding a position with one of the companies setting up in the Far East. But there was no point in that unless Dorothea would divorce Curtis and marry me.

When I dared to voice those hopes, she cut me dead. No, there was no possibility of divorce. The scandal would be unbearable, and how would she manage the business? Besides, there was Nicholas to think of in London.

I began to think the business and Nicholas were a ready excuse. My old fear, that I was simply not good enough for her, reared its ugly head. Tormented by it, knowing my career was the only thing between myself and that tradesman's boy from Hanley, I tried to imagine giving it up. That I was even willing to consider it horrified me.

Consumed by desire, I thought it was love. Maybe it was. I wanted to believe that she loved me too, but that fantasy lasted only so long as I was at sea. Ashore, I was faced with reality. She did not want to share her life with me; the excitement of the moment was all that mattered. It went against everything I had ever believed of women – decent women that is – and made me feel rather less than the man I'd imagined myself to be.

Perhaps it was inevitable. We were no longer new lovers discovering the wonder of each other, but existing on snatched assignations; sometimes at the house, when Curtis was absent. I often wondered what the servants thought of my visits, but when I voiced such thoughts Dorothea said they were paid to work, not to think. And anyway, she added pettishly, they were Chinese, so what did it matter?

That was unlike her. I knew she relied heavily upon Li, the elderly retainer who seemed to combine the duties of butler and major-domo: certainly he kept the other servants under control. He'd been with the family since her father's day, so I imagined his allegiance was to Dorothea rather than to Curtis – but that didn't mean he agreed with what she was doing. No matter how differently the Chinese lived, as I understood it, adultery was adultery, no matter the race or creed.

Dorothea's husband might have abandoned his marital responsibilities, but I have to say I was never easy in that house. The portrait of Dorothea's mother hanging in the drawing room seemed to watch me at every turn. Although Curtis left little impression on the place, I saw David Lang in every shadow, felt the power of his fortune like a weight on my back.

Often, I found myself reflecting on that hot afternoon at the garden party, when David Lang had dismissed me like some tradesman's boy. I had so wanted to prove that I was better than that. And yet here I was, in love with the daughter he'd warned me against, and behaving like some unprincipled scoundrel in a cheap romance.

I wasn't the first, but what did that signify? I'd lost most of the pleasure in my job; I moped one way across the Pacific, and battled with the weather and my desires on the way back.

Hines the Swine proved his epithet. Needling me about Dorothea, on occasion he used fo'c'sle language. The first time I almost took a swing at him, and it was only a swift word and Cooper's grasp on my arm that stopped me. After that, knowing what he was after, I schooled myself to walk away, to shut him out. On a less personal level he constantly found fault, warning me that if I didn't buck up, I would be in trouble. Did I want *Decline to Report* written in my Seaman's Discharge Book? That would scupper any ambitions I might have had.

He was right, of course. There were occasions when I'd been late back to the ship and less than meticulous about my duties. Worse, leaving Hong Kong for Shanghai on our next return to San Francisco, I found it difficult to sleep and hard to rouse myself for my watch. But what angered me was the way Hines managed to insinuate that I was lazy, not up to the job, not White Star material.

He must have had a word with the Old Man, because a few days after we left China I was summoned to his presence.

'Sit down,' he said gruffly, waving me to the seat beside his desk. He was a man I respected; tough but not unkind. Mostly, discipline was left to the Mate, which was how it should be; only when things were serious did he intervene, so I knew I was in for some hard talk.

'I want to keep this informal, Mr Smith, because in spite of evidence to the contrary, I believe you have a future with this company.'

That was an opening to gain my full attention.

'I do not like to presume upon a man's private life,' he went on, eyes glinting beneath bushy brows, 'but in this case, I gather your private life has become public knowledge in Hong Kong.' He paused to let that sink in. 'I tried to warn you before, but I fear it is starting to impinge. Not just upon your reputation, Mr Smith, but upon the reputation of this ship – and, by association, White Star.

'We cannot allow this situation to continue. The woman you are consorting with...' I noticed he used the word woman, rather than lady, 'is married to an important Hong Kong resident. I cannot comment on their personal arrangements – that is beyond my knowledge – but if necessary I can prevent you from continuing an association that I consider detrimental to good order...'

There was no need for him to spell it out. As the ship's Master he could refuse permission for me to go ashore; and if I should be foolish enough to disobey, the reprimand would be official, and entered in the ship's log book to be submitted the Registrar General of Shipping at the end of the voyage. That would mean dismissal. An end to my career as a ship's officer.

'It hasn't gone that far – yet. But from what I hear it seems to be heading that way. Your work is suffering. I imagine as a result of this unfortunate liaison. Am I right?'

I swallowed hard. 'Yes, sir.'

'Well then, Mr Smith. I advise you – most strongly – to end it.'

I nodded and made to rise. He waved me back down. Addressing me again, his tone was a degree or two less frosty.

'Life, for a seafarer, is hard. You know that. You're not a boy, you've been a shipmaster yourself. You know the pitfalls. If you were faced with this situation you would say what I am about to say: do not let this woman ruin you. No matter what you think and feel at the moment, she isn't worth it.'

'No, sir.'

'I want your word, Mr Smith, that when we return to Hong Kong, you will behave with discretion, be prompt about your duties, and give me no more cause for concern.'

I nodded, weak with relief. There was only one answer. 'You have it, sir.'

'Good.' The Captain turned to his desk. The interview was over.

Returning to my cabin, I sank down on the bunk and buried my head in my hands. There was no choice. I knew the truth of what the Old Man was saying. In a way, it was almost a relief. He was right: I would say the same to any man in my position.

I had no claim on Dorothea. No future. She'd made that plain. And the Old Man had made it clear that I couldn't have her and my career. But how was I to give her up?

I rolled over, smothering painful gasps in the pillow. That it should come to this! She had me, right where she wanted me – only had to crook her finger for me to jump and do whatever she wanted. What was I to her? Excitement to liven the dull days, something to look forward to when the ship returned. And when we lay together, bathed in each other's sweat, while I pleasured her, loved her, longed to make her mine, did she ever think what she was doing to me?

Time was running out. She knew that as well as I did. Two, maybe three more visits and *Coptic* would be leaving. Did it matter to her? It didn't seem to. That was my problem, the reason I was in such a mess, not sleeping, making mistakes, barely able at times to drag myself out of my bunk. The Old Man was right: it had to stop.

It was one thing to make that decision, another to live with it. After leaving Shanghai for San Francisco, I expected we would be back in Hong Kong within our usual nine or ten weeks, but it was longer than that. In the vicinity of the China Sea on our return we were hit by an early typhoon, the engines struggling against the battering of enormous seas. Sky and sea were one. Impossible to see further than

100

a few yards as wind and rain lashed great clouds of spume across the open bridge. We were pitching and rolling, a dangerous spiral motion that lifted the stern clear while the prow buried itself, sending huge green waves rolling down the foredeck.

Each time the propeller came clear and raced madly, the engineers below struggled to control the revs. When she smacked down, the engine groaned like an animal in its death-throes. There was a danger she would break in two. With every massive sea the Old Man yelled warnings to the Chief down the chartroom telephone. I couldn't think what conditions were like below – it was a bare-knuckle fight on deck.

The quartermaster's veins stood out with effort as he fought to control the wheel. An hour was as much as he could stand without a break. Changing lookouts every two hours, we officers did the usual four-hour stint in our oilskins, clinging hand over hand from one side of the open bridge to the other.

Just like sailing-ship days, I thought; not exactly enjoying it, but finding a perverse kind of satisfaction in a hell that mirrored my inner turmoil. Until, that is, *Coptic* pushed her nose into the kind of wave that had turned *Lizzie Fennel* on her beam ends.

Luckily, I was off watch and in my bunk when it happened, but the force of the blow landed me on the deck. I scrambled to my feet. A few paces to the bridge and I saw Hines was down and bleeding profusely, the lookout trying to hold him as he slid about amidst great shards of glass. The chartroom windows were shattered.

The Old Man was all right but Hines was out cold, his face badly cut. He came round a minute or so later, but the doctor discovered he also had a broken arm. After that, the Old Man and I hardly left the bridge, and when he did, to grab a couple of hours' rest, he left me in charge.

Suddenly, after two full days and a night of it, the wind died away. By the second evening we were still being thrown about on disturbed and massive seas, but the rain had stopped, the clouds had lifted. We even saw the stars again. As young Cooper and I attempted to establish just where we were, Hines staggered to the bridge, his splinted arm in a sling.

We were all grey with strain, but Hines, his face criss-crossed by scabs and stitches, looked infinitely worse. 'Thank God that's over.' Through swollen lips, the words came out like a groan.

I shook my head. 'I doubt it, sir. Give it a few hours, we'll be in it again.' He denied it, said I was wrong; in his opinion we were through the typhoon. But past experience told me there could be a hellish couple of days yet to come, and I was too tired to be tactful. 'No, sir. Just look at those seas – coming from every direction. It's the eye of the storm. I'd get back to bed if I were you. Get some sleep while you can.'

He eyed me for a moment, disliking my tone I think, as much as the contradiction. I half expected a caution for cockiness, but he let it go.

We had much to follow, though not as bad. But if the first blast had caught and measured my anguish, strangely, that small respite in the eye of the storm was a turning point. There had been no time to think while we were battling for survival – I'd simply accepted that the Old Man had to grab an hour's rest here and there, and with Hines laid up, I was the logical replacement. But the fact that the Old Man had trusted me – after his reprimand – was almost overwhelming. I knew at last that I'd begun to redeem myself. Not just in his eyes, but in my own.

Between Shanghai and Hong Kong I was deeply apprehensive. Fearful, yes, but mainly of my own emotions. Dorothea could be cold and cutting when she chose, and I almost prayed for it, knowing it would make the parting easier.

After much deliberation I sent a note ashore shortly after we docked, asking her to meet me at one of the better hotels in town two evenings hence. Circumstances, I added, made it impossible for me to come ashore earlier than that. I hoped she would read the message between my brief lines. I wanted her to be prepared.

The chosen evening did not augur well. It was mid-June, bucketing with rain as I left the ship. Despite a borrowed umbrella I was soaked before I arrived. Booking a room, I asked for some drinks to be sent up and poured myself a stiff gin, adding a splash of tonic water as I rehearsed what I would say. Something along the lines of my career and future against no future at all. We must say goodbye, because even if I ditched White Star and tried for a position out East... But no, that must not be said; that direction was a blind alley. I must stick to goodbye.

Having arrived early, I felt my heartbeat quicken as the appointed time came. It passed, and I poured myself another gin, consulted my pocket-watch, checked the time every few minutes for more than an hour. Concern mounted to anger, and descended to anxiety. I went down, enquired at the desk: there were no messages. Undecided, I stood by the door for a while, knowing I could not return to the ship without finding out what was wrong. If Curtis was at home – well, so be it, I would face him too. Since the rain was passing, I set off to walk up to the house.

Apart from one small light, the place was in darkness. I rang the bell and Dorothea's Chinese manservant answered, his smooth old face impassive as he asked me to wait in the hall. He left me there a moment or two, returning with two envelopes: one that I'd addressed to Dorothea, the other bearing my name.

'Madam gone to London,' Li said as I gazed at it. 'Brother sick. She say sorry, Mr Smith.'

Speechless, my head full of questions, I could only turn the envelope over in my hands. The old man bowed, indicated a chair, asked if I would like tea. I said yes and sat down to open the letter. It was just one page and dated some three weeks previously.

'Dearest, this will come as a shock I know, but I have to go home to England. Nicholas is very ill. So things must be arranged with regard to the business. With no idea when I might return I have closed up the house as far as possible and left Li in charge. Curtis will come and go as he sees fit. He has taken up residence in the apartment above the office – says he prefers it so while I'm away.

'I know your time with the ship is coming to an end. We would have had to say goodbye sooner or later... better we part now...'

Several words were smudged. Suspecting tears were the cause, I felt my own throat tighten as I struggled to make out her meaning.

'... may not believe me perhaps but it is true. What we had, my love, will never be again. I shall remember you always. Ever yours, Dorothea...'

Tension leached away as I read. Re-read and read again. Drained, I sagged forward, staring at the paper between my hands. It was over. She had ended it, and I thought my heart would break.

Li brought tea and went away. It was only as I roused myself to push the letter back into its envelope that something fell out – a fine gold chain, one she had often worn around her neck, but minus the small gold locket I had given her.

On the back of the letter she had written a post-script: *'The chain for you – the heart for me.'*

13

Next time round in 'Frisco, I behaved like a fool, drinking and whoring my way round all the sea-front taverns and bordellos. At the time I thought it made me feel better. Certainly it relieved a lot of anger, although I'm not proud to think of some of the things I did. And then, regretting it, I went through a mawkishly sentimental patch, wearing Dorothea's gold chain all the way back to Liverpool.

With the familiar waterfront ahead of me, the tower of the Sailor's Church looked like a beckoning finger. As soon as I had a free hour I went in, as I had with Joe as a boy, and thanked God for bringing me home. Counting my sins while I was at it, I knew I would never willingly go back to Hong Kong. Dorothea and my frustrated longings were too strong. I put the gold chain in a small box at the bottom of my sea-chest and decided it was best forgotten, but it was years before I ceased to think of her. Every now and then I'd come across it, or something else would remind me, and I'd be back in that small hotel with Dorothea beside me...

Gradually, as these things do, it ceased to hurt.

I didn't go to London, didn't try to look for her. There was nothing to be gained, only the opening of wounds not yet healed. The affair was over. One lives and learns, and no doubt Mr Dickens would have had a thing or two to say about it. Joe too, except I kept it to myself. Remembering what he'd said in the beginning, *pretty coral will rip your keel out,* I was too ashamed to tell him what a fool I'd been.

104

Now, all these years later, I had questions in my mind, and wished I could have confided in him.

By the time *Coptic* and I reached Liverpool, Joe had swallowed the anchor, opened a chandlery business in Birkenhead and, with his wife and sons, become quite the family man. Susanna was a kind woman, unflappable it seemed, willing to make my mother as welcome as she did me. And Mother was not the easiest guest.

Nor was Mother the easiest company for me. I cannot say that we had ever been close, yet of all the family, she it was who saw the change in me. She held me at arms' length when I went home to Hanley, examining me for an uncomfortable moment with those sharp blue eyes of hers.

'She turned you down, then.' It was a statement, not a question.

My breath caught. How could she know? 'Please, Mother...'

'Oh, don't worry,' she said, releasing me. 'I'm saying nothing. It's your business, not mine. But whoever she was, I'm sorry. We all go through it, you know.'

I could not speak for the lump in my throat. She patted my arm and turned away. It was never mentioned again.

If she said anything to Joe, he never let on. Mostly, I stayed with him and Susanna when I was in port and, somehow, the hours spent reminiscing over a pint or two in Joe's local were just what I needed. Brought me back to reality.

Another Pacific voyage had been mooted, but I refused, asking to be returned to the New York run. Apart from a couple of interruptions, I've been crossing the Atlantic ever since. A few trips on one ship, a few years on another; every new liner bigger than the last. *Olympic* was almost twice the size of her predecessor; but somehow Tommy Andrews had found a way of making this one even bigger.

Next year – or the year after – there'd be a bigger one still. I didn't want to be around for that.

Except – except for some strange reason the past was becoming stronger, making me examine everything in an attempt to solve the mystery of who I was, what I had been, and where I would go from here. Was it just age and retirement beckoning, or was it the girl I'd seen with Stead? I hadn't thought of Dorothea – consciously, that is – in years. Yet now, all the old questions arose. What had happened after we parted? Had she gone back to Hong Kong? Was she still living there? I couldn't imagine her as a woman of my age. In my dreams – and yes, once in a long while she came to me in sleep – she was as young and lovely as the girl in the lavender gown.

Mesmerised by the ploughing of the foam, I pictured the engines below and wondered where this journey was taking me. But I'd lingered too long. Reluctantly, I turned away.

The navigation lights were on, the officers' accommodation suitably darkened. Having done a round of the Boat Deck, I went down by the portside steps, unhooking the chain with its sign, *Ship's Staff Only,* to access the softly-lit Promenade, where Bruce's plate glass windows allowed passengers to walk in what he was pleased to call safety. They still gave me a shiver when I thought of those massive seas smashing through *Coptic's* chartroom window. If I'd been in Belfast while this one was fitting out, I might have prevailed upon him to change his mind. But no, Bruce wanted me to remain aboard *Olympic* while the Atlantic weather was so bad. *The passengers feel safe with you,* he'd said, overriding all my arguments.

Well, at least the weather so far was calm. If a storm blew up, I'd simply ban the passengers from walking here, and Bruce could protest till he was blue.

I glanced to left and right, my eyes accustomed to what was normal, ready to notice anything untoward. Ahead, two couples were coming towards me, catching the light from a pair of bay windows. With the blueprints in mind I guessed they were passing the Smoke Room, while the bay window to my left must be the Reading Room. Glancing in to confirm it, I paused, noticing a pale figure against a kaleidoscope of moving shadows. I was almost certain it was Mrs Carver in that distinctive gown. Others were present, arranging chairs – what were they doing? Was that Frank Millet? And Stead was there too – what was he up to?

Aware of people approaching, I forced myself to move on – it wouldn't do to be seen spying on my passengers. I bade them goodnight as we passed and wondered when I could decently go back. Telling myself they had every right to be in the Reading Room, I tried to reason it out. The Smoke Room was no place for ladies, while the Palm Court was lively and popular for its music. Perhaps they wanted to talk. But why not the Lounge, where both sexes tended to congregate? Why the Reading Room? It didn't make sense.

I went in through the Palm Court entrance. The orchestra was playing something soothing, the strains of which could be heard in the Smoke Room next door. In there, the Philadelphia banker, George Widener, was drinking with Charles Hays, the railroad king;

as they spotted me I knew I should have avoided cutting through. I stopped by their table, said I just had a few minutes as I was doing my nightly rounds, but before I knew it I was involved in a discussion about the next new ship, already under construction in *Olympic*'s old berth. George Widener – a major shareholder in White Star's parent company, IMM – was in sentimental mood, singing my praises and bewailing the news he'd heard of my retirement.

'The only way to say goodbye,' he insisted, breathing whiskey fumes in my face as he grasped my arm, 'is to have commanded each of these three great ships. Next year – think of it! Another maiden voyage – another success! Then you can retire, sir!'

My heart plummeted at the thought. I forced a smile. 'It's tempting, Mr Widener – and I thank you for the compliment. But I think my wife would divorce me!'

Wishing Bruce could have kept quiet, I bade them goodnight. Best get done, I said to myself. It was almost 11 and I was tired. One deck down, and a quick check of the Restaurant – staff setting up for tomorrow – and Café Parisienne. Through to the 2nd Class Smoke Room, typically quiet with just a few men at the bar and a table of dedicated card players in the corner; then down to the deck below. The 3rd Class public rooms were lively – there were even children running about in the Common Room, where a fiddler was playing some foot-tapping music. The atmosphere was relaxed and friendly – no trouble there.

On my way up in the electric elevator I felt odd, suddenly. Light-headed, dizzy. I glanced into the mirror and saw a grey, gaunt, hollow-eyed reflection. An old man's face. A chill passed over me, followed by a wave of heat. Running a finger round the inside of my collar I realised the elevator had stopped. The boy was holding back the gate.

Emerging by the Palm Court I was glad to step outside for a breath of air. Exhaustion, no doubt. Ellie had been telling me for months that this relentless pace was no good, and urging me to rest as much as possible. But there was no chance to relax. Every hour at sea was a working hour, even while sleeping. And I didn't seem able to get much of that.

After a minute or two, feeling better, I remembered the odd little group I'd seen earlier. Walking back along the deck I saw the Lounge was lit but empty, while the other window seemed darker than before. I slowed my steps, already anticipating something – I don't know what – but hearing a cry I abandoned all pretence and hastened indoors.

A woman was prostrate in her chair, the others crowding round.

They all turned in the half-light, like guilty children caught in some unpleasant game.

Questions could come later. In the chair I recognised Mrs Burgoyne, pearls all awry, mouth open, head lolling back. For a moment I thought she was dead, but then I touched her neck, felt a pulse racing beneath my cold fingers. Her breasts heaved. She was breathing.

'What happened?'

'She fainted,' one of the women said, sounding as though she might be on the verge of it herself.

'I can see that. But I heard someone cry out. Was it Mrs Burgoyne?' Answered by a chorus of affirmatives, I asked why, but only Frank Millet replied, and that was just to give a flippant, 'Hard to say.'

'One of you ladies sit her upright – get her forward, head down. Yes, that's right,' I said as Mrs Carver took the lead. She was deathly pale but seemed the most capable of the three. 'Stay with her – all of you – while I call Doctor O'Loughlin.'

Along the corridor was a telephone below the stairs. Something untoward had been going on, that much was obvious, but while Billy tended to Mrs Burgoyne, I would deal with the others. What Frank Millet's role was, I couldn't guess, but I knew Stead would be the instigator.

Within a couple of minutes Billy came hurrying up the stairs. He had his doctor's bag, but was still buttoning his uniform.

'I think she's had some sort of fright,' I said.

'What were they doing in there?'

'I've yet to find out.'

We went in, to find Mrs Burgoyne half-conscious and weeping. Every now and then she gave little shrieks, shaking her head and fending people off.

Millet and another man – big and owl-like behind his spectacles – looked on, distinctly uncomfortable, while Stead leaned against the fireplace as though in his own front room.

'Come now, Mrs Burgoyne,' O'Loughlin murmured, taking her pulse and gently chafing her hands. 'Back to your cabin, I think. Can you stand, my dear? It will be so much easier if we can make you comfortable.' With no discernible response, he opened a bottle of sal volatile and wafted it beneath her nose.

She came to at once, her eyes wide and terrified. She took one look at Billy's kind face and started shrieking in earnest, hitting out at all around her. Reaching for his bag, Billy asked Mrs Carver to stay and the others to leave. Realising he was going to sedate the hysterical woman, I ushered the others out and towards the Lounge. While they hovered, guiltily, I called one of the stewards and asked for some tea.

'Shall we sit down? I should like you to tell me what was going on before I arrived.'

The two ladies in black I recognised as friends of Colonel Gracie – sisters, both in their middle years. They gave me their names, as did Mr Futrelle, the owlish-looking gentleman in spectacles. Stead sank back in his chair, eyes veiled like someone exhausted, while Frank Millet, on the edge of his, said apologetically, 'Well, this might sound a little odd, Captain, but we were having a séance.'

Appalled, I closed my eyes and took a deep breath before replying. 'And who, pray, was conducting this séance?'

Stead spoke then. 'I was.'

Hardly a surprise. We had never met before this voyage, but Mr Stead had impinged upon my life many times. Almost from the first time I met Ellie, her fears for me had been racked up by his sensational tales. Since she never hesitated to inform me of his latest nonsense, I was very much aware of his stance on spiritualism. As I'd made clear to McElroy when I first saw Stead's name on the passenger list, I wanted no truck with that kind of thing. With an effort, I controlled myself, disciplined my words.

'Would you care to explain what prompted this exercise?'

Normally self-confident, he seemed unusually reticent, as though having difficulty with words. 'There was a discussion. Yesterday, I believe...'

One of the ladies broke in. 'It wasn't Mr Stead's fault,' she said nervously. 'We came across on the *Olympic* – you won't remember us, sir, the weather was very bad, Eloise and I hardly left our staterooms. We came over for our sister's funeral...' She worried her necklace, looking so distraught I felt my anger soften. 'Some strange things happened in England, and we...we wondered if Mr Stead could help us.'

'To do what?' I asked gently.

'To find out what was wrong. We felt – Eloise and I – that our dear, departed sister was trying to tell us something.'

'And was she?'

Miserably, she shook her head. 'I don't know. Mrs Burgoyne screamed, and...'

Frank Millet broke in. 'It was very cold, suddenly.' Futrelle agreed and said, 'The temperature dropped sharply, within a minute, no more.' The ladies nodded.

'Anything else? I'm wondering what it was that made Mrs Burgoyne so hysterical.' When no one answered, I said, 'Something must have happened.'

'She saw what I saw,' Stead murmured. 'At least, I believe so.'

'And what was that?'

He glanced at the ladies. 'I'd rather not say just now. I doubt it would be helpful.'

'Very well,' I said, taking his point. 'But you've caused harm this evening, Mr Stead. To Mrs Burgoyne if no one else. Let there be no more dabbling in this kind of thing – at least aboard this ship. What you do ashore is entirely up to you – but I won't have it here. Is that understood?' I looked at him particularly, but they all nodded.

'Perhaps we gentlemen could discuss this tomorrow? Shall we say nine o'clock, after breakfast? In the meantime, I urge you to keep it to yourselves.'

As I stood up, Frank Millet made to follow me out. I cut him short. 'In the morning, Mr Millet, sir – I'm sure you understand. Right now, I must see Mrs Burgoyne.'

I turned away and it was at that point – by the door – that I came face to face with Mrs Carver. For a moment our eyes locked. Hers were blue. My anger drowned in a wave of astonishment.

Clearly troubled, she stepped back and dropped her gaze. 'I do apologise,' she murmured. 'What we did – it was foolish.'

Suddenly I realised I was holding the door, blocking her path. I drew breath, moved aside. 'It's Mrs Carver, isn't it?' As she nodded, I bowed and introduced myself before asking if she had the number of Mrs Burgoyne's stateroom.

'I can't remember the number – let me show you.' And before I could protest, she was walking ahead of me, down the stairs.

Some detached quarter of my mind noticed she was neither as young nor as slight as I'd imagined. She was taller than Dorothea and her figure in the fashionably cut gown was fuller, more rounded.

'Did you come down with the Doctor?' I asked. 'How was Mrs Burgoyne then?'

Mrs Carver paused on the half-landing and looked up. 'She was a little calmer, I think, but still very upset.' I began to say something reassuring, but she broke in with another apology. 'I'm truly sorry for what happened. If only I'd realised...'

110

'It can hardly be your fault,' I said. 'Surely Mr Stead organised it.'

She shook her head. 'No – I asked him to do it. The dear ladies were upset about their sister, and I thought he could help.'

That took the wind out of me. 'Mr Stead is a friend of yours?'

'An acquaintance. We were introduced in London.'

'Ah, I see.' But I didn't, not at all. I took another step towards her. 'I'd like to know a little more about this evening. Could you tell me about it tomorrow?'

Glancing over her shoulder, she said, 'Really, sir, there's very little to tell.' Her profile – it was her profile that was so like Dorothea's.

'However little that might be,' I said as we reached the foot of the stairs, 'it would help me to understand the situation.'

I followed her down the carpeted corridor with staterooms to either side. She stopped outside a door at the far end. I tried again, lightly this time. 'I promise you, Mrs Carver, coffee with me will be no High Court enquiry!'

For some reason that made her smile. I felt my heart skip a beat as she softened and agreed to meet me in the Lounge at 11:30 the next morning. Watching her as she moved away, only then did it register that she was English, not American. My mind racing with questions, I took a moment before tapping on Mrs Burgoyne's door.

Billy O'Loughlin stepped out to me. 'She's calm now,' he murmured. 'I've given her a sedative. Sure and she'll be away with the fairies in no time.'

'Is she still awake?' As he nodded, I asked if she'd said anything, and for a moment he looked uncomfortable. 'Look, Billy, I met her, years ago, when she was just a girl. She's a strange one, but I'd like to hear what she has to say. That is, if I may?' Aware of his reluctance, I said, 'Unless you think it's dangerous, I'd like to hear the story now. By tomorrow it could be different.'

With that he opened the door and we went in. The stateroom was done out in traditional style, with twin beds, a dressing table, and a sofa that looked somehow out of place. When I entered, Mrs Burgoyne's companion was seated there, book in hand, while Adelaide was in bed, propped up by pillows, her eyes closed. The lights were dimmed, and for the first time I saw something of the girl she'd been, and felt a surge of sympathy.

Perching himself on the edge of the bed, Billy took her hand. 'My dear, I have the Captain with me. You know him, don't you? Do you feel able to tell him what happened?'

Her eyes opened, unfocused at first. 'Cold,' she said to Billy. 'I was cold.'

'Yes, you said so. That must have been alarming.'

'Something,' she breathed, 'in the mist…' She broke off, gulping, her hands gripping Billy's convulsively. 'A figure… couldn't see who it was… wet through. Hair, dress, running wet…' Voice rising, she clung to Billy's arm. 'It was my sister – she drowned off the bayou – I thought she was coming for me!'

A ripple of ice went down my spine, but Billy was calm as ever. 'No, my dear, it was just a bad dream. You fell asleep and had a bad dream. That's all it was, now, a bad dream… Tomorrow you'll wake up and you'll have forgotten all about it… ' Soothed, she subsided at last upon the pillows, closed her eyes and appeared to sleep. Billy turned to me, his jaw set.

Mystified, shaken by that revelation, I hardly knew what to say. Or think. What did it mean?

Rubbing her arms, the young companion seemed frightened. I went over to her. 'Please don't be alarmed, Miss…' I'd forgotten her name, if ever I knew it. 'Mrs Burgoyne was with some friends, playing silly parlour games. It seems to have got out of hand. I've had words with the people concerned, and believe me, it won't happen again.'

She nodded, reminding me again of a little sparrow, all nervous, fluttery movements. 'Thank you, sir.'

O'Loughlin was reassuring. 'Mrs Burgoyne will sleep late – that'll be the sedative working. When she wakes, she may well think her fright was just a dream – if so, I should leave it at that. You understand me, now?'

'Yes, Doctor, of course.' She smiled up at him, trust and confidence restored.

'That's a good girl.' With that he patted her hand.

As the door closed behind us, Billy's frown returned. I waited until we were clear of the staterooms. 'I knew Marcia – the sister. Thirty years ago.'

He looked up sharply. 'Did you? I'm sorry. Did she drown?'

I shook my head. 'I don't know. To be honest I'd forgotten her – until Adelaide made herself known to me. But she didn't say Marcia was dead.' I hesitated for a moment. 'Back there, Billy – do you think that's what she saw?'

'Well now, there's no denying she's had a bad fright.' He paused as we reached the stairs. 'But the mind is a strange creature – who can say how it works? Memory, imagination – a lot of suggestion – we're all susceptible to some extent.' He shrugged. 'Those we've loved and lost – somewhere, there's always a slice of guilt.'

While I was pondering that, he smiled and turned to go. 'You want my honest opinion, sir? I'd say he's a clever fellow, our Mr Stead.'

14

It was after midnight when I reached my bed. I read for a while, but not even Arnold Bennett could distract me from the buzzing round of questions and anxieties. Adelaide Burgoyne, her dead sister Marcia: the dreadful image she conjured. Marcia, who had married a man called Beau. What happened there? Why had she drowned? And Mrs Carver, persuading Stead to hold a séance: so many questions, and no answers. I found myself reading the same paragraph over and over. Eventually, I dropped into sleep, only to wake moments later with a ghastly face in the mirror before me. My face: distorted, pale as death, but recognisably mine.

Gasping, I switched on the reading light and tried to bring my mind under control. The bedroom was as normal. Ellie's gaze met mine from her portrait by the bed, her sweet smile undisturbed. I reached for the carafe and poured myself some water, telling myself it was just a dream. No doubt Billy O'Loughlin, with his mind-theories, would say it was based on some memory from the past. And heaven knows, I'd seen enough to know what drowned men looked like. Too many. I shuddered, told myself they'd become one with the image in the mirror.

The time of Adelaide Burgoyne's fright must have been close to mine. Had she really recognised her sister in the figure she described? And if so, were the two visions connected? That idea unnerved me afresh. I reached for my book, taking refuge in the commonplace events of Arnold Bennett's *Clayhanger*. In the Five Towns of Stoke-on-Trent, such things did not happen.

Next morning, needing warmth to restore me, I drew a hot bath. The water revealed a slight list which raised fresh anxieties about the bunker fire. Last night's note from Joe Bell said it was still burning.

Paintin came in with my tea as I was dressing. Ordering breakfast in my quarters I went through to the wheelhouse, exchanging greetings with Mr Lightoller as I checked the early morning star sights.

Philips, the senior Marconi man, came into the chartroom with some wireless messages as he was going off watch. They were mainly greetings and congratulations from eastbound liners. *President Lincoln* and *Saint Laurent* were added to yesterday's *Empress of Britain* and *La Touraine*. Lined up like calling cards, ready to be posted on the bridge notice board, they all mentioned ice off the eastern seaboard. But that was almost as much a courtesy as the greeting. At this time of year ice was to be expected and, after the wild winter, there would be plenty of it.

Generally, the ice drifting down on the cold Labrador Current melted rapidly on reaching the warm Gulf Stream. Avoiding that area was easy enough when steaming to New York: the separation of shipping lanes meant we were following the southernmost route, anyway. Returning on the more northerly track was a different matter. The warnings already received came from ships heading back to Europe. Hardly surprising that they were encountering ice off Halifax and in the region of the Grand Banks; doubtless we would on the return leg. Fog too, more than likely.

Fields of small, broken-up bergs presented few difficulties for large passenger ships. Pack ice was a problem though. Stopping overnight in that was a dangerous temptation: it could close in and freeze hard, squeezing an iron hull until it literally squeaked. I'd heard enough to know that getting out of that without damage would be something of a miracle – hence most shipmasters preferred to keep moving.

The big bergs – those looking like New York city blocks cast adrift – were an awe-inspiring sight. In the 25 springs I'd spent crossing the Atlantic, I had encountered several, always further north and mostly at a distance while we were threading our way through less imposing stuff. The ones to be feared were the smaller, greyer, tired-looking ones. Sinking, with most of their bulk below the waterline, they were deceptive and dangerous. Impossible to see in fog.

Across the Grand Banks, billowing fog was a hazard most of the year. That was the real problem. So far there'd been nothing, not even a whisper. *Please God, may it stay that way.*

The message I'd been anxiously waiting for was delivered by hand from the Chief's office as I was finishing my breakfast. Joe Bell, in his usual terse prose, was pleased to inform me that the fire was out, the offending bunker now empty and cooling down.

Thank God.

Until the wave of relief washed over me I hadn't realised the depth of my anxiety. The terrible fear of fire. All at once my breakfast revolted. I dashed to the bathroom and was violently sick.

Stead was the first of my visitors, arriving some 15 minutes before the rest. That he had recovered from the strain of the night before was obvious. Then he had been withdrawn, unsure of himself, even a little shaken. Facing me now he seemed confident, pale eyes gleaming, hair and beard bristling, ready to face a challenge.

Taking a chair, he adjusted the creases in his trousers and crossed one leg over the other. Only the swinging of his foot indicated that he was in any way apprehensive. He had the grace, then, to ask after Mrs Burgoyne, and to apologise for having been the instrument of her collapse.

'How is the poor lady this morning?'

'I've not yet seen Dr O'Loughlin. He will advise me later.'

'Ah.' He seemed slightly discomfited. 'Do you mind if I smoke, Captain?' he asked, noting the ashtray on the table.

'Please – go ahead.' As he opened a gold case and lit a cigarette, I opened the discussion. 'So, Mr Stead – what was it that you couldn't tell me in front of the ladies?'

Having discarded the match, he viewed me through a haze of smoke. On a little laugh, he shook his head and said, 'Forgive me, Captain, but it feels strange to be on this side of the interview. Usually I'm the one asking questions.'

I looked at the clock. 'You came early, Mr Stead, so I imagine you'd prefer to talk before the other gentlemen get here?'

He was suddenly serious. 'Yes. Yes, of course.' He flicked ash from his cigarette. 'Allow me to apologise again for what happened. It was most unexpected – I've never had anyone collapse on me before. Most upsetting.' After another pause, he said. 'We went through the preliminaries. I like to give instruction beforehand, to avoid running into trouble. I remember we were in the quiet time, concentrating hard on the people we wished to make contact with. I was seeking Julia, my usual guide...'

'Julia?'

'Yes, Julia, my spirit guide. She helps me make contact with the world beyond.' He talked of this Julia – an American journalist who'd passed over some years before – as though she were still alive. It was all beyond me, but I waited for him to continue.

'After a little while I felt a disturbance. Several spirits struggling to get through. I couldn't see anything, you understand, just felt the distress. They were troubled and impatient, all of them keen to be heard. But something was preventing them coming through.' He drew hard on his cigarette, stubbed it out. 'For once, Julia was no help. Eventually, I sensed it was a woman. I thought she must be the sister who had so recently passed over...'

'The sister? I interrupted. 'Whose sister are we talking about?'

'Why, the ladies in mourning, of course – that's what the séance was all about.'

'Ah – I thought you meant... I'm sorry – go on.'

'They don't know how to behave, you see, when it's been a sudden passing. They think they're alone and come through quickly – it can be very confusing. So I asked her name... No answer, just...' he broke off, seeming genuinely moved. 'I can't describe it, except as an overwhelming sense of loss...

'But then the mist came – a dark mist, obscuring everything. The room went cold. Like ice.'

He paused, head bowed. After a moment he looked up. I had thought his eyes penetrating when I first met him, but now they bored into me, invading my mind. 'And then I knew. It was ice – ice at the heart of the mist.'

With an involuntary shiver I tore my glance away. 'Did you see it?'

'No. But the ice was there.'

'Did the others see it?'

'Not the men – maybe not the sisters. Mrs Carver – possibly, I'm not sure. Mrs Burgoyne experienced it. She probably saw it – that's why she screamed.'

'Yes, indeed.' I'd no intention of revealing what Adelaide Burgoyne had seen, but I was about to ask how she'd come to be involved, when Stead leaned forward, pale eyes intense.

117

'I had a presentiment, Captain, years ago. One of the reasons I don't like crossing the sea. But what we experienced last night was more than that – the sorrow, the confusion, the icy cold – it was a clear warning...'

Just as I held up my hand to stop him, there came a discreet knock at my open door. I looked up and Frank Millet was standing there, Futrelle close behind.

Enquiring after Mrs Burgoyne, they came in, apologising afresh for the disturbance of the night before. Stead, clearly frustrated, sat back in his chair while they settled themselves. As it transpired, there was little they could add to what I knew already, but they were keen to explain their presence in the circle. Frank Millet said he had always been interested in the occult – years ago he'd experienced some strange happenings at his English home in the Cotswolds.

'The ghost of a lecherous former innkeeper, would you believe?' His smile broadened. 'Used to caress my wife when she came into my studio – other ladies too. I had the devil's own job keeping my models!'

Futrelle – a novelist, I'd been told – chuckled appreciatively before giving his own account of weird, real-life coincidences that had inspired his fiction. With my daily meeting at ten, I looked twice at the clock while they were speaking.

'Yes, very interesting, gentlemen. What is it Shakespeare says? More things in heaven and earth than man can possibly know?' I paused to measure something Joe had impressed upon me years ago. I wanted them to understand how deeply felt it was. 'Out at sea,' I said heavily, 'we seafarers are like children in the face of the Almighty. We are alone with his power and his might. We do not play with the Devil.'

Allowing a moment for that to sink in, I drew things to a close. 'Thank you for coming, gentlemen.' I rose to my feet. 'I will let you know how Mrs Burgoyne is faring when I have a report from Dr O'Loughlin.'

Stead, as I suspected he would, hung back. 'Captain – a moment more.' His voice was low, urgent, his pale eyes afire with conviction. 'As I was trying to tell you before – the chill, the fog – it was a warning. I feel it most strongly. We are in danger.'

'No more than usual, Mr Stead. Now, if you'll excuse me...' I urged him towards the open door. Whatever he had to say, I didn't want to hear it.

'You don't understand. Let me explain about the presentiments I've had – they've always come true. This time...'

118

'This time?' I repeated. Suddenly furious, I pushed the door shut. 'What about the time you organised a campaign to send General Gordon to the Sudan? That was right, was it? Got a good man killed – and nothing was achieved! And *The Truth About the Navy?* Turned out to be an invention that got the country into hock! That's the trouble with you, Mr Stead – you *feel* things, and just because you can string a few words together, you imagine you know better than the rest of us.

'Oh, and forgive me,' I went on, tapping my forehead for effect, 'didn't you once go to prison for falsifying evidence?'

'It was not falsified!' With a burning glance he brushed past me, reached for the door. 'But I see you are a bigoted man, Captain Smith. I fear you will regret it!'

'Come now, Mr Stead – this isn't one of your stories – this is real life!' I recoiled as he slammed the door behind him.

After a moment I opened it again, hooked it back. My hands were unsteady. I lit another cigar, tried to calm myself before anyone else arrived. *A warning.* Did the man think I was as deluded as he was? As if there weren't enough real problems to deal with, he had to go about inventing more!

As O'Loughlin remarked dryly when I released a head of steam a few minutes later, Mr Stead was a prime example of a man who carries the power of conviction.

With one of his ironic, *I'm a Catholic, raised by priests,* expressions, he said, 'A shame he's not travelling in Second – we could steer him towards Father Byles – he'd soon point out the error of his ways!'

For once, Billy's dry asides failed to amuse. I was still rattled when we set off on our morning's tour of inspection. Having inspected the watchkeepers' cabins and officers' mess abaft the bridge, we headed as a group down to B Deck, where, as chance would have it, we bumped into a young stewardess coming out of Tommy Andrews' stateroom. She lowered her eyes as she spotted Mr Latimer and me coming down the alleyway, and, with a bob of acknowledgement, hurried away with an armful of towels. Tommy, I thought, looked a little pink about the ears. I felt unaccountably irritated. I said nothing – he was not a member of the crew, after all – but raised an eyebrow and turned to Mr Latimer. Words were unnecessary. He nodded, and I knew the stewardess would be reminded of her position and her duties – which did not include flirting with Harland and Wolff's chief designer.

If Tommy's greeting was overly hearty, he was as keen as ever to share his latest assessments, button-holing the Chief about bringing the additional boilers into play. I wanted to get on. Any more talk and we'd have Mr Ismay joining us.

'Inspection, gentlemen,' I said briskly, whereupon Tommy bowed and stepped aside. We did not enter the staterooms, but I was sharp-eyed in the bars and galleys, with random checks of conditions in store-cupboards and cold rooms. Latimer had his own methods of keeping an eye on stocks.

Finally, having worked our way through the victualling department's accommodation – deck and engineering staff to come on Monday – it was just the Chief and I and the engine room. It was a relief to see things looking how they should. With the fire out, and the bunker cooling down, we could concentrate on what these engines might do under optimum conditions. Of the 29 boilers, 20 had been up to pressure from Southampton, and it was almost time to bring the reserves into play. The turbine was taking its power from the main engines' exhaust system, and at the right moment the Chief could increase the revs and see what speed she would do.

The calm seas were a bonus we could not have envisaged. But in order to obtain maximum speed for a test run, we needed those who'd slaved to kill the bunker fire, fit and able to put in more effort.

'When we do decide,' Joe Bell said, pausing with his hand on the engine room door, 'we'll need those furnaces fed to capacity. I'll need some warning, sir.'

'Of course you will.' I considered the options. 'Today's no good?'

'No, I'd rather not. The lads have put their backs into killing that fire. They could do with normal duties for a watch or two.'

A quick calculation put Sunday out of the equation. 'Well, providing this weather holds, how about Monday morning? I expect Mr Ismay will approve. He might even like to suggest it,' I said with a dry smile.

The Chief grinned. 'Monday it is, sir.'

Eager to convey the news before I met Mrs Carver, I called Bruce's suite from the Chief's office. His secretary said he was out on deck, taking the air. A few minutes later I spotted him on the Boat Deck, leaning against the rail in the sun.

'By the way, sir,' I said quietly, after we'd exchanged the usual pleasantries, 'you'll be pleased to know the bunker fire is out, and no damage done as far as we can see.'

He straightened at once. 'Thank heavens for that!' With a rueful grin he said, 'I don't mind telling you, EJ, I've been quite anxious about it.'

It was on the tip of my tongue to say, *you think the rest of us haven't?* I bit it back. 'Yes, the Chief's done well. He deserves congratulations.'

'Absolutely!' Bruce agreed, smacking the rail for emphasis. I waited. There was a slight pause, then he frowned and said, 'So where does this leave us with regard to the speed test?'

I explained that we would be leaving the Great Circle and changing course somewhere around tea-time the next day, followed by a potentially difficult few hours as we met the cold Labrador current.

'There could be ice, there could be fog. Possibly both.'

'Grand Banks Sunday night?' His sharp eyes studied me, the ends of his waxed moustache twitching as he pondered the situation. 'Hmm. Tomorrow's out, then. What about today? Can we really not fire her up today?'

I shook my head. He was not an engineer and I knew I shouldn't be annoyed by his lack of perspicacity. Remembering his position it was necessary to humour him, although while a ship was at sea and I was in command, my word was law. Bruce Ismay was well aware of the fact and I did not need to confront him with it. Of course, it did not prevent him from trying to impose his will.

'I doubt the Chief will want to stretch his men further at the moment,' I observed, repeating Joe Bell's words. 'They've worked double shifts on that bunker...'

'That's too bad.' His eyes roved over the horizon as though seeking an answer out there. Finally, thrusting his hands into his pockets, he said, 'Better be Monday then. I suppose we can do it on Monday?'

'I'll speak to the Chief Engineer, Mr Ismay.'

'Very good.' And with that he strode away.

I cursed him silently. Without any increase in speed we were already on schedule for arrival before dawn on Wednesday, the 17th. Bruce was keen to beat *Olympic*'s record on her maiden voyage, and in this calm weather we could probably do it. But the fact remained that it wasn't practical to arrive after midnight, when shoreside officials weren't available. Anyway, the Chief knew his job. He would fire up the rest of the boilers when the time was right.

15

I was a little late for my appointment, and Mrs Carver was waiting at a table by the window, watching people stroll past along the Promenade. Another lurch of the heart as I noted her profile. Crossing the room I reminded myself that people do have doubles: this lady was a stranger, not Dorothea. She could not be expected to understand the emotions she aroused in me.

'Mrs Carver,' I greeted her with a warm smile. 'How are you? It's kind of you to see me – sorry I was delayed.'

'How is Mrs Burgoyne?' Betraying her anxiety, they were almost her first words.

'A little better, I understand. Still resting, but the Doctor assures me she's much recovered from last night.' Disconcerted by the openness of her gaze, afraid she might see too much, I looked away, signalled to a steward. 'Will you have coffee?' She nodded, I ordered, and then, bringing my mind back to the séance, I said, 'Tell me, how did Mrs Burgoyne come to be with you last night?'

'Why, she's acquainted with the Enderby sisters, Marianne and Eloise. But I don't think she was at the funeral.'

'No, she joined in Cherbourg.' I thought for a moment. 'She didn't mention her sister by any chance? No? I just wondered. But the séance, you said, was your idea… How was that? What made you approach Mr Stead?' As she hesitated, I apologised for being so direct. 'It's only that I'm trying to understand how it came about.'

Mrs Carver looked down, studying her hands. Against the rich blue material of her skirt, her fingers were long and slender, the nails oval; she wore a ring set with pearls and rubies above her wedding band.

'Well,' she said at last, 'it was simply that I thought a séance – something like that – might help. It was talked of, you see, when I was in London. My cousin – Emily – had read some of Mr Stead's *Borderland* journals. She thought I might be interested. We were going to attend the *Bureau*...'

'The bureau?'

'*Julia's Bureau* – it's a meeting place for people interested in spiritualism. Mr Stead gives lectures there. I wasn't in London long enough for that, but as chance would have it he attended a soirée given by a friend of my aunt's. We were introduced.'

Intrigued, I asked her opinion of the man. The question surprised her. 'Well, I must say Mr Stead has a powerful presence. People are drawn to him.' She hesitated, gave a rueful smile. 'To be honest, he makes me feel a little uncomfortable.'

At that, I chanced a bold question. 'As though he knows what you are thinking?'

As our eyes met, she nodded. I agreed it was a disconcerting trait. 'But – forgive me – I'm still curious. You said something about the ladies, and trying to help?'

Our coffee arrived. She poured, asked if I would have milk. I noticed she was trembling slightly as she handed me the cup. She was clearly anxious about something. Was it the séance, or was it me? I'd almost forgotten my question when she began to explain.

'Yes, Captain, as I said last night, they were upset. Their sister had passed away, and the funeral was held over until they could get to London. It probably sounds silly, but... they said strange things were happening at the house. The dead sister's house, I mean, where they were staying.

'The telephone kept ringing – but no one was there. Marianne said she woke to see a figure at the end of her bed – and then Eloise heard the piano playing in an empty room. There were other things, I forget now. But they've been so distressed by having to return home with this mystery hanging over them, it's almost all they've talked about. Well,' she smiled a little at my expression, 'it may sound unlikely, but they've been so kind to me, I simply wanted to help. So,' she added with a gesture of appeal, 'when I saw Mr Stead was aboard, I offered to speak to him.'

'I imagine he was eager to oblige?'

'No,' she shook her head. 'He was reluctant at first. But I'm afraid the ladies and I were rather persuasive.' After a moment, with a quick glance, she asked, 'Do you dislike him?'

'I think he's…' I stopped to amend my words. 'What he does, I think, is dangerous.'

Her cheeks suffused with colour. 'Again, sir, I can only apologise.'

'Mrs Carver,' I said gently, leaning towards her, 'I attach no blame to you. The matter's been dealt with now, so it's unlikely to raise its head again. I ask only that you do not discuss it with other passengers.'

'Of course. I understand.'

I sipped my coffee. She sipped hers. I could see she felt rebuked. In an attempt to bring the conversation round to less distressing subjects, I said, 'You were just visiting London?'

She relaxed visibly, her mouth curving into a smile. 'Yes, I have family there. But I married an American – and now I'm going home to New Haven and my little girl.'

'You must miss her,' I said with sympathy. 'Have you been away long?'

'Just a month – but it feels like forever. I can't wait to see her.' She looked down, half-shy, half-amused. 'She's only two. I hope she hasn't forgotten me.'

I smiled and shook my head. 'I doubt it. I have a daughter too – ever since she was born I've been away for weeks at a time. She never forgot, not even when she was very small.'

We talked about our daughters, her little Daisy, and my Mel. The conversation moved on to New England. She'd been living in Connecticut for four years, and I had come to know something of the area in my time, so it was pleasing to discover we liked the same places for similar reasons. But then, in telling me how she'd met her husband, a lawyer, she mentioned her family in London.

When she said they were bankers, the Langs sprang to mind. Aware that time was pressing and there might not be another opportunity to ask, I was more direct than polite. 'Forgive me, Mrs Carver,' I began, 'if I seem to stare – but you remind me of someone I used to know…'

'Really?' In her flush of pleasure I saw the resemblance afresh.

'The surname was Lang.'

She exclaimed with surprise. 'No! But that's my family name too!'

The moment seemed to stretch itself. As I struggled for words, she looked up. I turned my head and there was Bruce Ismay, one eyebrow cocked quizzically, bowing to Mrs Carver and begging to be introduced.

I found my professional self from somewhere. Civilities over, I checked my watch and said I must go to the bridge – the ritual of the noon sight. She must have sensed something, because Mrs Carver excused herself too, saying she'd arranged to meet her friends for lunch. I bowed as she left us, too stunned to think straight.

16

Leaving Bruce to make of it what he would, I caught up with my guest in the atrium. 'Forgive me, Mrs Carver – I really do have to get to the bridge. But, would you – would you care to…? I mean, it would please me enormously if we could talk later?'

'Yes, Captain,' she said warmly. 'If you have time, I'd really like that.'

'After lunch?' She nodded, surprise and pleasure in her eyes. 'Here, then, at two o'clock?'

Buoyed by the prospect as we parted, the day seemed brighter, my fatigue a thing of the past. Indeed, my body seemed not to belong to me. As for my mind, it was so far elsewhere I was barely aware of the daily ritual. While Murdoch and the juniors took their sextants to shoot the sun on the stroke of noon, I was staring at the horizon, thinking of Lucinda Carver.

She had to be Nicholas's daughter: she would know something of Dorothea. What had happened in the years between?

As my officers set about their calculations, I noticed the boy on the starboard side. The one who was going to go to sea one day. I knew he was waiting to catch me again, but there was time to stand and chat to him for a few minutes. He asked how far we'd travelled, so I told him our position, and that we'd covered 519 nautical miles since noon the day before.

'Why do you always say, *nautical miles*, sir?' he asked. I liked this boy, and thought him old enough – he was about twelve – to understand the difference between land miles and sea miles.

'Well now, if you make a circle on the surface of the earth, and divide it up into degrees, you'll find – once you've done all the maths – that a degree measures 60 nautical miles. A minute is one sixtieth of a degree, so a minute equals one nautical mile. And that nautical mile measures 6,080 feet. Rather longer than a statute mile, which is…?'

'1,760 yards,' he answered.

'Or, 5,280 feet,' I added, watching him consider the maths.

'And *knots*,' he said triumphantly, 'are nautical miles travelled in an hour!'

'Exactly,' I agreed, delighted to hear yesterday's lesson repeated back to me. 'So we have travelled 519 nautical miles, in the last 25 hours. Remember, we gain almost an hour each day, travelling westwards, so our average speed has been a little over 21 knots.'

He beamed. 'Thank you, sir!'

I ruffled his hair. 'You'll go far, young man. Now then – get along. Your mother will be wondering where you are.'

'That's all right, sir – she knows!'

I chuckled, pretty sure she did know. Feeling like a boy myself, I returned to the chartroom to resume my duties.

Light from the glass dome cast a radiance around her as she came towards me. Aware of how lovely she looked in her velvet coat, I smiled with pleasure. 'Mrs Carver.'

'Captain,' she said warmly, extending her hand, 'I can't tell you how pleased I am that you could spare the time to talk.'

I assured her the pleasure was all mine. As we reached the Boat Deck I donned my cap firmly while she tied a pink chiffon scarf around her hat. Stepping out into the sunshine, she said lightly, 'If you knew Dorothea – and I imagine she's the person you were referring to over coffee – I'd love to know more about her. You did mean Dorothea,' she added, 'when you remarked on the resemblance? Uncle Nicholas says I'm the image of her.'

My step faltered. 'Yes – you are indeed.' I moved towards the rail, leaned against it, turned my eyes to the distant horizon. *Uncle Nicholas?* I was suddenly confused. If he wasn't her father, then what was her relationship to Dorothea?

'So you knew her!' she exclaimed happily. 'I can scarce believe it after all this…' But whatever she meant was covered by a gesture. 'Never mind,' she went on quickly, 'do tell me how you met? If you knew her as Dorothea Lang, I imagine it must have been in Hong Kong? Lang's the family name, of course – her married name was Curtis.'

'Curtis – yes.' I was nodding like a donkey, unable to take in what she was saying. I cleared my throat. 'Yes – Curtis – I met him once.'

At that she seemed equally taken aback. Gazing frankly, we shook our heads at the same moment. As the wind whipped pink chiffon across her face, she looked out over the dappled sea. Grey-green waves, a grey-blue horizon. 'Ah, so you met Mr Curtis. When was that, do you mind my asking?'

Something in her voice had changed. I wondered why. 'Well now,' I said slowly, pretending that year wasn't etched on my mind. 'It must have been '82 or '83, when I was on the Pacific route. We were in and out of Hong Kong regularly then.'

'Oh. I see.'

'But I first met Dorothea,' I went on, gathering myself together, 'back in '70, when she was serving tea at a mission hall.' At that, Mrs Carver stared in surprise. 'I met her father, that same afternoon. They talked about Nicholas,' I added, deliberately bringing him back into the conversation, 'but I never met him.'

'Uncle Nicholas worked in London. He was my guardian.'

'Your guardian?' Confused, I said, 'But who was…? Forgive me, I don't understand. What is your relationship to Dorothea?'

She studied me. After what seemed a long pause, she said gently, 'Dorothea was my mother. I'm afraid she died when I was just a child.'

My shock must have been obvious. I felt winded, in need of a hiding place. I bent forward, shielding my eyes. When I had my voice under control, I said, 'I didn't know. To be honest, I didn't even know she had children.'

'Just me.' As I looked up she smiled. A rather tight little smile. She looked exactly like Dorothea then. 'I was the only one.'

In the space of a few moments, I felt the world had changed. Dorothea, who had sworn to me she could not have children because of a botched miscarriage – or deliberate abortion, I was never sure – did have a child after all. But whose child was she? What about Curtis?

I couldn't ask. Mindful of being in a public place I suggested we move on. Perhaps Lucinda Carver was nervous too, because as we walked she started talking about her childhood. Clipped, rapid words that I found hard to take in – hard to bear, sometimes. 'I didn't really know either of my parents, Captain. Dorothea left me in London with Uncle Nicholas and his family – the climate in Hong Kong, you understand. At least, that was the reason given. She came back for a few months each year until I was – six, I think.

'After that,' she went on sadly, 'I didn't see her again. She died in Hong Kong when I was seven. Fever, they said. I imagine it was malaria.'

Hearing it like that gave me a queer sensation in the pit of my stomach. I had never thought of Dorothea gone, always imagined her continuing to live as she had when I knew her, with strings of lovers and quite invulnerable. In my imagination she had never suffered, never grown old.

'Oh, forgive me,' her daughter apologised, 'I've put it badly.'

'No, it's all right. I'm a little shocked, that's all. And so very sorry.' With a mote of soot in my eye I stopped to find my handkerchief. Struggling to keep my voice even, I said, 'Like her mother. Her mother died of Hong Kong fever too.' I took a deep breath. 'And your father?'

Lucinda drew back at once. 'Curtis?' she said, just as Dorothea had, and shrugged in the same way. Curiously, I'd seen in Dorothea only a couldn't-care-less gesture; in her daughter I suspected it hid a wealth of pain. 'He came to see me,' she went on, 'a few months later. I'd not met him before.'

As I stared, aghast, she shrugged again. 'You say you met him. Didn't you know he had a Chinese family?' As I nodded, she asked bleakly, 'What would he want with me?'

'He only came to see you? Not to take you back to Hong Kong?'

'Oh, no. He'd come to contest the Will. My mother had left her share of the business to me, but he was claiming it, you see.'

I nodded, said I was aware of both business and domestic arrangements. Despite the stiff breeze along the Boat Deck, more and more people were coming out to stroll in the sunshine. Ahead, two ladies in black were passing the funnels and coming towards us. Recognising the Enderby sisters, I knew we had to speak to them.

They looked enquiringly at my companion, but – like her mother before her – she seemed able to dissimulate without effort. I was a little stiff, I'm afraid, and they may have thought I was still displeased with them. Anyway, after a brief exchange of platitudes we each walked on.

After a few yards, aware that she was having difficulty with her scarf, I said, 'Why don't we have some tea?' And so we found ourselves a corner in the pretty Palm Court, shielded from casual gaze by fronds of greenery.

'You were saying that Curtis contested your mother's Will,' I

129

reminded her as we were served.

'Yes, and it might even have gone his way. In law, you see, Curtis was entitled to his dead wife's estate.'

Understanding the difficulties of such a situation, I nodded and waited. When she'd poured the tea, Lucinda said, 'But it transpired that he'd installed his Chinese son as manager out there. Uncle Nicholas – as you can probably imagine – was afraid Lang's would lose control of the Hong Kong end, which was where his father had started the business. He wasn't going to let that happen.'

'No, I can imagine. What happened?'

'He fought Curtis and won,' she said with satisfaction. But then, raising her brows, she added, 'Not that there was much left of her estate after that...'

I knew enough about the law – and the situation out there – to understand that it must have been a dirty fight. 'Oh what a tangled web,' I murmured, shaking my head, thinking back on how the bank and bullion business had been the top and bottom of everything that was wrong with that marriage – and also between Dorothea and me. 'That must have been hard for you...'

'It was.' She paused, considering, her blue eyes veiled. 'Very unpleasant.' I noticed how tightly her hands were clasped.

Wanting to take those slender hands in mine, I said, 'And you were just a child...' With a dozen questions on my tongue, I forced them back. Rarely had I felt so constrained. 'A strange man,' I added, with possibly more feeling than I intended. 'To think more of the business than he did of your mother...'

'You saw that?' Under her earnest gaze I felt my opinion was being weighed against some kind of measure. Suddenly, she said, 'He was not my father, was he?'

Startled, at a loss for words, I shook my head. Before I could speak she took it for confirmation. 'No, I don't think so, either. There was too much – I don't know – talk, cruelty, accusations.' Her voice was suddenly husky with emotion. 'Oh, Captain Smith, I'm so sorry, I shouldn't be saying such things, involving you in all this ancient history. You don't know me...'

I reached across to pat her hand, but the gesture seemed to worsen the crisis. As she reached for a lacy handkerchief, I drew back. 'It's all right, my dear, think nothing of it...' She was Dorothea's daughter. Now she'd begun I wanted to know everything. 'Do you mean Curtis? What could he accuse you of? You were just a child.'

'It was the day I was taken in to the drawing room to meet him.' In a taut voice, she said, 'He drew me close – I thought to bestow a kiss. He was, after all, supposed to be my father. Until then I'd regarded Uncle Nicholas as my father, so it was a difficult moment… I didn't like the look in this man's eye. I tried to pull away, but he held my shoulders, stared hard at me. And then he said, *Oh, yes, I can see whose child you are.*'

Shocked by her words, I was almost afraid to speak. 'What did he mean?' *That she was the by-blow of one of his friends?* 'Did he ever say?'

'No. That was it. I was sent away. Dismissed.'

Stricken for her, I hung my head. When I could trust myself, I looked up. 'But my dear, you are the image of your mother…'

With a wry little smile, she said, 'You're very kind, sir, but I don't think that's what he meant. Later, when the estate was being fought over, my cousin David said I wouldn't inherit a penny, because I didn't have a father and my mother was… a tramp, I think was the word he used. He must have been listening at doors.'

With a huff of disgust, I shook my head. 'She was never that.'

'I'm afraid things came out at the court hearing which were hard to misinterpret.'

'My dear, believe me, courts are places where things are deliberately misinterpreted! Folk swear on the Holy Bible and proceed to lie through their teeth!'

'You think so?'

'I know so!'

Leaning towards her I proceeded to do a bit of falsifying myself. I couldn't bear to think of her burning with shame and sorrow over an accident of birth. Lucinda Carver was Dorothea's daughter: that was enough for me. So I gave her my view of the situation between her mother and Curtis, and told her that David Lang was the one to blame for it, with his insistence on putting trade and money above all else. Way above his only daughter's happiness.

'But it rebounded on him in the end! I swear, if Curtis blackened your mother's name, it was for his own gain.

'And it's ironic,' I went on, 'when you think David Lang married for love – a Portuguese beauty from Macau. Her portrait was still hanging in the main room of the bungalow when I was last there. He should have known better than to talk his daughter into a marriage of convenience.'

'Portuguese? I didn't know that – Uncle Nicholas never said.'

'Another little secret,' I commented dryly.

She viewed me keenly. 'But you know so much…'

'Yes.' Too much, perhaps. Afraid of what she might see, I turned away, studying the surrounding tables through the veil of palm fronds. 'Your mother was a girl of 18 when we first met, and I was less than a year older – 3rd Mate on a sailing ship out of Liverpool. I thought Dorothea was the most beautiful girl I'd ever seen…' Swamped by memories, for a moment it was hard to go on. 'I was over 30 when we met again, and she was married, of course – still beautiful, but life with Curtis had changed her.' I paused, searching vainly for words to explain the sudden passion that had flared between us.

'Did you marry for love?' I asked, knowing she had from her warm response. 'Well, my dear, you'll understand how powerful such feelings can be.' As she agreed, I cleared my throat, suddenly shy, finding it difficult to say that I had loved Dorothea, and she had loved me – I'd never been sure of it anyway. 'Perhaps it was wrong, but…' Even as I tried to shrug emotion away, the truth hit me like a physical blow. I could hardly breathe. Looking up into her eyes, all at once I knew what Curtis meant.

'I can see that you loved her…'

I blinked and nodded, swallowing hard as my vision blurred. 'Forgive me,' I managed at last, 'I know a gentleman should never ask the year of a lady's birth, but…?'

We read each other's thoughts. The silence seemed to vibrate as it stretched between us. Her words were so soft they were barely there. 'I was born on the first day of December, 1883…'

When I last saw Dorothea it was April.

Overwhelmed, aware of people close by, I found my handkerchief, made a play of blowing my nose. 'Might we talk later, my dear? For now, I'm afraid you'll have to excuse me…'

'Of course.' Her eyes were brimming too. 'I understand,' she whispered, and I saw then that she did.

'Thank God,' I murmured, and pressed my daughter's hand.

17

I made my way blindly to my quarters. Once inside I closed both doors. If anyone wanted me they would have to knock.

Choked by emotion, I took refuge in my bedroom, sank down in the chair and wept. Pulling myself together, I imagined the bout was over, only to be overwhelmed afresh moments later. It went on for half an hour or more, a release of grief and joy coupled with anguish. Lucinda – my daughter! But Dorothea – I could barely contemplate what she'd been through. I remembered the letter she'd left in Li's hands, understanding everything now. Recalling the way I'd blamed her, I wept again.

Hypocrite. I'd gone to the house to bring it to an end, anyway. So what would have happened if she hadn't run off to London? If she'd stayed to tell me she was expecting my child? I couldn't have abandoned her then. Had she known, the last time we met? That day of the picnic: was the tale of an aborted pregnancy just an attempt to throw sand in my eyes? I remembered her face, its stony expression; her hands on the reins, the casual shrug as she told me about losing a child. As though I, a mere man, could know nothing of such pain. Well, I thought, I'd learned since.

Memory cast up painful images, venting emotions I'd imagined were dead. That last night at the hotel, the way she'd wept in the aftermath of love, body-wrenching sobs that were as startling as they were sudden. I thought I'd hurt her, but she clung, wordlessly, stroking, kissing,

133

wrapping herself around me as though she would never let me go. And when, at the last, I had to leave, she held on to my arm, my hand, the very tips of my fingers, like someone afraid of drowning.

Yet all unknown to me, she was the one making plans to leave.

I thought of that letter, the smudges on it. *Better we part now,* was clear enough; and then the indecipherable line. Did she say *I love you,* and then think better of it?

Dorothea – oh, my love, how you almost destroyed me. I wept again, remembering.

No point wishing it could have been different. If I'd stayed, given up my career for her, could it have worked, would we have been happy? Suspecting not, I dried my eyes, tried to banish the regrets.

Even so, I had a terrible aching void where my heart should be; an ache for the daughter I'd not known about, the years we had missed; not least the suffering she had experienced. I longed to hold her, tell her I was sorry.

Needing to pull myself together, I poured a stiff, restorative measure of whisky. With Lucinda in mind, I remembered that amongst the books and thick jerseys at the bottom of my sea-chest there had been a small box. Had Paintin unpacked it when I joined, or was it now locked in the hold with the officers' luggage?

Hastily, I checked the place where my studs and cufflinks were kept. I felt to the back, even pulled the drawer out, but no, it was not there.

Having gone through every drawer I sat back on my heels and swore. It would mean a trip to the hold. Paintin would think I'd gone mad. But with woollens to prompt me I turned to the deep drawer beneath the bed. Inside were two thick white knitted jerseys with a pile of sea-boot socks. Underneath, in the back corner, I found it: the little box. Inside, a scrap of soft, discoloured cotton protected the gold chain that Dorothea had given me almost thirty years ago.

As I ran it through my fingers, I caught Eleanor's gaze. It seemed I even felt her presence in the room.

Squeezing my eyes shut against the sudden burn of guilt, I wondered how I would tell her. What would she say? I had always kept Hong Kong and Dorothea to myself – not just from a sense of shame, but because of the connection with Harry Jones.

134

18

Strange tales, unseen forces, coincidences. That was what Futrelle and Frank Millet were talking about when they came to see me. Frank claimed most people had at least one odd story to relate. I wondered what their reaction would be if I were to tell them mine.

That the death of Harry Jones had led to a passionate liaison with Dorothea was one thing, but for years I'd felt uneasy about the link between Jones and Eleanor. Now, faced with the consequences, I burned with remorse, not knowing how to explain. Once, not long after our first meeting, she'd asked about that first trip. I was suitably vague, brushing off any suggestion that I'd been at all heroic in caring for young Harry, a man she'd never met. So he disappeared, conveniently for me, into the wash of time and memory.

It wasn't exactly guilt that stopped my tongue; not then. If I'm honest, at that time Dorothea was far from forgotten, and I had no wish to reveal the agonies she'd inflicted. Besides, it seemed to me that if Eleanor had known about Dorothea, she might have felt diminished; and there was no need for that.

Eleanor was everything Dorothea was not. They were both beautiful, but where Dorothea was sharp, Eleanor was soft; where one's glance was veiled, secretive, the other's was fresh, open, honest. But then, Eleanor had nothing to hide.

Eleanor's smile – well, that was the first thing I noticed when I saw them waiting to cross the road. I can see her now, talking and laughing as though she hadn't a care in the world. I thought then, *what a gorgeous girl*. It was one of those moments when you long to know everything there is to know about a woman – and it must have been obvious because when I caught her eye she blushed and looked away. Her companion hurried her on. I followed them with my eyes, admiring the neat shape of her waist, the slight sway of her hips, until they rounded a corner and disappeared from view.

I was feeling good that day but she put a tune on my lips and a spring in my step as I continued towards Lime Street to meet Joe's train. He'd been to Hanley on family business and we had much to discuss. The girl went from my mind.

We were planning to share a meal before he continued home on the ferry and I went back on duty. It was back in '85, and I'd just been promoted again – this time to 1st Officer of the *Republic*. The liner was not new – in fact at fifteen years old she was getting to be an old lady, but she was on the Atlantic run, and that to me was all that mattered. We were due to sail for New York the following day, and I knew I'd not be back in Liverpool for several weeks.

My brother had kept in touch with the Jones family in a casual way. They were wine and spirit merchants, with premises close to the docks, but by the time Joe came ashore, the business was in the hands of Harry Jones's elder brother, Thomas. Although I ran into members of the family occasionally, in the aftermath of Dorothea I kept well clear of the shop on Castle Street.

It was not difficult – as a navigating officer with White Star, I had nothing to do with the purchasing of victuals. Since coming ashore, however, Joe had become quite the businessman, supplying various small shipping companies with their requirements, from bacon to bolts and barrel ends, including the best in Scotch and Irish whiskies. My brother's ambition was for a way in with the bigger companies, and since White Star was part of the story, he wanted me to meet Mr Thomas Jones again. 'Just to remind him,' he said, 'of who you are and which company you're working for.'

I would have preferred not to, but it was hard to refuse. So we made our way towards Castle Street, a broad thoroughfare running parallel to the docks. *Wm Jones & Sons* occupied an old building, the entrance set back between bow-fronted windows. As I set foot on the step, the door was opened by someone inside; and there, about to leave the premises, was the gorgeous girl I had set eyes on not half an hour previously.

136

We stood and gazed at each other, she with her sister at her shoulder, me with my brother at mine, locked on the threshold like clockwork figures.

Thomas Jones jerked us into motion. 'Good morning, Captain Hancock, Mr Smith,' he said cheerfully. 'Do come in, if my nieces will allow it. We try not to conduct business in the doorway!'

By then I had taken in every aspect of her appearance, fine features, pretty mouth, beautiful eyes – were they grey or dark green? – and the glossy brown curls which framed her face. She was wearing – well, something that echoed the mysterious colour of her eyes. Her cheeks deepened to rose as she stepped back for us to enter.

I bowed and thanked her and moved forward into the shop. Thomas Jones embarked upon a round of introductions. Eleanor Pennington was the remarkable one – the other was her sister, Mary Jane. We stood in the shop and chatted for several minutes, during which time Thomas explained – to my deep embarrassment – our connection with his younger brother Harry. It was a profound relief to discover the girls had no memory of either Harry or the tragedy, and that Thomas was not a blood relative but their uncle by marriage. After that I felt able to relax a little.

The sisters were in Liverpool for the day. They planned to do some shopping in town, but Uncle Tom had promised to escort them along the Landing Stage first, to view the ships, before going on to have some dinner at the George Hotel.

Joe, bless him, hardly missed a beat. 'My brother, here,' he said, 'is 1st Officer aboard the *Republic*...' He turned to me. 'If the ladies like to look at ships, Ted, perhaps we could have a look at yours?'

'By all means,' I agreed. 'If they have time?' Of course I was looking at the lovely Eleanor, who was blushing and looking to her sister. But she seemed more concerned about their shopping list.

'Come now, Mary Jane,' her uncle chided, 'it's not every day you have chance to see one of White Star's famous liners!'

She gave in at that, and a few minutes later we were all walking down towards the quays, past George's Dock and onto the Landing Stage. *RMS Republic* was alongside, her sails furled, masts and buff-and-black funnel impressive above the white superstructure and black hull. She dwarfed the other vessels berthed nearby.

It was gratifying to receive compliments, although having only recently been appointed I couldn't claim praise for how the ship looked on that sunny September day. As we boarded, cargo and stores were still being loaded; the 2nd Officer raised his eyebrows as he saw me coming along the deck. 'I thought you were off today, sir?' Then he noticed the ladies and smiled.

'On duty later,' I said equably, and led my little party up the external steps to the bridge. By then I was used to showing people around ships, and had no difficulty keeping up a commentary. Miss Eleanor, I could see, was paying particular attention. As I finished explaining the various instruments, she asked tentatively, 'But how do you know where you are, Mr Smith, when you're out of sight of land?'

Hoping to impress, I showed her our navigating instruments. 'You see, Miss Eleanor, we know where the sun, the moon, the stars and planets are, every second of the day. So we take sights with our sextants – at first light, noon and evening – and work out the latitude and longitude mathematically. We mark the position on the chart, and from there it's a simple matter of fixing direction and course by the ship's compass.'

Most people were satisfied with that. Miss Eleanor was different. With a nod and a shy smile she thanked me; but then, biting her lip and colouring to the roots of her rich brown hair, she looked up and said, 'I hope you don't mind my asking, but is it always accurate? I mean, how easy is it to be wrong?'

Mary Jane clicked her tongue, and on the edge of my vision I was aware of the sharp look she gave her sister. I could have lied, said we rarely made a mistake, but gazing into Eleanor's eyes I felt she deserved better.

'Very easy,' I said. 'Which is why all the deck officers take sights. If there are discrepancies, we check each other's figures. A small error in the middle of the ocean doesn't matter much over a day or two – but it does matter close to land. Especially,' I added, 'if the weather is poor.'

'Yes,' she said thoughtfully, 'I can imagine. It must be very difficult. Thank you for being honest.'

I felt ten feet tall at that. Then Mary Jane wanted to know how long it took to cross the Atlantic, and Thomas Jones was interested in the ship's speed, so I found myself explaining that too.

'She'll do about 14 knots using sail as well as steam,' I said, 'and depending on the weather, it's about a six week round trip. Of course we're always keen to make faster crossings. Quite apart from the satisfaction of getting there in good time, we carry the Royal Mails across to New York, and the US mail back again. The contract pays well – we don't want to lose it by being unreliable!'

We were on the main deck when Eleanor asked what the cold frame was for. Joe and I smiled when we realised she meant the skylight over the steerage accommodation, but I loved her keen interest.

Looking down, we could see the outlines of tables, bunks and benches. 'No separate cabins, I'm afraid – just dormitories. But there are portholes along the side of the ship, and this skylight – as you see – has wooden shutters to protect it in bad weather.'

'But I thought...' She looked around. 'It's not very far down, is it?'

'No – it's the same deck as our Saloon.' Suddenly, I realised what she meant. 'Steerage only means aft, close to the steering mechanism. It can be noisy, especially in rough weather, which is why richer folk choose to travel amidships.' But while the lovely Eleanor Pennington was giving me her entire attention – which pleased me enormously – I could tell she was still mystified.

'Weight goes in first,' I explained. 'The engines and boilers are on the double bottom plates, then the heaviest cargo goes in fore and aft in ways to ensure it won't move. It has to be worked out carefully otherwise the ship could develop a list and turn over. Don't you see,' I went on, 'people are very light, they move about all the time – so they can't be lodged far down in the ship.'

Joe said something about it being a pity in some cases, which made us laugh. As I used my master key to open one of the staterooms, he commented that passenger cabins had changed beyond recognition since his days at sea. With their proper beds and curtains, there was no comparison with the Spartan facilities offered aboard sailing ships. At that, like a magician performing his favourite trick, I flicked a switch and the lights came on – to my delight, the girls gave little squeals of astonishment. Electricity was a rarity ashore.

Having repeated the trick a couple of times, I led my little party on, through *Republic's* main reception area and down a fine oak staircase to the dining saloon. With its lamps and paintings and long refectory tables, I thought the room worthy of a gentleman's residence. When Miss Eleanor whispered, 'Isn't it *grand*?' I could have kissed her.

She was so clearly enjoying herself – even looking into the galleys where all the food was prepared – that I could have kept things going all day. But the mention of sumptuous meals prompted Mr Jones to glance at his watch. He asked if Joe and I would like to join them for dinner at the George Hotel – it was the least they could do, he declared, after such a fascinating morning. Joe deferred to me, but there was no need. He could see I was smitten.

139

As I was locking up, Mary Jane asked, 'Do you have family in Liverpool, Mr Smith?'

I smiled. 'No, miss. Just my brother in Birkenhead.'

'I see,' she replied, but it was hard to decide whether she thought my single status a good thing or a bad.

A little while later, as we followed Thomas and his nieces into the hotel, Joe nodded in Miss Eleanor's direction. 'A shame you're away tomorrow,' he murmured. 'You could have made some progress there.'

His words echoed my thoughts. I was already wondering when and how I might see her again.

I'm sure we enjoyed an excellent meal – the food at the George was always good – but my attention was on Miss Eleanor Pennington. She had such an expressive face, I found myself watching emotions come and go like light across the ocean. The joyous nature of her smile set my heart dancing. Having spent the last hour spouting forth about the ship, I was content to sit back, to look and listen while the girls chatted with their uncle.

I gathered there was a brother, John, and a younger sister, Martha. Their mother, Sarah, was elder sister to Thomas Jones's late wife, and their father, William Pennington, was a farmer. Home was at Winwick, about halfway between Liverpool and Manchester. I had journeyed in that direction a few times by train. Knowing nothing of farming I could not have said whether it was good land or bad, but since the girls were well-dressed and well-spoken, I imagined it was good.

It seemed all the Penningtons were involved with the farm in some capacity or other. Their work depended on the time of year.

'We make butter and cheese all year round,' Eleanor said. 'Not big amounts, you understand. At the moment we're bottling fruit. September is always a busy time, so it's nice to have a day off,' she added with an impish smile for her Uncle Thomas, who was quick to praise the samples they'd brought.

Joe was drawn forth about his experiences as a sailing-ship master – Thomas Jones had clearly been entertained before, and was happy to let his nieces share the more exciting aspects of my brother's early life.

'Were you born in Liverpool, sir?' Eleanor asked Joe. 'Have there always been seafarers in your family?'

'Not that I'm aware of. My father was a potter from Stoke-on-Trent – he died when I was a boy. Then my mother married Ted's father, and when I left school I was expected to go into the potteries too. I didn't want that,' he said frankly, 'it wasn't for me. So I ran away to Liverpool, to a seafaring cousin of my mother's, and signed on aboard his ship.'

'Joe went off to sea when he was fourteen,' I said. 'As you can imagine, our mother was not best pleased when I wanted to do the same.'

Eleanor smiled and nodded sympathetically. 'In winter-time, when Mother complains about Father coming home soaking wet and covered in mud, he always tells her to be thankful he chose the land and not the sea for a living...'

'That's true,' Mary Jane said pointedly. 'From what we hear it's a dangerous profession.'

'It can be,' I agreed, sensing some kind of undercurrent. I wondered how she could resemble her sister and yet be so different. 'But I imagine farming has its dangers too. You're at the mercy of wind and weather just the same.'

'Not quite,' she replied primly. 'We knew some people who took ship for America. It went down somewhere off Canada, I think, and everyone drowned.'

Joe and I exchanged a look. Suddenly, much was explained.

Blushing, Eleanor frowned at her sister, and turned to me. 'The Prestons lived in our village,' she explained. 'They had five children. Their daughter Lizzie was my age.'

On the periphery of my vision I was aware of Joe's eyes on me, but my gaze was for Eleanor. 'I'm sorry to hear that. What ship, can you remember?'

'Yes. It stuck in my mind because they were crossing the Atlantic on a ship of the same name.'

I knew it at once. In Liverpool at the time, studying for my Mate's Ticket, I'd heard the newspaper boy calling out details no seafarer could forget. 'The *Atlantic*, yes – she foundered off Halifax in '73. A terrible tragedy – almost 600 people lost their lives. I'm so sorry,' I added gently, 'for the loss of your friends.'

The morning's good beginning seemed liable to collapse. When Eleanor said she'd always wondered what the ship was like, Joe shot a warning glance in my direction, but something told me she would never accept a lie or half-truth. Even so, I weighed my words. 'Well, Miss Eleanor,' I began, clearing my throat, 'the *Atlantic* belonged to White Star. We've just been looking round her sister-ship. I have to say, *Republic* is as close to her in looks as makes no difference.'

There was a silence. Eleanor's eyes widened. I wondered how much more would be helpful. 'Nothing wrong with the ship,' I said firmly, as Mary Jane began to protest. 'There was a terrible storm, it was the middle of the night and they were out of fuel. No doubt an error of navigation took them onto the rocks.

'Marine engines have been modified in the last ten years,' I assured them. 'They're much more reliable. And lessons have been learned. Nowadays, the amount of coal we take on is always over and above what we need.' I forced a smile, eager to play down the worst aspects. 'There are dangers, I cannot deny it. But we do all in our power to keep everyone safe.'

'I'm sure you do,' Thomas Jones said.

'Sadly, a disaster always makes the headlines. But think of all the voyages that pass unremarked, the ships and passengers you never hear about.' As my listeners nodded, eager to be reassured, I added lightly, 'I swear to you, every time I come into Liverpool, the traffic is worse. These days, I reckon crossing the road is riskier than crossing the ocean!'

With rueful laughter, everyone agreed, and the serious talk was over. The deep-sea grey of Eleanor's eyes was suddenly greener, catching the light when she smiled at me.

As we were leaving, under cover of more general conversation, she said quietly, 'I confess I haven't thought of Lizzie Preston and that awful tragedy in years. But something in the newspaper brought it to mind the other day. And suddenly, here we are in Liverpool, meeting you, Mr Smith, and invited to look round your ship. Almost a twin of the other. A strange coincidence, don't you think?'

Aware of more than that, I nodded.

'And I've never been aboard a ship before…'

'What did you think of it?' I ventured.

Glancing up at me, she blushed and smiled and began pulling on her gloves. 'It was very exciting,' she said demurely.

19

I wanted to talk to her, listen to her, know her. The seemingly impossible question of how tormented me that night.

I'd been on the New York run for a year and a half, and had adjusted to the fast turnarounds, but although my new position paid well it left little time for leisure between voyages, and even less for the gentle pursuit of courtship.

Unable to sleep, in the early hours I took pen and paper and scribbled a few lines, changed my mind and scribbled a few more. The final version, expressing pleasure at our meeting, and looking forward to renewing our acquaintance, was copied onto a sheet of the ship's headed notepaper. Could I hope, I wrote, that if she should happen to be in Liverpool at the same time as myself, I might be granted the privilege of taking her to tea? It was difficult to name a precise date, but as soon as my ship docked, I promised to be in touch.

Other than the final sentence, it was very formal, very correct. I felt that was what Miss Pennington – and most especially her parents – would expect.

My only means of contact was through her uncle, but the connection with Dorothea – albeit a tenuous one – caused me more than a moment's hesitation. Telling myself it was the only way, I addressed it to Miss Eleanor Pennington, c/o Mr Thomas Jones, Castle Street, Liverpool. With the ship's mail I handed it to one of the juniors as I went in to breakfast, instructing him to see it posted.

All the way across the Atlantic, Eleanor invaded my dreams. Making my way to and from the bridge for my watch, supervising work on deck, occasionally passing through the saloon, I pictured her eyes, her smile, her every reaction as I showed her my world. Equally, I tried to visualise her world and failed; could only see her demure figure bending towards me as she asked a question and listened wide-eyed to my reply. I thought I would go mad if I didn't see her again.

Joe had always spoken well of Thomas Jones, so I was sure he'd post the letter. But whether he would promote my cause with Eleanor was another matter. I was at least ten years older than his niece, and perhaps not quite what the family had in mind when it came to suitors.

I'd included Mary Jane in my invitation, and hoped that would sway things. But all the way back from New York, every time I tried to imagine Eleanor and me taking tea together, my fantasies were quashed by thoughts of her kill-joy sister. If only she could be detained by some emergency at home – but in that case, Eleanor would be similarly detained. Unmarried young ladies were usually keen to keep their reputations intact.

Eleanor's note of acceptance – waiting for me when we docked – was as formal as mine, but it bestowed an almost euphoric anticipation. On the afternoon in question I spent an age before the glass, trimming my beard and brushing my springy fair hair into submission. I donned my best shoreside suit of clothes, tied a blue silk bow purchased in New York at the neck, set my hat at a jaunty angle and set off for Castle Street. I was on time and Thomas Jones was waiting in the shop, quietly informing me as we went upstairs that Eleanor was here but Mary Jane was indisposed and had remained at home. For a split-second I was overjoyed; then he said that his sister-in-law – Mrs Sarah Pennington – had come with Eleanor instead.

'Do not fret,' he added as my heart plunged off some internal cliff, 'she's merely concerned to meet you. But with your permission we'll have our tea here.'

My smile was frozen to my face as I was shown upstairs to his office. The two ladies rose as I bowed, a pink-faced Eleanor bobbing a nervous half-curtsey as her mother inclined her head. If I had thought of Mrs Pennington at all, I probably imagined an old lady like my mother, stiff with rheumatism, emphasising her wishes with the aid of an expertly wielded walking stick.

I could not have been more surprised. Plump and well-corseted,

Eleanor's mother looked to be younger than Joe. Thomas covered an awkward moment while I collected myself. I glanced at Eleanor, taking heart as her eyes implored my understanding. Finding my manners, I enquired solicitously for Mary Jane while expressing myself delighted by this opportunity of meeting her mother. Oh, I was very correct, very much aware that this was staid, merchant class Liverpool, and not the wild, heady place that was Hong Kong.

Our host brought another chair to a table before the window which had been set for tea. There were cakes and scones and silver cutlery. Mrs Pennington granted me a smile as I took my seat but her glance was coolly appraising. I knew at once who Mary Jane resembled and, as it turned out, the resemblance was not confined to looks. Mrs P seemed just as suspicious as her elder daughter. 'My brother-in-law tells me you are a Master Mariner, Mr Smith. Forgive me, but we are unacquainted with seafaring at Winwick, so perhaps you could tell us a little about what you do.'

'Certainly,' I agreed, aware that I was being interviewed for the position of suitor to Miss Eleanor. In such circumstances it was difficult not to sound either glib or boastful as I launched into some familiar phrases, but with Eleanor as my goal I was desperate to impress. I wanted her mother to know that I followed a respectable profession.

'The term Master Mariner,' I began, 'is just a qualification. It proves a man has served the required time at sea, studied the right books, and has satisfied his peers that he's competent to handle a ship.'

'And what does that entail?'

'Well, ma'am, he must be able to navigate by the stars, forecast the weather and conduct the ship's business – oh yes, and understand maritime law as well. Above all,' I concluded, with what I hoped was a deprecating smile, 'he must prove himself a fit person. Because once promoted to Captain he will be responsible for everything – the ship and its cargo, and every soul aboard.'

She was surprised. 'Ah. I see.' Studying her daughter for a moment, she switched her glance back to me and said, 'I understand you have already attained this position?'

'Well, yes – and no.' I went on to explain my four years of command aboard the *Lizzie Fennell*, and the subsequent move from Gibson's to White Star; that having gone from ships with sails to ships with engines, I'd spent the last few years learning my trade all over again.

'I'm presently studying for a further qualification,' I said, and noticed Eleanor's eyes widen with surprise. 'An Extra Master's

Certificate covers all the major subjects in greater depth, but the main part of it concerns the handling of steamships.'

Mrs Pennington wanted to know about my present job. As I described my responsibilities for the cargo and the crew, she raised her eyebrows. 'It seems they keep you busy, Mr Smith. Do you enjoy your work?'

'I do, Mrs Pennington. I enjoy it very much. With diligence, I hope to regain a position of command within a year or so.'

'If what Thomas tells me is true,' she conceded graciously, 'I'm sure you will.'

I thanked her as Mr Jones's man arrived with the tea. Mrs Pennington poured. While I perspired inside my collar Eleanor asked whether the voyage had been a good one. I said the weather had been rather trying for some of the passengers on the outward journey, but not really bad. Remembering our last conversation, I wished I'd kept off the subject of weather, but to my relief, she asked next about New York.

'I've read that everyone over there has ice boxes – is that true?'

'And washing machines to do the laundry?' her mother asked.

By our host's expression, he was amused – but Mrs Pennington's sense of humour was so well-hidden I was forced to answer in serious vein. 'I don't know whether washing machines are common as yet, but I have seen them in the stores – worked by a handle, I believe, to agitate the clothes. But everybody has an icebox. New York gets very hot in the summer. Over a hundred degrees sometimes, and humid too.'

'A *hundred* degrees?'

'I'm afraid so. Very uncomfortable. But having such tall buildings, at least the streets are shady.'

'Maybe so,' Mrs Pennington acknowledged with a frown, 'but imagine the stairs. It must be dreadfully wearing going up and down, especially in all that heat.'

'They have elevators – lifts.' At their incomprehension, I said, 'Like a dumb waiter only bigger – powered by electricity.'

As Eleanor and her uncle exclaimed in amazement, Mrs Pennington looked horrified. I assured them that being whisked up and down was quite entertaining. 'Except when the thing breaks down between floors – you never know how long it will take to start up again.' Suddenly envisaging being stuck for an hour in a lift with Eleanor, I forced myself to think of something else.

The one thing to dominate my mind during the voyage had been how to court her. Aware that my suggestion might be badly received,

I said, trying not to stammer, 'The ship will be in port for a few more days… I wondered… I wondered if Miss Eleanor would be free to accompany me to the theatre? An afternoon performance, of course,' I added quickly.

I might have been suggesting something improper, although my original plan had been to include Mary Jane. Mrs Pennington, however, was a different proposition. As Thomas Jones raised an eyebrow, his sister-in-law shook her head emphatically. 'The theatre?' She made it sound like a den of iniquity. 'No, Mr Smith, I don't think so. Even were it something elevating, like Shakespeare, there would be the problem of getting home afterwards. We are some miles, you know, from the railway station at Newton. Mr Pennington would have to make a special journey, which is hard for him at the end of the day…'

There was a long pause in which we all raised our cups and appeared to study the prettily-set table. Eleanor replaced her cup in its saucer and set it down. 'That's a shame, Mother, because I would like to go. Couldn't John pick me up from the station? Surely Father wouldn't mind?'

She looked appealingly at her uncle, and he appealed to me. 'Is there something special showing?'

'A Gilbert and Sullivan opera, at the Grand.'

'Ah, yes, *The Pirates of Penzance* – I saw it advertised. It should be entertaining – very witty, these things.' He looked to his sister-in-law, but, taut with disapproval, she said the matter would have to be discussed. He turned to the window. A weak sun was shining through the haze. 'It seems a shame,' he said, 'to spend all afternoon indoors. While I ring for some fresh tea, why don't you young people get yourselves out for a walk? Blow the cobwebs off.'

Before Mrs P could protest, Eleanor had retrieved her coat and we were descending the stairs with unseemly haste. As the shop door closed behind us with a jangling of the bell, she looked up at me with a mischievous smile. With one accord we hurried along the street, crossed over and came out on the Strand. Before us were the docks, Canning and Salthouse, with the Basin and Albert Dock beyond. A forest of masts and spars, funnels here and there, bustle and activity wherever we looked.

'Which way?'

'Any,' she said on a long breath. 'I love being here – it's so exciting. All these ships, where are they going? And their cargoes – where do they come from? I do envy you, Mr Smith, travelling the world.

Mother doesn't understand, I'm afraid, but this was always my favourite place as a child.'

I could have hugged her for that. 'Mine too.'

I led the way, cupping her elbow as we crossed the Strand's broad expanse, avoiding cabs and drays and an omnibus heading for the ferry. The contact felt intimate. We crossed by the locks to watch a ship being hauled into the Basin, and she wanted to know where it was from.

'Could be the West Indies,' I said, giving her a sidelong look, 'with a bonded cargo of rum and molasses...'

'Really?'

'Just guessing. The Customs warehouse is over there...'

She laughed and so did I. Because I longed to fulfil some recent daydreams, I deliberately avoided the Landing Stage and the *Republic*, and took her in the opposite direction. I felt ridiculously happy with this girl at my side, could have sung for joy just because we were together. We walked half a mile or so along Wapping, past the old docks, enjoying the smell of hemp and tar from the repair yards. Just a few tall ships in, but it was only mid-October.

'They'll be busier next time,' I said, 'in late November, December, when they're starting to lay up for the winter...' Thinking about it made me sigh. Meeting her quizzical glance, I said, 'Wishing I was due for some leave. A few days off every six weeks is better than most, but it makes for an odd kind of home life.'

'It must,' she agreed. 'Where do you stay when you're ashore?'

'I used to go to my brother's in Birkenhead, but my mother has just moved up from Hanley. She's living with Joe and his family now, so I'm presently staying aboard.' I went on to explain that if I needed to get away from the ship for a while, I knew of a good lodging house in town. 'It's clean and well-run and will no doubt serve its purpose.'

'But not nearly so homely,' Eleanor commented sympathetically. 'It seems a strange kind of life to us, who live on the land – especially to someone like my mother. You must forgive her for asking such direct questions.'

'She has your interests at heart, Miss Pennington,' I said magnanimously. 'But I hope she'll agree to our trip to the theatre.'

Eleanor gave a puckish smile. 'If anyone can talk her round, Mr Smith, it will be Uncle Tom!'

She was right. With permission granted, two days later we dropped the formalities. We were Ted and Eleanor, and getting to know each other a little better. The show was witty and funny and we laughed a lot – in fact, *Pirates of Penzance* remained a favourite for years. It was gone five when we came out and already dark. With catchy tunes still echoing, we had some tea before making our way to the station; and then, simply because I couldn't bear to say goodbye, I found an empty compartment and boarded the train with her.

'Ted – what are you doing? The train's leaving...'

'I'm coming with you,' I said as the guard banged the door shut and blew his whistle. 'It's all right, don't panic, I shall come back on the next train.'

She laughed out loud as the train lurched into motion. 'What about your ticket?'

'I'll throw myself on the guard's mercy. Anything,' I declared, capturing and kissing her hand, 'just to be with you.'

Blushing at that, she started to giggle. 'You can't come home with me – Mother would have a fit.'

'I've told you, I'm going as far as Newton and catching the next train back. After which,' I added with mock anguish, 'I shall most likely pine away until I see you again.'

'Six weeks...'

The rhythmic clacking of the wheels was like time itself, measuring out the allotted span. Alone in the dimly-lit carriage, we were serious suddenly, and wordless.

Gazing into those grey-green eyes was like looking down into the sea, a dizzying, hypnotic moment in which a fall is almost inevitable unless you pull away. I bent and gently touched my lips to hers; as she sighed I drew her into my arms. She was as innocent as I imagined, kissing like a twelve-year-old with lips firmly closed. But that, for me, was just as exciting as an eager, open-mouthed response.

Patience, I said to myself as she broke away with a little gasp. Her cheeks were flushed and her eyes sparkling as she pulled back to look at me. With an unfathomable expression she laid a finger against my lips before turning to draw the blind at the window.

'Now,' she said shyly, resuming her seat, 'you may kiss me again...'

It was probably just as well that we gained some company at the next station.

20

Inexperienced but not prudish, Eleanor was fun-loving, generous, clear-sighted and loyal, and I doubt she could have lied to save her life. I knew she was for me.

Even so, it was not an easy courtship. I think her parents – particularly her mother – did not quite know how to deal with the situation. It seemed too impulsive, too hasty, not the way things were done in their world. They lived their lives according to the changing of the seasons; as farmers, they'd had the same neighbours for generations. On the other hand, a seafarer's friends and neighbours were Board of Trade acquaintances – a large but shifting band of people, known and met from time to time on different ships. Family was a constant, but the time available to keep up with individual members was short. Finding a wife, making a family – that was the difficulty. No wonder seafarers ashore had a reputation for being impulsive.

Eleanor and I met in the first week of September. We spent two afternoons together in October – including the trip to the theatre – and three in November. It could not have been more different from my time with Dorothea.

Speaking in general terms, I'm sure the most committed of lovers have moments of hesitation, of needing time alone to think. We had too much solitude. We had time to burn. Time was our enemy, keeping us apart when my ship was riding the Atlantic storms, walking hand in hand with propriety during the few days we were in port.

Nothing could be casual. Eleanor couldn't play hard to get – which is what her mother felt was right and modest in a young woman – she had to acknowledge that she wanted to be with me by coming to Liverpool when the ship was in, or by inviting me to Woodhead whenever possible. Although she was 24 years old, meetings were difficult to arrange without her parents' consent. Nevertheless, we did manage one remarkable afternoon in Warrington towards the end of November. She'd gone there to shop, and I – well, I just happened to be alighting from the Liverpool train as hers drew in from Newton. That apparently casual meeting had taken some working out with the aid of a Bradshaw; how we laughed about it, feeling like conspirators in some railway-centred plot. It made our closeness closer.

Sharing my umbrella, her arm tucked in mine, the intimacy of our walk through grey and drizzly streets was somehow heightened by the glow of lamplight from doorways and shop windows. Pausing here and there along the way, we entered a churchyard, pretending to view the rows of black and weeping memorials. In the shelter of a deeply carved doorway, hidden by the umbrella, we turned to each other and embraced. Her lips tasted of the rain at first, cool and glassy, before longings fuelled by solitude ignited and passion flared. For a moment – again, so briefly – I had a glimpse of the woman beneath the surface and wanted all of her. I drew her closer, the umbrella dipped, and suddenly rain was tapping me on the shoulder to remind me of where we were.

As breathless laughter caught us both I raised the makeshift canopy, embracing her with one arm while she pressed her lips again to mine.

Clinging to each other, attempting to be sober while dizzy with love and desire was like climbing the shrouds in the teeth of a gale. 'It's no good,' I said at last, and emotion had me somewhere between laughter and heartbreak. 'You'll have to marry me, Ellie…'

I had thought of it: in fact in terms of being together I'd thought of little else. But I hadn't planned it. Not like that, flat and practical, a salve to this burning. I'd imagined buying her a ring – perhaps in New York – and begging her to accept it as a token of my love.

But life catches you out.

'Will I, indeed?' she exclaimed, eyebrows raised, laughing up at me. 'Is that what I must look forward to, Ted Smith, a bit of no-nonsense courtship followed by a no-nonsense wedding?' She tapped me lightly on the chest. 'I could have that any day of the week from the lads in the village. I thought you were different.'

She made to walk away, but I caught her arm. 'Ellie – Eleanor – please. I didn't mean it like that.'

'What did you mean, then?'

Hamstrung by the damned umbrella, I cast it aside and tried to embrace her. 'No,' she said, fending me off. 'I want you to tell me what you meant.'

What did I mean? What could I say? *I'm in hell living like this, hardly ever seeing you, when what I want is to be with you all the time, from the moment my ship docks to the moment it leaves again. I want to take you to bed and not stir for three days, I want to take you to New York, I want -*

Standing there in the rain, feeling like a small boy, I said, 'I wanted to buy you a ring. I wanted to tell you how much I love you... I wanted to ask you to be my wife.'

There was a silence in which she gazed at me, her eyes, more grey than green that day, brimming with sudden emotion. 'You could still ask. It doesn't matter about the ring.'

'Then let me hold you,' I begged softly, reaching out to take her hand. 'I need you to give me courage.'

Slowly, I drew her towards me. 'I love you, Eleanor,' I said as she came into my arms. 'I want you so much... Marry me, tell me you'll be my wife...'

'Yes,' she whispered against my lips, and the rain dripped a joyful tattoo beside us, while the fickle umbrella turned cartwheels across the graveyard.

My heart turned as many cartwheels as the dratted umbrella, but Eleanor's answer was not without its reservations. I would have liked to marry at once; but, as Eleanor explained, her parents would never agree to that. And weddings take time to arrange, she said gently; we would have to wait, at least until spring.

Rather than the full-blown family wedding she envisaged, I'd have been happier midweek with a special licence, a parson, and a couple of witnesses. But that was never going to be. I had to be thankful that when we dropped the bombshell, Eleanor's father welcomed me as a prospective son-in-law, while her mother could find no serious objections. Mary Jane, I thought, viewed us with envy.

Before I could begin to chafe at the bit, however, my impatience was knocked flat. At the beginning of December, just days after I left on my next trip across the Atlantic, Mr Pennington died unexpectedly, and my engagement to Eleanor became a period of mourning.

One way and another she had worked alongside her father most of her life, from helping with harvest and haymaking in childhood to working in the dairy as an adult. She was devastated by his death.

Having Eleanor's letter from White Star's office, as soon as I left the ship I took train for Newton. We met at the farm. Displaying a tact and generosity I'd not imagined her capable of, Mrs Pennington showed us into the drawing room, left us alone and closed the door. Holding Eleanor close, breathing in the scent of her hair, her skin, I tried to stroke away the grievous hurt.

'He didn't come in for supper,' she said, repeating words she'd written to me, words that I had read only that morning. 'He'd been seeing to a cow that wasn't milking right, and – well, he just didn't come in. So Mother sent John to see what was keeping him – supper was on the table – and John came back white as a sheet. *He's gone*, he said, but he couldn't make Mother understand. She kept asking *where* had he gone, what did John mean…'

'Shock,' I murmured, still in the throes of it myself. 'She couldn't accept it.'

Eleanor nodded, wiping tears. 'Still can't. He was her life.' She sniffed and I handed her a fresh handkerchief. 'A heart attack, the doctor reckons. We'd no idea…'

The engagement ring I'd bought in New York, all unknowing, was tucked away in my pocket. I'd planned it as a New Year present, but it was hardly a time for celebration. 'You remember that day in Warrington?'

As she raised her head I had the reward of a small, watery smile. 'How could I forget?'

'Just remember that I love you – that we have each other…'

Even as I did my best to console her, it seemed other forces were at work. Come the spring, the time we'd hoped to be married, Eleanor happened to read a short story in a batch of journals passed on by a neighbour. The story had acted upon her imagination while I was away, casting her into an additional maelstrom of anxiety on my behalf.

The story, by W.T.Stead, *'How the Mail Steamer went Down in Mid-Atlantic,'* was melodramatic and even nonsensical in places, but still there was enough in it to set my teeth on edge. *Mid-Atlantic* was a misnomer though. Western Ocean would have been more correct and Grand Banks more specific. The area is notorious for thick weather, and major collisions were distressingly common. There was also another hazard: fishing boats from St John's, Newfoundland, small and ill-lit and difficult to spot.

I'd had near-misses there. I'd often seen a mast sweep past the bridge – no lights aloft, only the glow of a lamp in the wheelhouse. Heart-stopping until I saw the vessel bobbing safely in our wake.

But of course that old story of Mr Stead's was meant to illustrate something else entirely. The inadequate provision of lifeboats was a subject which came up every time a ship went down and people lost their lives. Circumstances seemed not to matter. The first question to be asked was always regarding the boats. Were there enough to rescue the ship's company? The answer, generally speaking, was no. And while the non-mariners threw up their hands in horror at such lack of concern for human life, the seafarers raised their eyes to heaven.

'It's part of a campaign,' I told Eleanor with a huff of disgust. We were sitting together in the farmhouse kitchen, at the end of a long day in which I had been clearing ditches with her brother John. I was cold and tired and the story I'd just read made me angry – largely because Eleanor was so upset. I resisted the urge to screw up the pages and toss them into the fire.

'Mr Stead thinks by frightening people he'll get the law changed.'

She stared in amazement. 'But surely it *needs* to be changed?'

'Well,' I said, 'it's a debatable point. Even if he succeeds, I shouldn't think it'll make much difference in the long run.'

'Ted, why do you say that? It *must* make a difference, surely?'

'Look,' I sighed, leaning forward to take her hands in mine, 'you don't know what it's like in a storm. Even in a gale, getting a boat down in an emergency is next to impossible. The davits...' She stopped me there, not understanding, so I began again, demonstrating with my hands. 'First of all, the boat must be raised by ropes off the chocks which hold it in place on the deck. The davits are the arms above the boat. They have to be swung out one at a time until the boat is parallel to the ship's side...'

The boats were big and heavy. I knew from experience that even in good conditions, hauling each boat up and out and level with the deck could take a well-trained crew 10 or 15 minutes – and that was with the aid of steam winches.

'There'll be a gap between the deck and the boat – and a long drop to the water. That fact alone,' I added weightily, 'can be daunting. Then, having got our people aboard, we must wait until the waves are right before lowering away, unhooking the falls and letting go – otherwise the boat can be swamped and overturned. And then those same men must tackle the next...'

154

'I see.' She looked dismayed as I sat back. 'What are you saying, Ted?'

'Frankly? I'm saying lifeboats are often useless because of the time it takes. In this case,' I added, brandishing the rolled-up journal, 'he's got a collision in which the ship is so badly holed she's heeling over – and that's going to be the norm, by the way. Believe me, Ellie, at the height of a storm, trying to create a lee side in order to get the boats down safely is a skill to challenge the most experienced seaman. Yet in this story the passengers are behaving like rabid dogs in their panic to get to the one remaining boat, while he gives no idea of how it's to be launched, only to say some bully-boys are hacking at the ropes...'

Opening the paper again, I searched for the place. 'Ah, yes. *The ruffians did not know how to lower away, and one of them began to lash at the forward fall with an axe...* But in spite of all this, by some miracle the boat is lowered, and our hero survives.

'And then, as a sort of postscript, Mr Stead has the gall to say, *This is exactly what might take place and what* will *take place if the liners are sent to sea short of boats.*'

With another huff of disgust, I said, 'We practice drills – yes. But with seamen, not passengers. Try to imagine the reality. How do you persuade panic-stricken people to leave a large, familiar deck for a tiny, storm-tossed boat...?' I drew breath and shook my head. 'It's not the easy answer he thinks it is.

'Believe me, dearest, lifeboats are an effective way of getting people off a ship in ideal conditions – but ideal conditions in an emergency are so *rare* as to be almost unheard of. Mr Stead might just as easily campaign for a flat calm...'

Eleanor was by this point looking quite sick. Angry with this Stead character for upsetting my darling, I was even angrier with myself for not knowing how better to allay her anxieties. And, if I'm honest, I was angry because it made me remember the *Lizzie Fennel*, and the hurricane in which I'd almost lost the ship, the crew and my life.

I sat back then, pulled her close, told her something of the near disaster we'd experienced. Mentally reliving the worst of it, I said, 'The boat went – it was just hanging, battering the hatch. We had to cut it free, let it go. Don't you see?' I finished passionately, 'in the end, as a seaman, you have to concentrate on saving the ship. Why? Because the ship is the best lifeboat you've got!'

Two days later she clung to me as I was leaving, trying so hard to control her grief, my heart broke for her. 'Trust me,' I whispered,

155

'believe me when I tell you I know what I'm doing. Darling Eleanor, these steamships are a feather bed compared to sail. Besides, I've no intention of throwing my life away – or anyone else's – just to prove someone like Stead right…'

That trip was one of the worst I can remember. Not just bad for weather but full of uncertainty. On top of her father's death, to be convinced that I stood in grave danger of my life every time I put to sea, was too much. Loving her, I did not want her to be distressed. Hurting, I was afraid she would change her mind, tell me she could not bear the anguish of marrying someone like me, a man she imagined to be in danger every moment of the day and night.

Bereaved or not, Eleanor's family worked every day because they had to. As she often remarked during that long, sad year, cows still had to be milked, animals fed, planting and harvesting had to be organised no matter how exhausting the effort. I saw how they depended on one another, how foolish it was to wish that Eleanor and I could have met and married sooner. Even if I'd tried to take her away to Liverpool, she would have had to come back to help out. They were a team, like any ship's crew, and, like a crew with a new Master, they were finding things were different.

At 26, John became not just the man of the house, but the farmer, responsible for all decisions pertaining to the running of the farm. His mother meant well, but did not make things easy: she was forever trying to tell him what his father would have done, which was not always helpful. He was aided by some experienced farm workers but he was the boss; the responsibility was his. I felt for him. John was the age I'd been when I first took command of the *Lizzie Fennell*.

One day when I was visiting, the lad seemed bowed down. We were alone, so I ventured to ask what was wrong. It seemed the men resented him and were dragging their feet over the simplest of tasks.

'Yes, but they were used to your father,' I reasoned. 'Used to his ways. I'm sure they miss him as much as you do.' Remembering how it was for me as a young shipmaster, dealing often with older men, I said, 'Why don't you try asking their advice? Do it their way for a while. Give the old boys a chance to get used to you before starting on the new ideas…'

I don't know if he did, but by my next visit things had settled down. For John and for me. As Eleanor's grief abated, her fears for me lessened.

156

Of necessity, I found myself spending most of my free days at Woodhead. Being there meant working hard but it was different kind of work to what I did at sea, and besides, it was a joy simply to be with Eleanor. I helped with the spring sowing of peas and beans and potatoes, and caught the last couple of days of haymaking in June. The weather was glorious, with just a few thunderheads roaming the horizon, but John had chosen his time well; the scented, flower-strewn hay was turned and aired and stacked and spread until it was fit for pressing and baling. Back-breaking work but that sense of working with the weather – remembered so well from my sailing ship days – was hugely invigorating. Rarely since the *Lizzie Fennell* had I worked as hard or intensively as I did that year. But I enjoyed every minute.

It was good to stay at the farm, to be with Eleanor. I got to know her, how hard she worked, how kind-hearted she was and how short-tempered she could be. Perversely, perhaps, I rather liked that. At least I knew where I was with her. And I got to know the other members of the family. I never did feel entirely comfortable with Mrs Pennington, often having the feeling that she was looking just beyond my shoulder, hoping for a better man to come along. Eleanor said I was wrong, that it was my own modesty made me think I fell short in her mother's eyes. Well, I wouldn't have called it modesty, but maybe there was a grain of truth there.

When I looked at the extent of the farm buildings, when I walked the fields, and most especially when I accompanied the family to church, I felt my lack of background. Eleanor and her siblings had been educated at the Rectory with the parson's children, young people who became their friends. These connections were not paraded, but I was aware of the fact that they called on each other, and shared certain obligations.

The parish of Winwick covered a wide area, and the building itself was grand indeed with a new chancel designed by some famous London architect. From the floor tiles to the highly coloured ceiling it was new-Gothic and much admired. I thought it a bit overdone myself, but forbore to say so. The patrons were some titled family whose pedigree disappeared into the mists of time. Well, they featured strongly in the Wars of the Roses, or so Eleanor said, and that was enough for me.

Then I came across Pennington Lane. On the far side of Newton, to be sure, but it surprised me. I wondered if Penningtons had been on the field when Richard III lost his crown, and whether Eleanor's pedigree could match that of the local grandees. She laughed and said not, but in the light of some of her mother's comments I did wonder.

With the sad year behind us, and stronger bonds to tie us, Eleanor and I were married in the New Year of 1887. Sure enough, as the Americans would say, we had the grand church at Winwick, a solemn parson to do the deed, and Cap'n Joe, Thomas Jones, John, Martha and Mary Jane all as witnesses. The second-degree cousins were there to fill the church and eat their way through a sumptuous repast. My mother came too, and, for reasons which will constantly elude me, she and Mrs P got along very well. Businesswomen both, Eleanor said.

We married to coincide with the month's leave that was due to me. Instead of battling my way across the Atlantic, I spent a more productive and enjoyable time renovating Spar Cottage.

Much of the heavy work had been done earlier, but hanging pictures and curtains and arranging our bits and bobs of furniture – mostly donated by relatives – were jobs we were happy to do together. I fetched my boxes of books from Joe's, and made a set of shelves beside the chimney breast. Eleanor's collection of novels and journals and slim volumes of poetry, sat beneath a row of china plates in the other alcove, while her notebook of recipes never left the kitchen. She was an excellent cook.

The cottage was close enough to the farm for convenience, but distant enough to allow us a degree of privacy; and although we promised ourselves a few days in the Lake District when the weather improved, whenever possible we made the best of what a wet winter could throw at us by being cosy together indoors. We learned a lot in those first delightful weeks, and not least about ourselves. My impatience was calmed, and as trust grew between us, Eleanor blossomed.

A few adjustments were necessary – marriage was a first trip for both of us, after all – but on the whole we managed very well. Eleanor was used to housekeeping, but at the farm there had been many hands to share the domestic tasks. The only outside help we had was with the laundry, so I endeavoured to assist with simple chores, like scrubbing saucepans and polishing cutlery. Like being a deck-hand again, I said with mock complaint, scrubbing decks and polishing brass.

Playing house was fun, but I worried about leaving her when I went back to sea. I was afraid she'd be lonely with no husband coming in each evening, and none of the family around. Eleanor said she'd be all right, while her sisters assured me they would visit often. Their mother said she could come back to the farm while I was away.

I was not too happy with that idea.

When my leave was up and *Republic* was ready to sail I did not want Eleanor to see me off. I'd seen enough weeping women on docksides, I said, to last me a lifetime. Being there to greet me on my return was a different matter though. It turned the last leg of the voyage into one of eager anticipation, and made the boarding of the Mersey pilot something to smile about.

I was rather taken aback on my first return to be greeted by tears. My dear girl wept like a child in my arms.

'I prayed,' she sobbed, 'all the time you were away...'

'But I've been away before,' I reasoned, 'and come back safe. Why should I not this time?'

'I don't know. It wasn't the same before, we weren't married, we weren't... And I've missed you so much.' She wept even harder. 'I'm sorry. I was all right until I saw you – and I'm so happy. I don't know why I'm crying like this...'

Having only a few days together, the reason did not become apparent until my next time home. Eleanor was expecting a child – *our* child – which seemed to me the most incredible and astonishing thing ever. Absolutely the best news since the day she agreed to marry me.

It turned out that she'd suspected, wasn't sure, felt terribly emotional, hadn't wanted to tell me in case she was wrong. But now she was sure, and besides, everyone said she looked like she was, and didn't I think so too?

I was over the moon with delight, but to be honest I thought she looked pale and wan, as though she'd been doing too much. Not that I said so. I just tried to make her sit down, put her feet up, let me see to things. And when I'd cosseted her a bit, and we'd made wonderful plans for this wonderful child of ours, we ate our supper and went to bed. No mad passion this time, just a gentle holding, a gentle loving, while it seemed to me the whole meaning of the world was contained between us.

At the end of April I returned from New York as Master of the *Republic*. A temporary appointment while her Old Man was recovering from a broken leg in a New York hospital, but I was cock-a-hoop when Thomas Ismay himself told me I was to cover the Old

Man's absence for the duration. I had four months as Captain of a first-class Atlantic liner. I felt I had arrived, that after this they would surely not bump me down.

But they did. They said it was because I had not yet taken my Extra Master's Certificate, for which I had been studying at sea for almost two years. Patience was the word, Thomas Ismay said. To help me exercise it – and to enable me to complete my studies – I was sent to relieve the 1st Officer on the *Britannic*.

In one sense it was an achievement of an ambition – I'd lusted after the *Britannic* the day I first saw her, sweeping out of the Mersey when I was urging my waterlogged *Lizzie Fennell* into port. But I'd imagined being her Master – going aboard as Mate was a blow to my self-esteem. But that blow was as nothing compared to the personal tragedy that followed.

The honeymoon baby Eleanor was carrying was stillborn at seven months. It was harvest time and she'd been helping out at the farm. I blamed that. Her mother blamed me. Indirectly, of course. It was a terrible time. Eleanor was distraught, kept asking *why*, in such a bleak little voice it tore right through me. I couldn't answer. Who could? We would have had a son. It was no consolation to be told by all and sundry that we could try again. Seeing Joe at that time, with his fine sons, was hard.

Worse, Eleanor lost the second baby, this time at two months, just before Christmas.

Why? Now I was asking the question too, but their family doctor couldn't answer, nor the specialist Eleanor consulted later. These eminent gentlemen made similar comments, that we were young – well, Eleanor was, at 26 – and recently married, and that time and patience would produce the children we wanted. In the meantime, a period of abstinence was recommended.

21

There followed a difficult period of time. After some intense studying, I submitted myself for the Extra Master's examination. That all-important certificate was awarded to me, but it was hard to celebrate when Eleanor was grieving the loss of two babies. When, to be truthful, we were both grieving.

My bright, happy darling was absent. In her place I found this low, sad girl, given to lethargy and misery. The cottage was a mess, but if I set to, she yelled at me and wept. Concern was misinterpreted, love was rejected, she seemed to want nothing from me. Once my studies were over I found solace in being back at sea, in some foul Atlantic weather which mirrored my feelings exactly. I was glad to have no more than a few days off between trips. If it was solitude she wanted, I said, there was plenty of that on hand.

Except she didn't. She wanted her mother and her sisters, which I suppose was natural in the circumstances.

Although it was not a good time of year to take a holiday, I was due some leave and felt if we didn't get away our marriage would never recover. I decided to take her to Paris, exotic and foreign and – if American passengers were to be believed – the most romantic place on earth.

I'd been to London before, but Paris was a first for both of us. As to conversation, Eleanor knew a little French, courtesy of the governess at the Rectory, and I'd picked up some patois in Quebec and Louisiana, but I can't say either was much use. Fortunately she saw the funny side. Despite our struggles with the language – and the bone-chilling cold outdoors – we enjoyed our few days in that beautiful city. It even snowed while we were there, turning Notre Dame into a kind of Camelot on its island in the Seine, and the Luxembourg Gardens into a place Lancelot and Guinevere might have enjoyed.

Our hotel room, with its splendid views and gurgling hot-water pipes, was almost too warm, but taking advantage of the sub-tropical heat, I pursued my darling wife with every lover's trick at my disposal. I'd hoped the holiday would turn out to be the honeymoon we'd postponed, but she kept putting me off, turning away, sliding out from every embrace as though there were something deeply wrong in my desire for her.

She was not a prude, and having been raised on a farm had known from childhood what procreation entailed. But that was it. That was the problem. In her view, a man and a woman coming together, be it pleasurable or not, was for the purpose of getting children. Since we had been told to put our desire for a family aside for a while – an unspecified period of time, incidentally – she seemed to think we should cease all contact. On the principle that kissing and touching were bound to give rise to forbidden desires.

That such desires might be indulged purely for pleasure, without reproduction in mind, appeared to be an uncomfortable idea. Sinful was the word she used, which I put down to the Rectory education, but it was difficult to counter without sounding like a – well, like a rampant male with just one thing in mind. And, in fact, she came close to saying that – not in so many words, but the inference was there.

'I thought you loved me,' I remember saying towards the end of our last night in Paris.

She was crying, huddled on her side of the bed. 'I do.'

'No, you don't, Eleanor. If you did, you'd know I married you for yourself, not just to make children.'

I was staring through darkness at the ceiling, remembering Dorothea's hedonism, wishing some of that careless, self-indulgent passion might find a root-hold here. As my thoughts ran on, I realised that in marrying Eleanor I'd imagined I would broach her virginity and teach her the ways of sensuality and passion as they had been taught to me. I never envisaged resistance to such lessons, or that her ideas of love and marriage would be different from mine.

Sorely tempted to tell her about Dorothea, I stopped myself.

Had Dorothea loved me? At the time I thought probably not. I was just an apt pupil who'd gained a few distinctions in the art of love: distinctions that were useless here.

Bruised and despairing, I was glad to be going back to sea. At least I knew where I was with a ship under my feet and the ocean before me. There was consolation in the wide skies and rolling green seas, in the scent of salt on the wind, even in the mournful cries of sea-birds as we left land and Liverpool behind. As ever, those old mariners seemed to be saying, *forget the land, the lass, the dusty road – forget the tears, come fly with us…*

There was little time to dwell on sadness. Keeping discipline aboard, making sure the men were constantly up to the mark, was always a challenge. With passengers aboard everything had to be spotless and shining, the decks Holystoned and smooth, the brassware gleaming, paintwork untainted by rust or salt. It was not an easy task.

Then, in the spring of 1888, I was promoted to Master, and everything came under my command. *Master under God*, as Joe had signed himself. With that power came the full weight of responsibility. But a certificate that declared me competent did not give me the experience needed to bear that weight. Yes, I'd been Master before, often responsible for a handful of passengers in addition to the ship and its cargo. In comparison to my new job, however, it seemed small beer indeed.

If I was reasonably at ease with wealthy Americans, the English upper classes daunted me. I'd been brought up to respect authority and revere those who by tradition ruled at home. Lords and ladies and landed gentry were the upper crust; well-educated, knowledgeable, used to regarding themselves – and being regarded – as better than the common herd. It was hard for me as a potter's son from Hanley to put myself in the same bracket. To sit at the same table, if you like. At the head of it, no less, when my sort had always been decidedly below the salt.

Eleanor urged me to remember, when I was feeling short of the mark, that what I did none of them could do. They had to defer to me. I was the ship's Captain, and they were in *my* care, not the other way around.

I'm not sure it worked every time, but it helped.

Like all newly-appointed White Star shipmasters, I spent the next eighteen months or so relieving the more established ones while they were taking their annual leave. So I was in turn Captain of various liners, and – for just one voyage – my old ship, *Republic*.

On the approach to New York, either by misjudgement of the pilot or some neglect of the dredging company at Sandy Hook, we ran aground. Frustrating, even though we floated free with the next tide. Tragedy was to follow, however. Alongside in New York we'd cleared the ship of passengers and the engine room was shutting down all but essential power for the next few days, when one of the pipes fractured, shooting superheated steam in all directions. Several men were badly injured, arms and faces ballooning with blisters even as they were dragged free.

The engine room was a place where accidents of one degree or another were always happening. Since we carried our own surgeon, most were dealt with professionally and quickly, but no one had seen injuries on that scale before. They were appalling. Two engineer officers died from their burns, as well as one of the firemen.

Republic was getting to be an old lady by then, and whether that fracture was due to the grounding is impossible to say. Even so, the responsibility hit me hard. It was worse for the Chief because they were his men. Attending the inquests and arranging for burials was a harrowing experience.

Feeling mangled, I came home to a summons from the Royal Naval Reserve. It had become part of White Star's policy to have their officers trained by the Royal Navy in case our passenger liners should be required for transporting troops. With rumblings of war in various parts of the Empire it seemed a not-unlikely eventuality, and I'd volunteered for the RNR some months previously. I groaned at the thought of wasting my precious days off with a bunch of Jack Tars, but in fact, the week spent learning to fire guns and brandish cutlasses aboard an old wooden frigate, turned out to be like playing pirates. Just the kind of light relief I needed.

My next assignment was to another liner on the Atlantic run – after which I was due for leave myself. Arriving back in Liverpool on a muggy late summer's day, I took the ship's papers into the office on Water Street, whereupon one of the clerks told me that Mr Thomas Ismay wanted to see me.

It was rare to be summoned by the owner, and I wondered if something was amiss, but Mr Ismay greeted me cheerfully as I was shown into his office. 'Would you consider,' he asked, waving me to a chair, 'taking command of the *Coptic*?'

164

He must have been dismayed by the way my face fell. Offered a ship to call their own, most Masters were overjoyed. But for me *Coptic* was synonymous with Dorothea. 'A year's run,' Mr Ismay added quickly. 'Probably not even that. I see from your record you did two years in the Pacific Service – this is just a New Zealand trip. Out via the Cape, and back by way of South America...'

My blood started pumping again. For one panic-stricken moment I'd thought he was going to send me to Hong Kong. I could hardly have refused, but it would have been unbearable. New Zealand was different though – I'd never been there. 'Thank you, sir,' I said, summoning a smile, 'I'd be delighted. I hesitated only because my wife and I are about to move house...'

'Then there isn't a problem,' he beamed. 'We won't need you until the autumn – we might even have a small job for you in the office in the meantime, which should give you plenty of time to get settled in. Where are you moving to, by the way?'

Suddenly embarrassed, I cleared my throat. 'Waterloo, sir.'

He gave a bark of laughter. 'Not Marine Crescent? Nice little houses,' he allowed as I nodded, 'and I must say fine views! Mine, as you probably know, is just a little way along from there...'

Of course I did. Our new home was barely a stone's throw from his large stuccoed villa overlooking the estuary.

After Spar Cottage we had resided in a pleasant enough part of Liverpool. But Eleanor hated being hemmed in. Waterloo, on the other hand, was ideal for its sea breezes and healthy, open aspect. Even better, it was a short journey by rail from there to Liverpool's Tithebarn Street Station. Added to which Eleanor would know when my ship was coming in, because she'd be able to see it from the upstairs windows. See it and hear it, since Thomas Ismay liked his Masters to blow the ship's whistle when they passed his villa.

'Not as a salute to me, particularly,' he said with a twinkle in his eye on the day I was appointed. 'A good long blast lets me know you're back safe, and your wife will know you're on your way!'

Ellie and I had fallen in love with the row of white-painted cottages. The long front gardens, the formal park they faced, and something about the windows gave Marine Crescent a Regency look. Elegant, attractive, bathed in sun for most of the day, it would be a good place for...

Refusing to put hope into words, to even listen to the superstitious whispers of *new house, new baby,* we had agreed with the landlord to rent the property for a year, with an option to extend the lease.

Our house was one of the smaller cottages near the end of the row. Happy there from the outset, we took long walks along the beach, identifying the occasional steamer amongst all the barques and brigantines passing in and out. We'd been there a month or so when Ellie paused while dressing to look out of the bedroom window. 'I do like being here,' she said contentedly. 'Just seeing all those ships, sailing back and forth, means I'm thinking about you all the time.'

'Didn't you think of me before?' I teased.

'Of course I did, silly.' She gave me an affectionate smile. 'No, what I mean is, inland I felt cut off from you. At the farm it was too easy to forget what you were doing. And in town, well,' she shivered, 'in town I lost sight of myself, never mind you and me…'

I felt humbled by her words, realising, perhaps for the first time, just how closely her life was centred on mine, how she depended upon me. The robust and healthy girl I'd married seemed so fragile after all the illnesses she'd suffered, I felt guilty for leaving her. Drawing her into my arms, I kissed her hair, inhaled her fragrance. I wished I could make her happy. Wished I could give her a child. A healthy, full-term child. She would not be so lonely then.

Our marriage, which had been suffering, began to mend in the four months I spent working in the White Star office and living at home. We met Mrs Thomas Ismay at our local church. That generous lady took Eleanor under her wing, introducing her to other White Star officers' wives. Through them she became involved in the general welfare of crew families. As she often remarked, we were fortunate, whereas those deprived of a breadwinner for any reason were quickly reduced to difficulty. Rapidly gaining in health and confidence, Eleanor took on a bloom I hadn't seen since the earliest days of our marriage. The cloud of doubt and guilt I'd felt hanging over me began to lift.

To my mind, the most important thing of all was that Mrs Ismay introduced Eleanor to a lady painting instructor. During the year I was away aboard *Coptic*, Eleanor started painting, from the dunes when the weather was good, from the spare bedroom when it was not.

She'd had lessons years ago with the girls at the Rectory, but she said she wasn't any good – watercolours were difficult to control, and she didn't think she'd ever master them. Nevertheless, she enjoyed her weekly lessons. When I came home, the spare bedroom walls were covered in half-finished pictures of the dunes and the sea, with ships skimming by on the breeze. I knew nothing about art but I could see her progress. I thought she was good.

Over the next few years, as Eleanor's skills grew, the hobby absorbed her more and more. We had resigned ourselves to the idea of no children, doing our best to avoid distress. Even so, we gained a live-in maid and a housekeeper, largely to look after Eleanor when she was ill. That was how we termed it. We did not talk about miscarriages.

If we had no children, at least we were able to get away whenever we wished. The Lake District was almost on our doorstep and we enjoyed some delightful sailing holidays there. Eleanor was also keen to see the city I visited every few weeks, so one year I took her to New York. Travelling as Saloon passengers aboard the *Britannic*, we met one of White Star's regular passengers en route – a widower who often visited his daughter in England. This charming Long Islander insisted on entertaining us to dinner in New York and a musical show.

Dear Ellie could not get over such generosity, but as I kept saying, Americans are like that: often demanding, frequently overbearing – but kind and generous to boot. It was an honour and a treat, but we did things for ourselves too, visiting the Metropolitan Museum, walking in Central Park, eating in some fine restaurants. We walked Broadway from Battery Park to Washington Square, and criss-crossed Manhattan as the mood seized us. We chuckled over her mother's reaction to skyscrapers, laughing some more as we rode in an elevator. I told her what had gone through my mind the day we'd had tea at Uncle Tom's, and by some weird coincidence the elevator stopped between floors as I was speaking. Only a minute or two, but long enough for me to kiss her and whisper a few sweet nothings.

Eleanor enjoyed the trip so much we planned to do it again but, as things turned out, we never did.

The following spring, going about his business in the middle of the day, Joe collapsed and died on Lime Street.

It was a terrible shock. He was still a fine looking man, and at 62 years old had rarely suffered a day's illness in his life. A bit of indigestion now and then, Mother said, but nothing more. She was stunned. We all were. I'd just arrived home, hardly unpacked my bag when the news came. I couldn't believe it. My half-brother had always been such a rock. I couldn't imagine him not being there.

With Susanna and my nephews I helped to organise the funeral.

It was held at the parish church in Wallasey, not far from where they lived. Mother, in her eightieth year, was lost to herself that day and for a long time afterwards. She kept saying distractedly that it should have been her – she was old, why hadn't she died? Why did it have to be Joe? Her eldest son – no age at all...

And he'd been her favourite. He was the firstborn, so I suppose it was natural. Not that I was jealous, only sometimes I longed to see honest affection in my mother's eyes, rather than the critical gaze she generally bestowed. I couldn't understand it. I'd followed Joe, had even outrun him in some respects, but even so, I seemed to fail in our mother's expectations. I wanted to tell her she had me, she could lean on me; but she never had. Joe had been the one. I could never take his place. It upset me more at that time than any other. I wanted to share her grief, comfort her, have her comfort me in my loss; but – inevitably, I suppose – it was to Susanna she turned, and with Susanna she remained.

As for me, burying my brother and closest friend, it seemed an arctic wind was blowing that mild May day. I felt it all the way down one side of me. How I grieved for him.

A few months later, a double-fronted house that we had long admired – midway along the Crescent – came up for sale. It had four bedrooms, attics and outbuildings as well as the usual offices, and – best of all as far as Eleanor was concerned – a glazed Regency awning over windows and door. I thought it rather grand; she thought it rather elegant. Like two excited children, we decided to buy.

Having never owned a house before, I found it an extraordinary experience organising a mortgage and moving in, but becoming a property-owner was a wonderful feeling. I thought Joe would have approved – my father, too. And Mother, being such a businesswoman, would surely be pleased by this step forward. But when she came for her usual week's holiday in the summer, instead of admiring our new home – our own bit of freehold – she poured cold water on it.

'Don't know why you had to buy old property,' she grumbled, 'it'll cost you more every year. Anyway, what d'you want with a place this size? Just the two of you?'

With Thomas Ismay's grand house just a minute's walk away, I felt she was accusing Eleanor and me of trying to ingratiate ourselves. But before I could reply, she added querulously, 'It's time you had a family!'

With all the rage of childhood locked inside me, I could not reply.

168

She made me feel a failure as a man. What was worse, she made Ellie cry. And then, when I remonstrated later, pretended not to know what it was all about.

We could not supply a family to order, not even to please my mother. Once she'd dried her tears Eleanor refused to discuss it, pointing out instead that we could at least indulge our daydreams. In the new house she could have her painting studio and I could have the book-lined study I'd talked about for years. We could afford to expand a little.

22

As it transpired, expansion was a good word. My dearest Ellie, always
neat-waisted, started to put on weight. After several weeks away I
noticed that she was becoming plump. More than that, she was
blooming, with rounded breasts and a rosy glow to her skin. She was
36 and she looked wonderful, just like the beautiful girl I married.

I hardly dared ask. I was enraptured by her beauty but so afraid.
Coward that I was, I left the secret with her until she was ready to
tell me.

We were in bed. I was curled around her with my arm across her
waist, almost asleep when she turned, suddenly alert. 'There,' she
said, 'did you feel that?'

Drowsy, I struggled into wakefulness. She took my hand and
placed it, very firmly, on the rounded bow of her stomach.

'Our baby is kicking,' she whispered, 'isn't it wonderful?'

I felt it then, a stirring beneath my palm, then a sudden movement
under my fingers, like the tiniest of protests. Awake and overwhelmed, I
felt myself grinning in the darkness. 'Yes – I do feel it – just there...'

'Oh, Ted,' she turned, burying her face against my neck, 'I've been
wanting to tell you for ages, but... I'm so happy – and so frightened...'

Her words broke off in a series of little gasps. I kissed her cheek
and tasted the saltiness of tears. 'I know,' I murmured, drawing her
close against the length of my body, 'I know...'

'It's been five months. The longest time, since...'

'I know,' I said again, not wanting this conversation to go on, yet understanding the need for it. Now the dam had burst she would be unable to stop going over the possibilities, the fears, the hopes, the anguish of this wonderful, incredible event.

How could I leave her, my dearest love?

I had to. It was my job. But Ellie was constantly on my mind. That year was our tenth anniversary; also the Queen's Diamond Jubilee, one of brilliant illuminations, of parades and celebrations everywhere. We joked about it, said how kind it was of Her Majesty to organise it just for us. As if drawn by magnets, visitors came from all over the empire; and if the number of our Saloon and Cabin Class passengers was anything to go by, the majority came from the old colony of America. After fighting to be independent, it seemed they were prepared to fight again for the privilege of being dazzled by our Queen and the entire Royal Family.

Aboard my ship, *Majestic*, we even carried the ambassador chosen to represent the United States at the official celebrations. Filled with patriotic pride that trip, I felt *Majestic* was singularly well-named.

Nevertheless, those of us in the Atlantic trade took a knock that summer. As though to upstage everything British, the first of Germany's Atlantic liners, *Kaiser Wilhelm der Grosse*, made the fastest eastbound crossing in under five and a half days. It wasn't much consolation to us – or our rivals, Cunard, for that matter – to discover that this big, fast, luxury liner carried too much top-hamper; although her nickname, *Rolling Billy*, did go rather well with a sneer.

Thomas Ismay in his usual, down-to-earth fashion, reckoned the Germans had pinched the idea from our sister-ship, *Teutonic*. The Kaiser had been so impressed after inspecting the new liner at the Spithead review, he'd decided he had to have one too. Bigger and better than anyone else's, of course.

Built to Admiralty specification, *Majestic* and *Teutonic* had strengthened decks and hull plating, and more efficient engines. The latest forced-draught system gave greater power, greater speed – and cut the fuel consumption by ten tons a day. Such economies in a competitive market were important. But in addition to cold rooms for on-board provisions, these modern vessels had the best innovation yet. Refrigerated cargo space. Some 40,000 cubic feet of it.

Passenger liners had always carried general cargo in the holds, but the freighting of chilled food was a new and lucrative business. With their huge capacity the two new ships transported quality meat from the United States to feed the growing number of mouths at home. Liverpool alone had doubled in size since I'd first gone to sea.

Also, to please the up-and-coming middle classes, these liners were the first to carry three-tier accommodation – Saloon, Cabin Class and Third – instead of the old two-tier system. Most impressive of all, they carried no sails. *Majestic* was my first command of a ship driven purely by steam. I thought of Joe and smiled, albeit wryly. He'd have shaken his head while I took over with a grin that rivalled the Cheshire Cat's.

After all our tribulations, Eleanor came through her pregnancy with barely a hiccup. Had I been a betting man, I'd have put odds on my being away when baby was born, but I was lucky. I came home on the last day of March 1898, and our daughter, Helen Melville, hurried into the world two days later.

She was a little early – only two weeks, but it meant she was tiny and red and rather cross, and seemed to spend her waking time shaking a threatening fist in my direction and howling for her mother. She had a good pair of lungs, I can testify to that, and a grip like a sailor up aloft. But when she paused to view her surroundings she was really rather beautiful with her seal grey eyes, silky brown hair, and pretty little mouth. I was besotted from the start.

Ellie was the most adoring mother ever. I hardly got a look-in to begin with, but I didn't mind, I knew she had a lot of catching up to do. And she was so determined to do everything right, I worried about that. 'Babies survive,' I declared heedlessly, at which she promptly railed at me and burst into tears. I realised then how afraid she was that Little Mel would be taken from us. Having got her baby at last, Ellie's next anxiety was that our darling child wouldn't survive infancy.

I looked into my daughter's eyes, I listened to that demanding yell when she was hungry, and I knew she was here to stay. Difficult, however, to convince Ellie of that. We hired a nurse to give her some respite, and I'm glad to say that as the months passed and our little one thrived, gradually Ellie stopped being quite so anxious.

It was a rarity for me to be in Liverpool over the festive season, but for Little Mel's first Christmas, heaven be praised, I got home with a couple of days to spare. By then our baby girl had blossomed into a rosy-cheeked angel with glossy curls and eyes just like her mother's.

She was still imperious and demanding, but we were so proud of our little beauty we had a family photograph taken and sent to all our friends and relatives.

The last year of the old century blew in for me on the wings of a storm, but that was nothing new. I was feeling good and the future looked fair. Especially with new ships on the horizon.

For decades, British shipping had dominated the transatlantic market, but the German line, Norddeutscher Lloyd, was posing something of a threat. In response, Thomas Ismay placed orders with Harland and Wolff for two additions to the fleet, managing to attract a government subsidy by having these new ships designed with gun platforms, ready to be transformed into armed merchant cruisers should the need arise. War was in the air.

Perhaps surprisingly, it did not break out as a result of European rivalries. Not directly, anyway. It came from southern Africa, where trouble with the Boer farmers had been simmering for years. In October an armed and united force from the Transvaal and Orange Free State invaded the British province of Natal. Our side did not fare well in the exchange. A month later, while the question of troop transports was being discussed at high level, the second of the White Star liners on order from Harland and Wolff was cancelled. Not because of the war, but in deference to the death of our Chairman, Thomas Ismay.

All unknowing, we were returning from New York, cock-a-hoop because we'd heard *Majestic* was to be one of the first liners to go to the Cape. And then, as we took the Mersey pilot aboard, we heard of Mr Thomas's recent demise. His health had been poor for some time, but the news of his death came as a shock. It was like losing a revered relative, one whose wisdom and benevolence has long been taken for granted. To me, his passing left a chilly emptiness at the helm just at a time when we needed his experience to see us through. As Managing Director, Bruce was perfectly capable, but, as Ellie and I often remarked, he lacked his father's touch.

The funeral was barely over before we were preparing for South Africa. *Majestic* had been requisitioned for the transportation of troops and equipment to Cape Town. Guns were fitted, floors boarded over, bulkheads which created cabins both forward and aft were taken out to make way for mess accommodation. A hospital was equipped and, even though officers were lodged in the staterooms, the most vulnerable fittings and furnishings were removed for safe keeping.

The whole job took two weeks.

Stores were loaded and bunkers taken, we were allocated a troop transport number, and with all my officers and crew – although minus most of the cabin stewards – we prepared to greet our new passengers. 2,000 of them, mainly from northern regiments.

Soldiers, I have to say, make a different kind of passenger, and after three weeks part of me was relieved to see them go. For airs and graces certain officers could have put a duchess to shame, while others were the kind of gentlemen I was proud to have aboard. Amongst the men we had the usual mixed bag of humanity; but apart from the NCOs they all seemed alarmingly young to be going to war. Watching as they clomped down the gangway at Durban, strung about with rifles and kit-bags, I wondered what the next few weeks would hold. The enemy, it seemed, was proving wilier than anyone expected.

While they marched out to acquaint themselves with death, we returned to beautiful Cape Town and a two-week break. Our crew headed for local beaches while the Chief, the Doctor and myself did a little sightseeing and hotel visiting. Sitting outside on a shady terrace overlooking green lawns with blue seas beyond was, I'm sure, the most perfect way to relax. Had it not been for a shared edginess and apprehension.

It was almost a relief when the holiday came to an end. Then we loaded the wounded. Not from any recent battle – indeed most of them had been injured a month or more previously. Our 200 passengers were those who had been patched up on the field, transferred to local hospitals while they recovered sufficiently to travel, and were now bound for military hospitals in England.

Making the rounds on a daily basis as I continued to do, it was impossible not to be stricken by these poor fellows. So much suffering, so much courage. Every face I looked into became that of Harry Jones. I felt their lives like a weight bearing me to my knees every night. I prayed as though they were my own.

My pleas were answered in that the weather was kind on the way home, at least until we reached Gibraltar. Rounding Cape Finisterre into the Bay of Biscay at the end of January was a fight though, and one that did not ease in any marked fashion until we were into the Channel proper. Then there was something of a fiasco when we arrived in Southampton. The special train detailed to take the wounded to the Royal Victoria Hospital at Netley was waiting in a half-completed shed, which, in view of the bitter weather, was a ridiculous place for disembarkation. Thank heavens someone took note of our protests. Directed then to a more sheltered berth, it meant a long delay for those poor lads, ready and waiting since dawn. At last though, they were able to leave us for better facilities.

I thought of them a few days later as we steamed down Southampton Water, carrying another 2,000 men bound for the Cape. The hospital grounds were covered in snow, the red-and-white buildings – almost a third of a mile long – stood out behind a veil of spidery trees and tall Scotch firs. Quite a few men were waving from the pier as we passed, and as our chaps began waving back I wondered at their thoughts. Were both sides thinking, *poor devils*, or were they cheering each other on?

It was Easter before *Majestic*'s stint as an army transport was done. Eventually a medal was issued to thank those of us who had served in that capacity, and, as I said to Ellie at the time, I felt I'd earned it. Not because I came under fire or did anything heroic, but simply because the strain of those four voyages was greater than anyone could have imagined.

That the war had been a shabby, ill-judged affair, did not come out for some time. But it was too late then for regrets or the kind of crocodile tears that men like William Stead indulged in. Men of his ilk earned their living promoting causes of one sort or another, or exposing the follies of politicians. To my mind, it was almost shamefully easy to find the wickedness in war. Enough, as I saw it, to say, *I did my best. I served my country.*

As the war began, we lost Thomas Ismay, the man who had made White Star what it was. In 1900 my mother died, peacefully in her sleep, which was how we should all end our mortal lives. Guilt weighed on me as I realised what little time we had spent together in my adult life. She was sharp and outspoken, and too often we rubbed each other up the wrong way. I wished it could have been different. Looking back it seemed I'd spent my entire life trying to win her affection. All I'd wanted was to please her, make her proud of me. Ellie said she was, but I couldn't quite believe it. I missed knowing my mother was there, but most of all I was sorry for what we had lost. The arctic wind which had blown for Joe whistled past my ears again.

These personal losses seemed magnified by the national one. Before the war had truly ended, in January 1901, we lost our Queen as well. She had been our monarch for 63 years and few people could remember a time before her reign. With Victoria's passing it seemed a way of life had gone forever. The whole country was in mourning, wondering what the new century had in store.

I imagine great thinkers would say our moral foundations had been shaken by the Queen's death. Certainly, it was a time of political unrest, with workers' strikes and demands for women's suffrage. Ellie agreed with their aims – yes, she said, she'd like the chance to vote, and to see women in Parliament – but she was appalled at the way some of these so-called suffragettes carried on. Beyond telling her these things were happening in America as well, I thought it best not to comment.

By contrast, life in the Atlantic service seemed to go on much as before. I made it home in time for my darling Mel's third birthday, but was in New York for her fourth which was a disappointment. Shortly afterwards, Mr Lightoller joined me as 3rd Officer and served aboard *Majestic* until the end of that year. I liked him, although he sometimes set me wondering. To hear him speak you'd swear he was a Newfoundlander, yet according to his history he was born and bred in Lancashire. Of course, he'd knocked around the world a good deal – more than most, I'd say. Had a streak of independence a mile wide – not always a good thing – and he could certainly tell a good story. Having asked about his route to White Star, I was astonished to hear that he'd abandoned his sea-going career a few years previously for gold-prospecting in the Yukon.

I wasn't even sure where the Yukon was. With a rueful grin, he enlightened me. 'Just about as far north-west as you can go, sir, without falling into the Arctic Ocean!

'I met old diggers there with crabbed noses and hardly a finger between 'em! So obsessed with the next big find, they didn't care what else dropped off. Honestly, sir, they scared me. After three months, I came home before the winter set in – didn't want to lose *my* family jewels to frostbite!'

I laughed at that. Broke, young Lightoller had seen sense and headed south again, become a cowboy in Alberta, and then a wrangler, working his passage home aboard a cattle boat to Liverpool. The following year he'd joined White Star.

That amused me even more. Clearly, Lightoller was a man who'd never be stuck fast, and the Superintendent who'd interviewed him must have seen his potential. I was rather sorry when the end of the year saw a parting of the ways. I forget where he went next, but when *Majestic* went into dry-dock for a major refit, I went home for a spot of leave.

We had a wonderful family Christmas, made better by the knowledge that I'd arrived home well in advance and did not have to dash off immediately afterwards. Eleanor's mother and Thomas Jones came to stay for a couple of nights, both of them eager to spend time with our little Mel, and to watch her opening her presents on Christmas morning. As ever I was her adoring slave, eager to do her bidding; even at four years old she knew it. Ellie got quite cross, telling me – and Uncle Tom – not to run around after her, or she would imagine that was what men were for.

Mrs Pennington sniffed at the rebuke, encouraging her grand-daughter in all her imperious little ways. 'She's a true Pennington,' she kept saying, 'a Pennington from before the fall...'

Quite what she meant, none of us knew – it sounded vaguely biblical to me, and this, coupled with a passion for churchgoing, made me wonder whether Mrs P was developing religious mania. But Ellie said not to be silly, it was only Mother's delusions of grandeur from which she'd been suffering for years.

The biggest change of that year, of course, was on the shipping front. As Managing Director of White Star, Bruce Ismay had been running the company for some time, and that he was in favour of expansion was no secret. With his more cautious father gone, Bruce was able to put his plans into action. In the person of the banker John Pierpont Morgan, he'd been courted by the Americans for some time. Morgan wanted to monopolise the Atlantic route, absorbing it into his group of railroads and shipping lines, and Bruce knew he was prepared to offer almost anything to see those dreams come true.

With his younger brother James, Bruce Ismay eventually sold out for £10,000,000.

'Pounds, that is, not dollars,' I said to Ellie. Her eyes went wide with astonishment. 'Quite a bargain,' I added dryly, 'when you think he's managed to rake in the money but remain in charge...'

'But I thought the rest of the family were trying to stop the sale?'

'They were, but the shareholders voted in favour. Besides,' I added, feeling a twitch of excitement even as I said it, 'With all this money, Bruce will be able to order new ships...'

'But what will happen to the company? Will it still be British?'

With that, Ellie put her finger on the problem. It was just a trifle sticky – and most of us felt this – that although White Star's ships remained under the British flag, it was no longer a wholly British company. It was in effect owned by a New York trust whose investors were mainly American. Of course, we'd been seducing wealthy Americans from the beginning, but the Government didn't like the new agreement. There were some very high-level negotiations before the deal went ahead.

New ships, yes, it sounded good. The lads would continue to be employed, the shipmasters would continue drawing their excellent salaries, and Bruce could still be boss. Looking back on that time, I can almost hear Joe saying, 'Careful now – they'll take their pound of flesh…'

23

A pound of flesh. I'd been feeling the truth of it all winter. The price of ambition – not just mine, but Bruce Ismay's too. Until last September, aboard *Olympic*, I'd never imagined how much I would be forced to pay. The last few months had left me in no doubt that it was time to say goodbye to what was, after all, a younger man's game.

Longing for this assignment to be over, suddenly I'd suffered a sea-change. Meeting Dorothea's daughter – my daughter – was like being cast up on some tropical shore. Strange, beautiful, exotic – and utterly foreign. Uncharted territory to a man who had confined himself to the grey-green waters of the Atlantic.

After the storm of emotions, I found the evening a trial. The Saloon was gently buzzing with conversation as I joined my guests for dinner, but with Lucinda at the forefront of my mind it was difficult to keep up. While I longed to have her by my side, almost anyone would have been preferable to the strange Mrs Charlotte Cardeza.

Tall and gaunt, her raised chin and haughty expression gave the impression that all around her were beneath notice. In Reception I thought she was some dowager duchess McElroy had forgotten to tell me about, but Mrs Cardeza was an American widow, rich beyond most people's conception of the word.

She was daunting – and different. Of the millionaires' wives I'd met, most were society hostesses, devoting their time to charitable causes. Mrs Cardeza's hobbies were ocean yacht-racing and big-game hunting. And, I guessed, indulging her son, the equally remarkable Mr Thomas Cardeza. Attempting to engage the lady in conversation, I asked about her yachting experiences. 'I understand, ma'am, that you've skippered ocean-going yachts?'

'One,' she said in clipped tones. 'The *Eleanor*.'

'Ah, my dear wife's name.' I smiled encouragingly while tackling my *coquilles St Jacques*. 'And where did that voyage take you?'

'Hardly a voyage. We were off Cuba.' She paused, studying the arrangement of smoked salmon on her plate. I thought she'd finished speaking, but then she said, 'Came through a hurricane.'

Amazed, I hardly knew how to respond. 'Well then, dare I say it, ma'am – you are lucky to be here to tell the tale.'

'Yes. So they tell me.'

I tried prompting for further details, but it was her son who provided the story. Almost swamped by wind and waves, they'd battled for most of the day and half the night – mainsail ripped to shreds and the rudder barely intact. But just as they thought all was lost, the wind suddenly dropped and they were able to make it to Havana Bay.

'Lucky as always,' Thomas Cardeza said, smiling fondly at his mother.

He was probably in his thirties. Although not present aboard the *Eleanor*, he had accompanied his mother on most of her big-game-hunting expeditions. That did surprise me, since it was hard to imagine him roughing it in a safari tent. Even less could I see him stalking lions across the savannah. He seemed more of a lounge lizard, monocle in place, hair slicked back with pomade, lips as pink as a girl's. My other lady guest – the elegantly-dressed couturier, Lucile – flirted with him outrageously. Fortunately her husband, the champion fencer Sir Cosmo Duff-Gordon, appeared more amused than concerned.

I had decided to tease the Duff-Gordons by pretending I didn't know who they were, referring to them as Mrs and Mrs Morgan, the name under which they had registered; but my little joke fell on deaf ears. Only when young Cardeza returned to the subject of his recent trip through Africa, did it seem to have been noticed.

'I must say Egypt's getting to be like Broadway,' he said dismissively. 'We bumped into everyone, didn't we, Mother dear?' He listed several well-known names, including the Astors. '*And* Mr JP Morgan. *He* said he was intending to travel on his brand new ship, but he's not aboard, is he?'

'Sadly, no.' I replied. 'Business matters, I understand.'

'Sir – if you'll forgive me for saying – I think it more likely Mother upset him. Insisted on buying the Pharoah's death mask he was after. Wouldn't give us the time of day after that.'

The young man evidently found that a satisfying tale, and Lady Duff Gordon laughed appreciatively. Mrs Cardeza raised an eyebrow. Only when I asked if she and her son were enjoying the voyage, did she give me a clear response. Hardly complimentary, since she judged the trip so far to have been rather dull. 'A storm or two,' she said, 'would have been more exhilarating.'

Feeling murderous, I responded with a taut smile. 'Perhaps next time...'

I was thankful when the meal came to an end. I thought I detected a sigh of relief from Sir Cosmo as Mrs Cardeza drifted off with her son – he still talking, she making no discernible response.

My eyes turned towards the far end of the room, where Lucinda was sharing a table with her lady friends. Earlier, I'd despatched a note, begging her forgiveness for my abrupt departure that afternoon, and suggesting we might have lunch together the next day. As I caught up, she shot me a grateful smile and said she would like to do that.

'By the way,' she added quietly, 'I hope you don't mind, but I've been saying you knew my parents in Hong Kong – the ladies were curious, you see. Mr Clinch Smith too. I said it's been rather special to hear so much about them...'

That tactful explanation covered a multitude of questions. I thanked her for it and asked if I might join them later. By the time we parted at the head of the stairs my anxious and uncertain mood had departed. I felt calm, restored to my old self, less daunted by the difficulties ahead.

While the ladies went into the Palm Court for coffee, I headed next door for my after-dinner cigar. Despite its newness, the Smoke Room gave the impression of an old-established gentlemen's club. Leaded glass, carved and inlaid panelling, leather armchairs and a discreet but well-stocked bar, made for a popular rendezvous. Frank Millet and Major Butt followed me in, and, as we looked for an empty table, Jacques Futrelle stood and offered us seats. Noticing Stead nearby, I hesitated; but the morning's interview seemed an age ago. I took a seat next to the Major, my back to Stead, and, as the steward took my order, reflected that after all I owed the newspaperman something. Except for the séance, would I have met Lucinda Carver? Stead had played his part. I should be thankful.

181

Gratitude, however, did not make for liking. Stead's voice, high-pitched, with its echoes of the north-east, intruded so much I could barely follow the conversation at my own table. Oddly enough, Frank Millet and Futrelle, both of whom had been journalists, were discussing their early days, while at the next table Stead was holding forth on the virtues of free speech and a free press.

I heard him say how proud he was of having introduced the personal interview to journalism – and claiming he'd educated the American newspaper magnate, William Randolph Hearst, in what he called revolutionary reporting. I thought revolution a good word, considering the campaigns he'd run on the *Pall Mall Gazette*. But as Stead was taken to task on this very point, I realised my companions' ears were also attuned to the debate.

'Hearst is nothing but a promoter of sensational stories!' one man protested – John Jacob Astor, I saw when I turned my head – while another spat the words *yellow journalism* as though they were fever-ridden.

'But Mr Hearst,' Stead responded, 'put newspapers within reach of ordinary people. He made newspapers popular by publishing the truth about crime and politics and financial corruption. The kind of truths that ordinary people – the ones who vote – ought to be made aware of! It's what I've been doing for more than thirty years.'

There was some grudging assent. From our table Futrelle broke in with, 'Don't forget Hearst gave us Jack London and Mark Twain – you have to admire him for that.'

'What about the truth, though?'

'Yeah, Hearst sure don't let truth get in the way of a good story!'

Everyone laughed. Turning, I caught Astor's eye, but with a wry smile he shook his head as if to say, 'Don't I know it!' His divorce and subsequent marriage to the young Madeleine Force meant that his name – in certain American newspapers – had been trawled through the mud.

I knew enough to be sympathetic. After the *Hawke* incident my name had been in print too. It was not something I'd enjoyed, but at least the newspapers had been kind to me. No comment from Stead as far as I knew, although he'd had plenty to say about ships in the past. Little of it worth repeating, in my opinion, but it was bound to come up. Good sense said I should finish my drink and leave before I became drawn in. Even as it went through my mind, someone mentioned Stead's interest in spiritualism – and then I couldn't leave. I had to be sure last night's episode did not get an airing.

I met Frank Millet's glance as well as Futrelle's – the Major too was suddenly alert. So he knew. Well, I imaged the President's right-hand man could be trusted.

Turning my chair, attempting to catch Stead's eye, I heard an English voice say, 'Didn't you write a story about one of the White Star ships, Mr Stead? The *Majestic*, wasn't it? How did you come to write that?' And before he could answer, someone else turned to me. 'Have you read it, sir – what did you make of it?'

Privately, I objected to the way he'd used the name of a real ship – my old ship, *Majestic* – as the centre-piece in a fanciful but alarming tale. I would have preferred not to comment but everyone was looking in my direction.

'Mr Stead wrote his story before I took over the *Majestic*, so I don't know what my predecessor thought of it. Was he the model for the sea-captain in your story?' I asked, throwing the ball back to Stead.

With a sniff, he said, 'Never met the chap. The whole thing came to me in a dream.' He lit a cigarette, viewing me with narrowed eyes through the smoke.

After the morning's sharp exchange, it was obvious – to me at least – that the man was throwing down a challenge. I was weighing my reply when Frank Millet said – with a mischievous glance at me – that they couldn't be content with such an answer, Mr Stead must explain.

My adversary looked to me for permission. Refusing to play the spoilsport, I nodded, wondering just how far he would go. He knew he had his audience – by then the group had grown – and without further ado proceeded to give us the outline of the tale.

'An old sailing ship, the *Ann and Jane* of Montrose, encounters fog while crossing the Atlantic – a common enough phenomenon as I'm sure the Captain here will testify.' He paused to draw on his cigarette. 'But lurking inside the fog bank is an iceberg. They are on it almost before it is seen. The ship runs along the berg's hidden reef, and with her keel laid open….'

Swept by superstitious dread, I held up my hand. 'Mr Stead,' I protested, 'remember where we are – spare your listeners, please!'

There was laughter, but I caught flashes of alarm. Evidently, Stead did too. After a brief apology, he continued. 'Well, in short, six men and a boy succeed in gaining a foothold on the ice – the rest go down, never to be seen again.'

'Really, Mr Stead – I don't think this is suitable…'

But the story-teller knew his audience. Chilled or thrilled, they wanted him to go on, while I was forced by some unwritten law to keep my seat and listen with the rest. Every nerve was stretched, awaiting the tale's conclusion, anticipating the connections he might make.

'Meanwhile, some hundred miles or more to the east, the crack liner, *Majestic,* is ploughing on through the Atlantic seas – and, as with this great ship of ours, passengers of various ranks and callings are aboard. There is an Irish lady, a Mrs Irwin, gifted with clairvoyance, and a man by the name of Compton, who is able to communicate with certain friends by means of automatic writing.'

'Automatic writing?' Astor queried, but Stead waved it away and carried on.

'Compton and Mrs Irwin, although strangers to each other, have each received knowledge of the tragedy by occult means. By virtue of clairvoyance, Mrs Irwin had seen it happening. She is able to tell Compton the name of the ship, and to describe those who've managed to save themselves. One is a giant of a man, she says, with a red beard.

'Startled, recognising the description, Compton tells Mrs Irwin the man is an old friend. Furthermore, at noon that day, he'd received a message from him, giving the ship's name, and calling for help. Stranded on the ice, they are in urgent need of rescue – they were following the liner route, and must be close to the line of outward steamers.

'Mrs Irwin insists on going to the Captain at once, to beg him to search for them. Compton is simply relieved to have what he sees as confirmation of his story from someone else. Otherwise, the Captain,' and here Stead looked straight at me, 'would almost certainly have ridiculed his story...'

There had been a case of survival on an iceberg, widely reported when I was a boy. I doubted most people's ability to last more than an hour in such conditions, especially after being dunked in the sea. However, I nodded to Stead and he carried on.

'It was fortunate that Compton was known to the Captain as a regular passenger – and that he had, *more than once*, been able to give the Captain information that had enabled the Captain to avoid certain danger...'

'And what was that, I wonder?' Frank Millet muttered from close by. If he heard, Stead ignored him.

'As they meet the fog, Compton asks to speak to the Captain, telling him what he and Mrs Irwin have learned. *But what do you imagine I can do?* the Captain replies. *I have 2000 passengers and crew aboard this ship, I cannot risk them all just for the sake of half a dozen castaways who may or may not be stuck on an iceberg somewhere in this great ocean...'*

Everyone looked to me. 'Just so.'

'*Majestic's* Captain was about to change course for a more southerly route – to avoid the danger, you understand. But he is persuaded to keep to the course they are on, negotiating his way through icy clouds of mist. At last, dead ahead, the lookout spots the berg, and there, on the verge of death, are the survivors of the wreck. A boat is lowered, and the folk Mrs Irwin had *seen*, and with whom Compton had *communicated*, were hauled aboard and rescued...'

Astor raised his hand. 'But *how* did they communicate with Compton? Am I right in saying this was before wireless?'

'Yes, of course,' Stead replied, barely batting an eyelid. 'As I said, the message was received by *automatic writing*. I'm sure you've heard of it – as I'm sure most people could do it, if only they bothered to train themselves.'

'Do explain, Mr Stead.' Millet's air of weary patience prompted smiles and a few smothered laughs, but Stead rose to the challenge.

'Wireless – we all accept that it works on electro-magnetic waves, do we not?' In response to general assent, he said, 'Thought can be transmitted in the same way – just as animals communicate without speech, so do we, only half the time we don't realise it.

'How many times have you begun a sentence,' he went on, 'for your wife to finish it? Or felt impelled to do something or go somewhere, quite against your normal routine?' He made an impatient gesture. 'One of those situations where logically, you should stay at home, but you go out, and thence meet someone, or discover something that changes your whole life...?'

'But what about the automatic writing,' Millet declared, bringing him back to the point. 'Tell us, Mr Stead, how do you do it? How does it work?'

Stead sat up straight, took an audible breath and prepared to inform us. 'Simply by making a habit – as I do, every day between one and two o'clock – of relaxing and waiting with an open, uncluttered mind, for messages to come through. It's like wireless, except no equipment is needed, other than a pencil and paper.'

Astor spoke for everyone, I think, when he asked from whom the messages came.

'Friends of similar mind – we attempt to receive and transmit in that hour.' He shrugged. 'Sometimes we get through – sometimes not. It often seems to depend on the urgency. One friend, for instance, was coming to see me on a particular train – but it was disrupted by the recent coal strike…' At this there were nods and rueful smiles. 'So she sent me a message from the train, saying not to bother travelling to the station as she was stuck outside Watford…

Like the entertainer he was, Stead joined in the laughter. He waited for the amusement to die away. When all was quiet, he lowered his voice. 'Sometimes, the messages come from other realms. How do I know? Well, they are clearly not from friends in this world. They are often specific and relevant to things happening today. Some messages are for other people, while others are prophetic…' Stead looked hard at me when he said this.

Gritting my teeth, I waited for some reference to the séance, or even to our earlier spat, but he closed his eyes and seemed deep in thought for a while.

Another message? That question seemed to go around the table. Looks were exchanged. Were we receiving extraordinary insights by a man of genius, or being taken in by a charlatan?

'People might not always have agreed with the things I have written,' he declared at last. 'I have been mocked for my beliefs and even imprisoned for things I've done.' Again, his eyes bored into mine. 'But I'm proud of it. The campaigns I've waged have been from the heart. I have always *known* that what I was doing was right. And I've been sure,' he said, 'because the message has come to me from above.'

He would never be wrong, then. He didn't just look like a biblical prophet, he sounded like one. I felt he'd argue the point with Moses, but I did wonder why, of all the liners crossing this ocean, he'd chosen *Majestic* for his unlikely tale. That, however, was a question for another time. Seizing my opportunity to escape, I thanked Mr Stead for his story and said that I, too, would be receiving messages from above if I didn't take myself to the bridge.

Amidst some appreciative chuckles, I bade the gentlemen goodnight. What was it Futrelle had asked me earlier? Would I be persuaded to change course under similar circumstances? He was joking, of course. At least, I hoped so. I could picture Bruce's face if I said we were making an alteration in response to one of Mr Stead's messages. *And how did he receive it, pray? Oh, well, sir, it came to him automatically, as he sat there with pencil and paper…*

He'd think I was mad.

As if responsible shipmasters could afford to be swayed by some crackpot scribbler. Only a ship in distress, or an emergency call over

186

the wireless, could warrant a marked deviation from the prescribed course. Such messages came in the form of a series of electronic sparks, the dits and dahs of Morse code, which the Marconi men translated into words for our benefit.

However, as I heard someone say as I was leaving, not every ship had such modern equipment. Sailing ships, tramp steamers, fishing boats, whalers – in fact just about any non-passenger ship – would not have wireless. In trouble, they had to fend for themselves, take to the boats if possible, and pray.

Prayer? Maybe that was what he meant. Ah, well, at least Stead hadn't gone on about lifeboats and Board of Trade regulations. I'd have had difficulty holding my tongue.

Relieved that the encounter had passed without ghosts, ghouls, or spirit guides being mentioned, I glanced at the time and went through the swing doors to find my neglected ladies. It was almost nine o'clock. Mortified by the delay, and only partly relieved to see they were being entertained by Gracie and Clinch Smith, I was surprised to feel a pang of jealousy.

They made room for me and we chatted for a while, Clinch Smith and I indulging in a long-running bit of banter about our names and whether or not we were related. It was unlikely: his people owned half Long Island and even had a town named after them, but we kept up the pretence. On the other hand, he was related – albeit distantly – to the Carvers of New Haven, and seemed eager, I thought, to cement that link with Lucinda. I recalled talk that his marriage was failing, and at once – like some aging knight – wanted to stand between them, protecting Lucinda's honour.

Before long, the sisters were making their apologies. 'These lovely evenings, Captain!' Marianne explained with a smile. 'We often say we could do with 25 hours in a day, but when we get it, we're exhausted!'

The gentlemen said they'd been keeping late hours too, what with the fine weather and pleasant company aboard. Amidst desires for early nights and promises for the morrow we all headed towards the stairs. I turned to Lucinda, knowing she must be fatigued even though her smile belied it, but to my relief she shook her head. 'It's such a beautiful evening,' she said, slipping a velvet wrap around her shoulders. 'Could I beg a few minutes, Captain, and walk along the deck with you?'

The air was sharp and clear. I was afraid she might be cold but she denied it, leaning against the rail with her head back, staring up at the array of stars. All around us, from the arc above to the far horizon, the firmament was sparkling. 'Like a Grand Duchess's tiara,' I said with a smile.

Wanting to share my knowledge, I pointed out the Pole Star and the Plough, and named some of the great constellations: Orion the Hunter, with Sirius the Dog Star at his heels; the group of 55 stars which made up Cassiopeia, seated in her Chair. Way off to the north, just visible, was Andromeda, Cassiopeia's daughter.

'There are lots of Greek myths attached to astronomy,' I mused, 'but the one about Andromeda claims she was chained to a rock and left to drown. Perseus rescued her, and afterwards they stayed together – when they died they were turned into stars. His constellation is close to Andromeda there – like a guardian…'

She sighed. 'If only we could all be turned into stars when we die.'

'Or sea birds,' I said, smiling. 'I used to think that, when I was a boy.'

'Maybe it's true.' She sounded so like my little Mel, so young and wistful, it touched my heart.

'It's all a matter of believing,' I whispered, thinking back to that moment of knowledge when it seemed the world stopped spinning and left us weightless.

'And do you believe?' She turned, suddenly intense, the stars forgotten.

I wanted to say that after the wonder of finding her, I was ready to believe anything, even that we might have a future as father and daughter. But she was too quick for me. 'That the spirit goes on, I mean? Do you think there's any truth in what Mr Stead says?'

'Well,' I said, struggling for an answer, wishing we could talk of things closer to reality, 'if there is an afterlife, why would a contented soul wish to return? An unhappy soul, restless and tormented, might still be earthbound and willing to talk – but, given an audience, might not be so willing to depart. That's my view.'

'It's just that I keep thinking of Dorothea…'

With a murmur of acknowledgement I felt for my small cigars, thinking how strange it was that after all these years she'd chosen to return like this. I recalled the strange vision I'd had, of the man and the young woman standing on deck just yards from where we were. Two nights ago they'd seemed so real. I'd thought the man was Joe. Could the girl have been Dorothea?

'Was she very unhappy?'

Startled, I shook my head. It took me a moment to gather my wits. 'Unhappy? I think we both were. Happy one minute, miserable the next. Isn't that the way of star-crossed lovers?' With a wry smile, I said, 'Besides, we were not often together – and she was married, of course.' Striking a match, I set the flame to my cigar and drew deep, releasing a long, pale cloud of smoke which hovered for a moment, curiously, like a wraith.

As it disappeared, Lucinda turned to me, eyes wide and dark with appeal. 'I hope you'll forgive me, sir, but I have a confession to make. I did offer to help the sisters in their trouble, but I thought – hoped – Mr Stead might put me in touch with Dorothea. Maybe it was foolish, but…' She broke off, bit her lip.

'You hoped she might tell you something? Give you a name?'

Miserably, she nodded. I saw then how important it had been for her to know the truth. She was shaking with cold, and no doubt tension and tiredness too. Concerned, I put an arm around her shoulders. Beneath the velvet she felt slight and vulnerable.

I begged her not to go down that avenue. 'Don't you see? Dorothea *has* brought us together. Less directly, perhaps, than Mr Stead would lay claim to, but still…'

With a sudden, grateful smile, she said, 'You think so? I hadn't thought of it like that. But you do understand?'

'I do. Of course I do. But we should talk about it tomorrow. In the meantime,' I said firmly, 'I'm going to see you to your door. Take my advice and ring for your stewardess – ask her to bring you a hot drink. One way and another it's been a long day – and at a guess I'd say you didn't sleep well last night.'

'How do you know that?' she asked with a little laugh.

'Because I didn't sleep well either!'

We parted by her stateroom, I think with lighter hearts. Reminded of the night before, when I'd walked this corridor with heavier step, I reflected on the last 24 hours. In spite of fatigue and the day's stormy upheavals, I was feeling better than I'd felt all winter. Doubtless it was down to Joe Bell's good news as much as to my meeting with Lucinda, but, for the first time since leaving Southampton, I was in good spirits.

Building castles in the air, I made my way back up top. By the main entrance, like the bad elf in a fairy tale, a small, white-haired figure crossed my path.

Considering the way I'd insulted him that morning, Stead's

greeting was surprisingly civil. But perhaps he felt he'd delivered his message in the Smoke Room.

'It's a fine night, Captain – we've been fortunate with the weather so far.'

'Indeed we have,' I said briskly. 'Makes a pleasant change.'

'Could it lead to fog, later, d'you think?'

'Fog? I doubt it. See for yourself...' I showed him the stars. 'Look at all that. See how clear it is. We don't often get nights like this.'

He was not convinced. 'Calm, though? That often leads to fog, doesn't it?'

'Look, Mr Stead,' I sighed, summoning all my reserves of patience. 'I'm sorry we had our little spat this morning. It was unforgivable of me to be so rude, and I do appreciate your civility this evening, but...'

'I'm proud of that prison sentence,' he declared, as though we were just speaking of it. 'You might not be aware of this, but I didn't just claim – I *proved* how easy it was to buy a child and sell her into slavery. I did it! Where I fell down,' he added sardonically, 'was in not paying the child's father as well as the mother. But then I didn't know he existed until my enemies dug him out.

'Nevertheless,' he went on, halting me before I could interrupt, 'my actions – dubious though some people thought them at the time – changed the law, raised the age of consent by *three years* to sixteen. You won't find many child prostitutes on the streets these days – and that's down to me. So yes, I'm proud of it.'

Surprised in spite of myself, I glanced at him, met that challenging gaze. I expected him to ask what I'd done that was half so important. He didn't, but my own bristling sense of pride made me tell him anyway. 'And I've spent 25 years ferrying people safely across the Atlantic, Mr Stead. Allow me to know my business.'

He gave a grunt that I interpreted as disbelief. 'There really is no need to concern yourself,' I said sharply. 'If there should be fog ahead, we'll have ample warning from other ships.'

As we parted, he turned his gaze to the dark ocean. 'Hmm. Reliable, is it, the wireless?'

'I've found it so, yes.'

Breathing hard with suppressed irritation, I stepped smartly up to the bridge. The 1st Officer was on watch, marvelling at the clear night.

'Everything all right, Mr Murdoch?'

'Yes, sir,' he replied, giving me a keen glance. 'A fine evening, good visibility, very little wind.'

I stood outside for a few moments, watching the ocean, steadying myself. 'It's certainly calm.' Indoors, I checked the course the helmsman was steering, studied the barometer. 'Remarkably steady, Mr Murdoch – what do you make of it?'

'I'd say it's good sleeping weather, sir,' he replied with gentle humour.

'For which we must be truly thankful!' As one of the juniors gave an involuntary grunt of agreement, I smiled. 'Aye, lad, but you must always keep a weather eye open. You never know what's coming next!'

It was good to be up here, amongst the kind of men I respected and understood. Trust and confidence: that was what ship-handling was all about. With a smooth, gentle swell under the keel, barely a ruffle on the surface, there was nothing to worry about. I might even get a decent night's sleep myself tonight.

Almost like the Doldrums except for the temperature. Not really cold though. Not yet. We'd get the chill tomorrow, once we hit the cold currents off the American coast. I would never have admitted it to Stead, but no wind could well mean fog tomorrow night. That would slow us down. Bruce would fret his socks off at that.

Hearing footsteps coming along the deck I turned to see one of the Marconi men. The thin-faced one – he looked about twelve years old – Bride, I think his name was. No doubt he was used to being teased.

He spoke in an undertone to Murdoch, handing him a slip of paper. 'What's that?' I said, intercepting him before he could slide away.

'I'm sorry, sir, I didn't – '

I held out my hand for the message slip and went into the chart room to read it. In the dim light I saw that it was not a greeting from some passing liner, but a bald announcement that the wireless was out of commission. I bit back a curse.

'What's wrong with it?'

'It's – er – it's the transmitter, sir. Mr Phillips thinks one of the condensers has gone.'

'How serious is it? Can it be rectified?

'I – that is, we think so, sir. I mean, it could take a while, but Mr Phillips and me, we're working on it. Sir.'

'I'm glad to hear it. Carry on.'

As the skinny lad hurried away a chill entered my soul. We'd become used to having wireless facilities aboard. What had once seemed no more than a novelty had proved its usefulness, especially with regard to weather and sea conditions. Friday, there had been

reports from other ships of ice in the vicinity of the Grand Banks –
way ahead of us, and well to the north of our track. Nothing to get
excited about as yet. But if there should be fog, too…

With Stead and his oracle's warning still ringing in my ears, I
swore under my breath.

Whatever the problem with the wireless, I hoped these youngsters
could fix it.

24

Swathed in fog, like a blind beggar fumbling with Death, I paced from port to starboard and back again. Rolling billows of eerie, silent mist took the decks from view. Aft, the red and green haze of navigation lights; ahead, two silvery triangles, cut-outs in a sheet of black, lit up the haze.

Our deep-throated horn gave out its warning blare. There came the muffled groans of an answering signal. And then another, closer this time.

Fog muffles everything, distorts sound, but still I strained to hear, trying to identify distance and direction. Two steamships, one maybe on the starboard beam, the other further away. The junior spoke: I shushed him. Holding my breath I listened with all my being. No air, no light, nothing to be seen inside this dense, smothering blanket. Another groan, another echo. Was it close? How close? On the back of it I heard the ringing of a bell. Fear gripped, and all at once to port came the whisper of a wooden ship, her bulwarks grazing as the helmsman fought with the wheel, spars catching the bridge.

I ducked, heart pounding like a steam hammer; and at once glimpsed the phantasms of nightmare. I was tangled in bedding, fighting to free myself, twisting away from the image of Death at the helm, searching for me.

Gasping, I found the light-switch, slaked my thirst with water from the carafe. Listened, all was silence, the ship moving steadily. No fog signals. Of course not: they would have called me. Even so, it was a while before I drifted off again. When I did it was to dream of Mel as a small child, climbing into my sea-chest like a stowaway.

'Daddy, don't go,' she cried, repeating the words each time I lifted her out. 'Don't go!' But then she was on the dunes in bright sunlight, with Ellie and a crowd of neighbouring children, getting smaller as I sailed away. They were waving flags as I sounded the horn... but that sounding of the horn threatened to take me back to nightmare... I fought it and suddenly I was awake again, breathing hard, thinking of my wife and child, thinking of our home. Our home by the beach at Waterloo.

Did I do the right thing? The question leapt like a cat out of the darkness, pouncing on reasons I'd thought were so right. Leaving the Mersey, leaving waters I'd known since boyhood, for ambitions that pushed me further and further away from all I held dear. I remembered how happy we'd been after Mel came along, and how much had changed since the move to Southampton. Mel was growing up, at boarding school now. I hardly saw her, except in the holidays.

I saw my life like a voyage away from the smoky, small-town confines of places like Hanley. Like Joe, I'd wanted to see the world, wanted to experience the wonders of the ocean – the thrills and excitement of rolling waves, the open sky. Sky all around – if I could have been an untamed seabird, I'd have chosen that. Instead I aimed for the next best thing – the freedom of being a Master Mariner in charge of my own ship, my own destiny. I didn't know that there is no such freedom in this world – we are all answerable. To ship-owners, passengers, lovers, children.

Some say the sea is a mistress, she gets in your blood and won't let go. Maybe that's right. If so, I was lucky, meeting Eleanor, marrying her. She understood, wasn't jealous. She never seemed to regard my work as a rival. Well, if she did, it was rare. If she was unhappy, it was for other reasons. But even in that, thank God, we were blessed in the end. We had a daughter who was everything we could have hoped for. And I can see it now, looking back, how our home was part of the contentment...

Having taken command of one brand new ship, within a couple of years I was in line for the next. The talk was not just of new ships – it was to be a new port, a new route. The only snag was that we would have to move.

When I told Eleanor, in confidence, her face fell.

'But you know how difficult things are,' I reasoned. 'The Germans are picking up more and more of our business, and Cunard are beating us hands down at home. White Star wants the rich American trade to and from the Continent, but whilst we use Liverpool as our home port, we're losing them to Norddeuscher Lloyd and Hamburg Amerika.'

'So Mr JP Morgan wants us all to move to Southampton, does he?'

'It makes sense – you must see that? From Southampton, with new liners, we can hop across to Cherbourg for the Continental trade, and still pick up the Irish passengers from Queenstown.'

She stared out of the window. Across the dunes a stiff wind was blowing, whipping sand into a miniature storm, obscuring the Estuary beyond. I knew what she was thinking: if I accepted, we would lose this house with its beautiful outlook, lose the friends she had made. 'Mr Ismay must be turning in his grave.'

'Ellie!' I swallowed an exasperated sigh. 'He was a businessman, first and foremost. He'd be the first to say we have to move with the times.'

She turned a cold, grey glance upon me. 'So we must move too – is that the case?'

Hating the idea, she dug in her heels and refused to discuss it. For a while after that, with the recession biting, the whole thing looked more than a little shaky. Eleanor cheered every time doubts arose, and she was not the only one. When the deal was done with the railway company owning Southampton's docks, the men – sailors and firemen alike – claimed they'd been betrayed. Liverpool would lose at least four ships, and, with several hundred crew employed on each one, jobs would be at a premium. Yet the men still had families to support. They could not afford to move south – and why would they want to? They were Liverpudlians born and bred.

Most affected would be senior officers permanently attached to liners on the new route; but, as Eleanor was quick to point out, they were not the problem. Used to travelling the world, they could settle anywhere. But not the wives.

'I sincerely hope,' she declared mutinously, 'that you've given Bruce Ismay no such promises, because I have no wish to leave here!'

For once, Bruce was not the instigator, it was JP Morgan, the force behind IMM.

'I like your style, EJ,' that growling, distinctive voice declared. We were relaxing over brandy and cigars – the very best – in the library of his Madison Avenue home. I'd just retired from the Royal Naval Reserve, and, as was the custom, had been bumped up a rank.

195

'Commander Smith, RNR,' he repeated. 'That's great, EJ. It says background, discipline, Royal Navy, Britannia Rules the Waves – you know the score.' He sucked on his cigar and raised another finger. 'Second, you have the talent as well as the ticket – I have never seen a man drive a ship through a storm the way you do. What's more, EJ, you put confidence in the hearts and minds of White Star's passengers.' He smiled and ticked off a third point. 'And speaking as a guy who is surely known for his pug-ugly mug, I just want to say this – you look the part. And the silver beard is perfect. Puts all these impressionable Yankees in mind of your great King Edward…'

That made me smile. I didn't imagine the monarch would be too pleased, but I was flattered. Flattered, yes. Good word, that. So is vanity. And pride. I should have remembered they were two of those seven deadly sins Billy O'Loughlin was so fond of joking about.

Oddly enough, it was through Billy that I got to know JP Morgan. The financier travelled a lot but hated rough weather, so he mostly clung to his stateroom. During one of his early crossings aboard the *Baltic*, he was particularly ill and, somehow, Billy O'Loughlin worked his magic, made the great man feel better. After that they were firm friends. Of course, the reason he was so fond of Billy's company was that he loved to discuss his ailments and Billy was a good listener. The great cure-all, he called it.

'The man's as strong as an ox,' was our doctor's private opinion. 'Doesn't he work everyone else to a standstill? I tell you, he'll still be kicking when the rest of us are feeding the fishes…'

JP barely touched a drop, but his nose was as red and craggy as a Colorado cliff. Told Billy he could have had an operation to improve it, but he'd refused. Said folks knew him by it, it was part of his character. And JP was strong on character, proud of the fact that he'd bought and sold entire railroads on the strength of his personal judgement. When he related stories like that, you felt he was paying you a compliment. Yes, for all he looked like a pantomime ogre, the man knew how to charm.

Most significant of all, during the crisis of 1907, when there was a real threat of the New York banks collapsing, he called in all his chips and bailed out the American government. Oh yes, Teddy Roosevelt owed a lot to old JP Morgan.

So when he talked about building new ships, and outlining the opportunities for advancement, I listened with all the attentiveness of an acolyte.

Fired with enthusiasm when I got back from New York, I faced an icy silence. In vain did I try to persuade Eleanor to see things from my point of view.

'But JP wants me for the next new ship,' I declared. 'It'll be bigger than *Baltic* – more powerful, too. It's just the beginning, don't you see? At this rate, I could be the senior master within a few years!'

That appeal, strong to my mind, fell on stony ground. I wanted that position and expected Eleanor to understand. But all she could see was disruption ahead. Disappointed, even angry that she was being so obtuse, next time round I tried the practical approach. It would be a terrible waste, I said, to spend two whole days of my precious leave changing trains between here and there.

'As a family,' I said unwisely, 'we need to be together in Southampton.'

'As a *family*?' she repeated, her voice low with suppressed anger. I turned to find her glaring at me, fists clenched at her sides. 'We're together five or six days out of the month, Ted – at best. When the weather's bad you hardly manage a couple of days between trips. So don't talk to me about family. *Your* family is aboard whatever ship you're on!'

The accusation struck with all the force of a javelin. She and Mel were all I thought of, all I worked for. Unable to speak I stared at her, wondering why she was behaving like this. So set against me it seemed hate was in her heart.

'My life,' she said in that same taut voice, 'is here with Mel. We have friends. We take the train to see our relations. Mel loves the farm. It would be cruel to take her away from her school and her friends and all she knows…'

I was feeling like some species of snake when Eleanor went on, 'And what about my mother? It would kill her if we went away…'

At mention of my mother-in-law all sympathy evaporated. Mrs Pennington spent a lot of time with my wife and daughter. Indeed, there were times when it was difficult to dislodge her and send her back to her cottage at Winwick. She had a knack of making me feel like an intruder in my own home, and now it seemed my wife was regarding me in the same light.

'Your mother has a son and two other daughters, several grandchildren and a perfectly good home of her own. She doesn't have to spend all her time here. Anyway, we're not talking about going to Australia!'

'She's getting old, Ted.'

'She's not that much older than me!' I retorted, hating the fact that we were separated by not much more than twelve years. 'Don't

I deserve consideration too?'

'You're a man,' she said, turning away. 'You don't understand.'

'I'm your husband,' I said heatedly, 'and I'll thank you not to forget it!'

Furious, Eleanor pushed past me, heading for the stairs. Mel was at school, fortunately. Grabbing my coat and a lead I left with Ellie's golden retriever at my heels. For good measure I gave the door a hearty slam. I didn't give a damn about the servants.

I walked along with Wagstaff, until the sandy road before the house became a track behind the dunes. From the highest point I could see the great expanse of the estuary, the dark line of the tide rushing in, and the lightships marking the dangerous shallows. How many times had I left the great River Mersey, to steam out into the Irish Sea and beyond? I could no more answer that than I could say how often I'd returned, always safely, but not often unshaken by my experiences. For all the route was the same, the ships changed and every single voyage was different.

Why did I do it? It was not something I often thought of while under way, but ashore – when Eleanor was making me ask such questions – I knew it was the challenge. The need to prove I could do it, that my skills were still sharp. There was nothing quite like coming safely into port after facing the worst weather the Almighty could throw at you. The tingling thrills of relief and satisfaction were euphoric. Like nothing else. Not alcohol nor tobacco nor the pleasures of sex. It lasted for days, made a man feel alive from his scalp to his toes.

Of course, once that feeling wore off, it was like losing the wind and drifting into the doldrums. With no control, at the mercy of hidden currents, life could be quite difficult. Even miserable at times, although it had nothing to do with Eleanor or Mel. I was glad of the retriever on days like that, glad of an excuse to walk. Eventually, it would pass, my spirits would surface and I'd feel tolerably easy with my lot. But I could never recapture that feeling of intense satisfaction except by going back to sea.

At three o'clock I gave up, pulled on some clothes and went through to the bridge. Henry Wilde was on watch, taciturn as ever, but good at understanding the need for tea and company in the middle of the night.

Calm, no fog. The atmosphere was clear, the constellations moving on their ordained paths across the firmament. Out there, all was as it should be. Only aboard did things seem set to go awry.

'Any news?'

'Not yet, sir. They're still working on whatever it is.'

With modern communications we had the answer to safety at sea. I'd been so sure of that. Yet in the space of a day, Mr Stead and his doubts had not only lodged themselves in my mind, they seemed to have been transmitted to the collection of generators, valves and tuners that made up the wireless equipment.

'I don't suppose you've come across Mr Stead – little fellow, bushy white hair and beard?'

'The newspaperman? I've seen him about,' Wilde said as the quartermaster handed us our mugs of tea.

'He's an odd fish – big opinion of himself. Reckons he's a medium or some such nonsense – receiving messages from the great beyond.' At that my Chief Officer gave me a keen glance. Remembering his wife's death, still so recent, I could have bitten my tongue. 'And the live and kicking,' I added quickly. '*Automatic writing*, he calls it. Reckons it's better than wireless!'

'Aye, Mr McElroy said. Forever talking about it, apparently. If he's that clever,' Wilde observed dryly, 'maybe we should set him to work?'

'Maybe we should,' I chuckled. Taking our tea, we strolled outside, viewing the magnificent array of stars. 'He was warning me about fog, earlier. The old fool even had me dreaming about it!'

Wilde grunted his disparagement. 'Not tonight, sir.'

'No, I said so.' We stood in silence for a while, but I couldn't get Stead out of my mind. Was he ill-wishing us? Acting as a channel for something malignant? I shook my head at that, thinking I was becoming as addled as he was. 'Do you know, I couldn't get over the feeling that he was just longing for something to go wrong?'

'Maybe the weather's been too good this trip, sir. He should have been with us last time round – he'd have been praying for his life like the rest of 'em, not dreaming up mischief.'

I nodded, seizing on the word. 'Mischief – you're right – that's just what it is. Going on about fog, he was, and then the wireless. I couldn't believe it, not five minutes later, the lad came up to say the wireless was out of commission!'

I caught the startled flash of light in Wilde's eyes. He said, 'No wonder you couldn't sleep, sir.'

'Oh, not that – it was dreaming of fog that woke me. I'm just hoping they get the ruddy wireless fixed. Otherwise he'll be sticking a feather in his cap and saying he can affect electrical circuits, too!'

25

Hauling myself out of bed a couple of hours later, I rubbed the tiredness from my eyes. It seemed years since I'd had a full night's sleep.

On the bridge just before 7:00, Mr Phillips – the senior of the two wireless operators – came to give me his report. He'd feared that repairs would have to wait until New York, but after working through the night he'd managed to fix the problem himself.

I felt my stomach weaken with relief. For a moment I couldn't speak, although no doubt the breadth of my smile conveyed much. These boys were used to working nights when the signals were strongest, but it proved their dedication. Of course, without being cynical, as we approached the eastern seaboard we were also coming within range of the wireless transmitting station at Cape Race. Passengers would be queuing up to have both personal and business messages sent on to New York, and each one of those telegrams came with tips over and above what Marconi paid them.

My sense of well-being was dimmed a little when I returned after breakfast. At 9 o'clock an envelope marked *Captain* was handed to me from the young lad I'd spoken to the night before. Inside was a telegraph form bearing a message from the Cunard liner, *Caronia*: 'WESTBOUND STEAMERS REPORT BERGS GROWLERS AND FIELD ICE IN 42°N FROM 49° TO 51°W APRIL 12. COMPLIMENTS BARR.'

Having sent an acknowledgement via Mr Bride, I studied the

position. Close to our projected route, and roughly 300 miles ahead. That was not good news. Westbound steamers encountering ice meant it was much further south than usual. Taking our usual course and speed, we'd be in the area sometime before midnight. Like every other westbound liner, we were on a modified Great Circle Route which ended at 42°N and 47°W. We referred to it as the Corner. From there, the route to New York turned almost due west, towards the Nantucket Shoal Light Vessel.

No doubt there would be other reports to come, but it would be prudent to change course a little later than usual, taking us further south and west of the ice field.

In the meantime, the sea was calm, the propellers were ploughing along at 75 revs, the engines were performing well, most of the boilers were running, and the Chief and Tommy Andrews were looking to bring them all on line for a full-speed run on Monday. Once we were clear of the ice-field.

Sundays were exempt from the round of morning inspections. Instead, our religious services – two Catholic Masses and two following the practice of the Established Church – were held at various times. McElroy took the 2nd Cabin service, while mine was held in the Saloon at 10:30. Tables were moved to the far alcoves, the small orchestra placed close by on my right, with chairs facing the lectern. That morning, as I walked in, the sun was shining through the stained glass windows, throwing rainbow beams of light across the carpet. Almost like a real church, I remember thinking – there hadn't been such a bright, steady Sunday for months. The size of the congregation reflected it, some 200 passengers rising with a shuffling of feet and chairs as the orchestra struck up the chords of the first hymn.

> *'God moves in a mysterious way*
> *His wonders to perform;*
> *He plants his footsteps in the sea*
> … calm again today, thank God…
> *And rides upon the storm.'*

The voices rang out, some fine sopranos and a few heavy bass voices amongst the enthusiastic majority:

> *'Judge not the Lord by feeble sense,*
> *But trust him for his grace;*
> *Behind a frowning providence*
> *He hides a smiling face…'*

I scanned the crowd for Lucinda, and found her three rows back.

Wanting to smile just for her I dragged my eyes back to the words on my service sheet:

> 'His purposes will ripen fast,
> Unfolding every hour;
> The bud may have a bitter taste
> But sweet will be the flower.'

I thought of Dorothea, and the agonies we'd bestowed on each other – but in Lucinda there was sweetness. How she came to be aboard my ship was a mystery to me; and that we should find each other, even more so.

As the service moved on, I led the prayers according to White Star's direction.

> 'We beseech thee to hear us, Lord… That it may please thee to preserve all that travel by water… and grant that in all our troubles we may put our confidence in thy mercy…'

Another hymn, and then those words from the psalm which always reminded me of Joe:

> 'They that go down to the sea in ships: and occupy their business in great waters: These men see the works of the Lord: and his wonders in the deep… When they cry unto the Lord in their trouble…. he maketh the storm to cease… and bringeth them unto the haven where they would be…'

Even at the worst of times those words seemed to calm everyone's fears. My homilies were often based on it, but my address that day was largely in praise of the calm weather with which the Lord had seen fit to bless us on this maiden voyage, for the comfort we were enjoying as a consequence, and for the dedicated staff upon whom we all relied.

Afterwards, John Jacob Astor came up to say how much he had enjoyed the service, and his young wife gave me a shy smile. With colour in her cheeks I noticed she was rather pretty. Effusive as ever, Mrs Margaret Brown stopped to chat – and then came Adelaide Burgoyne. I asked how she was and in response received a very searching look. I was afraid she was going to tell me again that I was supposed to be dead. Fortunately, the sisters ushered her along. Lucinda's shining smile warmed me; and as she pressed my hand I reminded her, lightly, that we had an appointment for lunch. Frank Millet, overhearing, made some comment about the privilege of rank which made the group around us laugh. *If you only knew*, I thought as they disappeared in the direction of refreshment.

And then I saw Stead.

'I was raised a Methodist,' he declared. 'But I came this morning because I wanted to hear you speak.'

I found a smile. 'I trust it was worthwhile?'

'Do you truly believe?' he asked when the last stragglers were out of earshot.

'Come now, Mr Stead – do you think me insincere?'

'Not at all. In fact your sincerity leads me to wonder why you refuse to listen.' When I forbore to reply, he went on with quiet intensity, 'I sense something in you – what is it? Surely you believe that beyond this material world lies another, as yet unseen?'

'I do, sir, but where we differ – if you'll permit me to say so – is with regard to what I see as the folly of trying to contact this *other world*. You're very convincing in what you say, but how do you *know* – how can *I* know – that these messages and premonitions you refer to are real? Or if they are, that they mean us well?'

'You expect me to take notice, but I cannot do that.' Rather more lightly, with Billy O'Loughlin in mind, I said, 'I'm not a priest or a parson, I'm just a plain old seafaring man. I don't have words to explain the dangers you run with this hobby of yours. I can only repeat what I said yesterday – we at sea do *not* play with the Devil.'

'No more do I!' As I tried to move away he turned with me. 'What if the message is genuine – from a place where time means nothing? Where the future is as clear as the past? What then, Captain?'

'Then I can only put my trust in God,' I retorted. 'And so should you, Mr Stead!'

Seething as I headed for the stairs, it took me a while to calm down. I was in my office as another message was brought in. It did nothing to ease my mind, but at least the warning was realistic. From the Dutch liner *Noordam*, reporting ice in much the same place as before. I went through to the wheelhouse and spoke to Murdoch. I'm afraid I was a trifle curt, and he viewed me with surprise. But having drawn his attention to the ice warning and pinned it to the board, I returned to my charts to work out the change of course for later in the day.

The ice would be drifting south on the cold Labrador Current. After some thought, I figured we could delay the alteration by half an hour, making our turning of the Corner a dozen nautical miles south and west of the usual turning point. I thought that should keep us clear of the ice field, without deviating too much from the westerly shipping lane. Having marked it on the chart I drew Murdoch's attention to it.

'We would have altered there – but instead I want to alter here...' As he studied the position, I said, 'I'll pin the note to the board, but please inform Mr Wilde when you hand over.'

At noon we shot the sun, worked out the position, and laid down the new sector of the Great Circle course to be followed for the next few hours. I calculated that we had travelled 546 miles in the previous 25 hours, which indicated a speed of 21.8 knots. Bruce should be satisfied, I thought, inscribing the figures for the notice board outside the Purser's Office. The whistles and telegraphs were tested according to Company regulations, after which Boxhall wrote up the log book and I signed it.

The ritual of everyday tasks calmed me, and with those completed I could turn my thoughts to Lucinda. I knew there would never be proof that we were father and daughter – only Dorothea could have said for sure – but I had certainty in my heart, and that was what mattered.

With only a couple more days ahead of us, I wanted to spend every available minute with her. Sadly, those minutes were few: from this evening I would be thoroughly occupied with professional matters. The speed test on Monday, the busy shipping lanes off Nantucket and Long Island on Tuesday, followed by Sandy Hook and the approaches to New York, taking us through into Wednesday's early hours. Barely time to eat or sleep, much less be sociable.

As chance would have it, just as I came down to A Deck I bumped into Bruce and George Widener. George could be a bit of a bore on the subject of finance but he was one of IMM's major trustees; so when he asked would I join them for a drink in the Smoke Room, I felt I must accept. We took seats at a pleasant table in the bay window, and, as the steward brought me my usual ginger ale, I made a point of saying I had someone to meet for lunch.

Industrial unrest on both sides of the Atlantic was still a frequent topic, and the two men were soon discussing President Taft's appeal for more brotherly love and understanding in the workplace. They were cynical in the extreme. I was on the point of making my excuses when I noticed the thin-faced Marconi man hovering in the doorway, evidently looking for me. I raised my arm and he came across, rather self-consciously, with an envelope.

'Thank you, Mr Bride,' I said as he stood watching me open and read the message, 'send my acknowledgement, would you?'

It was from Ranson, who had succeeded me on the *Baltic*. They were en route from New York to Liverpool. He reported moderate winds and clear, fine weather since leaving. Then:

'GREEK STEAMER *ATHENAI* REPORTS PASSING ICEBERGS AND LARGE QUANTITIES OF FIELD ICE TODAY IN LAT 41°51'N LONG 49°52'W. LAST NIGHT WE SPOKE GERMAN OILTANK STEAMER *DEUTSCHLAND* STETTIN TO PHILADELPHIA. NOT UNDER COMMAND SHORT OF COAL LAT 40°42'N LONG 55°11'W. WISHES TO BE REPORTED TO NEW YORK AND OTHER STEAMERS. WISH YOU AND *TITANIC* ALL SUCCESS...'

Not under command – in other words, unable to manoeuvre. Ice was a hazard, but if the German steamer was without coal, without power, and in the midst of the busy shipping lanes, she was a positive danger. At night, with just her red NUC lights showing, she'd be difficult to spot. But still, from the co-ordinates it looked as though she was well ahead of us. We should be through the ice field tonight, but if Bruce was after a speed run tomorrow, we would have to watch out for two things: one, that we didn't waste *our* precious coal, and two, that we didn't run into that drifter.

Hoping it might change the subject, I passed the message across to Bruce so he could take it into consideration. But he was listening to Widener expounding on some theory or other. He took the slip from me, but as I waited impatiently for him to read it, a flash of light made me turn my head. Outside, on the promenade, Lucinda was walking past.

'Would you excuse me, gentlemen? I've just spotted someone I need to speak to...' Like a bored schoolboy, I made my escape.

Not everyone went down to the Saloon for lunch – the Palm Court and Café Parisien were popular too. When Lucinda and I reached my table, the Saloon was almost empty, which was how I'd planned it. For a moment I simply sat and looked at her: winged brows above startlingly blue eyes, high cheekbones, a short, perfect nose, an expressive mouth above Dorothea's determined little chin. Apart from the colour of her eyes, I could see little of myself in her – except she was clearly taller than her mother. Perhaps that was down to me.

We ordered and, while waiting to be served, she asked how long I'd been at sea, and if I would tell her something of my career. Inevitably that took us back to Hong Kong, but the tale I told of Harry Jones was very much an abridged version of events. As to how I'd come to be with White Star – again, regarding the *Lizzie Fennell*, I drew a veil over the worst and put a humorous gloss on our passage back to Liverpool. We were having quite a jolly conversation until she asked about Eleanor.

'Well now…' I poured some water, wondering why it should feel so strange talking about my wife with this new daughter of mine. But almost before I knew it, I was telling her how I'd met Eleanor, and about the connection between Dorothea, the Jones family, and the Penningtons. Making the confession, I realised I would have it to make again – to Eleanor next time. How else could I explain about Lucinda?

Suppressing that thought, I asked about her husband, the lawyer. He practised in his father's law firm, she said, and evidently did not always see eye to eye with him. But the way she described Richard Carver – a kind man, espouser of causes, someone who took on cases of injustice, often for people who could not pay – made me warm to him. It pleased me that she admired him so much. Wives should admire their husbands, I thought – and then suffered another pang of guilt wondering how Eleanor would view me when I finally told her the truth.

Lucinda began to explain her reasons for visiting London. 'Only after I was married and living in Connecticut – and about to become a mother myself – did I really begin to wonder about Dorothea and her life in Hong Kong. It became very important to me. I thought Uncle Nicholas would be sure to help – that he'd feel able to tell me the truth now I'm no longer a child. Or at least throw some light on things.

'Sadly, he couldn't. Or wouldn't, I'm not really sure. He said my mother had never confided in him – and anyway, my aunt refused to have the scandal brought up again. As far as the world was concerned, my birth certificate named Henry Curtis – it was all anyone needed to know. He said I'd be wise to leave it there…'

'He was no doubt trying to protect you,' I suggested gently.

'But you do understand how important it was? You see now why I turned to Mr Stead?'

'Yes, of course.' Keen to get away from that particular subject, I said, 'But tell me about your aunt.'

'Hilda?' She shrugged. 'Not a very kind woman. She didn't like Dorothea, I understood that from an early age. What's more, she didn't like Nicholas speaking of her.'

'Disapproving?' I asked. 'Or just plain jealous?'

'Both, I think,' Lucinda replied with a wry smile. 'Aunt Hilda is very correct – she was even appalled because I'd travelled alone, without a maid – she couldn't imagine what my husband was thinking of to allow it!'

I chuckled at that. 'Clearly, she doesn't know many American ladies!' After a moment, I said, 'Dorothea was never constrained by propriety. And why should she be? In those days Hong Kong was more like a frontier town. It certainly wasn't England. People there made their own rules.'

There was a small silence. Lucinda looked at her plate, broke a few more pieces of bread. I saw the colour in her cheeks deepen as she appeared to struggle with something. 'Last night,' she got out at last, 'we talked about believing. But I never asked the really important question...' Her eyes were glistening and suddenly she was looking for a handkerchief. I handed her one of mine, while she tried and failed to control those wayward emotions. 'Sorry – can't help it...'

'I know, I know.' She was sitting across from me and I couldn't reach her even if I dared. But I wanted to hold her close and tell her it didn't matter – none of it mattered. By some miracle we had found each other – everything was going to be all right. Over her shoulder I saw the steward approaching. I shook my head and he retreated.

'I think,' I said slowly, 'that I am going to break a few of my own rules here. I am going to ask you to come up to my quarters. I'll get my steward to make some tea, and we will stop being polite and say what we really think. And if we shed a few tears, it won't matter because we'll be private there. Is that all right?' She nodded, and I pushed back my chair, going round to assist her.

A little while later, when Paintin had brought the tea and gone away again, I unhooked and closed both doors. I was beyond worrying what others might think, only certain I did not want our conversation overheard.

Regaining my seat, I tried to find the right words. She seemed so vulnerable, her eyes searching mine for answers. I could see myself in her, all those years ago, longing for things Dorothea would never say.

'When we were at the table,' I began gently, 'were you trying to ask me whether I truly believe you are my daughter?'

Tears sprang afresh as she nodded; she had to set down her cup. 'I'm sorry – I was all right yesterday. But it keeps overwhelming me. I hardly slept for thinking about it – then suddenly I was doubting everything. Wondering if I'd imagined that moment, when... when it all seemed so clear.' She broke off, only to exclaim in distress, 'How I hate that man's name on my birth certificate!'

'It wasn't Curtis,' I said, reaching out to her. 'He must have known all along that you weren't his child. That marriage was no marriage in the true sense, Lucinda – it was a business arrangement.' I took her hands in mine. 'Look at me. Never mind the tears. Do I believe you are my daughter? Yes, I do. I was sure yesterday. I'm even more certain today. I hope you don't mind...?'

'No – no, I'm happy – so happy...' With that, suddenly I was by her side, embracing her as I would Mel. She clung like a little girl, as though she would never let go. 'I felt as though I knew you,' she said between gulps and sniffs, 'as soon as you smiled at me. As though I'd always known you...'

She smelled like her mother. Flooded by memories, for a moment I held her tight, then on a deep breath put her away from me. 'Yes, I felt that, too. But...' I added with shaky amusement, 'For me it's understandable – after all, you are very like your mother.'

My daughter smiled back at me. Like sunshine after rain. 'But Dorothea had dark eyes, like the rest of the family. My eyes are blue,' she said, 'like yours.'

That small observation went straight to my heart.

She wanted to know all about her mother; but it was difficult for me to describe the Dorothea I knew without pain creeping into my voice. I didn't want to say how very much she'd hurt me by her secretiveness, her inability to confide the things I longed to know. Most of all, that she'd loved me, that I meant more than Curtis, the business, and yes – more than the other lovers who'd come and gone before me.

'Dorothea kept a lot to herself,' I said at last. 'In the beginning I think she was afraid that if she revealed too much, I would go away, never come back. And later – well, maybe I threatened to wreck the boat. So she only told me what she thought I needed to know.'

Struck by an irony, I said, 'Looking back, it seems to me Curtis could have been plotting to seize your grandfather's fortune from the beginning. David Lang trusted him – and the man took advantage. But even if your mother had suspected – and I don't think she did – it would have been difficult for her to divorce Curtis. Especially out there. Too much tit-for-tat, I'm afraid. We discussed it once. But I would have stayed without marriage – if she could have borne it. I would have resigned from White Star, signed up with some other company. We could have moved to India, Singapore – even San

Francisco. People need not have known our circumstances…

'But the business…' With a shrug I left the rest unsaid, turning away as memories threatened to overwhelm me. Jealousy and bitterness were long gone; looking back, all I could feel was sadness. 'For all her waywardness, Dorothea had a strong sense of duty – she couldn't bear to let Nicholas down. Or, I suspect, the memory of her father.'

'Yes,' Lucinda whispered, 'that's what Uncle Nicholas said. That she stayed in Hong Kong with Curtis because of the business. At what cost, though…'

'A terrible cost.' I was looking at Lucinda and thinking of her upbringing – the fighting over Dorothea's will, the casual cruelty of Nicholas's wife and son.

'What happened in the end? Can you tell me?' When I hesitated, she said, 'It doesn't matter – if you argued, parted badly, I'll understand. I simply need to know.'

'We didn't argue.' I struggled for words to explain. 'Not as such. In the end I lost heart – as sad and simple as that. Nothing I could say would sway her – and I was suffering. My work was suffering…' Describing my interview with the Old Man, the choice that was set out so plainly, I stopped, mid-sentence, caught by an aspect of the truth never before considered: I had abandoned Dorothea for the very reason she could not commit herself to me.

Overwhelmed by sudden shame, it was difficult to go on. 'So, in the end, faced with a choice between her and my livelihood, I chose the latter… It hurt,' I confessed with painful honesty, 'like nothing else before it. But after all the intensity – all we'd been through – in some ways it was a relief.' Unable to bear my daughter's steady gaze, I reached for my cigars, lit one, drew deep and tried to be calm.

'I was given leave to explain when we got back to Hong Kong. But Dorothea had gone by then. To London, the letter said, because Nicholas was ill.' I looked at Lucinda, knowing she had to be the real reason. 'Because – well, because of things she'd told me before, I never suspected the truth. Although I did suspect Nicholas was just an excuse. To get away from me, I thought at the time. I thought – well, that she'd just decided it was over.' I struggled to control my voice. 'Now, I can only imagine she'd realised she was expecting a child – you, my dear – and knew she had to leave before scandal wrecked everything.'

After a little while, Lucinda said, 'It must have been terribly hard for her to do that.'

209

'Yes, it must.' A fresh wave of shame silenced me. The unknowing had hardened inside me like a lump of ice. Understanding, it melted like a tidal wave. Awash with sudden grief, I whispered, 'I wish I'd known…'

I had to get up, shake it off. Gazing from my window, I waited until it had passed. When I had myself under control, I felt in my pocket, found the gold chain Dorothea had enclosed in her letter.

'She left this for me.' The long gold chain glinted between my fingers. 'I burned the letter, but was never able to part with this. I think you should have it. A small memento of your mother.'

'Are you sure?' she whispered, her eyes alight with concern for me. 'After all these years, are you sure? I would love to keep it – not just because it was hers,' she added quickly, 'but because it makes a link with both of you.'

As she wound it through her fingers I felt the drawing together of past and present. I touched her hair, drew my fingers along the line of her cheek. So soft, so perfect, so like Dorothea. 'Dear girl, you are the only link that matters.'

26

So many links in the chain of a life. If Lucinda was living proof of the love I'd shared with Dorothea, *Olympic* forged shackles which dragged me down. I struggle to see the point where I might have broken the chain, unhooked myself from the sequence of events. Maybe only with Dorothea, in Hong Kong or 'Frisco or some such place: only then might I have avoided what was to come. But we each made our choices: hers, the bank and bullion business out East; mine, White Star and the Atlantic trade.

I was ambitious, so I chose my career. I married Eleanor, a woman who supported that.

I thought about her, my love, my wife. Every marriage has its difficulties, but we'd been together 25 years, and mostly we'd been happy. For us, the worst time was the impending move from Liverpool. Pulling in different directions, then.

I should have listened to Eleanor.

Even Mel managed to make me feel bad. We were in the garden one sunny afternoon. I was seated in my favourite wicker armchair with the papers, reading a piece about the Hamburg-Amerika Line. It outlined the business they were taking from British companies, emphasising the need for a south coast service.

As though she read my mind, eight-year-old Mel wormed her way in beside me. Looking intently into my eyes, she said, 'Daddy, I don't want to go to silly old Southampton... I like it here.'

I set my newspaper aside. 'So do I, little girl, but it's Daddy's job.'

She pouted prettily. 'But your job takes you away all the time. Why can't you just go there and do it, and leave us here?'

It was a child's question, a child's reasoning. 'Because I want to be able to spend as much time as possible with you and Mama.'

Frowning, Mel studied me, her head on one side. For a moment, disconcertingly, she looked just like her grandmother. 'But Daddy, you don't spend hardly any time with us.'

Banishing the image, I drew her towards me, kissed her forehead. 'I'm sorry, my angel, but going away to sea, driving big ships – that's my job, it's what I do.' Fishing for names, I said, 'Your friends – Sarah, is it, and Bertie? Their fathers go away too.'

Such similarities cut no ice. She gave me the benefit of her grey, Atlantic gaze. 'Don't you miss us?'

'Of course I do – I miss you all the time.'

'I miss you too,' she said, giving me a little hug and sliding off my knee. 'But you know,' she added over her shoulder, 'I'm going to miss my friends lots more.'

That stung. I stood up as she closed the gate, watching her cross the path to join a group of neighbourhood children, perhaps half a dozen young ones in the care of a couple of older girls. One of them waved to me. 'We're just going to the beach, Mr Smith!'

Automatically, I took out my pocket watch. 'Be careful of the tide – half an hour, it'll be coming in.'

'We will!'

They were well-intentioned, but I didn't trust them entirely. Going indoors I called to Eleanor from the front hall, saying I was going to have a walk, keep my eye on them. Closing the gate, I looked back at the long white Regency terrace: fifteen years of our lives had been invested here. Mel had never lived anywhere else. It seemed too cruel to drag her away.

In her withdrawing of warmth and approval, Ellie had been making her feelings clear for months, while I'd felt badly-used and resentful. It seemed all our domestic difficulties hinged upon the forthcoming move. The argument went round and round in my head, but every time I considered turning down the new route and staying in Liverpool, my desire for new ships, new challenges, won the day. Ambition had always fired me, and in the past Ellie had approved of that. She loved greeting me when I came ashore: enjoyed the excitement and euphoria of each safe return. It kept our love alive.

212

With each new liner she was keen to come aboard, see my quarters and the bridge, just so – as she said – she could imagine me there, doing my job and doing it well. She was proud of me, she often said so. It kept me going, refuelled my enthusiasm, made me want to find new challenges to conquer, just to see that sparkle in her eye. She'd reaped the rewards, too. She couldn't just tell me to stop, take a step back. It wasn't fair. More to the point, it wasn't me.

Wedged in a cleft stick, I did not know what to do. Perhaps, as my daughter suggested, I should leave them here? It would mean travelling at either end of every voyage – a compromise that left me slack with dismay – but it was beginning to look like the only way forward. I missed Ellie, missed her badly. The Eleanor I was living with seemed another woman entirely, one who had taken all warmth into herself, leaving me out in the cold.

Preparing for bed that night, I tried not to think of the following day. Another Atlantic crossing, six days in New York, and then another week back again. I was tired – wearied, in truth – not so much by the challenges aboard, but by the trials at home. I hoped, tonight, that Eleanor wouldn't turn away. It had been a long time and I wanted her so much. Wanted to know we were still one, and not poles apart.

To my surprise, she pushed back the heavy curtains and raised the blind. The warm afternoon had changed, and half a gale was rattling the window. Frigid air chilled us both. I wondered what was wrong.

'Look out there,' she said at last. 'Can you see them?'

Bending, I could see our faces and the candle's flame reflected in the glass. Moving closer, blocking out the room, I spied navigation lights beyond the darkness of the dunes. 'Ships passing...'

'Yes.' She turned and looked at me. 'You know, Ted, I watch them coming and going in all weathers. I think of you, and I pray for you – especially nights like this, when I cannot sleep for wondering how you are, and what...' As her voice caught, she took a deep breath and turned away. 'When I'm wondering what trials you're facing...'

Feeling bad, I laid a hand on her shoulder. 'Ellie...'

'I'm afraid, Ted,' she said bleakly, looking up at me. 'Time goes by so quickly, you're no sooner home than you're away again...and it seems to me we're like those ships – just passing. Sending signals when half the time nobody's looking.'

'Don't say that, Ellie, please...'

'It's how it is, Ted. You have your ships – I have my life here. If we were moving to Southampton to be together, I'd go – willingly. Anything to be with you…' She turned, and came into my arms, her eyes pleading. 'I'm just afraid to be alone in a strange place. Not knowing anyone. Starting again, like it was when we first came to Liverpool – that's how it will be. Can't you see that?'

I said yes, I understood – and it was true, I did. Here she had friends, the support of other wives whose husbands also worked for White Star. Southampton was new territory; it would take years to build the kind of life she had here in the village. It hurt, but I was beyond trying further persuasion: I knew I had to leave them here. We made up and we made love, and it was intense and heart-breaking, like a last farewell, as though next day's leaving was for the far side of the world.

Neither of us slept well, and I was aware at one point that she'd risen and gone downstairs. But in the morning, just as I'd kissed my daughter's solemn face and waved her on her way to school, Ellie came softly to my side.

'Have we time for a walk?' she asked. I nodded and she called the dog. After last night's storm it was a fine, if windy, morning with white horses racing in the Estuary. Watching the brown and buff sails of vessels bouncing across the waves, I thought of my passengers and hoped they were good sailors.

We passed the Ismays' old house with its view of the green Wirral and the headlands of North Wales beyond. I wondered what old Mr Thomas's reaction would have been to this new move. It was important for the company, but did I really want it? Logic said yes; but, recalling last night, I was suddenly unsure.

'It's not really fair, is it?' Ellie said suddenly. 'Of course the whole thing's unfair, Ted, but I couldn't sleep last night for thinking about it.

'I mean the practical side of things,' she added, meeting my quizzical gaze. 'I know you've been saying it for months, but I got the Bradshaw out and checked the journey myself. You're right, it will take 4 trains and the entire day to get from here to Southampton Docks.' As I nodded, hardly daring to breathe, she went on, 'And of course, as soon as you board, you'll have the ship to take out to sea… Or perhaps you'll have to travel the day before, cutting short your leave? So I thought – realised,' she added sadly, 'that it was wrong of me to expect you to do that.'

Disbelieving for a moment, I had to ask her to explain, and when she said, 'Well, there's nothing for it, we'll just have to move – all of us,' I was so relieved I couldn't speak. For a moment, as she gazed at me, tensely waiting on my reply, I couldn't even move. But then I did, enfolding her silently in my arms.

Very quickly, we started looking for a home in Southampton. Although we would have loved something similar to the house at Waterloo, with views of the sea and open country to hand, it was not to be. Having turned several down, almost at the last minute we were shown a house on the northern edge of town, just a few years old, large with every modern convenience, close to Southampton's wooded Common, yet within a few minutes' walk of shops on the Portswood Road. The house, red brick with gables and turrets and deep bay windows, was much bigger than our old home. It was also more expensive, but with its large, private garden at the rear – terraced and south-facing – it was the best we'd seen.

I worried that it was too big, that Mel and Ellie would rattle round in such a place, but, 'I love the bathroom,' Ellie breathed. 'Imagine – a shower-bath! And water-closets upstairs and down – what luxury!' She looked up at me with shining eyes. 'Oh, Ted – could we?'

With more than a dozen rooms it would cost a fortune to heat the place, but it was the brightest smile I'd seen on Ellie's face for months. The asking price was just affordable, although it would take most of our savings and I hated not to have money behind me. On the other hand I wanted her to be happy. For what felt like an age the pros and cons went back and forth in my head, while Ellie fairly bounced with expectation. At last my anxiety burst forth into laughter. 'Yes,' I said, shaking my head at the folly, 'yes, of course we will...'

Having handed over my old command, I prepared myself for a journey to Belfast. While I stood by for the final few weeks of the new ship's fitting out, Ellie was packing for the move south.

I got home in time for moving day. The house we'd loved was as bare as the day we bought it. Taking a final look round, somehow it felt very sad, as though we were leaving our best years behind. In what had been our bedroom, looking down at the neat little park with the untamed dunes beyond, for a moment I wondered what we were doing. All these years I'd lived within sight and sound of the sea. It seemed inconceivable that I should give it up.

'I shall miss this.'

'Me too,' Ellie confessed.

'I hope we've made the right decision,' I muttered, turning to take her in my arms.

'Why, Ted,' she whispered, 'of course we have.' But she couldn't quite meet my eyes when she said it, and a moment later I saw her wiping away tears.

Despite my forebodings, we became familiar with our new home. If Mel and the family dog missed their daily frolics on the beach, at least our garden here was much bigger and more secluded. We were surrounded by trees, and when Ellie suggested naming the house *Woodhead*, after the Penningtons' farm, I wasn't sure if she was really reminded of her childhood home, or because she was homesick.

Between trips, with Mel, we took advantage of train rides through the New Forest, and I must say, compared to the rather austere watering places of the Lancashire coast, the quaint little port of Lymington had an old-world charm that captured us both. Even better, from there we could take the ferry to Yarmouth on the Isle of Wight; and, as Ellie said with a teasing smile, that was *almost* like going abroad.

As for me, that summer, each time we came up Southampton Water, I found the intense greens of the woodland on either hand a kind of shock to eyes attuned to the tones of blue and grey. It was a pleasure, a tonic, uplifting to the spirit.

I grew used to the new ship, the new port, the new passage in and out. Passing the Hamble with its fishing boats, and the Royal Hospital at Netley, I often thought of *Majestic* and my time in South Africa. It seemed such a short time since, and yet, as I fingered my service medals I realised it was almost ten years ago. Time seemed to be speeding up. Certainly, between voyages, my days off flew past like swifts on the wing. Before we knew it, we were celebrating Mel's tenth birthday and our first anniversary in the new house.

Ellie took frequent trips home to begin with, but gradually the visits became less. She and Mel settled in, made new friends. Life was sweet.

But then came *Olympic*, and with it a class of ships named to evoke the gods of ancient Greece. Olympians, Titans, masters of the universe. Grand in name, grand in concept; but like many such ideas it came to birth at a bad time. The world was in recession. The fight for domination of the Atlantic trade was increasingly centred on profit and loss. Faced by commercial rivalries, Bruce Ismay, backed by JP Morgan, was determined to grab the world's attention. This new class would be bigger and better than anything else afloat. The rich and famous would clamour for tickets, eager to be seen and photographed against backdrops so luxurious their friends would scarce believe they were afloat. Gods indeed. With White Star's best crews working night and day to maintain the illusion.

At 45,000 gross tons, *Olympic*, the first of the new trio on order, would be almost double the tonnage of the previous Big Four. By far and away the biggest ship in the world, she was already on the drawing board before they thought to consult the men who would be handling her. My early effervescence quickly gave way to a not inconsiderable anxiety.

It came down to some very practical and unromantic issues. I had to explain to Bruce – and to Lord Pirrie in Belfast – that the increase in length and depth presented their own peculiar problems. Handling something so big would be a huge challenge, for me as well as the pilots. The approaches to most ports were generally along narrow channels, dredged to keep them clear. As it was, Southampton's Bramble and New York's Sandy Hook required some tricky navigation to avoid grounding. A new vessel with much deeper draft would be looking for a lot of dredging. Port dues would be more expensive.

Then there was the length of the berth to consider. Not a problem at the new White Star dock in Southampton, but Pier 59 in New York was only just big enough to accommodate the current big liners. Discharging passengers and cargo from a vessel whose proposed length was close to 300 yards from stem to stern would be impossible from the present pier. The New York Dock Commissioners would have to be consulted; although as far as I understood it, the ultimate decision rested with the US War Department.

'And if they refuse?' Bruce demanded, suddenly anxious because he hadn't given that aspect much thought.

'Well, we might have to move.'

'Where to?'

I shrugged. 'Brooklyn, probably.'

'Brooklyn?' It might have been Outer Mongolia.

'Or Staten Island.'

'Oh, *please*, EJ, be serious.'

'I am, sir.'

'No, it won't do. We *must* remain on the Hudson – our passengers won't tolerate having to travel into town from such outlandish places…'

Such matters were perhaps not the concern of Harland and Wolff – their job, after all, was simply to build a seaworthy vessel. But Bruce's conviction that he just had to express a wish and all would fall into place infuriated me. I knew my job, and I knew the officials of the Port of New York. White Star was just one company amongst dozens. They would not be told, by Bruce Ismay or even JP Morgan, what they must or must not do. Applications would have to be submitted with due formality, and in good time.

I knew it would be a last minute job. The unresolved situation made my blood boil. I would be the one held to account if things didn't go well for the maiden voyage. There we were, with the world's biggest ship in the final stages of her fitting out, and across in New York the new pier – for which we had *temporary* permission only – was just begun.

By the beginning of May, 1911, I had spent the greater part of two months standing by ashore, dividing my time between Southampton and Belfast. Discussing draft depths and dredging with George Bowyer and the Harbour Master at one end, and getting to know the ins and outs of this massive new ship at the other. Cargo holds, lifting gear, winches, anchors, chain lockers, capstans; fresh water tanks, pipes and electricity circuits; cold rooms, dry stores, galleys and laundries, Royal Mail post rooms and crew accommodation, all to be checked and fixed like a mental map. New navigation instruments to be installed, telegraphs to test and compasses to correct, maintenance manuals to read and certification to be sure of.

The Chief Engineer was with me, and two White Star Superintendents – but, as we kept saying, *Olympic* was a huge ship, 882 feet long and immensely deep. 'Who needs the gym and Turkish bath?' was a regular complaint as one or other of us arrived, gasping, having climbed nine decks and innumerable flights of stairs from the engine room to the bridge. The alleyways seemed to go on for miles.

Sailing day – the 31st of May – was getting closer, and the date for the maiden voyage, two weeks later, was already emblazoned across every major newspaper in the known world. Pictures were appearing in illustrated periodicals, showing *Olympic* in various stages of completion, her iron hull painted white to show more clearly on the photographs. She was a graceful ship with long, elegant lines and a lovely 18th century stern, and I couldn't wait to get these interminable preparations over. After all the hard work I wanted some pleasure, to get away to sea, discover how she would handle.

It didn't help that Bruce was fretting like an expectant father, suddenly afraid that his civic welcome in New York would be spoiled by unsightly scaffolding on an unfinished pier. Meanwhile he was busily contacting Lord Mayors' offices and organising grand send-offs from both Liverpool and Southampton. As if that were not enough, additional pressure was suddenly applied by the threat of a general strike. And the heart of the trouble was being fomented in Liverpool.

The day we sailed from Belfast for our courtesy visit to *Olympic's* port of registry, the new Transport Workers Federation held a massive demonstration, marching through the city to St George's Hall. The Sailors and Firemen's Union, together with the Union of Ships' Stewards, Cooks, Butchers and Bakers had called a strike and the TWF was calling for the support of *all* transport workers. The march was evidently a ploy to attract publicity just as a civic welcome for White Star's grand new liner was going on. Certainly it took the edge off things, and needless to say, Bruce was furious. You'd have thought it was personal.

It was certainly cleverly organised. But there was a vast amount of trouble that day, and with a hand-picked crew we only just managed to escape the consequences.

A few days later, on the 14th of June, with the aid of 5 tugs, our pilot, George Bowyer, took us gingerly, stern first, out of Southampton's White Star dock. I was with him every inch, but he was so careful I did begin to wonder whether we'd ever get under way. Finally we did. With all Southampton and half the world's press turned out to cheer us, the excitement was overwhelming; and with every ship in the harbour sounding as we turned and moved forward, it seemed the noise would raise the dead.

As everyone said, the view from the bridge was like gazing down from Mount Olympus. I looked back to see the old walled heart of the city spread out like one of those medieval maps, dotted with towers and spires. Steaming down Southampton Water in daylight was another new experience: everything seemed so much smaller. We took the turns around Calshot Spit and the Bramble like a duchess curtseying to royalty. Ahead, on the Isle of Wight, Cowes, with its hundreds of onlookers, looked like Lilliput as we came round into the Solent.

Friends of ours had driven Ellie and Mel down to Stokes Bay, from where they could see the extraordinary array of warships gathered in the eastern channel at Spithead. We were only a matter of three weeks away from the Coronation of our new king, George V, and in the last week, while we had been taking on stores and cargo, dozens upon dozens of British and foreign warships had been arriving at the anchorage between Portsmouth and the Isle of Wight for the Coronation Review. More were yet to arrive, but the sight was already awe-inspiring. George had warned me, but for a moment I simply gaped; and then he said: 'Hope they've left us room to get past...'

Mr Murdoch, my 1st Officer, had drilled the most junior deck officer in the etiquette of salutes between naval and merchant vessels. It was a pleasant formality, generally. But in this instance there were rather a lot of navy ships before us.

'Right, young man,' I said to the 6th Officer standing just a few feet away, 'off you go. Don't forget – you dip our ensign first, and don't you dare raise it again until the other fellow's dipped and raised his...'

'Yes, sir. Every single one, sir – Mr Murdoch said, sir.'

'Off you go, then.' I couldn't help but smile as he hurried away.

George chuckled. 'You'll need new ropes by the time you've saluted this lot, Captain!'

'Worth it, though!'

I was as proud as the King himself as we progressed between the rows of warships at anchor. With whistles blowing their distinctive *whoop-whoop*, every single one responded to the dipping of our blue ensign, ratings stood to attention as we passed, the officers saluting. Our passengers were out in force on every deck, their voices a wordless babble of excitement. This was a maiden voyage with all the extras.

Looking through binoculars towards the Island, I could see Ryde, thronged with onlookers, while across on the Portsmouth side the crowds were almost as thick. I searched for Mel and Ellie; suddenly, right on Gilkicker Point I spotted the open-topped car, bonnet gleaming in the sunshine, with figures standing up and waving. I waved back, hoping they could see me, knowing they'd be thrilled by this display of courtesy to a wonderful new ship.

As we reached the Nab, George Bowyer left us, his handclasp warm and firm. 'Have a safe voyage, Captain.'

'Thank you, Mr Bowyer...'

Watching the pilot cutter drop back and the warships recede as we picked up speed, I heard Mr Ismay call me from a few yards away on the Boat Deck. As was his privilege, he was making this maiden voyage with us.

'We won't be able to lay this spread on again, more's the pity.'

I looked at him, still thinking of George and the admirable job he'd done, easing 45,000 tons of ship and cargo around the inverted S of the Bramble, not to mention our slow passage before all those warships.

'The Coronation, EJ – the Naval Review. Can't arrange one of those for every new ship, you know...'

I told myself that Bruce was Bruce and tried hard not to wish him over the side.

Maiden voyages can be difficult, I knew that from experience, and the sheer size of *Olympic* was a problem. The crew – sailors and firemen alike – kept getting lost, while the stewards – our front line where passengers were concerned – seemed to take an age to find their way around. Bruce was annoyed by the number of complaints.

To balance that, with mainly fair weather and little fog, we averaged just short of 23 knots on the crossing. A speed to be proud of. Arriving early off Sandy Hook, we picked up the pilot at first light, and took the turn into the Ambrose Channel with care. While our passengers were enjoying their breakfasts we proceeded in stately fashion through the Narrows, which since my previous trip seemed so much narrower, as though a giant had been out and pulled Brooklyn and Staten Island together. I was sweating like a man in a fever by the time we got through. Fortunately, I'd cooled off by the time we reached the Quarantine Anchorage. Port Health officials boarded; and with the crew examined and cleared, we were able to proceed to Manhattan.

Passing Liberty and Ellis Islands as our First and Second Class passengers were being cleared, fifteen minutes later we were passing the Castle and Battery Park. At the foot of Broadway, where the old shipping offices had stood for most of my life, I could see the bulk of the new US Customs House, flanked by a variety of tall buildings. Like foamy waves, crowds of cheering sightseers lined the shore, eager to greet *Olympic*, the world's biggest and greatest ship. Overwhelmed, we felt like gods indeed.

Like a royal procession, with horns and whistles blowing, *Olympic* headed a following of tugs and small boats up the Hudson River to White Star's Pier 59. The pilot had assured me it was fine, but it wasn't until I saw the pier for myself – looking complete and perfectly sound – that I was entirely convinced. Coming in, amidst orders being called back and forth, I prayed we wouldn't disturb so much as an inch of its paintwork as the tugs nudged us gently alongside.

Against the barriers a great crowd was waving and jostling, impatient for us to tie up.

Avid with friendship and curiosity, they flooded around the passengers as they disembarked, almost as though they would swallow them whole. Watching from the bridge, a strange sensation seized me. Maybe it was relief. Maybe I was simply overtired – it had been a long night on the bridge – but needing time to recover my balance I felt unnerved by all that humanity. I longed to escape, but as soon as US Customs and Port Officials were done, newspapermen flocked aboard. For the next hour or so, at least a dozen of these scribblers were constantly on hand.

'How many dinners do you serve, sir, on an average day?' This to Hugh Latimer, the Chief Steward.

'Sir – Captain Smith – how far do you walk to conduct your daily inspections?'

'Well,' I replied, 'at a sixth of a mile long, and taking into account our walks fore and aft, and up and down eight decks, I should think we walk two or three miles at least – although we haven't actually measured it. Keeps us fit!' I said with a smile; but while O'Loughlin and McElroy indulged in their usual witty repartee, I longed for the privacy of my quarters.

One fellow, having asked about the ship's dimensions, went on to press about lifeboats and safety at sea, and how would we deal with, say, a collision in fog, which had claimed so many lives in the past. I don't recall the questions exactly, or quite how I replied, but I was reminded of how – thanks to the modern miracle of wireless – passengers on the *Republic* had all been saved after a recent collision. The Master escaped with his life just before she went down. I'd been standing by aboard *Baltic* as his passengers were brought into New York.

That extraordinary story had captured the attention of the world's press, and I wanted to emphasise the progress we'd made in recent years. Also, I'd just been given command of the world's newest and biggest liner. The modern design, with watertight compartments in the engine room, was just another step forward in shipbuilding.

Maybe I was too confident in my reply. Next day, in black-and-white, I was reported as having said, *'Modern shipbuilding has gone beyond the absolute disasters of yesteryear,'* and, *'Whatever happens, there will be time enough before the vessel sinks to save the life of every person on board...'*

Whatever happens? I never said that – I was still seaman enough and superstitious enough not to tempt fate with such a statement. Re-reading the piece, I wanted to grab the idiot who'd written it and give him a good talking-to.

'It'll be wrapping tomorrow's hot dogs,' McElroy said easily, 'don't let it bother you, sir. They write what they please and call it news.'

'But folk believe it,' I retorted. 'How often have you heard a man utter complete nonsense, before telling you it must be true, he read it in the paper!'

But newspaper coverage was good for business, as Bruce Ismay was never slow to point out. Americans had evidently taken to this new ship. Our passengers for the return journey were almost twice the number we'd had coming out, and when it came time to leave we were given a marvellous send-off. Thousands lined the sidewalks along the Hudson, and Battery Park saw thousands more, waving flags, handkerchiefs, scarves. It was a tremendous sight, giving a great boost of pride and confidence and satisfaction. I hoped enough of the crew could see it: after all their trials on the way out, they deserved this accolade.

Back home it was a different story. By the time we arrived in Southampton, the Shipping Federation had caved in and acquiesced to the seamen's demands, but then the dockers went on strike, followed by the railwaymen, making travel impossible. That hot summer of 1911 was a nightmare of discontent. According to the newspapers, revolution was in the air. It was easy to believe. In Liverpool in August men took to the streets again, the Riot Act was read, police were armed and troops called out. It was all rather ugly, a minor war in fact, with several strikers brutally attacked and killed.

Ellie's sympathy was rekindled. She knew how poor these families were, even with a man in work – without, their situation was unthinkable. I had been used to taking a tougher attitude, my argument being that I'd come from nothing and pulled myself up by my bootstraps – so why couldn't the rest of mankind? But Ellie insisted that the value of what people earned had gone down, while the cost of living had gone up.

'Even I can see the difference in what we spend, and we're not poor.'

'No wonder costs have risen,' I retorted, 'when the dockers won't lift a finger and food is rotting on the quays. If that's not a sin, I don't know what is. Do you know we're having to load food at Cherbourg? There isn't enough in Southampton to complete a stores list. Of any quality, that is.'

That stopped the debate. 'Really, Ted? But that's terrible.'

'Yes, it is. Worrying. Time the government got it sorted out.'

The government was battling it out, but no sooner was peace achieved in one part of the country, than disputes and rioting broke out elsewhere. Everyone remarked on the use of guns; even our American visitors were unsettled by the belligerent atmosphere in the country as a whole.

Come September, two trips later, in the midst of worrying about strikes and stores and diminishing passenger numbers, something happened which blew all else to the distant horizon. Just as we made that turn by the Bramble, out of the haze off Cowes appeared a warship, *HMS Hawke*. And that was where my career, largely uneventful, began to take on a different hue.

27

The 20th of September, 1911. The date was etched on my memory. In that collision with HMS Hawke, Olympic suffered grievous damage. It took two weeks to patch her up enough to get to Belfast and dry-dock, and another six weeks to do the repairs. Worse, in a difficult year, was the expense to the company in time and revenue and reputation. What I failed to understand at the time was the personal cost.

For weeks, while *Olympic* was under repair, I felt as though there had been a death in the family. Eleanor tried her best, but not even she could fully understand my grief and remorse. I felt I'd let myself and every shipmate down.

'The biggest ship in the world and a Royal Navy cruiser – a collision on our own front doorstep!' My bitter exclamations must have driven Ellie mad. 'Laughable if it wasn't so bloody serious!'

'You mustn't worry,' she kept saying. 'They can't blame you – it wasn't your fault.' Logically, she was right – it wasn't. Nor George Bowyer's either. But that was beside the point. It had happened.

Dumbfounded, I kept going over it. *Why* hadn't *Hawke* crossed astern of us when she had the chance? George, Wilde, Murdoch, all said the same. It was what *we* would have done in similar circumstances. What each and all of us had done on innumerable occasions in the past. It was not just safe practice, it was common sense. You see a big ship in a tight manoeuvre, you give her a bit of space. She's bigger than you, she can't just *stop* in a seaway with all that force behind her. With years of experience you just know the sensible thing to do. Keep clear. Do the safe thing. Give her a bit of leeway.

And her commander wouldn't even have had to slow down. That was the crazy thing. He could have altered to port, passed astern, and continued directly to Portsmouth.

Why hadn't he? What in hell was he trying to prove? That His Majesty's Navy had right of way, no matter what?

A strict interpretation of the *Rules* might suggest that we should have slowed to let him past. Fair enough, two small ships in that situation could have obeyed the relevant rule to the letter – but we were not a small cruiser. *Olympic* was huge, and the navigable channel was narrow.

Trying to stop – or even slow – in a sharp turn can be dangerous. You need speed to get round – to push water under the keel and over the propellers. Without it, any ship is difficult to manoeuvre. In those circumstances, slowing down could have put us up on the Bramble Bank. Or aground off Egypt Point.

A professional seaman would have understood that.

The official enquiry began on 17th November and went on for a week. I imagined it would be in Portsmouth, but the Admiralty tries its cases in the Royal Courts of Justice, a huge Gothic building on the Strand. George Bowyer, with Wilde, Murdoch, the Chief Engineer and myself, had been up to London previously to consult with the solicitors acting for White Star, so we were prepared for the ordeal. But on the day, faced with a cathedral almost, I think we were all quaking.

The case was heard before the Right Honourable Sir Samuel Evans, Solicitor General and President of the Court, sitting with Captains Thomson and Crawford, both Elder Brethren of Trinity House. The ancient guild had evolved to become the country's pilotage authority and maintainer of lights around our coasts. Trinity House also happened to be George's employer.

The Oceanic Steam Navigation Company Limited – White Star's company name – was the plaintiff, suing for damages from Commander Blunt, RN, for faulty navigation. The Admiralty was the elephant behind the mouse, of course. Blunt could hardly have afforded to pay the fees of the man they bagged for the defence: Sir Rufus Isaacs, Attorney-General.

Nor did it help me that the leading King's Counsel for White

Star was a Mr Laing. Not the same spelling as Dorothea's name, but whenever he was referred to I could not help but make some unsettling associations.

The bare facts of the case were indisputable. Blunt had inexplicably turned his ship to port and rammed *Olympic* in her starboard quarter. What was at issue was how and why the collision had occurred. It depended on an interpretation of the *Rules and Regulations for the Prevention of Collision at Sea*. In essence, which of us was the overtaking vessel, and thus bound to keep out of the other's way. To my mind that was *HMS Hawke*. But the defence claimed that Blunt was not attempting to overtake, that we were steaming too close and that *Olympic*'s size and speed had caused *Hawke* to be sucked in by the wash.

White Star's case rested on when and where *Hawke* was first sighted, and how we were navigating the confines of the deep-water channel leading from Southampton Water, around the Bramble Bank, and into the eastern Solent. These facts had been presented to the court earlier, backed up by log books and charts illustrating the relative positions.

I was the first witness. Called from the anteroom I felt the queasiness of nerves. Like taking my Master's Certificate over again, I thought. Until I went in.

If the outside of that imposing building was like a cathedral, the court put me in mind of a Puritan chapel: wood panelling and box-like pews, the bench itself a high, broad pulpit from which sinners could more effectively be damned. Climbing up to the witness box, preparing to give evidence before the red-robed President and uniformed Elder Brethren, was daunting. Being questioned was doubly so, even by a bewigged Mr Laing, the man on our side.

Two months had passed since that fateful day, and I prayed that memory would not let me down. Allowing for nervousness, Mr Laing took me through the events outlined in our plea, enabling me to present the situation as clearly as I could recall.

Having taken me easily through various points and positions, Mr Laing moved on to the question of time-keeping. I confirmed that both bridge and engine room worked with electric clocks, synchronised from the ship's master clock. 'And do they record seconds, or do they jump?'

'They jump once every minute.'

That turned out to be an important point in the assessment of speed. Speed was a question that his opponent, the Attorney General, was to return to, over and over again. As was the following question:

'Where was the cruiser when you first saw her?'

I could see *Hawke* in my mind's eye: a slim grey shape cutting the foam as she came up from the west. We had rounded Calshot Spit and were on the straight between the North Thorn buoy and Thorn Knoll, slowing for our turn around the West Bramble. It was 12:40 pm. *Hawke* was almost directly ahead of us.

'Three to four miles away,' I said. 'From half a point to a point, I should think, on our port bow.' I noticed the Elder Brethren glance at each other, as if to say *Hawke*'s commander should have allowed us a bit of sea-room in such a situation. The red-robed President was making notes.

'Was she coming up the Solent Channel?' I confirmed that she was. 'And your steamers come out by which channel?'

'By the east channel,' I said.

Mr Laing had the facts to hand, enabling me to give simple affirmatives to his short, clear questions. Yes, we rounded the West Bramble Buoy to get onto our course; and yes, we were keeping to the deep-dredged channel. I said that we gave two short blasts on the hooter, the regulation signal for a turn to port.

'Can you give me the time you steadied on your course?'

'About 12:43.'

'Are you able to tell me from your personal observation where the *Hawke* was at 12:43?'

We had completed our turn. *Hawke* was now astern of us and coming up fast. The last I'd seen of *Hawke*, I said, just as we steadied on our course, she was about 2½ points on our starboard quarter, about half a mile away.

Again, I caught a glance between the Trinity House men. No doubt their thoughts echoed mine: that was the point where *Hawke* could have altered her course slightly to port and passed safely astern of us. Safely on her way to Portsmouth.

'Had you any anxiety at that time?'

'Not at all.' I hadn't, not then. I went on under questioning to say that *Hawke* had continued to overhaul us until she was almost abreast of our bridge, running a parallel course. She had continued for some appreciable time to keep up. Then, either our speed increased or she dropped astern – which was it? the President interjected, but I couldn't say.

'Either way,' I said, 'we gained on her, and immediately afterwards her

228

bow came to port, she turned very quickly, and struck us on the stern.'

'And had you heard any signals from *Hawke*?' the President asked. 'Did she sound her whistle to signify that she was turning?'

'No, sir.'

As to our speed and position when she struck, I said about 15 or 16 knots, and we were abreast of East Cowes at the time. I said I could not fix our position by the Prince Consort Buoy, because *Hawke* obscured my view of it.

Having elicited my opinion, that there was plenty of room for *Hawke* to have passed on either side of us, Mr Laing sat down. I felt myself relax, confident that I had presented the situation clearly and honestly. It was then the turn of the Attorney-General, and the whole situation had to be gone over again.

Sir Rufus Isaacs was tall and thin-faced with penetrating eyes. Pleasant enough to begin with, but despite that smooth manner he was a man with a rapier mind. And like a swordsman he switched back and forth between aspects of the case with the intention to trip and confuse. He went back and back – and back again – over the smallest point. The clever way he twisted the estimates appalled me.

'Let me understand what you say was your maximum speed – is it 22-23 knots?' As I said 22½ , he went on, 'You were going full speed, of course, with all your engines?'

I had already stated to the court that we were on reduced steam, making easy way, but he made it sound as though we were ripping along at full ocean speed, when in fact we had just rounded the Bramble on something like half. But I had to remember not to argue. We had been warned beforehand to answer the questions directly without protest.

'Yes,' I said.

After a raft of questions about the various buoys we were negotiating, he said, 'I just want to know, generally, how long does it take, if you are making a speed of 11 or 12 knots, and then give the order for full speed ahead – how long will it be before you reach your full speed?'

'Well,' I replied, wondering where this was heading, 'we've never had any experiments of that kind, but I should think probably three or four minutes.'

Checking his papers, he asked pleasantly, 'According to the statement in the Pleadings, *Olympic* was going 16 knots at the time of the collision, do you agree that?' *I agreed.* 'At the time of the collision you were drawing ahead of the *Hawke*?' *Yes.* 'Of course you were a very much larger vessel?' *Yes.* 'Did you observe her carefully?'

There'd been no reason to. We had been in *Hawke*'s view for several minutes. I expected she would keep clear. 'No,' I said. 'After we steadied on our course and she was on our quarter I turned round and looked forward.' To see we were steering true, I might have added, but he was already asking the next question.

'How long before the collision was it that you observed her again?'

'Some little time.' Unable to give it exactly, I said, 'Probably a minute or so.'

'So how fast were you going, when she was coming up very quickly on you?'

I caught a glance from one of the Elder Brethren. 'It's very hard to say. Our speed was increasing all the time.'

He pursued it, but the questions were too vague – precisely when, where and at what moment did he mean? Even the judge, wearing a frown, intervened to make the question clear. So I gave an estimate of maybe 14 knots when we steadied on our course – but then, hard on that, Sir Rufus Isaacs wanted to know what speed I thought the *Hawke* was doing. Pressed, I said maybe a knot and a half faster.

Next he handed me a chart, asking me to mark where I thought *Hawke* was at that moment. I hesitated then marked it to half a mile distant from what I'd given – two months ago – as our position at the time. That opened a convoluted back-and-forth series of questions about the Bramble Bank. Exactly *when* did I consider *Olympic* to have been abeam of the West Bramble Buoy?

I felt the sympathy of the Trinity House men at that impossible question. I hoped they'd explain to the judge that ships do not follow a set of wheels, they move crabwise in a turn, and what would be a circle for a cart is more of an ellipse for a ship – elastic too, being subject to the effects of wind and tide. Every passage is different – they knew that. But the Attorney General wanted it exactly. He had me demonstrate with ship models on the chart where I thought we were. Then, having pinned me down to his satisfaction, he turned to the question of time, managing to prove – apparently – that I was mistaken in my estimate of a half mile distance between *Olympic* and *Hawke*. With only nine minutes to play with, he claimed she must have been closer than I thought.

A lifetime's experience of judging distances at sea was not enough. Log books were consulted afresh, charts were studied and marked and studied again. While the President – a landsman, after all – peered at the evidence and strived to follow the point, I lost count of the times the Attorney General repeated, 'I just want to get clear...' while proceeding to confuse everyone.

This issue of time and speed, position and distance, went on interminably. I bit my lip so hard and so often it's a wonder I didn't spit blood. Complex questions were fired, one after the other, as if absolutes were possible. The exact time of the first sighting; our precise speed at that precise moment; were we gaining or losing speed during the manoeuvre? Question after question, warping around the facts of seamanship.

I wanted to ask if he knew of any ship with a facility for measuring speed under way? It was all very well for him to introduce mathematical possibilities, but you can only assess a ship's passage through the water by measuring the distance between two fixed points and dividing it by time. Taking into account the forces of wind and tide as we came first around Calshot Spit, and then the West Bramble, it was at best a flexible sum. I had a very good idea of our speed at the time of the collision, and said so. About 16 knots, I estimated, and stuck to it.

Well, he pursued that to its nth degree – trying to prove that we were proceeding with reckless disregard. I repeated forcibly that we were *getting up* to our speed in that area. Which was something rather less than the 20 knots he implied.

Before I could congratulate myself on making that point, the Attorney-General switched without warning to the question of headings, suggesting that if we were on the course S59ºE when we steadied, and *Hawke* was on S74ºE, we would be crossing vessels, according to the *Rules*.

What? I felt my wits were starting to flag. I couldn't see how that was possible. As the two Elder Brethren exchanged a glance, I did a hasty calculation. *Hawke*'s heading did not make sense to me, but I had to agree that we would indeed have been crossing vessels, had that been the case. With that claim, he was introducing a whole new argument.

I tensed, wondering what was coming next. But after a short pause my interrogator went back to the distance between us when *Hawke* was running abreast. I said it seemed perfectly safe; he pursued the point, suggesting I was mistaken and that our close proximity had caused *Hawke* to be drawn in by suction. Had I not considered this possibility?

'No,' I said. 'Absolutely not.' I could not believe he was introducing that argument as a cause of the collision. It was ludicrous.

When pressed about the effects of suction in confined areas, I agreed that if a vessel was particularly close I would be concerned. At that, the President admonished Sir Rufus for introducing theories into the argument. Changing tack, he returned to the issue of time. To the moment when I noticed *Hawke* had dropped back and was starting to turn. How long did it take from that observation to the moment she struck?

I could see it when I blinked, like a fragment of nightmare: *Hawke*'s stem dropping back, turning in, a great spume of foam leaping along her port side. Starboard side sweeping round, looming close – bridge, masts, funnels; guns angled as though for attack. Catastrophe inevitable.

'Under a minute,' I said, drawing breath. 'It seemed a long time, but under a minute.'

'It must have appeared to you the maddest thing possible for this vessel to have come round at that moment.'

I nodded. 'Inconceivable.'

What more was there to say? But the Attorney General had not finished. He drew my attention to the chart, and, like a swordsman cornering his victim, pressed that I might be a cable out – some 200 yards – in my estimate of the position. He seemed to be implying that *Olympic* was closer to where the channel shelved, and had thus given *Hawke* no sea-room.

I had no clear reference for the point of collision. All I could see was the cruiser's burgeoning shape, closing in by the second. Skewed by the impact, unable to stop dead, *Olympic* had ended up in Osborne Bay.

I said, 'I can only give my impression immediately beforehand.'

'Having regard to some fixed object?' the President asked.

'Yes, a general view – looking over Cowes Harbour.'

With that, to my surprise and relief, the Attorney-General nodded to the bench and sat down.

After a short but welcome adjournment, our KC, Mr Laing, returned to the fray, enabling me to state my long years of experience as a shipmaster. He asked whether I had noticed any effects of suction while traversing narrow channels in the past. I said not. He enquired the width of the Ambrose Channel, going into New York, and I said, 1,200 feet.

Looking mystified, the judge raised his pencil. 'Is it a channel between walls?'

The Elder Brethren chuckled. After a lifetime spent navigating that awkward stretch of water, I had a mad desire to laugh. 'No,' I said, 'it is a dredged channel.'

When Mr Laing resumed his seat, I hoped the interrogation was over, but then the President himself took up the enquiry, returning to all the vital points already made. He finished with the question of clocks and time. I repeated what I had said in the beginning, that our bridge clock jumped visibly from minute to minute. As did the engine room clock by which the engineers kept their log. Therefore, as the judge himself was at pains to make clear, our recorded time could be up to a minute out in every case. Which would mean an appreciable difference in the average speed as worked out by the Attorney-General.

'So when you put down 12:40,' the President said, 'that may be 55 seconds out?'

'Yes, sir.' *At last!*

'Or,' he added with the ghost of a smile, '5 seconds out only...?'

My spirits plummeted. Dismissed, I climbed down from the witness stand.

Passing George Bowyer going in, I wished him luck. In the waiting room my legs suddenly gave way and I almost fell into a chair. I looked at my watch and was astonished to find almost three hours had passed. Trying to light a cigar, I realised I was shaking like a man with palsy.

Next day it was the turn of *Olympic*'s officers, starting with Hobhouse, the young junior who'd been taking notes that day. I told him to stick to his guns, and not let them rattle him. It was the most I could do. Then there was an adjournment while the top brass went to the National Physical Laboratory in Teddington to watch some scientist's experiments on suction and displacement. Apparently it boiled down to laws of attraction and repulsion between the wakes and bow-waves of vessels of differing sizes. It was a fascinating point, explaining things I'd observed in the past – but somehow it failed to convince when distance came into the argument. Both George and I were adamant – there had been too great a gap involved to affect the *Hawke* in such a way.

Then it was the turn of Commander Blunt and his officers, counterclaiming that we had damaged their boat by excessive speed and faulty navigation. Sir Rufus Isaacs and his supporting legal brains were trying to prove that we were negligent, while making out that the RN officers were the true professionals because they had their answers pat.

A little too pat, if you ask me. I didn't hear their evidence, of course – one doesn't. But I read in *The Times* afterwards that their Navigating Officer lost his notebook through what he described as, *the shock of the collision*. How very convenient! I bet that caused some roars of laughter over the breakfast-tables of the world. Odd too that no one had written up their bridge log immediately after the event. We had our log, as well as knowledgeable, independent witnesses – both aboard and ashore – to describe what they saw: namely, that *Hawke* was running parallel and dropping back, before suddenly and inexplicably turning to port.

It was interesting to read that the 20-year-old cruiser had just come out of refit and was undergoing speed tests on the day of the collision. The Navigating Officer was on loan from some other ship, and Blunt, a destroyer man, had only recently been assigned to *Hawke*. The speed trial was their first trip together. And their first acquaintance with the cruiser.

They said their helm jammed. Maybe it did. Refits are notorious for leaving spanners in the works. But Blunt also said they were not attempting to overtake, and that we were steaming too close. Arrant nonsense. Blunt would not have it that he'd miscalculated or given a wrong order – or even that the helmsman had turned the wheel the wrong way. Furthermore, the Admiralty claimed we were the overtaking vessel and – by maritime rules – should have kept out of *Hawke*'s way.

But still I worried about that question of headings. George could scoff all he liked – and his reaction to the question of *Hawke*'s heading, S74°E, had caused merriment in the court – but nonsensical though it seemed, I felt threatened by it. *Crossing vessels*: if that was the way the argument was going, they could have us for not slowing down and allowing *Hawke* to pass.

28

Olympic's repairs were being completed as the court case ended. For White Star, speed was essential. Every day she was out of service, *Olympic* was losing money. To save time at Harland and Wolff, they raided the new sister ship – still fitting out in dry-dock – for spares, and diverted the work-force to the more immediate task. *Olympic*'s water-tight bulkheads and outer plating were repaired and the sister-ship's unused prop-shaft fitted. I remember thinking that this would cost time elsewhere. The next maiden voyage, due in March, would have to be delayed.

As *Olympic* came out of dry-dock, I travelled north to Liverpool and across to Belfast to take her out on trials before steaming back to Southampton for the next Atlantic crossing. By the end of November she was bunkered, stored, and loaded with cargo, ready to welcome the next set of passengers.

For many years we had operated a four-week schedule – roughly two weeks at sea and six days in port at either end. It was a rhythm that worked. It allowed for delays due to bad weather, it gave the people who crewed and ran the ships on a 24-hour basis, time to recover between voyages that were sometimes extremely difficult. And it gave ample time for cleaning and replenishment at either end. Bad weather not only slows the ship, it affects everyone from the Master to the lowliest galley-boy. And lack of sleep affects passengers too. Added to which, on the eastward journey, an hour is lost every day. Even on a relatively calm crossing that can result in fractious passengers and a worn out crew.

Maybe it was a necessary way of recouping the losses, but when White Star's board decided to change the four week rhythm in favour of a three weeks' round trip for the foreseeable future, it felt like they were taking a pound of flesh. Our liners were not Cunard's greyhounds, we were limited as to speed – and on the very first voyage we came straight out of Southampton into head-on gales. That trip was a slow, uncomfortable slog to New York. We did get blown back rather more speedily, but at both ends of the voyage we were left with just half a week to load bunkers, cargo and stores. It was a very tight schedule that didn't allow for unforeseen delays. On top of which the dockers didn't like having to work round the clock, while the crew wondered what they'd done to have seven days a month knocked off their shore leave.

Strikes? Ellie was ready to organise one herself.

I'd done one round trip and was preparing to set forth on the next when the verdict was delivered. It was 19th December. I got the news over the telephone from London.

It was a shock. Despite my fears and apprehensions, I had hoped that common sense would prevail. But, in his summing up, the President of the court had accepted conjecture as fact. He and the Elder Brethren found for the Admiralty, taking the view that the two ships were crossing vessels, and by such maritime rules, *Olympic* should have kept out of *Hawke*'s way. They even cited pilot George Bowyer as negligent in his navigation.

It didn't matter that the world's biggest ship could have ended up aground, blocking the main channel in and out of Southampton. His Majesty's Navy could not be seen to be in the wrong. That was the nub of it.

'Bloody rules!' I swore to Eleanor. 'Rules were made for the guidance of wise men, and the blind obedience of fools!'

I don't know what angered me most, the slur on George's reputation as one of the finest pilots it has ever been my good fortune to know, or the sheer bias of the finding.

The costs were massive. When Bruce Ismay came down to Southampton next day, he could barely speak for rage. But, as he ground out between clenched teeth, at least *Olympic* was under compulsory pilotage at the time. Chief Officer Wilde and myself

236

were not responsible in White Star's view; nor was George Bowyer, come to that.

'But we must be thankful for small mercies, EJ. At least we can blame the pilot and save White Star's reputation.'

'You can *never* blame the pilot,' I retorted. 'The pilot only ever tenders his advice. It's up to the master to accept it or reject it. I accepted it,' I added tersely. 'The *blame*, sir, rests with me.'

'Does it really, EJ? Well, don't let me hear you say that in front of a reporter!'

I'd been on my way out of the office, but I spun to face him. 'Do you want my resignation, Mr Ismay?'

For a moment I thought he was going to accept, but he lowered his gaze, the waxed moustache twitching as he pursed his lips. 'No, no, of course not – that's the last thing I need.' He looked up, light glinting in his eyes. 'White Star is supporting you, EJ – we stick together. Understood?'

It took a moment, but I nodded. 'Understood. Sir.'

White Star's reputation: that was all Bruce thought about. George Bowyer could have lost his job had Trinity House been so inclined. That they did not sack him said a lot.

The look on George's face; that travesty of justice; Bruce's self-centred concerns: I was reeling from a sense of betrayal. It seemed to me that all I had believed and trusted and worked for, the principles of honesty and right action by which I had lived, had just been thrown overboard.

I was getting old. My principles were no longer the common currency they used to be. I spoke to Eleanor about retirement.

'But not yet,' I said grimly as I was packing my things. 'I will *not* let these clever, conniving, truth-twisting blackguards destroy me!'

'You're right,' she whispered fiercely. 'How dare they!'

'I'll wait till I'm ready, Ellie – by God I will!'

She came to hug me and I held her tight, taking comfort from her strength, from her unquenchable belief in me. 'Just remember, dearest, everyone *knows* it wasn't your fault!'

'But a court of law said it was faulty navigation. That's damned hard to accept!'

The day I left was the day of the winter solstice, as short and gloomy as one might expect. In the dark before dawn I kissed my darling girls farewell, and – if only for form's sake – wished them a happy

Christmas. We were all wearing long faces.

Anger got me back on board and through the next trip to New York. Similarly, Wilde and Murdoch. Having thrashed it out over a couple of days – done our jeering, expressed our ridicule – after that the topic was barely mentioned. Except we were closer, somehow. Still professionals – always that – but, like good friends in adversity, they showed their sympathy in small ways. Considerate, kind, eager to spare me time on the bridge whenever possible. Billy O'Loughlin was clearly concerned; but in weather like that I couldn't take pills or medicine. A whisky before bed was as much as I dare risk. But as anger wore off and gave way to numbness, I felt exhausted.

Christmas Day 1911 was not particularly cold, although we were hammering into another gale. Tablecloths were damped down to prevent glassware and cutlery sliding; even so, a spectacular roll was often marked by a crash from some nearby pantry.

In my cabin, the books did a regular shunt against the batten holding them in; contents of drawers shifted back and forth; the wooden panelling squeaked in protest. I had so many slips of paper jammed in drawers and cupboards, my bedroom looked like a betting shop. But we could not slow down. With a deadline to meet we kept ploughing on, past Nantucket – no fog, heaven be praised – past Fire Island and on to Sandy Hook. All night on the bridge as usual, and finally to Pier 59. It was a relief to reach New York for a couple of nights' rest.

I hadn't forgotten the verdict: how could I? But I failed to consider its effects upon the maritime world. It sent shock waves everywhere: prompted heated debates for months. The number of napkins ruined by pencils drawing out the relative positions of our two ships must have run to hundreds. I'd ruined a few myself. Aboard *Olympic* I imagined it was still being discussed by passengers even as we docked, but if the decision was under appeal I had no faith in the outcome. As far as I was concerned it was over: the blame was on me, and that was that.

I did not wish to discuss it further, yet it was the one topic on everyone's lips. When JP Morgan's invitation to dinner arrived, I groaned inwardly. He would want the story from the horse's mouth, and in all conscience I could not refuse. It was with a heavy heart that I dressed the following evening.

Paintin, my steward, tried to cheer me. 'Never mind, sir – it'll be a good dinner at the Metropolitan, I'll be bound.'

238

'And a late night,' I grumbled as he fixed my waistcoat.

'Well, the good Doctor will see you home, sir, and you can lie in bed tomorrow.'

'You sound alarmingly like my wife, Paintin!'

He laughed. 'I do my best, sir.'

The story went that JP Morgan had founded the Metropolitan Club in '91 after certain of his newly-rich friends had been black-balled by the old-money Union Club. In response, JP had commissioned the eminent architect Stanford White to design the building. Whatever his outrageous private life – or perhaps because of it – Stanford White knew a thing or two about outward appearances. As Frank Millet once pointed out, seen from the Park, the Metropolitan's white marble exterior on 5th Avenue was as restrained and elegant as an Italian Renaissance palace; only the entrance on 60th Street gave an inkling of what it might be like inside.

Those wrought iron gates topped with gilded curlicues were high and wide, while the courtyard presented a barrier no uninvited person would dare to cross. Once inside it was a place to leave you slack-jawed with amazement. With its elaborate staircases, painted ceilings with clouds and cherubs, gilded pillars; dark portraits and classical landscapes, the interior had all of JP Morgan's taste for opulence. A taste he'd managed to impart to his newly-rich friends; and, more importantly, to Harland and Wolff's interior designers.

'Ostentatious, Frank Millet calls it,' I muttered to Billy as our cab pulled up. 'He reckons it's the kind of place that started the French Revolution...'

'Jaysus!' Billy exclaimed, laughing. 'After the summer we've had, he'd be wise to watch his tongue! Is he not a member?'

I shook my head. 'Oh, come on, Billy, Frank Millet's old money, he wouldn't be seen dead here!'

'Is that so? Well, sir, I don't know about you, but I'm not complaining...'

There had been unrest in America too, but amidst the opulence of New York's Metropolitan Club, the idea of insurrection seemed ridiculous. As our overcoats were taken, we were greeted by other guests in the lobby and ushered through to the lounge. Suddenly there were smiles and cheers.

Surprised, not a little confused, I looked over my shoulder to see who had followed us in. But no – the welcome appeared to be for us – no, for me. Billy's grin was as wide as the Brooklyn Bridge. He was in on the secret, that much was obvious – but until that moment I'd had no idea the dinner was being given in my honour. After a tiring voyage – after the trials I'd left in England – it was overwhelming. All the cheers and back-slapping, all the big smiles and *for-he's-a-jolly-good-fellow* bursts of song were almost too much. I could barely see for the salt in my eyes, could not speak for the lump of emotion lodged in my throat. It took a generous shot of bourbon to clear both, to enable me to do more than merely nod and smile. I think I swore under my breath as I dug Billy in the ribs, but all he would do was smile and nudge me towards the next man eager to shake my hand.

I spoke to most of the guests before we went upstairs to dinner, but later, when the speeches began, when it became clear that this sumptuous occasion had been organised as a – well, as a *vote of confidence* following the *Hawke* debacle – that almost unmanned me again. The court decision had been such a public embarrassment I had been truly afraid that people would believe we'd acted unprofessionally – worse, that I was somehow unfit and incompetent. This dinner assured me that the opposite was true. With the aid of another steadying drink I was able to say a few words of thanks. The words were heartfelt and perhaps fewer than some might have wished, but in the circumstances they were all I could manage.

29

Two days after the dinner, JP Morgan joined us for the return journey across the Atlantic, on his way to Egypt for the winter. We met up in my quarters a couple of times, but the weather was poor and he was not a good sailor. Mostly he remained in his suite, and mostly I was on the bridge or sleeping. Between the weather rolling us along and the loss of an hour each day, it was not a very sociable crossing for anyone. I doubt the other passengers realised he was aboard.

Blown back across the Atlantic, at home to recover my sleep for three nights, I heard that Commander Blunt of *HMS Hawke* had been promoted to Post Captain.

The news left me feeling quite sick. No time to dwell on it, however. On the 9th of January, we were at sea again.

It was relentless. Didn't matter that we gained an hour each day on the westward crossing, we were punching storms all the way. Impossible to sleep except in snatches. Whether it was my earnest prayers that did it, I don't know, but somehow we came through without serious damage. Late into New York, the tight schedule meant a late departure, too. Could only hope we'd make it up on the way home. Almost, not quite. Then a delay with the mails off Plymouth – bad weather again. Two nights in Southampton, porters, dockers, cleaners working full-tilt. Murdoch, Wilde and myself left the ship at dawn, each of us grey with exhaustion.

I was so tired when I got home, I couldn't eat. Ellie made tea, hot and strong, and toasted some muffins. I was dropping before I'd finished. Somehow she got me upstairs. All I remember for the next two days was being in bed, getting up for the bathroom, and falling back to sleep again. She made soup, I remember that – or was it beef tea? Something hot and savoury and comforting.

We barely spoke, but there again, she only had to look at me, her eyes dark with worry, her kind mouth drawn down, for me to know what she was thinking. How much longer could I carry on like this? It had been hard enough before, but this new schedule was a killer. And I was older now, not the hard young sailing-ship master I used to be.

Removing the dishes, Ellie came back to sit on the bed. She sighed as she reached for my hand. 'I think it's time, Ted, don't you?'

'To retire? Yes, I think it is.'

'What about…?' She hesitated. 'This new ship – they're expecting you to take it?'

'Yes, but I'll speak to them. Lord knows when – I hardly have time to breathe at the moment. I'll get a message to Bruce – maybe he'll come down to meet the ship next time we're in. If not I'll get him on the telephone.'

'What will they do?'

'Well, they'll have to promote somebody, won't they? There's plenty waiting to step into my shoes. Henry Wilde, for a start. Of course, he'll have to start on one of the old girls and work his way up.'

'What about Captain Cod?'

I smiled at her nick-name for Herbert Haddock. 'Old Codfish! If ever a man was destined for the sea…' Suddenly I started to laugh, and knew I was feeling better. 'He's been snapping at my heels for years. He'll be delighted to take over. And there's Hayes, too. They're not short, Ellie – they'll manage.'

At sea, two days later, while writing up the log I remembered it was my birthday. The 27th of January, 1912. I was 62 years old.

Mild winters are always bad for storms, and that winter was one of the worst. If February was bad on the outward crossing, the return was a nightmare. Two days after leaving New York, we hit a hurricane off Nova Scotia, the whole ship cork-screwing in turbulent seas. We had to slow down, reduce the revs, while the hurricane blasted us across the Atlantic, the seas coming up from astern, smashing down on the weakest point as the bow rode up and out, only to smash into the next wave as the stern rose free. Every few minutes the propeller was racing,

242

crashing, groaning. *Olympic* was such a long vessel, with every twisting turn, every slam as she hit the waves, I could feel the stresses and strains on her structure. I feared she might break in two.

Slowing as much as we dared, it seemed I did little else that voyage but hang onto the bridge front and pray for the weather to abate. The Almighty must have been busy elsewhere, because suddenly *Olympic*'s nose came up, her stern slammed down and something went. A propeller blade. It snapped. We felt it go, the whole ship shuddering as the crankshaft juddered under its uneven load.

Everything had to be shut down for a while, which meant more discomfort for the passengers, complaints, frustrating delays, slow speed back to Southampton and – sickeningly – further repairs. Delivering her back to Harland and Wolff's yard, I felt I never wanted to see Belfast Lough again.

'Must have caught a submerged wreck,' one of the shoreside wallahs said.

'Not in mid-Atlantic,' I snapped back. 'Not with hundreds of fathoms beneath the keel!' Sick of fancy theories, before the man could utter another word, I told him it was no stray growler either – we were too far east for ice.

'Faulty casting,' the Chief said, backing me up. 'Force of water,' said I. We both agreed that storm conditions would find out the weakness in anything new, even a bronze propeller. The shoreside wallah had the grace to look abashed.

But for all the fighting talk I was as close to despair as I have ever been. Tommy Andrews tried to cheer me by talking about the new ship, offering to show me round while the repairs to *Olympic* were under way. I shook my head, not wanting to even think about it. I just wanted to get home to my wife and daughter.

I had a few days in Southampton before returning to Belfast to collect the repaired liner. By then I was beginning to dread every effort. The journey to London, to Liverpool; the overnight ferry to Belfast; suddenly, I couldn't face it.

As the breath left me, I whispered, 'I can't do this any more...'

Ellie, packing essentials into my bag, stopped what she was doing. As I covered my face with my hands, she came to me, drew my head against her bosom and rocked me like a child. 'It's all right,' she murmured. 'You'll be fine, Ted – it'll pass.'

'I can't do it, Ellie – there's nothing left.' I felt her draw breath as her body stilled. Her arms were suddenly strong, her hands hard as she grasped my shoulders and bent to look into my eyes.

She went straight to the heart of the matter. 'Yes there is. You're still you. My husband – Mel's father – our Pole Star. *You* haven't altered, no matter what. The weather got that propeller, Ted – it wasn't your fault. You're dwelling too much on what those idiots up in London had to say.

'Couldn't let the Navy look stupid, could they?' she said fiercely. 'So it had to be you – and George, poor man. You've paid the price, you know you have. You've carried on, refused to give in – no wonder you're feeling mangled. You need some time off – and I don't just mean a few days...' She paused for breath, sat down beside me, was suddenly gentle as she stroked my hand.

I took a deep breath, wishing I could just stop. Grab the telegraph and ring down *Finished with Engines*.

'Did you speak to Bruce about the new ship?'

I shook my head. 'No. Haven't seen him. I think he's away. I'll write to him. Tell him straight – it's time for me to retire.'

But even a letter required effort.

The foul weather continued into March, a month renowned for its gales. Like a repeat performance of the last three voyages, the storm hit us when we were three days out from New York. That evening the saloons were deserted, most passengers battened down in their cabins; those who weren't were clinging to the nearest bar, seeing how many cocktails they could down before the drink slopped out of the glass.

I dined in my cabin, but didn't eat much; Paintin remarked on it as he cleared away. Listening to the myriad creaks and groans of the ship as she rolled heavily, I nursed half a cup of coffee and tried to banish anxiety.

For it to happen twice in succession was taking coincidence too far; nevertheless, with another new propeller fresh from the yard, I dwelt on the possibility, interpreting every squeal and groan as a precursor to some major or minor disaster. They say some ships are jinxed, and I was starting to believe that *Olympic* had my number. First *Hawke*, then the propeller. I found myself dwelling on the 5,000 tons of coal we'd loaded as a special cargo in New York, hoping it wasn't shifting in this storm and creating friction. Praying that fire in the hold wasn't going to be the third misfortune.

That'd be ironic. Carrying tons of coal to beat the miners' strike, just so the new ship could meet her sailing day – not much use if it should destroy us all in the process.

Aware that my thoughts were becoming morbid, I roused myself and went through to the bridge. In the chart room's half-light I checked the course and barometer readings, donning oilskins before stepping outside. As my eyes adjusted I made out the shape of the ship by the breaking bow wave, seeing the nose dive into the swell, throwing up heavy water and vast clouds of spray across the foredeck. The weather was coming hard from the north-west, and inevitably the ship was trying to turn, the quartermasters having a hard time keeping her steady.

It was wild out on the bridge wing, huge seas running close, a howling gale tearing spray from the tops like snow from Alpine peaks. Every so often a rising Matterhorn made my heart lurch. Looking aft along deserted decks, I watched the boats dipping down towards spume-flecked walls of water, surely closer with every roll. Thankfully no one was attempting to take the air; those daft enough to venture out in the afternoon had been corralled, as our Americans would say, inside the accommodation.

Torn between respect for the ship, concern for every soul aboard, and a driving need to keep to time, I knew there was little leeway in which to reach Southampton. Nor was it a question of satisfying passenger needs and company policy; this time when we docked, I had a deadline to meet.

Normally, I would have conducted a thorough handover in person to the new Master – old Codfish in this case – but he was in Belfast with Joe Bell, standing by the new liner while she was completing her fitting out. So I had written copious notes about *Olympic*'s habits and idiosyncrasies under various conditions; not least the power of her wash when the revs were increasing. Haddock would have to make the best of it.

Overnight, coming up the busy Channel, I was on the bridge, alert as ever for sailing vessels. Their navigation lights could be feeble, but even with the biggest, the real problem was that *Olympic*'s bridge was so high, we were invariably looking down on them, their side lights and mast lights often obscured by the extent of sail. Nantucket to New York might be a busy stretch of water, boasting everything from fishing boats to ocean liners, but it was nothing compared to what we in Britain had on our front doorstep. With craft from the

North Sea and Scandinavia meeting ships from the Baltic, Germany, Holland and France, the Channel was a bottleneck with the flow going in both directions. And with fishing boats and ferries crossing at various points, four officers on the bridge and two look-outs up aloft were barely enough.

We reached Southampton with the early morning tide on the 30th of March, docked at 7:00, and, with rare swiftness, I disembarked in time to catch the boat train up to London. Usually I went straight home once Customs and Immigration formalities were complete, but not today, there wasn't time. Ellie, bless her, had promised to meet me and was waiting on the quay, her lovely face marked by anxiety. Feeling the warmth of her embrace, for a moment I was overcome, could hardly speak for thankfulness.

As Paintin stowed my bags in a First Class compartment, Ellie and I climbed aboard. When he'd gone, I hugged her fiercely. She gave a breathless little laugh, but as we parted her grey eyes viewed me with concern.

'You look tired,' she said gently. 'Was it very bad?'

I nodded, reluctant to let her know just how dire things had seemed such a short while ago, how weak with relief I was to be safely ashore. An over-reaction to the pressures of the last few months, no doubt, but I was heartily pleased to be free of *Olympic*.

'One more round trip,' I promised, forcing a smile, 'and you'll have me home for the summer, pottering in the garden and no doubt getting under your feet. Then you'll be regretting it, and pushing me off to sea again...'

'Don't say that, Ted, I can't wait to have you home. If only it could be *now*.' She sighed and shook her head. 'Typical Bruce, insisting you do this one trip...'

'Please, Ellie – don't go over it again.'

She squeezed my hand. 'Sorry.'

We travelled to Eastleigh, just up the line, with hands clasped and eyes only for each other, the exchange of trivial news – our daughter's doings, events at home – masking deeper emotion. Desperate for time together, we even promised ourselves a relaxing few days on my return from Belfast. And we both knew that was unlikely.

Fifteen minutes, no more, and the train was drawing into the station, doors flying open as several people disembarked. Ellie and I said our farewells as I handed her down to the platform, but at the last moment she turned to clasp me again. 'Come home safe,' she said

246

with pleading in her voice. Doors crashed shut as the guard blew his whistle. Forced to regain my compartment I watched till I could see her no more, feeling bereft, hating this moment which seemed to have drawn all such moments into itself. For us greetings were always emotional, partings deliberately otherwise, and to have both thrust together was almost unbearable. For a few scalding seconds I think I even wished Ellie hadn't come, bringing with her the scent of home and then, with a swirl of her skirts as she left the train, whisking it away again. Like nothing else, her presence emphasised what I'd known for months. I should have been going home with her now, not girding myself afresh for another voyage, another new ship to break in for White Star.

I tried to turn it down. When Bruce came down to Southampton in answer to my letter, I told him it would be better if he gave the new ship to someone else. I said the new three week schedule was too much. It was knocking the stuffing out of the crew – and giving me no time at home with my wife and daughter. And I was due for retirement anyway.

'But you're the senior Master, EJ – the VIPs like you, they trust you to get them across the Atlantic safely and on time...' Leaning back in his swivel chair he went on at length in similar vein. 'Do the new one,' he pleaded, 'just the maiden voyage, and give Haddock a chance to get used to *Olympic*. It's a fair jump in size from *Adriatic* – although I must say *you* did brilliantly from the off, EJ, it's just that Haddock doesn't have quite your talent or your confidence...'

He finished with, 'And personally, I see it as a very public opportunity for White Star to prove its confidence in you. I know you took the judgement badly, but this should enable you to rise above the *Hawke* incident once and for all...'

And so, by a mix of flattery and cajolery and an unerring instinct for applying pressure in the right place, Bruce persuaded me to do the job. But all the way to Liverpool I knew I should have held out, stuck to my guns.

I'd squeezed one important concession out of him: told him in no uncertain terms, if I were to take this new ship, I wanted both Wilde and Murdoch with me. He didn't give in easily – it meant changes to those standing by in Belfast – but at last he agreed. That way, I hoped I'd be able to sleep at night.

I crossed London and caught the one o'clock train from Euston with only minutes to spare, arriving at Lime Street just after dusk.

It was raining, and as I waited for a cab I watched people hurrying by with umbrellas, all concerned with their own lives, their own priorities. What was I doing? How had I reached this point, this mad, rushing point, when all I wanted to do was go home and enjoy life with my family?

The cab driver dropped me by Pier Head. I stood for a moment looking back at the waterfront. The Sailors' Church was still there, its lantern tower still showing a leading light for the pilots bringing ships in from the Mersey. But the old familiar view had changed, marred by the overhead railway running along between town and docks. The smells had changed too. More soot and sulphur in the atmosphere, less wood and tar and canvas. Would I want to go to sea now, if I was starting over?

I thought of Joe, and my first trip on the *Senator Weber*. The evening before we sailed he'd taken me into the old church to pray. I had the strongest urge to do that now – something I hadn't done for years, not since giving thanks for the gift of my lovely daughter. I even looked at my watch and back at the ferry. But there wasn't time. Time, again, rushing me on.

With regret I turned my back and made my way down onto the Landing Stage, place of so many arrivals, so many leave-takings. As the ferry moved into the channel and passed the Bell Light, I looked out towards Waterloo and my old home, feeling deeply sad for some reason. Fatigue, probably. With a sigh I went below to find my cabin. Time to grab some sleep before the onslaught of tomorrow.

A brisk wind coming down the Irish Sea set the ferry moving noticeably, and my concerns running with it over the next day's engine trials. I slept only fitfully in the narrow bunk, mind churning like one of the propellers, anticipating meetings with builders and owners; then, providing all was well, the official handover. I hoped there'd be no problems. I'd had no time to get to know this new ship.

With something of a grimace I pictured Haddock leaving Belfast on the boat for Liverpool – rushing to complete the opposite journey to me – in order to reach *Olympic* in time to sail her on the 3rd of April. It would have been far easier to have him take on the new ship. After all, he'd been standing by for the last few weeks, overseeing the thousand-and-one details I'd taken care of when *Olympic* was fitted out. But Bruce would not be persuaded.

So it was up to me to see the new one through her paces, and – if all went well – to accept her on behalf of the company. My name on the ship's register, mine the responsibility.

It's easy to fall in love at first sight, but it seems to me maiden voyages are like virgin marriages, requiring tender hands and much respect. On the whole it's best to take the long view. *Majestic* was not mine from the beginning but we were together for nine years and I loved that ship, she was a wonderful old girl with lots of spirit. *Baltic* was my first maiden voyage, and even though she never had much go, I grew fond of her in the end. You do: the relationship is like a marriage: the awkward ones needing even more care than the willing. *Adriatic*, now, she was a pleasure from the start; you knew she'd never let you down, even in the worst of seas. After four years I really missed her when we parted.

Somehow, although *Olympic* was a truly beautiful ship with sufficient power and all the attributes – and even though my time with her began with great fanfares – she and I were never really easy with each other. It wasn't her size – I got used to that, barely noticed it after the first trip – and she handled well, I couldn't complain there. She had a fair turn of speed too. Had it not been for the *Hawke*, perhaps we might have settled down, reached an accommodation. There again, maybe it was me, reaching the age where past achievements were preferable to the challenge of the new.

In more ways than one, winter had taken its toll of us both. *Olympic*'s needs had pushed the other's moment of glory back and back. I felt the two ships were like human sisters, so similar in looks it was hard to tell them apart, the elder demanding precedence, attention, executing a tantrum here and there, while the other, equally remarkable, stood in shadow. Ready to make her debut, wondering if anyone would notice.

Was that her trouble? We sailors attribute human virtues and failings to what are, after all, inanimate objects – and yet they seem to have souls, these ships. And this one found a way, in the end, of outshining her elder sister, becoming a legend more evocative than any of the Greek myths.

Approaching her berth at Queen's Island, I was aware of apprehension. Nothing specific, it was just that our previous acquaintance had been slight, no more than a glance or two across the dock whilst my attention was absorbed elsewhere. And now here I was, getting ready to take this great ship to sea on the briefest of introductions.

Seeing her across the dock in the early morning light, I felt my heart beat faster. With smoke streaming from her funnels, she was a beautiful sight. A great ship alive at last and ready for action. At once my doubts were whipped away. There was even a pulse of youthful excitement as I glimpsed her port of registry, *Liverpool*, across the sweep of that elegant stern, and the gilded letters of her name, *TITANIC*, shining in the rising sun.

30

Our sea trials, scheduled for the 1st of April, were postponed because of high winds. Frankly it was a relief, giving me chance to spend the day going over the ship with the deck officers who had been aboard for the past few weeks, and with Joe Bell and the Harland and Wolff engineers. But time, more than ever, was the issue. The next day dawned fine and clear, but since we could not afford to waste another day on trials, the sea-trials were not entirely complete by the end of it. Although we satisfied the Board of Trade officials as to her turning ability, stopping distance and all-round sea-worthiness, we never managed the full-speed test. We did 20 knots for a couple of hours, but that was enough. By 6:00 in the evening the bureaucrats were happy and signed her off.

To maintain the schedule, we had to reach Southampton by the midnight tide on the 3rd of April, and we made it with little to spare. Desperate for sleep after another passage up the Channel, I disembarked around three in the morning and left for home. With so many last-minute details yet to attend to, those six days were hardly the relaxing time Ellie and I had hoped for. I'd missed Mel's birthday by a couple of days, but she was home from school for Easter and so excited by my arrival it broke my heart to see each morning's pleasure turn to disappointment as work intruded and the day wore on. We got out daily with old Wagstaff, showing his age these days; but sadly, the little holiday we'd hoped for on the Isle of Wight had to be postponed.

Mariners should know not to make promises. But in my mind I was already halfway home and dry. *One more round trip*, I declared, *and then I'll be home for good.* The kind of promise I'd spent my life refusing to make. I should have known better.

Mr Wilde was Officer of the Watch when we changed course at 5:45 pm on Sunday, the 14th of April. Previously, the sun had been on the starboard hand; as we steadied on our new course, we were sailing almost directly along its golden path. The sky was streaked with high, fine-weather cloud. The sunset would be spectacular.

At 6:00, Lightoller took over the watch and Wilde went off on his rounds. As the sun dipped towards the horizon it became noticeably cold. With a shiver I returned to my quarters to change for the evening. Thinking about Lucinda, I wished I could have turned the Wideners' party invitation down. There was so much to talk about, however would we fit it all in? But even without the Wideners I would have had to cut the evening short because of the ice reports.

I was in the bathroom when I remembered the lunchtime message from *Baltic*. It should have been pinned on the board in the chart room. I should have told them about it.

'Blast it!' I began a brisk towelling. Even so, it was almost 6:45 by the time Paintin had me buttoned into my mess uniform. I headed down to the Smoke Room.

Bruce and George Widener were together. Again or still? I wasn't sure. Apologising for my sudden departure at lunchtime, I said smoothly that I'd been trying to catch up with someone all morning, '… and suddenly, I spotted her…'

Bruce gave me a keen look, but the banker seemed not to have considered it amiss. He waved my apologies aside, called to the steward, and asked what I'd have to drink.

'I won't, at the moment, thank you, sir. In fact,' I turned to Bruce, 'I need to return to the bridge. Do you happen to have the telegram I showed you earlier, Mr Ismay?'

'Yes, I do.' He put a hand in his trouser pocket and brought out the paper. 'Wondered where you'd got to, EJ.'

With another apology I left them and made my way back up top. I went through to the chart room and was pinning *Baltic*'s message to the board when the lamp trimmer came up to report all the navigation lights lit. The junior officers were waiting with their sextants to take stars, but I heard Murdoch tell Lampy to go and close the fo'c'sle hatch properly – a light was showing.

'Where's Mr Lightoller?' I asked as Murdoch came in. 'He's late having his meal, isn't he?'

Murdoch murmured something I didn't quite catch, which left me suspecting some abrasion between the two men. I made a mental note to have a word later. The bridge was no place for personal animosity.

I tapped the message I'd attached to the board. 'Make sure everyone sees that – particularly Mr Lightoller when he returns. If he's in any doubt at all about visibility, tell him he must call me. I'll be in the restaurant for the next hour or so.'

'Yes, sir.'

Outside, it was dead cold, no wind across the ocean. The only disturbance was caused by our movement through the elements. The first stars were appearing above a horizon streaked with red and gold; reflecting the last of the light, the sea was like milky glass. That nightly show had drawn a small crowd of admirers, but I did not see Lucinda.

Returning to the Smoke Room, I was just in time to join the Wideners' party going down to the restaurant on B Deck. Mrs Ida Straus – a charming lady – said she and her husband had been able to send a wireless greeting to their son and daughter-in-law, heading for Europe on the *Amerika*. They'd had a message back, and Mrs Straus was quite thrilled about what she called this modern magic. Warmed by her enthusiasm, I found myself wanting to tell her my bit of magic: that I'd just found a daughter I didn't know I had.

Earlier, Lucinda and I had talked about our families. Richard Carver would be delighted to know she'd solved one of the biggest questions in her life, but, we both agreed, my dear Eleanor was not likely to share that happiness. As for Mel – she could be quite possessive. I didn't say so, but I had a feeling she would be both angry and jealous. And yet Lucinda, in her excitement at having found me, was eager for us all to meet.

Could *I* come to New Haven? Fired by her enthusiasm, I wanted to say yes. I wanted to meet Richard and little Daisy. My grand-daughter – how extraordinary! I wanted to revisit New Haven – I hadn't been there for years – see Lucinda's home, absorb something of her life. But reality calmed those desires.

'Dear girl,' I'd said as we parted, 'nothing would please me more. But it's not going to be possible just yet. We won't be in New York long enough…' Before she left I'd hugged her again, thanking her for the invitation and for her faith in me. Despite the calm seas, it had been a turbulent few days.

I made an effort to put personal matters aside. Champagne was being served. Needing to keep a clear head, I asked for a glass of my usual – ginger ale looked sufficiently alcoholic to fool most people. The Maitre d' nodded, and I knew he would make sure my glass was topped up with the right beverage.

The party was in aid of the maiden voyage, and everyone I talked to seemed to be bubbling with enthusiasm about the ship – smooth running, most sleeping like dormice, all enjoying the excellent food. Mrs Straus's news sparked a plethora of family stories, what everyone was going to do when they got to New York, where they were going for the summer. Now the ship was in touch with the Cape Race wireless station it seemed they'd all been sending messages home. The Marconi men would be busy tonight.

People circulated for a while, and a little later were seated. After so many years, these occasions tend to blur into one, so I do not recall what we ate, only that everyone commented on how cold it had become. The change in temperature was no surprise to me, but whereas my passengers were complaining about the chill, I was thankful that the skies were presently clear. Year round we faced the hazard of fog: June was the worst month, while April to August could be tricky for ice. In April and May though, you had a 50% chance of fog into the bargain.

With the unsettling Mr Stead on my mind I looked around me. No sign of him here, for which I was thankful.

Mrs Widener said the heating in their stateroom was not working very well – so I called Tommy Andrews over, asked him if the problem could be solved before Mrs Widener went to bed.

While he went off to telephone one of his staff, young Harry Widener, a collector of antiquarian books, buttonholed me, wanting to tell me about his latest purchases in Europe. He'd managed to acquire a rare edition of Sir Francis Bacon's *Essaies* at auction, and was cock-a-hoop about it. But then Mr Guggenheim managed to put a spoke in his enthusiasm by asking young Widener if he knew who'd bought Eliku Vedder's illustrated edition of the *Rubaiyat of Omar Khayyam*.

'I hear it went for a record price,' Guggenheim said with a sly smile. 'Of course the binding was particularly fine.'

'Yes, I heard,' Harry Widener said, trying to be dismissive. 'With solid gold and fifteen hundred precious stones it'd be hard not to shout its value. I go for content, myself.'

'I guess,' the older man said laconically with another sly glance at me. 'Someone said it's aboard this ship?'

It was indeed. In the ship's safe, together with innumerable jewel cases and Mrs Cardeza's treasure chest of emeralds, rubies and priceless pearls. But I was not at liberty to divulge such information. Anyway, I did not like smooth, bland Mr Guggenheim – he reminded me of Curtis – so I smiled and said it was possible, but as I had no knowledge of individual items I really couldn't say.

With my eye on the time, a little before 9:00 I made my excuses, expressed my thanks for an enjoyable evening, and bade my hosts goodnight. I didn't imagine the party would go on too much longer. Several 25-hour days were beginning to take their toll.

The Labrador Current was also making itself felt. I looked at the bridge thermometer: it had dropped by 10° Fahrenheit in the last couple of hours. Lightoller said he'd already spoken to the engineers about the water tanks and drinking water supply. Some of the pipes were vulnerable and would need draining down.

We stood for a few minutes looking out, commenting on the extraordinary stillness of the ocean, the lack of wind, the intense brightness of the stars in the firmament. 'But we mustn't forget that ice field, Mr Lightoller. The next hour or so, we could be seeing something.'

'A pity there's no breeze, sir.'

'Indeed it is.' The only disturbance of air was in the passage of the ship; there was barely a ruffle on the surface of the sea. It was as though the Almighty had exhausted his energies this winter.

'You see, Mr Moody,' I said, raising my voice to address the young man at the far end of the wheelhouse, 'even on a moonless night like this, breaking waves will catch whatever light there is. A small disturbance against the base of a berg will make it visible in the darkness. Isn't that right, Mr Boxhall?'

The 4th Officer emerged from the chartroom behind me, his smile just visible. 'To be honest, sir, I've never seen an iceberg.'

'And how long did you say you'd been at sea?' I asked with mock severity.

'Thirteen years, sir. Five with White Star.'

'In that case, Mr Boxhall, you're fortunate! Let's hope there are none to be seen tonight. Keep your eyes peeled. And remember,' I stressed, 'old bergs, growlers that have capsized or absorbed vast quantities of salt, can be a dull grey and hard to spot. Ice isn't always the blue-white you imagine.'

Crossing the bridge, I picked up the binoculars. 'Well, at least the stars are bright. If we come across that ice field there'll be a certain amount of reflection. Tell the lookouts to look for a shimmer, Mr Lightoller – nights like this, it's generally a giveaway.' I tried scanning the horizon but, with nothing to focus on other than stars, the binoculars were not much help.

I stood a few moments longer, assuring myself that the atmosphere really was as clear as I'd ever seen it. 'We should get ample warning – but if there's the slightest haze, we'll have to reduce speed. Any doubt at all, Mr Lightoller, call me. I'm just inside.' With that I went to my quarters. I called Paintin to help me out of my mess kit and asked for some coffee. I pulled on serge uniform trousers and thick socks, together with a woollen jersey. If I was to be in and out of the bridge all night, it was as well to be warmly clad.

Having written up the log book for the day, I found I couldn't settle. After a cup of coffee and a small cigar I donned my cap and shrugged into my jacket to do the rounds of bridge, wheelhouse and chartroom. We had two quartermasters on duty, one on the wheel, the other acting as lookout when not required for other tasks. There were two lookouts up the mast in the crow's nest. Young Moody was also using his eyes as he paced the bridge. Boxhall was in the chartroom, working out the 7:30 star sights, while I was in and out like a weatherman. Just before 10:00, I checked Boxhall's results and entered the position on the chart. He was doing all right, I thought – a steady young fellow, reliable. Then Murdoch came on duty and Lightoller went off to do his rounds of the ship before going to bed.

Murdoch and I had a similar conversation about the sea conditions. With our joint focus on the reported ice field, I repeated my comment about the likelihood of star shimmer on the horizon, asking him to pass that to the new men on lookout duty. There was little else to say. I knew Murdoch had experience in ice, so went back to my jug of coffee, now cold. I smoked another small cigar and thought maybe I should grab some rest. At 11:00, with still no sign of ice, I told Murdoch I was going to stretch out on the office day-bed for an hour, but to call me at midnight.

I took off my shoes, switched off the light and pulled a blanket over me. It was bliss to lie down, to stretch out my limbs. Physically, I was dog-tired, but my mind was alert, almost buzzing with awareness. In the darkness I could feel the movement of the ship beneath me.

Not the engines as such but the quivering they transmitted, like the pulse of a human heart.

The dream was vivid, reality distorted by the terrors of nightmare. Paralysed by foreknowledge, I was back on *Olympic*'s bridge, waiting for the worst to happen.

The cruiser closed on us with horrifying inevitability, the dreaded collision made worse by slow motion. *Thank God*, Wilde exclaimed as *Hawke* dropped back to slip round our stern. We all took breath. Then came the impact. Woken by my own cry of alarm, for one gasping, palpitating moment I was convinced there'd been a real collision. But it was just a dream, a nightmare. I calmed myself. Any normal ship would have sunk, but we stayed afloat. Listing, but afloat. *The watertight compartments held.*

Dreaming, I was dreaming. No, not a dream – we were turning. A prolonged shudder went through the room. The lights dimmed. Something had happened, was happening. It was real.

I shoved my feet into shoes, grabbed my jacket and hastened through to the bridge. To my horror, I saw Murdoch pulling the emergency lever to close the watertight doors.

'What's happening? What have we struck?'

'An iceberg, sir.'

I repeated the word as though I'd never heard of such a thing. *'An iceberg?'* I strode outside. *'Where?'*

Dear God. Murdoch and I peered aft, straining to see the thing; we smelled its dank breath but saw nothing to starboard, only blackness. Above and to port, the stars were glittering. *What* was it? *Where* was it?

And then something ghostly, like a frozen plume of smoke, appeared on the starboard quarter, slowly growing as we cleared the vicinity. The great berg showed its profile then, a pale shape in the night, drifting silently astern.

'Did you see it, Mr Boxhall?'

'I did then, sir.'

It was a quarter before midnight. I despatched Boxhall on a tour of inspection, keeping Moody close by for taking notes. I established from Murdoch what had happened: the lookouts up top had rung the bell and shouted, *ice ahead*, just after Murdoch saw the thing for himself. He'd shouted *hard over* to the man on the wheel, then dashed to the telegraph to ring *Stop Engines*. For a ship that size to respond takes time, and whilst her prow was moving to port she was also moving beam on – sideways – to the berg. Judging the right moment to call *hard over* the other way – to swing her stern clear of the danger – is a fine, fine art. You need to know your ship to execute such a move successfully. We all knew *Olympic,* but her sister was different. Nevertheless, Murdoch was very nearly successful. As it was, she turned that bit quicker than he anticipated – and ran over a submerged ridge of ice.

She bumped along for several seconds, he said. Yes, I had felt the shudder. The quartermasters described it as a grinding noise. There was a trail of ice on deck from where the berg had partially capsized under pressure and grazed the upper decks. Despite that, in those first minutes it seemed no more than a narrow shave.

Pitman and Lowe arrived for the change of watch as Boxhall hurried back, gasping a little, with his report. The 3rd Class singlemen's accommodation up forward was undamaged, and the passengers were safe. That was a relief. I sent him away again to find the ship's carpenter – the man responsible for taking soundings. A minute later he was back, expression tense. The carpenter had been on his way to the bridge to report the forepeak hatch blown off by air pressure – below was seven feet of water, and rising. If that was bad, hard on his heels came one of the postal clerks, to tell me the mail hold below the post office was flooding fast.

I sent down for a damage report and summoned Wilde to the bridge. It was seven minutes to midnight.

Chief Engineer Bell's report was not good. The forepeak, three forward holds and two boiler rooms had flooded already. I thought the watertight compartments should contain the damage, but my chief concern was to prevent panic breaking out amongst the passengers.

Fortunately, few had noticed anything amiss. Tommy Andrews, the architect, had been so engrossed in studying plans of the ship he was astounded to be told there'd been a collision. He looked stunned as he came to the bridge.

At once he and I went below to inspect the boiler rooms together. I didn't see Joe Bell but heard him below, snapping out orders. Firemen caught by the first flood had escaped just as the watertight doors were closing. Curses reached us, sharp with fear. Shocked and bedraggled, the men were being sent back down to draw out the boiler fires. The problem we'd sailed with had been just one undesirable blaze in a bunker: here were a dozen furnaces to kill; a dozen more after that. It had to be done. If freezing water hit those steel kettles, they would explode, killing us all.

It was a terrifying prospect. From the steps we could see steam and smoke and flame; the noise and heat were ferocious. Hard at it in the forward section, men were reaching in to rake out burning coals, hosing them down. Impossible to see the damage, but water was swirling in and rising faster than the pumps could deal with it. Gauging the rapid increase above the keel, we paused to discuss the options. Tommy jotted down a few figures, his expression grim. Too many spaces had been broached for the watertight compartments to be effective.

'She's designed to shut off three,' he said faintly. 'Three will hold. *Olympic*, now – only two compartments broached – she stayed afloat. But this…'

'Looks like five to me,' I snapped, eager to hurry him on.

'Too many.' Pale and sweating, Lord Pirrie's nephew cleared his throat. 'Strictly speaking, the compartments are not in fact watertight. You see, the bulkheads amidships only go up as far as E Deck, and as the bow sinks lower…'

'So the water will overflow into other spaces,' I ground out. The most basic of principles.

'Pulling the bow down even further…'

The biggest, most luxurious ship afloat, no expense spared to fit her out. And she had to be unsinkable too. It was a myth. Just a myth. White Star had never actually claimed that – somehow in advertisements the wording had been misconstrued. *Almost unsinkable* had become *unsinkable*, and the bitter truth was that *I* had contributed to the legend. Badly holed in the brush with *Hawke*, *Olympic* had stayed afloat. Inadvertently, I'd proved to everyone, from the richest banker to the humblest man reading his daily newspaper, that the White Star liners were the biggest and best, the safest in the world.

Unsinkable, though? No ship is unsinkable: at heart I knew that. But even I had embraced the fantasy.

I wanted to hit Tommy Andrews. Kind, charming, easy-going genius that he was, I could have killed him on the spot.

He must have seen it. He quailed under my gaze. Somehow I got the words out. 'How long have we got?'

'An hour,' he whispered. 'Two at most.'

The ship is your best hope: I could hear Joe saying it. Somehow, we must keep afloat. Get every pump working. Joe Bell was already onto it.

There had to be other ships in the vicinity. I left Andrews with the engineers and hastened up to the Marconi room. Spoke to Bride –

half-dressed for some reason – said we'd struck an iceberg and to get ready to send out calls for assistance. It was then that I saw the message form lying on the desk. I picked it up. It was timed at 9:40 pm, when I had been on the bridge. It was from *SS Mesaba* to *Titanic* and all eastbound ships:

'ICE REPORT. IN LAT 42°N TO 41°25'N LONG 49°W TO 50°30'W SAW MUCH HEAVY PACK ICE AND GREAT NUMBER LARGE ICEBERGS ALSO FIELD ICE WEATHER GOOD CLEAR.'

What? 'What's *this* doing here? Why wasn't it posted to the bridge?'

Terrified by the look on my face, Bride stammered an answer, something about it was not addressed to the Master. Philips had been on watch; he was just about to turn in.

'Well, get him out! We need you both!'

Too bloody busy sending passenger's telegrams! I thought furiously, heading for the wheelhouse. *No good – can't dwell on that now.* 12:13 by the bridge clock. Bruce Ismay was looking in from the Boat Deck, white-faced, shivering, an overcoat over his pyjamas, wanting to know what was going on. I spoke to my Chief Officer first.

'Get the boats uncovered and ready.'

'How serious is it?' Bruce repeated as Wilde hastened away. 'Can't the pumps handle it?'

I shook my head. 'Losing battle, I'm afraid. Find some warm clothes, sir – it could be a long night.'

McElroy and Latimer were standing by. 'Get all the passengers up and out, gentlemen – lifebelts, warm clothes, no baggage. Any questions, it's just a precaution…'

With a deafening roar, steam began venting from the boiler relief pipes. As my officers hastened away, I made a note of our position from the chart and strode back to the wireless room. 'Send the call for assistance.'

'What call shall we send?'

'The regulation call for help – just that!' I handed him the ship's position, then realised, as I hastened away, that we were some hours ahead of that calculation. What to do? Recalculate? It wouldn't matter for a while – we just needed to advertise our need for assistance.

On a sudden flood of emotion, I remembered Lucinda. Was she awake, did she know what was happening? Probably not. Fear chilled me. I must get word to her. I looked for my steward, but he was nowhere to be seen.

Turning my back on the roar of the steam I hurried down to C

Deck. By the main staircase, I met a large group of people milling about, many of whom had been with me at the party earlier. They were all in various states of undress and complaining about the noise, not one carrying a life belt. I spotted George Widener and John Jacob Astor, advising them to dress in warm clothes, with their lifebelts, and to make sure everyone else did the same.

Along the alleyway several doors stood open. I passed a steward and asked how the muster was going.

'Very well, sir.'

'Good man.'

Lucinda's cabin was empty. *Damn*. She could be anywhere.

On the service stairs I met Billy O'Loughlin. 'I've just seen Tommy Andrews,' he said in a rush, then stopped abruptly as he saw my face. His doctor's gaze stripped prevarication bare. 'It's true, then?'

'Yes, Billy, I'm afraid it is.' He was an experienced hand, there was no need to tell him to go quietly, or refrain from spelling things out to passengers. I leaned in. 'Do what you can. We've got an hour – hour and a half at most.'

Briefly, he touched my arm. 'I understand.'

Raising my voice above the din outside, I added lightly, 'At least the steam vents have roused everybody!'

'And they'll soon be on deck demanding to know the reason why!'

Back to the bridge. Looking forward I could see the nose was down and she was starting to list a little. I found Boxhall by the boats. The roar from the steam vents meant I had to get close to his ear to speak.

'Calculate our present position,' I said, urging him towards the chartroom. 'I'll be on deck.'

More folk were appearing, beginning to be quite a crowd, most with hands over their ears. Busy with the boats, the deck crew were using the steam winches to lift them from their cradles. Lightoller came up, shouting above the noise that the port side was ready, and should the boats be swung out? I said yes, swing them out, just as the beardless youth arrived from the Marconi room, all agog. He said the steamer *Frankfurt* had replied to the emergency call.

'And? Her position?'

At his blank look I clasped my hands behind my back. 'FIND OUT,' I mouthed, remaining just long enough to be sure he understood.

To the bridge wing, another look at the nose – yes, she was down a bit further. Across to the port side, along the boat deck, and then –

thank heavens! – the steam vents ceased their roar. Into the ringing silence men's voices sounded hollow, not quite real, while the women's were high-pitched, excited, anxious. And then the first notes of a well-known jig came floating across the deck. I looked round and saw members of the ship's orchestra, clad in hats and coats and mufflers, standing in a ring, playing a jolly, rollicking tune.

How to distract and sweeten a crowd! Mr Hartley would know, if anyone did, that a good tune can put a smile on the most miserable face. Momentarily, he even put a smile on mine.

I had to find Wilde, have a word about the boats. My Chief Officer was on the port side, looking grim as he supervised the sailors, but then he generally did. I thought about his four motherless children at home, and remembered Eleanor asking me not to take him this trip.

'Keep things steady,' I said, indicating what I meant by a look. 'Just a precaution – all right?'

Wilde nodded, mouth set, frown still in place.

There were not enough boats. There might have been. Everyone knew the original number for the *Olympic* class was three times the number we carried: 16 lifeboats, plus four Englehardt boats with canvas sides. But stacked boats made the upper deck look bulky, Bruce said. He was reluctant to clutter up the Boat Deck, where 'people like to promenade...'

We'll add more when we have to, he said. I remember him saying it.

But who am I to cast stones? Avoid panic: that was my chief concern. All of us who'd been at sea longer than a dog-watch remembered the tragedy of the liner *La Bourgogne.* She'd gone down in 40 minutes, in fog, after colliding with an iron-hulled sailing ship. Panicking, the passengers had erupted with knives and guns, the ships' officers powerless to control them. They'd gone down with at least 500 other souls, and of the 165 who escaped, only one woman survived.

At least we had wireless, and with any luck some nearby steamer would get to us quickly. I looked up at the wires strung out above the Marconi room and prayed for an answer.

As Boxhall came out of the chart room brandishing a slip of paper bearing his estimation of our current position, young Bride dashed up with a message form giving *Frankfurt*'s position. I compared the two, did a swift calculation and knew the steamer could not help. She was about 150 miles away.

'Keep sending,' I said tersely, handing over Boxhall's fresh calculation, 'using this new position.'

Where were they all? The times we'd crossed the Grand Banks with ships barely a mile apart. That generally was the danger.

I looked along the port side to check how things were progressing. Close by, Boat 4 was swung out and almost ready to load. A group of women with young children were standing by, watching, their faces taut with apprehension. And no wonder. The drop from Boat Deck to water was something like 70 feet – like looking down at the street from the top of a seven-storey building.

'Get them down to A Deck,' I called out to Lightoller, 'it'll be easier to board from there.'

I saw the women go down the steps and moved on. A minute later one of the male passengers dashed back and bellowed that the forward end of A Deck was glassed in. I had forgotten! On *Olympic* it was open. *Damn me! Damn Bruce!* I strode back to Lightoller, told him to get the people back, load them from here.

Boxhall called to me, binoculars in hand. 'Sir! I can see lights!'

Hope blazed as I took the glasses from him. Just a point or two to starboard I found them: what looked like two masthead lights showing just above the horizon. The ship could be seven or eight miles away, but if we could see her lights, then the man on watch should be able to see ours. Why wasn't he answering our distress calls?

'Should I fire the rockets, sir?'

'Yes, do that.'

The Boat Deck was thronged with people. Needing a clear space Boxhall moved them back to a safe distance while he fired the first rocket. It went off with an almighty roar and burst overhead with a great trail of white stars.

Over the next half an hour, as Boxhall and a quartermaster fired more rockets, we made out the port and starboard lights of what was probably a four-masted steamer coming directly towards us. Either without wireless or not keeping a watch. Praying hard, with every nerve stretched taut for a reply that must surely come in the next moment, I could barely tear my eyes away. Between rockets, convinced the steamer would come speeding to our aid, I ordered Boxhall to use the Morse lamp, to signal we were sinking. We strained our eyes through the binoculars, but gradually, despairingly, we were losing the green, and with the red port-hand light towards us, I knew he was turning. Please God, not sailing past, but preparing to come to our aid.

So close – how could the man on watch not see us? Did he think it was the 4th of July? November 5th ? Or the Chief Cook's bloody birthday?

No success with the wireless. Phillips was sending constantly, but responses were coming from too far away. Each time Bride came to me with a name and a position, my heart leapt and fell again as I worked out the distances. The closest seemed to be *Mount Temple*, about 70 miles to the south west. The Cunard liner *Carpathia* was a similar distance to the south east. Even *Baltic*, over 700 miles to the north-east had turned and was making towards us. As for *Olympic*, she was in touch with both of us. Old Codfish was making all speed in our direction, but he was still some 500 miles to the west.

My old commands. It choked me to think of them.

31

On the port side, all the boats were made ready. None were away yet, but women and children were being given absolute precedence. I understood the principle – in any alarm children were likely to panic and scream for their mothers, putting the mothers in a flap, which ran the risk of endangering everyone else.

I thought of Mel, my dear, brave little tomboy. She was going to have to be brave indeed.

Anxious for Lucinda, my eyes scoured the milling crowd for a glimpse of her. Crossing to starboard, I saw two boats were already away. Too late to intervene I saw Boat 1 – the small boat, the one kept permanently ready to launch – go down with Sir Cosmo and Lady Duff Gordon ensconced like aristocrats in a tumbrel, together with servants and a few men. It seemed Murdoch expected the crew to fill the rest of the seats with people from A Deck. But as far as I could see that did not happen.

The deck had a definite tilt, so I climbed a few rungs of the ladder outside my quarters, trying to grasp what was happening further along. It was difficult. Isolated in pools of light, groups appeared like actors on a stage. There was tension and confusion but surprisingly little panic – until I spotted Adelaide Burgoyne. With her companion at her elbow, she jerked away, fear written in every gesture. My heart sank. Even if I'd fought my way through to her, I knew she wouldn't brave that 70 foot drop. Like many more she would cling to the safety of what she knew.

While one of the men tried to coerce her, others clambered into a boat under Pitman's direction. Then there was a bit of a kerfuffle, which grabbed my attention. Bruce Ismay was trying to tell Pitman and Lowe to hurry, whereupon Lowe – a Welshman with a temper – spun round and told Bruce to shut up. That quelled him.

When I looked again for Adelaide, she was nowhere to be seen.

On the port side I found young Moody working with the Bo'sun's Mate. But they were lowering with what looked like only a half-load. The old regulations! Moody said they were afraid the boats wouldn't take the strain on a long drop like that, and they'd load the rest from A Deck or the cargo doors below.

'That's no good.' The cargo doors were surely inaccessible by now, and I didn't know what was happening on A Deck. 'Look, it's a risk, lad, but these new ones are supposed to bear a full load, for heaven's sake – 65, isn't it?'

He nodded, but didn't look convinced. 'Do it,' I said. 'And tell the seaman in charge to aim for those lights over there – unload his passengers and then come back. If you see Mr Lightoller, tell him.'

As stars erupted from yet another of Boxhall's rockets, I saw Mrs Straus being urged into the next boat, but she was another one refusing to go. Not that she seemed afraid. She wrapped her fur coat around her maid, pushed her towards the boat with the Countess of Rothes, and retired to a deck-chair with her husband.

Walking the length of the ship in the course of that dreadful hour, I saw many more like Mrs Straus. Especially the women in 3rd Class. Hanging back, choosing to stay with their menfolk or refusing to go without them. Less from fear, it seemed to me, than loyalty.

To starboard, McElroy was helping women and children – those who were willing – into the boats. Making my way through groups of people, I kept searching for Lucinda, finding it hard to see clearly beyond a radius of a few yards.

As the bow dipped even more, the slope on deck was increasing, together with a list to starboard. The musicians were playing ragtime, which cheered a body of 3rd Class passengers coming up from steerage. To my amazement, some of the girls were spinning and laughing as they formed a group near the band. With all the lights and music and people milling about, I dare say it seemed like a fairground. Even the deck was a cake-walk.

Our lights made viewing the horizon difficult, but it showed they were keeping things going below. My mind shied from thinking what it was like in the engine room. No bloody fairground, that was for sure. For us up top, Joe Bell and his team were manning the pumps and fending off darkness.

'Keep up, keep up,' I muttered under my breath, remembering *Lizzie Fennell*, the way we'd saved each other in the face of overwhelming odds. Praying we might do it again, even for an extra hour. But from the bridge the situation was obvious. The prow was on the waterline. Not everyone was going to get off before we went down. The heroes below knew that, but they were still giving us power for the winches and distress calls.

Past the Mess and through the alleyways, I crossed from side to side, all the time seeking my daughter's face. Aft, some kind of altercation was going on between Wilde and a bunch of foreign youths from steerage. He was trying to keep them in the well-deck, while they were jostling the women and children. I roared at them like a Bo'sun – they might not have got the words but they understood the meaning. With that they backed down.

'Will you give permission for the firearms, sir?'

'If you think they're necessary, Mr Wilde, you have it.'

'No sir, that's the point,' he said tersely. 'I wasn't in Belfast – I haven't got them.'

Lightoller had the keys. I had to get them, find the locker where he'd stowed the guns and hand them out. Just in time. The youths came bursting up the steps, jabbering and pushing to get to the top. Wilde fired a shot over their heads. With that they fell back again, allowing the women up to the boats.

The whole business was taking too long. And after the list to starboard, she developed a list to port, which became more pronounced as water flowed from one side of the ship to the other. At once the difficulties of loading and lowering increased. To starboard, gravity was inclining the boats to the ship's side, whereas to port they had difficulty holding the boats in so people could board.

I heard a gunshot. Lowe, alongside Boat 14 on the port side, fired to prevent some men – probably the same young fools as before – rushing his boat. Moments later I saw a crowd of firemen, black from the engine room, diving into another boat. Another roar ordered them out, but we needed women and children to board at once. Where were they? Thirteen hundred fare-paying passengers, and there can't have been more than a few score left on the Boat Deck. Then I saw a mass of people aft. Looked like a ruddy prayer meeting.

'Come on,' I muttered, moving as best I could in that direction, 'God

267

helps those who help themselves!' I saw a young couple in the light, hovering by the 2nd Class steps as though unsure of their right to be up here. I grasped the man's arm. 'Come along, sir – they need men who can row!' And then as he turned eagerly, I recognised him – and his girl. It was the pair I'd spoken to the other day. 'Glad to see you've got your lifejackets,' I said, ushering them to the nearest boat on the starboard side. 'Here,' I said to the Bo'sun, 'two more for you. See they get aboard.'

Buoyed by the moment, I went down to see how many more were waiting on A Deck. An unbelievable crowd on both sides. I moved downhill through stewards helping ladies into lifejackets, scanning every face. For some unaccountable reason, they still hadn't loaded Boat 4, yet I'd seen it being lowered from the Boat Deck ages ago – where the hell was Lightoller? What was he doing? I spotted Astor. He seemed to be pleading with someone – it was Lightoller, who, like some bloody knight in armour, was saying no, women and children only. But what about men to handle the boats?

I shook my head. 'Oh, for God's sake...' On the other side, Murdoch had allowed men in to handle the falls. Most had been firemen, brawny enough, if not the expert seamen needed in an open boat. If Astor had only gone across earlier, he might have got in with his young wife. The virtues – and drawbacks – of good breeding. *Don't push, don't shove, wait your turn like a gentleman...*

I dared not intervene. If I overruled my 2nd Officer now, there would be a riot. All the men so anxious for their wives would rush the boat and...

I caught his eye. 'I'm sorry, sir, it took an age to get the windows down!'

Bruce's bloody windows – that bloody promenade! I swallowed my anger. 'Well, hurry along there, Mr Lightoller – we must get this boat loaded and away.'

Where was Lucinda? Had she gone already? I gazed around before cutting through the 1st Class entrance. Climbing uphill to starboard, I glanced at my watch. Almost two hours since we foundered. How much longer? The thought was barely formed when I saw one of the 2nd Engineers, with weary difficulty, come clambering up from the poop. His blackened, bloated face was unrecognisable; his voice a hoarse whisper.

'Boiler Room 3's flooded, sir. We got out just in time.'

'Right.' Boiler Room 3, amidships. Tipping point. She'd start to go faster now. Much faster.

I thanked him before slithering and scrambling my way back to the Marconi room. Captain Rostron aboard *Carpathia* was close, but not close enough. Even at full speed, it would be another hour or more before he could reach us. While Philips, the senior man, promptly tapped out another message regarding our present condition, creaks and squeals, underscored by strange, unearthly groans, were making themselves heard from below. She was crying out in protest at the strain.

'Keep up, keep up...' Muttering my constant prayer, I clutched the rail and – God forgive me – willed my very soul into the steel heart of the ship. Anything to give us that extra hour.

Turning, I saw Boxhall preparing another rocket. 'Look lad, leave that. They're not going to answer now. Go on – get yourself to the next boat. You're a seaman – they need you.'

'Sir, I'd rather...'

'Don't argue, Mr Boxhall.' Telling him to aim for those lights on the horizon, I sent him on his way.

Back down to A Deck. Port side this time. I passed Colonel Gracie, helping ladies into one of the boats, and gave him an encouraging word; then saw O'Loughlin's tall figure in the light from the 1st Class entrance. He was with Paintin, handing out lifejackets. As we were speaking, I spotted the Enderby sisters, and suddenly to my relief and alarm there was Lucinda, her face so pinched and white I could tell she was terrified. The look in her eyes as she turned and saw me was like a knife to the heart. Aware that time was running out, I pushed my way through to her side.

Inside her fur-collared coat she was trembling badly. I wanted to enfold her in my arms and usher her to the front of the queue. I wanted to place her in that boat and personally oversee its lowering away. Under cover of the crowd, I found her hand and squeezed it.

'I'm glad to see you've got your lifejackets on, ladies. This boat should get away soon.' *So little time...*

'I saw you pass by earlier,' Lucinda whispered. 'I wanted to follow but the Doctor said we should stay here.'

'Quite right.' I hardly dared meet her gaze.

'I thought I wouldn't see you again,' she admitted with a catch in her voice. 'And I wanted to tell you how sorry I am...'

'Why? What is it?'

'I was afraid to say, before... I did see something at the séance. A ghost – a woman – standing behind Mr Stead.' With a fearful glance, Lucinda grasped my arm. 'It must have been Dorothea, trying to warn us...'

Even as a shudder ran through me, I shook my head, thrusting the image aside. This was no time for ghosts. 'A parlour trick, Lucinda –

269

that's all. He put the suggestion in your mind.'

'Could he do that?'

'Certain. It's all trickery.' I took a deep breath. 'Don't dwell on it, my dear – it will only torment you.' We moved forward in awkward steps. I held her close, trying to comfort her with a confidence I did not feel. 'There are lights out there on the horizon – a ship, not far, you'll soon reach it. You'll soon be safe.'

'Will you come with us?' She gazed up at me with such appeal I had to look away.

'No, my dear, I must stay for the moment. But when you get home – and you will, I know you will – remember this time we've had together. Write to me, won't you?'

Lucinda nodded. 'You'll come to New Haven?'

'Yes, of course.'

O'Loughlin wormed his way through to shelter us from curious eyes. A little cough reminded me that time was passing. 'I'll see her safe into the boat, sir.'

'Thank you, Billy.'

Gazing long and deep at this daughter of mine, I knew Dorothea lived on in her; that whatever happened, something of myself would continue beyond this moment. Bending closer, I hugged her to me. She felt like life itself. 'I will always love you,' I vowed, and knew those words were for Mel and Ellie and Dorothea too.

She reached up and quickly kissed me, her eyes full of life and fire behind the tears. 'Don't forget – New Haven!' She was like her mother then. 'I haven't waited this long to lose you now!'

'No fear of that,' I said, gently pushing her towards Billy. I managed a smile. 'I'll be there – it's a promise. God bless you, dear girl.' I had to turn away before the pain in my chest betrayed me.

The man overseeing Boat 4 was one of the quartermasters. 'Steer for the lights, Perkis,' I called when I could find my voice. 'Be sure you get into this boat and steer for those lights.'

'Right you are, sir!'

Pushing through the crowd with unseeing eyes, somehow I reached the Boat Deck. I leaned over the rail to be certain Lucinda did get away. The drop, thank God, was a quarter of what it would have been two hours ago, but the gap meant difficulty for the women in their long skirts. A couple of seamen were in the boat, hauling them in. I saw Mrs Thayer, Eleanor Widener – Madeleine Astor, weeping and distraught – hanging on to each other with grim anxiety as others scrambled over

270

them for seats. I counted some 40 women and children, amongst them the young boy I'd imagined would go to sea one day.

With a sudden lurch, the boat tipped and righted and began its drop. A cry went up. Lucinda appeared in a halo of light – looking up, finding me, so intense in that moment of recognition my heart thudded with love and fear.

I heard a man shout as the boat reached the water – then Perkis answered and shinned down the falls. Thankfulness surged through me – a good man, Perkis. Capable. He'd see them right.

I stared, my eyes peeling away the darkness until the lifeboat with its precious cargo disappeared from sight. It was the last one to leave: apart from the two canvas boats, the others were all away. If they stayed together, aimed for those lights… *Please God, keep them safe!*

With the binoculars I raked the night, seeing only stars, dimmed by our close, bright lamps. Searching for the lights of a ship… that was no longer there.

Hope deserted me then. I cursed the men aboard her.

The sea, black and gleaming, was alarmingly close. The first boats had lowered away part loaded. If those boats hung around, people could still be saved. Hauling my way along the Boat Deck I made my way aft, down through the prayer meeting on the well deck and – with difficulty – to the engine room access. The door was open, the steps at a crazy angle. Steam was pouring out like fog. I shouted down and one of the engineers emerged, black and bedraggled, like a spent devil from hell itself. 'Find the Chief. Give him my respects and tell him it's time to stop, get the men out…'

'Right you are, sir. Respects. Time to stop.' He disappeared.

I passed dozens of steerage passengers, huddling in corners, the women clutching bundles and precious items. Some had children clinging to their skirts. 'Come on!' I cried, urging them along with me. 'Get up on deck while you still have a chance!'

But they cringed away, not understanding.

Chest aching, I made it back to the wireless cabin, but no miracle had intervened. I told the two boys they'd done enough, it was time to quit. The port side was down at an angle. Water was swirling below the bridge. Not long now.

O'Loughlin staggered as he reached me. 'You sly old fox,' he said, adding, 'sir,' as an afterthought. I caught the smell of brandy on his

271

breath. 'Who was that lovely young thing with the pretty blue eyes?'

'My daughter,' I said without preamble. 'I didn't know about her until…' My voice suddenly grated, throat as dry as the Sahara. I had to think. 'Until yesterday.' It seemed an age ago.

'Jesus, Mary and Joseph,' he whispered, stepping back. The deck was at such an angle he almost fell. 'By all the holy saints. You're kidding me?'

'Now, Billy – would I joke about a thing like that? At a time like this?'

'No, sir, ye would not.' I knew he was drunk – he was sounding very Irish.

One-handed, I patted my pockets, realised they were empty. 'For heaven's sake, Billy – give me that flask you've got hidden away. And find me a smoke. I'm desperate. My office…'

Scanning the darkness, it struck me that we had seen nothing since watching that plume of frozen mist recede into darkness. Despite the arctic chill there was no ice to be seen. I looked around, trying to see Murdoch, wanting to tell him it was just a stray growler, when an ominous creak from below sent ripples of alarm through me.

I took a hefty swig from the hip-flask. Brandy. It cleared my throat and coursed through my veins. Just then I saw Stead inching down past the wireless cabin, his eyes focused on me. He waved a piece of paper in my direction.

'I have a message!'

At once, hope leapt. *Could it be?* Was it possible that this time, against all the odds, Stead had made contact with a ship close by? I was ready to embrace him with gratitude.

'I was wrong about the fog,' he gasped, sliding towards me. 'Completely wrong. I wasn't wrong about the ice though, was I?'

I shook my head as hope plunged beneath the waves. I wanted to curse him, yet the habit of civility remained. 'No,' I said wearily, turning away, 'you weren't wrong about the ice.'

He caught my arm. 'And I was right about the lifeboats too!' His prophet's eyes bored into mine. 'You see it now?'

'Believe me, Mr Stead, the irony is not lost. You know,' I confided, as though we had all the time in the world for this little chat, 'I used to tell my wife boats were not much good except in ideal conditions.' I heard myself laugh – it sounded strange. I wanted to weep with despair, with the knowledge that I couldn't change a thing. This was how it was. The antipathy between us mattered not; all was vanity. Stead was a fraud and I was a tired old man.

'And here we are,' I said expansively, the irony bitter on my tongue. 'Ideal conditions…'

A clear night, no fog. Everything perfectly still. No waves, no swell, no risk to those being lowered to the water. But even with boats aplenty, time would have been a problem – we still hadn't got the last ones away, and water was lapping at the bridge front.

We didn't practice often enough…

'If only you'd listened – changed course – I tried to warn you…' Stead pressed the paper into my hand. The message, whatever it was, was badly written. Clinging to the wheelhouse door-jamb, I didn't attempt to read it. As Billy reappeared, handing me my small cigars and a box of matches, I pushed them, with the paper, into my pocket.

'I'm not afraid of dying,' Stead declared, shrugging off Billy's attempt to persuade him towards the canvas boats. 'You know why? Because I *know* there is another world. And thanks to you, Captain Smith, that's exactly where we're going.'

That was too much. I lost control. 'Are you so sure,' I asked with bitter force, 'you didn't draw this situation down on us? You and your blasted table-rapping!'

My anger stayed him. Suddenly, he seemed sad and old, all his bombast gone. 'No, Captain,' he said quietly. 'I promise you, all I did was listen. I've known for years that I was going to lose my life at sea – why do you think I campaigned so hard for more lifeboats?'

Billy pulled him away. 'Come on, sir, let's find us both a drink…' The last I saw of them they were negotiating the steps – now almost level – to A Deck.

With an effort I calmed myself. The foredeck lights were underwater and the forward mast looked more like a bowsprit. With just a few feet to go I knew she was flooding rapidly below decks. I glanced up, seeing the funnels looming horribly over those working to free the canvas-sided boats. They'd go next.

Wilde and Murdoch were on the roof of the officers' quarters, with Clinch Smith and Colonel Gracie. They were struggling to free one boat, while Lightoller and Moody and several sailors were forming a ring round the other. Behind me, a tense crowd waited. Two chubby young children – not much more than babies – were screaming. A man passed them across the ring to a stewardess. Another woman picked up the younger one, its imploring hands like starfish reaching back, its cry one long wail of distress.

That finished me. I took shelter in the wheelhouse, propped myself against the wheel, and swallowed a long slug of brandy to stop the tears.

Out there, amidst the shouts of men, the shrill cries of women and children, music was still playing, but something gentler now.

Times without number I had crossed this patch of ocean, on occasion almost sick with anxiety, feeling my way through the fog. Sometimes, battered by storms and gales, I'd wondered if we would make it. And the snow. My God, the blizzards we'd encountered off this eastern seaboard. Unable to see a man on deck, never mind another ship on a collision course.

Every seaman has his moments of terror, the near-misses that make your heart pound and your bowels turn to water. I've had them in my time. Never imagined a collision on a clear night, with the sea as still as glass.

Never imagined one off the Isle of Wight, either – other than with a small, unwary yacht, perhaps – yet there we were last autumn, on our own front doorstep, rammed by a gunboat. Then, to have a propeller sheer in the midst of the ocean – that was bad luck too. Couldn't blame Stead for that one, though.

Driven by time, keeping the schedules, threading my way through ice, I'd dreaded collisions for 25 years. Somehow I'd come through unscathed. And enjoyed it, enjoyed the winning, enjoyed the accolades. Good man. Always on time. Until now.

A mild winter, winds to cut the bergs to bits. And a stray growler, unpredictable as a rogue bull, way out ahead of the rest of the field. Who would believe it?

If only we'd altered course earlier…

Or later…

If only we'd had more boats…

And more time…

It could have worked. We had the wireless, we had perfect conditions. It could have been a textbook rescue. We could still have got everyone away. If only that ship had answered… If Phillips had given me that last message…

Reaching into my pocket for a smoke, I found the crumpled paper. But in the light I saw it was Stead's message, badly scrawled, hard to make out. Something about endings and beginnings and the celestial wash of *time...*

The celestial wash of time... With those words it came to me – the mistake I'd made. That hasty calculation. It was my fault. My fault – nothing to do with Stead. It was all a matter of time. Dear God,

274

forgive me! In changing course those few degrees, *I hadn't allowed for the drift of current carrying the ice-field...*

Even now, close behind that stray growler, the ice-field was moving steadily south at something like a mile an hour. The boats would soon be in it. Would anyone survive the night?

Lucinda... Praying for her, praying harder than I'd ever prayed in my life before, I thought of Dorothea, struggling through time to warn her beloved daughter of what was to come. For a while I seemed to see her imploring figure like a reflection in the glass. She was calling me, but how could I go to her, how could I abandon my responsibility? How could I leave the myriad souls remaining aboard my ship? I shook my head, backed away. 'Forgive me,' I whispered. And then she was gone, leaving only sadness, a long, aching sadness, in her wake.

The musicians had stopped playing, the lights were going out, one by one. The sea was glassy and still, a reflection of night sky, with boats and lights bobbing here and there, just like a midnight fishing trip. Ellie and I had done that once. We'd planned to do it again one day. Now we never would. I thought of her and Mel, the news they would soon receive, and my eyes burned with sorrow.

Ellie, I'm sorry. My dearest, darling wife, I was wrong about so much, an arrogant fool. I made so many mistakes. Forgive me.

Titanic – mighty name, mighty ship. Built to defy the seas at their worst. How shameful that she should be defeated by this, my one small error of navigation.

Her name and mine have been linked together for all of a hundred years, always on someone's lips, always with a question attached. Whose fault was it? Was she badly built, poorly equipped – was she running a speed test? Biggest question of all – was the Captain competent? The only thing that matters is that people died – 685 of my brave lads, my chosen crew, and over a thousand passengers who trusted me to get them safely across the Atlantic Ocean. There were mistakes, yes. One upon another, adding up slowly to the final error. I paid for every one of them with my life.

Only right, I know, but notoriety is a wearisome thing. With every question I make the journey again. I wish they'd let me rest.

Those who went down with me have long since been released. And apart from me, who remembers Mr Stead? But I'm still here, still commanding the ship whose Articles I signed way back in April, 1912.

275

As Master, you see, I am responsible. It matters not who else fell short, who cut corners, who contributed to the disaster. I made the fatal mistake. I was in command. The blame will always rest with me.

I have time enough now – in this dark place where Time has no meaning – to repent, to atone, to build the ship of truth, as the poet said, in which my soul may sail at last.

Afterword

The ship that had shown its lights just a few miles away from the stricken *Titanic* has never been absolutely identified. It is thought to have been the Leyland Line's cargo ship, *Californian*, commanded by Captain Stanley Lord. At 11:00 p.m., on instruction from Capt Lord, the wireless operator tried to send a warning to *Titanic*, to say they were stopped in ice. Since they were close and the signal was no doubt powerful, he'd had short shrift from Mr Philips, who was trying to send messages via Cape Race. So, having been on watch since early morning, *Californian*'s wireless operator, Cyril Evans, retired to bed.

An hour or so later, over a period of time, eight white rockets were seen by various crew members on the *Californian*, but not positively identified as distress signals. A vessel had been sighted before Captain Lord quit the bridge, presumed by him to be a small cargo steamer of about *Californian*'s own size. He decided, subsequently, that the rockets were coming from there. From his cabin, Lord directed the officer of the watch to signal the ship by Morse lamp. No reply was received. 2nd Officer Stone, on watch after midnight, also reported what he judged to be a small steamer about five miles distant – but he too received no confirmation from his Captain, or response to his attempts to communicate by Morse lamp.

3rd Officer Groves did go to the wireless cabin to listen for a distress signal, but the operator was asleep and did not tell him that the mechanical signal detector needed winding...

Failing to respond to a distress call is the most heinous crime there is in the maritime world. Captain Lord was censured by the American and British enquiries for his neglect – indeed, for failing to view the situation for himself. Despite the ice around them, Captain Lord's defence was that both he and his officers failed to recognise the white rockets as a distress call, since coloured rockets were generally the norm. And anyway, he did not believe, nor ever would believe, that the lights of the steamer they saw could have been *Titanic*.

There were many inconsistencies in the evidence given and questions remain unanswered. An additional point concerns the lights seen from *Titanic*'s bridge. If the *Californian* was stopped in ice, between 10 and 20 miles away from *Titanic* at the time of the disaster, could she have been the vessel in question?

In 1962, the Mate of a Norwegian sailing ship, the *Samson* of Trondheim, made a sworn statement on his deathbed. Henrik Naess said he saw the rockets fired by *Titanic*, and that he and his ship were within sight of the stricken liner. His vessel was part of a sealing expedition in forbidden waters off the North American coast. With a hold full of illegal seal-pelts, they dared not stop to render assistance.

While others slept, doubted or simply feared to respond, *Titanic* sank deeper. The bridge went under just as the canvas-sided emergency boats were freed from their lashings. 2nd Officer Charles Lightoller and Colonel Archibald Gracie were just two of the men who had been struggling to free them – both were sucked down as the ship began her dive to the bottom many fathoms below. Extraordinarily, both were blown back up to the surface by a release of air, and separately managed to reach one of the canvas-sided boats – the upturned Boat B. They clung to it with about 30 other men.

They survived to write accounts of their experience. Young Lightoller wrote his story much later in life, but the 59-year-old Colonel Gracie began his book almost at once. Having interviewed and written to as many survivors as he could find, Colonel Gracie obtained details from the American Senate Committee hearing and put together an account of what happened that night. He did it in a little over six months – the book was not yet published when he died on the 4th of December, 1912. His former family home – the Gracie Mansion in New York – is now the official residence of the Mayor of New York.

The two Marconi men, Bride and Philips, were also sucked down but came back to the surface. They also reached one of the boats but Philips died shortly afterwards. Bride was injured but survived.

The two infants, seen latterly, were travelling in 2nd Class with their father under the name of Hoffman. Rescued, but having lost their father, they were thought to be orphans – until their mother, in southern France, recognised their photographs in a newspaper. Their real names were Edmond and Michel Navratil – and they had been abducted by their father.

The young couple spied talking over the gate by Captain Smith (and Lawrence Beesley, a young science master travelling in 2nd Class) remain unidentified, but may have reached safety.

Sir Cosmo and Lady Duff-Gordon – like Charlotte and Thomas Cardeza – got away safely from the starboard side, in boats 1 and 3 respectively, the former containing 12 people, the latter about 40.

Mrs Margaret Brown not only survived – after being lifted bodily into Boat 6 – she became an eminent fund-raiser on behalf of families left destitute by the tragedy.

Madeleine Astor, Eleanor Widener, and Mrs Thayer were amongst the 36 women and children in Boat 4, the last *big* boat to leave ship, and one of the last to reach safety.

The Countess of Rothes, with her cousin and a maid, boarded Boat 8 with 35 women, three male stewards and a seaman. Since the women had more boating experience than the stewards, Seaman Jones put the women to the oars and the Countess to the tiller. They were the last to reach the Cunard liner *Carpathia*, about 8:00 in the morning.

Bruce Ismay climbed into the canvas-sided boat C, the last boat to leave from the starboard side. It contained about 40 people, mainly women and children. Mr Ismay testified on oath that there were no more in the vicinity – by then most people had retreated to the stern. Shattered by his experience and the loss of the *Titanic*, he retired from public life to live in Ireland, and died in 1937.

JP Morgan, delayed in Europe on business, was a broken man. He died in 1913.

Thomas Andrews was last seen in the Smoke Room by the fireplace, gazing at the magnificent painting of Plymouth Harbour.

Presidential aide, Major Archie Butt, and his friend, the artist Frank Millet, helped women and children into the boats before retiring to the familiarity of their favourite table in the Smoke Room. Over a final nightcap, they no doubt met Charles Hays, and

George Widener with his son Harry. Benjamin Guggenheim, having discarded his lifejacket and donned his evening clothes, was, with his valet, preparing to die like a gentleman. The author Jacques Futrelle, having persuaded his wife into Boat 9, also took refuge amongst the friends he'd made. And, at the last, so did Mr William Stead.

John Jacob Astor was still on deck when the first funnel collapsed. His body was recovered by the *Mackay-Bennett* on 22nd April, and identified by the initials sewn into his jacket and the gold watch in his pocket. The *Mackay-Bennett*, a cable-laying steamer, was assigned the task of recovering the dead from the sea. 328 were recovered in all, 150 buried in the cemetery at Halifax, Nova Scotia.

3rd Officer Herbert Pitman, 4th Officer Joseph Boxhall, and 5th Officer Harold Lowe, were each assigned to lifeboats as practical seamen and navigators, to lead groups of boats towards the ships speeding to their rescue. 6th Officer James Moody could have gone with Boat 14 on the port side, but said he would go in the next one, and insisted Lowe take his place. With 1st Officer William Murdoch and Chief Officer Henry Wilde, James Moody remained aboard, launching boats right to the last.

Chief Engineer Joseph Bell's team below decks consisted of 35 engineering officers and almost 300 men, all of whom worked heroically to keep the generators going and the pumps working. 72 of the men reached safety, but not one of the engineering officers survived.

The ship's orchestra, eight men led by Wallace Hartley, played on until the lights went out.

Dr William O'Loughlin, Chief Purser McElroy and Chief Steward Latimer, after directing help and assisting passengers into the boats, stayed with the ship, as did Arthur Paintin, the Captain's steward.

Several other stewards and stewardesses survived, largely because they were ordered into the boats by their superiors.

Aboard the Cunard liner *Carpathia*, Captain Rostron urged all speed. The ship normally operated at something like 14 knots, but with every minute vital on that 70 mile dash, the engineers managed to squeeze more than 16 knots out of her, arriving at the last known position of *Titanic* around 4:00 am, just an hour and a half after the sinking. There were bergs and field ice all around. Small boats – and small distress flares – were difficult to spot in the darkness, but with the dawn all the boats were rounded up, the survivors taken aboard.

So few – a mere 711 out of the 2,210 souls aboard.

On both sides of the Atlantic, nations were plunged into mourning.

The port of Southampton was devastated. Every family lost someone to the tragedy.

Mrs Eleanor Smith moved to Cheshire with her daughter, and later, after Mel was married, to London. Captain Smith's widow died in 1931, his daughter Mel in 1973.

In 1914, in response to the sinking of *Titanic*, the United States Coastguard formed the International Ice Patrol, to monitor the waters of the Arctic and North Atlantic Oceans and advise shipping of the movement of ice into the shipping lanes between Europe and North America.

Nowadays, all vessels navigating within the area of the Port of Southampton, must ensure that a large vessel – greater than 220 metres in length – shall be given a 'clear channel' between the Hook Buoy (just north of Calshot Spit) and the Prince Consort buoy (off Cowes).

Author's Note

The tragedy of *RMS TITANIC* has exerted an extraordinary fascination for a hundred years, and doubtless will do so for generations to come. My novel would not have been thought of had it not been for Ron Hancock, manager of the Southampton Pilots' Office, who very kindly showed me the DockMaster's Log Book for 1912.

That large, leather-bound book logged ships inward on the left-hand page and outward on the right, under columns headed *Date, Time, Ship, Captain*, etc

The entries for March and April were quite extraordinary. My husband and I were shown the entry for April 10th, noon – the time *Titanic* sailed from Southampton – the destination New York, and the Captain's name, *Smith*. That entry alone was enough to give me a shiver, knowing what was to come.

But then the pages were turned back, and the elegant copperplate handwriting recorded Captain Smith as having arrived in Southampton on March 30th at 06:00 am from New York, aboard the White Star ship *Olympic*.

Five days later, Captain Smith's name appeared again. This time the log recorded him coming into Southampton at 01:15 am on April 4th, from Belfast – aboard *Titanic*. Six days after that he was sailing for New York.

My husband and I stared at the book, checking times and dates again. We worked out the journey he must have made. Arriving from New York aboard *Olympic*, he docked in the early hours in Southampton, took a train to London, another to Liverpool, and then an overnight ferry to Belfast – with a new ship to take out on sea-trials and then bring back to Southampton. And this after a winter spent crossing the North Atlantic.

Those brief entries were like alarm beacons. Personal experience is part of any response, and I had enough experience of life at sea to appreciate at once just how hard that must have been. As my husband – another sea-captain – shook his head, appalled by the pressure those entries conveyed, I wondered how many other people would understand.

Needing to express it, I wrote a short story. But the amount of research necessary for that, resulted in other aspects surfacing. Once I'd taken the *Hawke/Olympic* incident into account, events aboard *Titanic* began to loom very large indeed.

I had been about to start work on a novel set in a completely different era, but it had to take a back seat. My family wanted to know more about Captain Smith – and so did I.

THE MASTER'S TALE is based upon Captain Edward John Smith's life and career. But it is also a novel, containing all the imagined dramas that novels require. The newspaperman William T Stead was an intriguing man, with interests in spiritualism and thought transference, although whether he conducted a séance aboard *Titanic* is purely my speculation. Those interested in facts will appreciate that Harry Jones and Thomas Jones were both well-known to Edward Smith, although whether they were related, again is speculation on my part. With regard to other liberties taken, I hope both the Captain's devotees and detractors will forgive me, and appreciate that for the novelist, *all* the characters become real.

I would like to think that Mrs Lucinda Carver was rescued along with all the other ladies in Boat 4. Her name, however, together with that of the Enderby sisters and Mrs Adelaide Burgoyne, was not found on *Titanic's* passenger list.

Acknowledgements

Thanks first of all to Ron Hancock, who started the story…

A friend in York, Nigel Mitchell, was the first person to trust me with his books on the Titanic, including his edition of Colonel Gracie's account of the sinking. Dorothy Palmer gave me an original 1912 newspaper, Bill and Maureen Schofield lent books on Hong Kong, and Tom Lunn his book on collisions.

Graham Mackenzie, Managing Director of Solent Steam Packet (Services) Ltd, and Norman Tulip, Chief Engineer of the SS Shieldhall, were similarly generous with their books and their time, explaining much about steam engines that I did not understand. (Any errors are mine!)

Captain Peter Roberts, my wonderful husband, acted as technical advisor, putting me straight each time my steering went off-course.

'EJ' – Gary Cooper's well-researched biography, proved an excellent reference for detail about Captain E J Smith's life and career.

Hannah Cunliffe, historian and maritime researcher, obtained transcripts of the Hawke enquiry and relevant newspaper articles.

My family read the short story and persuaded me into writing the novel. My agent, Caradoc King, was as insightful as ever in giving creative advice, and my dear friends Maureen and Victor Morgan, with Anne Hodges, kept flagging spirits up with their enthusiasm for the early drafts.

En route, the Blue Room Writers' Group kept everything moving – providing the breeze when I was stuck in the Doldrums, hauling me back on course when the tale seemed set to go adrift. My warmest thanks go to Jenni Jacombs, Deanna Dewey, Donna McGhie, Claire Hanley, Mike Plumbley and Mike Hayward. Their support and advice were invaluable. Special thanks must go to my publisher, Tessa Warburg, for taking this book on when so many others shook their heads – and to Evelyn Harris, for her shrewd editorial advice.

Jenny Law, of Hamble, a brave and wonderful lady, has been an inspiration simply by being herself.

Ann Victoria Roberts
Southampton, 2011

Bibliography

'E.J.' - Gary Cooper (2009)

'TITANIC' – Colonel Archibald Gracie (1913)

'THE MAIDEN VOYAGE' – Geoffrey Marcus (Unwin 1969)

'THE VICTORIANS' – A N Wilson (Arrow 2003)

'THE MAKING OF MODERN BRITAIN' – Andrew Marr (Macmillan 2009)

'THE PRIVATE LIFE OF OLD HONG KONG' – Susanna Hoe (OUP 1991)

'LIVERPOOL' – Catherine Rothwell (The History Press 2009)

'SOUTHAMPTON' – Robert Cook (The History Press 2009)

'COINCIDENCE – a Matter of Chance or Synchronicity?' – Brian Inglis (Hutchinson 1990)

'AN AGONY OF COLLISIONS' – Peter Padfield (Hodder & Stoughton 1966)

'THE STORY OF THE TITANIC as told by its survivors' ed. Jack Winocour (Dover Publications, New York 1960)

'TITANIC SURVIVOR' – Violet Jessop, ed. John Maxtone-Graham (Sutton 1997)

'TITANIC – TRIUMPH AND TRAGEDY' – John P Eaton, Charles A Haas (Patrick Stephens Ltd 1986)

'TITANIC AND HER SISTERS' – Tom McCluskie, Michael Sharpe, Leo Marriott (Parkgate Books 1998)

'WHITE STAR LINE – A Photographic History' – Janette McCutcheon (Amberley 2006)

'STEAM AT SEA' – Dennis Griffiths   (Conwy Maritime Press 1997)

A Glastonbury Thorn

Out of the ruins,
out of mid-winter;
flowering!

The Thorn Press

Books in Print

The Dohlen Inheritance trilogy - Tessa Lorant Warburg

The Dohlen Inheritance
Paperback: ISBN 978-0-906374-06-1   £11.99
Hardback: ISBN 978-0-906374-03-0   £18.99

Hobgoblin Gold
Paperback: ISBN978-0-906374-08-4   £11.99

Ladybird Fly
Paperback: ISBN 978-0-906374-09-2   £11.99

A Woman's World, Hilary Jerome
Paperback: ISBN 978-0-906374-00-9   £9.99

Snack Yourself Slim, Richard Warburg & Tessa Lorant
Paperback: ISBN 978-0-906374-05-4   £8.99

Inktastic, Andrew P Jones
Paperback: ISBN 978-0-906374-04-7   £17.99

All available from Amazon UK, US and EU, and from good
book shops

www.thethornpress.com